James H. Graff, James Grant

Fairer Than a Fairy

A novel

James H. Graff, James Grant

Fairer Than a Fairy
A novel

ISBN/EAN: 9783337044497

Printed in Europe, USA, Canada, Australia, Japan

Cover: Foto ©Andreas Hilbeck / pixelio.de

More available books at **www.hansebooks.com**

FAIRER THAN A FAIRY

A Novel

By JAMES GRANT

AUTHOR OF

"THE ROMANCE OF WAR," "UNDER THE RED DRAGON," ETC.

LONDON:

GEORGE ROUTLEDGE AND SONS

THE BROADWAY, LUDGATE

NEW YORK: 416 BROOME STREET

CONTENTS.

FAIRER THAN A FAIRY.

CHAPTER I.

PROMOTED.

"'PRINCE CONSORT'S Rifle Brigade; Lieutenant Lancelot P. Rudkin to be captain, vice Paget deceased.' So says the *Gazette*," I added, after reading my own name and laying down the *Times* with a certain emotion of satisfaction mingled with honest regret.

"So you are a captain now?" said Henriette Guise, looking up at me with an indescribable smile.

"A captain, yes. But, poor Paget—I knew him well."

"What has he died of, think you?"

"Fever, too probably. Every fellow dies of fever where that battalion of ours is quartered at present."

"And shall you join it there?" she asked, in a sweet clear voice, and with a little anxiety of tone—at least, so I flattered myself.

"No; the battalion to which I shall now belong is up country in India—at Allahabad, I think."

"And you must join it there?"

"Undoubtedly."

The girl made no answer; but I could see that her breast heaved softly, her dark lashes drooped, and a little flush crossed her cheek.

" Will—will this promotion shorten your leave ?" she asked, after a thoughtful pause that implied a good deal.

"Oh, no."

Circumstanced as Henriette and I were, I felt that she had a right to take a greater interest in my movements and affairs than her simple words expressed, and that this was the time to say a great deal more than these two brief monosyllables ; but many pressing considerations fettered my tongue, and crushed the best emotions of my heart.

We were seated in an oriel window of the drawing-room of old Thorsgill Hall. The evening sun was streaming through it, lighting up the rare beauty of my companion—a beauty which was high in class and very remarkable in character, possessing what some one terms "the magic of luminous darkness" about it. "But," says another writer, "it is sorry work to attempt to describe beauty. Easy enough to write down a list of features, and say that, amalgamated, they look well ; but *expression* is not to be sought in so many words ; and without expression life is wanting."

In figure Henriette Guise was rather undersized, and—as she is *not* my heroine—I may assert with confidence that her general loveliness struck one chiefly by its rare quality, and it was purely patrician ; that her form was perfect, and her hands the finest I had ever seen. Her complexion was wonderfully delicate and white, though her hair and eyes were deeply dark, with long black lashes that turned upward at the tips, and strongly defined and nearly straight dark eye-brows, that almost met over her delicately-pointed nose ; and this imparted great character to her pale oval and animated face.

Her eyes, I have said, were very dark ; indeed, they were a kind of violet-black, if such a term can be used ; and they expressed all the purity, goodness, and honesty of heart which were fully hers ; though her short upper lip, which quivered at times when excited, showed that she was a proud girl, who had a little temper of her own, and with whom it might be unpleasant to have even a lover's quarrel.

The summer drills were over, and my comrade Stapleton and I had obtained a few months' leave of absence, two of which I had spent with General Dormer's family circle at Thorsgill Hall, a fine old place near the Tees, where his niece, Henriette Guise, who had completed her education at a fashionable West-end establishment, was now paying a farewell visit previous to rejoining her parents at Calcutta, for which city of palaces she and a cousin were to depart together.

For two entire months I had been there, having thus far exceeded what Sir Walter Scott used to term the "guest-week" which followed the "rest-week;" and though there were several other friends in the house, my intimacy with this most attractive girl had suffered no interruption, save when the General and I threw a line into the Tees, or, after the grouse and ptarmigan shooting began, took a turn over the moors. If I had played much at croquet, it was less for the love of the game than to obtain a glimpse now and then of a taper ankle, a well-bred foot, and a high instep that was suggestive of a good waltzer; if at chess, I saw less of the figures on the board than the delicate hands and softly-lidded eyes of my companion; and when we shot at the archery butts, my arrows flew wide of the target, for I thought only of her rounded bust and arm as she drew the bow, her lithe figure and wonderful grace.

I was then as much in love with her as any man could be, mewed up in a somewhat dull country house with such a girl. I had come but to stay a week or two; yet the time had rolled with marvellous quickness into months; for the General was an hospitable old Bengalee, and we had to visit and often picnic at, or near, all the "lions" of the neighbourhood, and all the ruins and scenes described in *Rokeby*—Barnard Castle, that overhangs the magnificent valley where the Tees flows through its trench of solid rock; "Egliston's grey ruins," that tower above the woodlands and the dell called Thorsgill; and Rokeby's glades and Mortham's Tower,

which by the way, is haunted by a female spectre; and often
did Henriette and I linger in the famous Rock-walk, and in
the bower which was a favourite resort of Scott, in a glen
so lonely and romantic that even his pen failed to describe
it; and many a scamper and scratch hurdle-race we had in
beautiful Raby Park. In all these expeditions I generally
contrived to be the companion of Henriette, who seemed
tacitly to expect me to be so, as we had many tastes and
thoughts and emotions in common; but the time was coming
now when these delightful days were to pass and to return no
more.

Henriette knew and felt that I loved her, and yet I had
never told her so. My attentions had been such, on a hundred occasions, that, in spite of myself and the guard I had
put upon my conduct, she had every reason to expect some
declaration; yet it was never made—for a stern necessity and
a conviction of hopelessness weighed down my heart and
sealed the lips that longed to tell its secret.

A married sub. might live in India on his pay and allow-
ances, provided that a great staff of ayahs were unnecessary.
True, I was a captain now; but could I ask *her* to share a
bungalow life with me up-country, Heaven knew where?

Could I have kept a house in town, my hunters in the
country, and a yacht perhaps at Cowes or Ryde, or even did
I possess much less than these pleasant accessories to life in
England, I should doubtless have been a much more confident and courageous fellow, and would openly have proposed to the wealthy Indian heiress—for such she was; but
as a captain in the Rifle Brigade, with only a limited allowance besides my pay, and with certain solid anxieties about
the contingent, batta, and tentage, it was not to be thought
of; so there was nothing left for me but to sigh "like a
furnace" and be silent.

Yet I doubt not my eyes and many a little action had
spoken eloquently enough; but with such limited funds as
compared with her lacs of rupees, as my brother officer

Stapleton said, " it would be the devil and worse, to be cross-questioned by the fair one's papa in the library, or the smug and smoothly-shaved family solicitor, about prospects, settlements, and pin-money.

"A captain at five-and-twenty," thought I (having purchased my lieutenancy), as all these miserable considerations flashed through my mind while gazing anxiously and with ill-concealed admiration on my fair companion, who was reclining in an easy-chair, with her dark eyes, shaded by the whitest of hands, fixed—as if she too were lost in thought—on the sunny vistas of the wooded chase that stretched in distance far away towards the Tees.

"Miss Guise," said I, smiling, and feeling the necessity of saying something, "you forgot to congratulate me."

"On having a scene of such distant service before you?"

"Distant! You forgot that you too are bound for India."

"True; for a moment I forgot," said she, colouring slightly; "but not for some months yet. However, to reside at Garden Reach is one thing; to march up-country is quite another."

My spirits fell lower at these words, though doubtless the girl spoke them inadvertently.

"Jungle fever doubtless killed poor Jack Paget," said I, thinking to excite her interest, and recurring to the *Gazette.* "I would rather not have gained my company through his death."

" He was your friend?"

"We chummed in the same hut before Sebastopol."

"Was he a nice fellow?"

"Nice is scarcely the term, Miss Guise; he was the king of all good fellows, and moreover a brave officer, who won the Victoria Cross at the storming of the Redan, when he served with the ladder-party."

"Then you are sure this promotion does not shorten your leave?" she asked after a little pause.

"Yes," said I briefly, as when she had asked the question before.

"I am *so* glad of that," she observed, with such genuine earnestness that I was tempted to take her hand in mine and say something decidedly rash, when she hastily added, "So glad—because—because——"

"Of what, Miss Guise?" I asked, lowering my voice, while my heart beat very fast indeed.

"You will see my cousin Blanche Bingham before you leave. She is a delightful girl, and everybody loves her. She comes to stay here until we sail together for India. We are the dearest friends in the world, and were boarded together in the same school in London, and were inseparable ; we sat next each other at meals, studied side by side at the same desk ; we practised the same duets, read the same books, and shared the same room, and indulged in all that romantic friendship so peculiar to young ladies, in general, and school-girls in particular."

"Until one finds a lover—when it ends."

"Perhaps so," she replied, growing, if possible, paler this time ; "but I am so glad that you will see her."

"Why specially so?"

"She is so beautiful."

"But we may meet in India," said I, feeling somewhat disappointed that this was her sole cause for satisfaction that my leave of absence remained intact.

"Scarcely," she replied, laughing, and showing a brilliant set of teeth ; "India is a wider world than Europeans have any idea of. At her last ball in London, Blanche was considered the loveliest girl in the room."

"Were *you* there?"

"Yes."

"Indeed, I could not have thought it."

"Now don't attempt flattery," said she, holding up a tiny forefinger ; "for even in a stupid country house it is intolerable. But there rings the bell to dress for dinner, so to punish you I shall retire at once."

And with a very sweet smile she bowed, and left me,

As her figure disappeared through the curtained arch of the outer drawing-room, a sigh of impatience escaped me.

"No, no," thought I, while slowly retiring to my room to make the necessary changes in my toilette, "it cannot—must not be! This affair of ours must be deemed only a flirtation, like any other—a flirtation to pass away, but I fear it will be a hard one to forget. Would to heaven that I had never, never come near Thorsgill Hall!"

CHAPTER II.

INDECISION.

Two lively London girls and their brother, Bob Howard, a somewhat priggish young barrister, formed a portion of the circle at the Hall; but as they have no share in my story, they need not be more particularly referred to; but Colonel Stapleton—Jocelyn Smyth Stapleton—as his cards had it— who came with me from Tilbury, requires some description, as the reader will hear a good deal of him at a future time in these pages; and it must be borne in mind that we were not friends but acquaintances only, who had come together on the General's invitation.

Though not quite six feet in height, he was a tall and splendidly made man, and had a very fair complexion, though it had been somewhat reddened by the Indian sun. His face was handsome, with regular features, and he was closely shaven, all save a thick light-brown moustache, which concealed a mouth that was so formed as to express both cruelty and hauteur, if not insolence. His eyes were a cold and pale dull grey. In manner he was calm, cool, refined, and apparently unimpressionable, though there were times when he assumed an air of *insouciance* that was somewhat repellent.

Yet ladies admired the Colonel, and generally liked his society, though he made no secret of the fact that he "was not a marrying man." He had won a reputation for courage, and was said to have done some dashing things (though no one knew precisely what they were) under Gough and Hardinge, when a sub. in the campaign on the Sutlej.

At dinner that evening I was congratulated by him on my promotion, and by our host, the General—a fine hearty old soldier, who had made more by indigo-planting than by his sword in India, though fond of boasting about Chillianwallah, the only battle he ever saw, and who had now settled down into an easy-going country squire and leading man of the district.

The Colonel used but a few well-bred words, and turned to address Miss Guise ; but the old General shook me heartily by the hand, while the butler poured out a libation of sparkling Moselle "to wet" the new commission.

By the little Misses Howard, whom the Colonel treated very patronisingly—for he was a blasé man of the world in his fortieth year—he was viewed quite as a hero ; for true it is that " no love broker in the world can prevail more in man's commendation with women than the report of valour ;" while his languid mien, and the industry with which he tugged his long tawny moustache, evidently had a great charm for them, though I could perceive that Henriette Guise and her aunt, Mrs. Dormer—a pleasant and motherly matron who had seen much of the world in the upper provinces—smiled covertly at his bearing, while I flattered myself that I was somewhat of a favourite with the old lady, chiefly perhaps because her son, Jack Dormer, was brother-officer of mine in the Rifle Brigade.

How sadly my mind wavered !

Half an hour ago I had silently resolved—yea, had vowed —to relinquish and forswear all hope of winning Henriette, and added the fervent wish that I had never set foot in Thorsgill Hall ; tormented too by hints the unwary General had more than once let fall, to the effect that her parents were as ambitious as they were wealthy, and had certain high views concerning her future in India.

If I remained silent, and buried my hopes in my own heart, might not another, no more moneyed or worthy than myself, step in and win the prize, even on the journey out—a journey affording a thousand opportunities to a lover of enterprise?

Amid the hum and routine of the dinner-table, the maze of hot-house flowers and wax-lights, the courses and entrées, and all the slow and stately process of a repast that was somewhat Anglo-Indian in its style, from the caviare to the curaçoa, while conversing on subjects the most irrelevant, and in which I had not the slightest interest, twenty times I vowed to put all to the issue on the first opportunity—that very night perhaps in the drawing-room or the conservatory—to-morrow at latest, and, if refused, would start by an early train for Tilbury.

Then, like a very craven, my resolution would wane away and die, till the nervous and very natural dread that another —perhaps Stapleton with his better prospects and superior rank—might supplant me through my own indecision, filled me with jealous bitterness and envy, and made me curse in my heart the ambition of her parents and the inequality of our fortune.

Otherwise, how sweet it would have been to abandon myself to the hope of being beloved by her!

The ladies passed in single file to the drawing-room, and when, after coffee had been drunk as a solemn and indispensable ceremony apparently, we had heard the General's usual reminiscences of Chillianwallah, anecdotes listened to with undisguised impatience by the Colonel, and much tugging of his long fair moustache—when, I say, we joined them at last, the night passed uneventfully for me, with music and much singing of the usually vapid kind.

I did much in the way of leaf-turning, glove-buttoning, bouquet-holding, and so forth, without having the opportunity I so earnestly sought: and when the time came, I laid my head on the pillow wishing that I had never quitted dull Tilbury by the turgid Thames to be thrown in the way of this terrible temptation, and conceiving, were it possible, to get up a counter-charm or counterfoil flirtation with some one—Sophy Howard, say—to fill up the time before embarkation; but I was past flirting moods now.

Then I began to nurse myself into a little fit of jealousy, as Stapleton had somewhat contrived to monopolise my idol for nearly the whole of the evening.

He was intimate with her family—would the views hinted at by the General be concerning *him* ?

Next, it suddenly flashed upon my mind that her little white hand lingered—or it seemed to linger—for a moment in mine, as I bade her farewell for the night ; and in the hunger of my heart I made all that imagination could contrive out of an incident so trivial.

I had now deferred my fate till next morning, but was late in coming downstairs ; and entering the breakfast-room, to my annoyance found Stapleton seated by her side, and engaged in the formation of a riding party to Rokeby Woods with her and the Miss Howards ; while the General had resolutely arranged that their brother, himself, and I, should " take a turn across the moors, and knock over a few birds."

Miss Guise was not a girl to show her feelings or make scenes, even on important occasions ; but I thought—it might be only fancy—that her quiet dark eyes brightened and their long lashes quivered as I approached and took her hand in mine.

So I was doomed to go shooting on this day—the eventful day which I had resolved should see me engaged to the pale, black-haired and dark-eyed Henriette—engaged till death did us part ; or off to Tilbury Fort, to musketry drill, and teaching "the young idea how to shoot" with a short Enfield.

This excursion to the moors would prove, I knew, in my present mood of mind utter boredom to me ; and, to make matters worse, she was to have Stapleton as her cavalier in these lonely woodland glades. So I agreed to accompany the General with a very bad grace. Orders were sent to old

Bagshaw, the gamekeeper, to get the guns and dogs in order, while the cattle were to come from the stable court for the riding party after luncheon ; and I knew that until then, too probably, the Colonel would be in close attendance upon Henriette, while I should be stumbling, knee-deep, among the heather at Hindon Edge.

The butler had just received his orders when he deposited before the General the despatch box containing the morning letters ; and, as the arrival of them is always a matter of interest at a breakfast-table in the country, all looked up severally from their coffee and grouse pie, as he drew forth and distributed the contents.

There were pink and yellow epistles, crossed and recrossed, and periodicals, with the latest fashions, for the Miss Howards; a letter for our host, concerning the county pack and certain melon frames that had been smashed at the last hunt ; " And such a smash we cannot, to use a Bengal phrase, score down to the flying artillery," said the General ; and there was one from India, on which the eye of Mrs. Dormer fell immediately with solicitude ; thus she did not open her own letters until the former had been hastily perused by her husband.

" From Allahabad, is it ?" she asked.

" Yes, from Jack."

" Our dear boy is well, I devoutly trust."

" Quite well, Louisa," said he ; " but he has the usual desire to draw on Coutts and Co., or the Agra, having, as he calls it, ' lost a pot of money on the Planters' Cup ;' and then he adds," continued the General turning to me, " ' that cholera has broken out in the cantonments, and that the sepoys are becoming greatly discontented, somehow, about the substitution of the new rifle ammunition for the old.' This sort of thing never happened in *my* time, though I remember at Chillianwallah——"

" I have here a letter from Blanche Bingham," said Mrs. Dormer, with nervous haste, for the General's reminiscences of that famous affair were seriously to be dreaded.

" From Blanche, indeed ! and what is her news ?"

" Shall I read it aloud ?"

" Do, please, aunt," said Henriette ; " her letters are always amusing, and seem so characteristic of herself."

" ' My darling aunt Dormer' (such a warm-hearted girl she is !), ' I cannot allow your kind invitation to lie over one moment longer. In the first place I must acknowledge to feeling quite vain on finding how solicitous you are all to see me—the gentlemen, no doubt especially ; and secondly that I long very much to be at dear Thorsgill Hall, where, by Henriette's accounts, you seem to be having a remarkably jolly time of it. Our chief excitement here is hunting. We were out three days ago—the Appleton girls and I—with the Brighton harriers, and rode the whole way to the meet with the master of the hounds. Such a handsome man, auntie, though getting grey, and he seemed to admire me immensely, as all the old fellows do.

" ' We started a hare, which was killed after an eight miles' run. I was in at the death, and saw the chopping, which shocked me ; for in a moment not a vestige of the poor animal remained but the blood on the dogs' noses. The M. F. H. and a couple of Lancers came to dinner, after which we had limited loo, and unlimited flirtation. At the former I lost horribly, as usual.

" ' Next evening we were all at a concert ; Titiens, as Lucia sang divinely, as you may suppose ; but the tenor, as Edgardo, squalled horribly in the churchyard. Yesterday saw us with the hounds again. We drew a fine fox from some gorse-bushes on the downs, and had a thirty-eight miles run without a single check ! Jacky Appleton and I were the only ladies there. We rushed our horses at everything, yet didn't keep cautiously behind any slow fellow who knew the country, the hedges, lanes, and so forth. The M. F. H. complimented us before the whole field ! The afternoon saw us at a pianoforte recital in the pavilion. Oh, how slow it was ! just like the conventional small talk of a kettle-drum that followed.

"'In the evenings we always "do" the pier of course. Thither comes Jacky's admirer and slavey, and I found myself playing Mademoiselle de Trop (a rôle which never suited your affectionate niece), till her mamma picked up for me a stray plunger on leave from Knightsbridge. For this I was thankful, as it is such a dreadful bore to superintend the flirtations of others.

"'As for poor dear Jacky's admirer, he is only a mild curate whom she caught at croquet; a lisping apostle in a long coat, with parted hair, and not brains enough to bait a mousetrap, otherwise I should soon have had him all to myself. Jacky's case seems a very bad one, but I don't think it will end either in "clandestine matrimony or charcoal."

"'Although I am very happy here, and my plunger, "made up by youth, by love, and by an army tailor," is very attentive and every one seems delighted with me, I quite long to be with you all, as my time in Europe is now, alas! so very short.'"

"She and Henriette go out with Mrs. Appleton as their chaperone," said Mrs. Dormer, parenthetically to me.

"'Give my love to the Howard girls. Has their brother Bob rejoiced in a brief yet?'

"Upon my word, Miss Blanche makes very free! And here is a message for *you*, colonel.

"'I am so glad that Colonel Stapleton is with you. I met him in London at one or two places, where he waltzed divinely, which—which—which—'" Mrs. Dormer paused with a perplexed air, and coloured perceptibly.

"Please, madam, to finish," said the personage alluded to, tugging at his fair moustache.

"'Which seems to be the only accomplishment he possesses, save playing with his moustache, if that be one.'

"How *can* Blanche permit herself to write thus!"

We all laughed at this, and none more heartily than Stapleton himself; however, that he was nettled was evident, as I heard him whisper to Howard:

" Gushing young female, by Jove !"

"Anything more?" asked the general, with mischief twinkling in his eyes.

"Only that she will arrive here this evening a little before dinner time, so the carriage must meet her at Winston Station," replied Mrs. Dormer, closing the letter in haste, as if she had read quite enough.

"Glad to hear it," said the general, rubbing his hands; "a dear good girl, and a beautiful one too! Gad, she'll bring a breeze with her! Blanche will take the house by storm."

To me the tone of the letter seemed a little too "fast," and but ill-calculated to give a favourable impression of the writer. I looked at the quiet, ladylike, and sweetly feminine Henriette, and thought, "Ah, *you* would never let your pen run on thus." But I give prominence to the letter here, because the fair writer will figure largely in the pages to come.

"I do not think it was quite just to the young lady, your reading that to me, Mrs. Dormer," said Stapleton, with one of his noiseless laughs, but letting his moustache alone for once.

"I stumbled on the passage quite suddenly," replied our hostess.

"And Blanche is somewhat of a privileged rantipole," added her uncle ; "we don't mind a bit what she says."

"Is it so?" I asked Henriette, by whose other side I had achieved a seat.

"Perhaps ; there is so much of the mere girl about her still : but with her winning ways, the waxen delicacy of her face and features will, nay must, be sure to charm you."

"I fear not, Hen—Miss Guise."

"Why?" she asked, smiling.

"Because I have ever had a preference for dark beauty," said I ; and lightly, and all unseen, I laid my hand on hers for an instant, and once again I saw a little flush like the tint of a rose-leaf, cross her cheek.

"How the time passes !" said the General, as a thoughtful

shade flitted over his handsome old face. "It seems but yesterday since she and Henriette—my own pet, Henriette! —came from India, little pale-faced and bleached, but prattling girls of five years old; so joyous and so innocent too! They used to climb from a hassock up my knees to kiss me. Now they are going out full-blown young ladies, to take the hearts of the Europeans by storm, and no doubt brides soon to be; for such wares soon find merchants in the Bengal market."

"O uncle!" said Henriette, deprecatingly, as she held up her pretty hands; "but I do hope that we are innocent still," she added, laughing, "though 'the years have rolled on,' as the domestic novels say." And, springing from the table, she put round the old man's neck two lovely white and tapered arms, that came softly forth from the loose and lace-trimmed sleeves of a very becoming morning dress of cerise colour, and kissed him on both cheeks affectionately while her eyes grew moist. I felt more than envious of the graceful caress, and more than ever solicitous about the proposal I had in view; more especially as, when she took her arms from her uncle's neck, her eyes first fell with a curious expression on me.

What a wonderful power those finely-lidded eyes possessed, and how graceful were all her ways and the action of her small delicate hands!

"And now for the moors!" said the General, rising.

With a glance causing my heart to quicken and throb, and to ban the shooting expedition which caused a fresh delay in my affairs, I ascended to my room to gaiter and accoutre; which I did in great haste, with the desire of having, perhaps, a parting word with one who was become so dear to me and so necessary to my happiness.

The breakfast-table was deserted. She was not in the drawing-room; but the subdued sound of voices drew me towards the conservatory, which opened off it on the south side of the house.

It was long and spacious, and more than one graceful acacia drooped there its feathery foliage overhead. There were two parallel passages, formed by a high pyramidal stand or frame in the centre ; on this stand was a mass of exotics in full flower. As I passed, almost noiselessly along the grated and matted floor, I paused, for the voices of Stapleton and Henriette fell on my ear, and my sole desire was to withdraw unnoticed ; for to her I had by this time indicated either too much or too little.

"Bring me a stephanotis," said she, "and take this for the button-hole of your riding coat."

"Oh, a thousand thanks!" he replied ; "but this—what is it ?"

"A camellia ; don't you see, Colonel ?"

"Here is the stephanotis. Do you know," he added in his most insinuating tone, "that what you have asked me for is quite a bridal-flower ?"

"Yes," said she, laughing, which might have assured me she had no grave or tender thoughts in her heart ; "but you have brought with it three rosebuds."

"Which mean," he added, "you know what, in the language of the flowers."

"A proposal, I believe."

What more followed I know not, as at that moment the General attired in a rough tweed suit, with brown gaiters, and with shot-belt and flask slung crosswise over his shoulders appeared at the entrance, saying noisily :

"Now, then, Rudkin—Lance, my boy--Howard and I are waiting ; the dog-cart is at the door, and we have a good hour's drive to Hindon Edge."

Then grasping my patent breechloader, I sprang into the vehicle in a very savage mood of mind indeed, and feeling the while that I was leaving the blasé Colonel in full possession of the field.

CHAPTER III.

THE SHOOTING PARTY.

THERE can be a conversation without words, or in which the words used—though mere commonplace talk—sink deeply into the heart, indicating that which if written, would fill ream upon ream of paper. Yet language has been given us for the purpose, too often, of concealing what we feel and what we wish for.

I had never told Henriette Guise that I loved her ; so barely even a pressure of the hand had passed between us. Each time we met and parted, words only of the commonest greeting and adieu had been spoken, yet our eyes had involuntarily established that silent conversation which says more than any human language can convey, and more than once it seemed to me as if we had actually looked into each other's hearts.

Then why did I linger in doubt and indecision? Why trifle with her and with myself, because the General had hinted that her parents were ambitious, and " had views," concerning her?

Alas, I could little foresee how all this was to end, and how a few short days would leave me no longer to be the arbiter of my own destiny !

How skilfully we can torment ourselves! As we drove through the beautiful wooded country, and past stackyards that teemed with grain, and shorn fields of tawny and rigid stubble, bordered by trees and hedge-rows presenting every variety of autumnal tints—of brown autumn, the evening of the year—my thoughts were all of her I had left behind me. I saw the Colonel—whom I knew to be very insinuating when it pleased him to act so, and, as compared with myself, to be most provokingly wealthy—lingering with her still in the conservatory, or, it might be, hanging over her at the piano ; and in fancy I furnished them with ample conversation, all about themselves, of course.

Then I drew a picture of the riding party, and Stapleton assisting her to mount, the departure, and he by her bridle-rein, with the confounded stephanotis in his lapel, and his three most significant rose buds, too probably, in the breast of her dark-blue riding-habit. How well I knew that habit, and the magnificent contour of her neck, bust, and shoulders in it!

All that I heard in the conservatory might only have been banter, which began and ended there—nay, sounded very like it; but I writhed at the idea that, even in jest, I had been anticipated. And so I dreamed on, amid the uniform patter of the horse's fast-trotting hoofs, and the hum of the wheels with their patent axle-boxes, till suddenly I became aware that the General had been talking to me for some time, all unresponded to, for Howard and the keeper were seated behind us.

"You know I told you how poor Herbert was killed at Attock?" he was saying. "I was first told of it by a Hindoo fakir—a horrid-looking fellow, half naked, and all smeared with white chalk, a gourd slung by a brass chain at his waist, and with a six-pound shot hung at his neck, by way of a perpetual penance."

"Where were you then, General?" I asked with affected interest.

"As I have already mentioned, we were on march to Chillianwallah. I had passed a devil of a night in a peepul tope, kept awake by beastly bats, winged foxes, and green bugs (it was the month of January, you know), and by the howls of the jackals foraging for carrion. I believe they knew what the rumble of the artillery-wheels portended on the morrow. I breakfasted on a little rice in a lotah, washed down by a glass of brandy-pawnee; and went to Gough, and told him we had no time to lose if an effective attack was to be made on those Sikh fellows.

"' I quite agree with you, Dormer,' said he ; ' we must overthrow them, and Chillianwallah shall be the scene of their defeat. Get your column in motion for Dingee.'

" I was then acting as brigadier in the field. The pink glow which always precedes sunrise in India was just coming in, you know—"

I didn't know, and still less did I care.

"— when the whole line broke into columns of march. The Sikhs, clad in red, with white flowing head-dresses, came on with their horse-artillery in front, and opened a fire on our line of skirmishers, till I recommended Gough—who always took my advice—to get up the light cavalry——"

And so on, and on, till old Bagshaw said :

" Here we are, sir, on Hindon Edge."

" Get out the dogs, then."

" The clouds look rather low, and the wind is southerly," said Howard somewhat apprehensively, as we alighted.

" We shan't have no rain, for all that, sir," said the veteran gamekeeper confidently ; " but I fear the birds are very wild to-day."

The butler had made ample provision for luncheon, as the contents of our picnic basket testified. The dogs, cramped by an hour's confinement, were brought out, and wagged their tails joyously at the familiar sight of the guns, which were now finally looked to.

Howard was to accompany the General on one side of the moor, while Bagshaw was to attend me on the other. The barrister was a somewhat taciturn fellow, yet I knew him to be very observant, and ere we parted, he contrived, quite unwittingly however, to make me feel more uncomfortable than ever.

" Why did not the Colonel accompany us ?" he asked me.

" Because he, more pleasantly, elected to ride with the ladies ; and perhaps he wishes to be at home to receive the new arrival."

" Why so ?"

" He paid her much attention while in town, I understand."

" I rather think it was to practise a certain duet with her cousin."

" What duet ?" I inquired.

" One called ' The Language of Flowers.' "

I started on hearing this ; but I remembered having seen a piece bearing that title lying on the piano.

" Oh, yes," he continued, " that was to precede the ride. Have you not perceived how much he has dangled about her for the last few days ?"

" No, not in the least."

" To be sure it was generally when *you* were not in the way," he added with a knowing smile.

At another time I might have been disposed to challenge the accentuation of the pronoun, but now I only laughed to conceal my own annoyance at the conviction that something had been going on that I had failed to see, and set off, with old Bagshaw, feeling all the bitterness of those " trifles light as air," which to young men afflicted with my then mental malady, are " confirmations strong as proofs of holy writ."

The sport proved to me most dreary and dull, unprofitable and uneventful.

The dense dusty heather was nearly knee-deep, and perilously full of old and half-hidden peat-holes, yet through it we toiled manfully, instinctively grasping our guns and looking sharply about us. We were on very lofty ground, and from Hindon Edge, as far as the eye would reach away to the northward, the vast extent of purple moorland stretched, all steeped in hazy but golden sunshine.

The birds were indeed wild ; for the dogs, steady and persevering, were scouring the ground at such a distance that they had to be recalled again and again by Bagshaw's whistle and the vicious cracking of his whip ; but it mattered little to me, for I missed every shot, as if bewitched, and the silver-haired gamekeeper held up his brown hands in pitying astonishment to see so much good ammunition expended on thin air without the least result.

But my thoughts were elsewhere, and thus, though usually a good sportsman and a trained rifle-shot, as a passed instructor in musketry, not a single grouse was mine, and the whole spoil that accrued to my prowess at the close of the day, greatly to the astonishment and amusement of the General, was one teal of the very smallest size !

Luncheon over—pâtés de foie gras and pie of boned larks—alas, for the poor bird that sings at heaven's gate, for even it cannot escape the gastronomic necessities of John Bull !—a long draught or two of champagne, imbibed after the bottles had lain to cool in a deep runnel ; and after hearing the General's report of his success—which seemed great, if one might judge by the distension of his bag, and also the delighted expressions of his legal friend, who had killed several brace of grouse—we separated again to plod over the moor ; and to me the day passed slowly amid the silence of that purple waste, broken only at times by a distant report, as the General or his companion " knocked over " a bird, or by the pitiful whistle of a curlew.

I was glad when the sun began to verge westward, and the Raby Woods to darken, and we were all once more in the dog-cart, and bowling homeward among the shady green lanes, where the yellow autumnal leaves lay deep beside the hedgerows.

Just as the old façade and pinnacles of Thorsgill Hall came in sight we saw the returning riding party, attended by two mounted grooms wearing orthodox cockades and belts, entering the gate of the avenue, and as my heart foreboded, Colonel Stapleton *was* with Henriette, the two sisters being left to ride together in their rear ; but, after all, this was not to be marvelled at, as she was certainly a much more attractive girl than either of the Howards, and as an alternative, decidedly the best.

Checking their horses in the avenue, a long and stately line of oaks, they halted till we overtook them ; and then ensued the usual inquiries concerning our sport, with congratulations

for those who were fortunate, and I had the additional mortification to find my unlucky teal the object of much laughter,
and to none more than Henriette, who seemed in unusually
exuberant spirits, and whose veil, as it was lifted by the wind,
showed that her normally pale face was flushed with exercise
—or was it with pleasure in the Colonel's society?

I gathered, however, a little satisfaction from observing that
the stephanotis was *not* in his button-hole, and that the three
buds were not in the breast of her habit.

Had they been declined, even if offered in jest, or accepted,
and then lost during the ride?

Alas, I had no right to inquire.

The grooms came up, and the party dismounted. Stapleton was off his horse in a moment, and assisted Henriette to
alight from her saddle. As he did so, I thought her fingers
rested for a moment on his shoulder, and then, giving her his
ungloved hand, he led her up the perron to the entrance-hall,
into which, with a smile and a nod to me, she swept with inimitable grace, and with the long skirt of her habit thrown
over her left arm.

At that moment of petty jealousy and distorted fancy, how
little could I forsee the change that was erewhile to come over
me, and the cold indifference that for a long, long time at
least was to replace the love and admiration which then filled
my heart!

"It can't be possible," thought I, "that she can admire a
fellow like Stapleton, with his sandy or straw-coloured moustache, large white hands, and pale China-blue eyes—one
long since looked upon as 'scratched' in the matrimonial
market."

CHAPTER IV.

WHY I DID NOT PROPOSE.

THORSGILL HALL is beautifully situated near an acute bend
of the river in the richly-wooded vale through which the Tees

flows from Milbourn Forest, on its way to the German Ocean.
A house of the Stuart times, that had been battered and burned
in civil war and more than once by Scottish invaders, it had
been patched up and repaired in different ages, thus adding
to its picturesque irregularity; and though extremely antique,
the older edifice and the more recent additions made thereto
in the same style of architecture, with mullioned oriels, were
all furnished in light and fashionable modern taste.

It was thoroughly a pleasant home, with an oaken library
that was tranquil and quiet with subdued lights, a cosy dining-
room with warm draperies, long corridors for promenades in
wet weather, and a stately double drawing-room, the brightly
tinted oriel of which looked out on a noble and far-stretching
chase, where the General's ancestors had hunted and hawked
in past times, had dallied with their brides in youth and with
their children in old age, and where now the brown deer found
a lair among the waving fern.

It was not without its quaint legends too, as it had a haunted
room in one of its old gable-ended abutments—a room which
existed without being seen, for a wicked Squire of Thorsgill
in times long past had been carried off there by the devil,
with a number of his friends who were gambling deeply,
drinking, and swearing profanely on a Christmas-eve, and
were never seen more; but it was averred that in stormy
nights, when the Tees was foaming over its rocky bed, when
the trees of the chase bent beneath the blast, when their torn
leaves and the rain pelted on the oriels, and the wind moaned
round the gables and clustered chimney-stacks of the old
mansion, the voices, laughter, shrieks, and curses of the lost
gamesters, with the rattling of dice-boxes, and the clink of
glasses, were heard in the mysterious room; but the General,
who laughed at the story, said that no such thing had happened in his time.

The proprietor's Indian tastes and proclivities were to be
seen on all sides, in the form of Bombay workboxes, Japanese
canisters all over flaming red dragons, Burmese idols squatted

on their hams, and in wonderful things carved in ivory.
There, too, were trophies of our Indian wars—Sikh tulwars
from Chillianwallah, Afghan juzails with inlaid butts ; gilded
Mahratta shields with brass orbs, and Goorkha cookries :
tigers' skins and skulls — which all told of the home of
the retired Anglo-Indian, and consorted curiously with
the fashion of the old English mansion—a house of the
fighting times, when the Scots were wont to come with axe
and spear as far south as the Rere Cross of Stanmore.

Having dressed for dinner on the evening after the shooting excursion, I chanced to stroll into the library, where to
my surprise and joy I found Henriette, and alone.

She was seated in the recess of a heavily-curtained bay-
window, an open book was in her hands and resting on her
lap ; but instead of reading she was gazing listlessly, or as if
lost in thought, upon the scenery without.

Then, declining behind the hill, the September sun was
throwing the long purple shadows across the green shaven
lawn and the stately trees in the chase, where the white sheep
in some places, and the deer in others, after having nestled for
hours among the feathery ferns, were rousing themselves for
a last feed among the tender grass, and causing the rabbits
and hares to glide to and fro like evil spirits.

Henriette's back was to me, and the soft Turkey carpet
enabled me to approach her unheard, till I placed my arms
on the top of the high chair in which she was seated, and
gazed down on her handsome head, with its wealth of black
silky hair, and its straight central division that was milky
white, her little delicate shell-like ears and beautiful neck,
which her attire showed to perfection.

What her dress was I cannot tell now ; I only remember
that with it she wore a black velvet body cut somewhat low,
but square at the neck and bosom, with a narrow stand-up
frill of white lace. She was without ornaments of any kind,
save a ring or two ; and her fine hair was coiled round a jet
comb, all save one long and negligent tress that fell down her

back. And as I continued to gaze with tenderness and admiration, I could see, with every respiration, the swelling of her bosom as it rose and fell.

We were alone, and I felt, while all my pulses quickened, that now or never was the time to have that told which I meant to tell.

Suddenly she looked up at me with a smile, and said:

"Now, Captain Rudkin, were I a nervous young lady, which I am not, your approach unheard might have startled me."

"Pardon me ; but I could not help admiring your profile and whole pose, as you sat ; but I fear I am disturbing a pleasant reverie perhaps. Of what were you thinking?"

"How peaceful the landscape looks, and how pleasant it is to hear the evening chimes coming from the old church-tower in the distance !"

"Then you have something of art and poetry in your nature," I observed, scarcely knowing how to begin, and feeling that I was becoming very commonplace.

"I fear that I have neither," said she, "I am rather prosaic and practical."

I could see that her eyes drooped under the unconcealed ardour of my gaze ; that she grew, if possible, paler after one tiny flush crossed her cheek, and that her respirations became quicker.

"How far did your ride extend to-day?" I asked after a pause.

"A sixteen miles' trot, to lovely Langley Dale. It was truly delightful ; the air was so bracing, and the view at times so extensive !"

"How I longed in my heart of hearts to be with you ! But the General insisted on my going to the moors with him."

"And you were most successful," said she archly.

"My thought and wishes were elsewhere."

"Then I would that you had come with us. I—that is,

3

we, all of us—did certainly miss you," she added, again looking out on the landscape.

I took caressingly in my hand the stray tress, and—as I thought, unseen by her—pressed it to my lips, forgetting as I did so that the shutter-panels of the bay-window were all mirror.

" I can *see* you," she said, laughing, while her colour heightened and paled again. " It is a very gallant action, no doubt ; but, Captain Rudkin, in these days it is perilous work to pull a lady's back-hair."

By this little action I had certainly "opened the trenches," and with all her self-possession Henriette seemed nervously conscious of what was most probably to follow

I drew a chair close to her side, and seating myself took her right hand in mine, but she withdrew it, and the action chilled and repressed me. A little awkward pause ensued, and I was silent when I should have spoken.

" Pardon me if—if I have offended you," said I, with a sigh that was irrepressible.

" Offended me ! Oh, no," she replied, in a low and breathless voice, and while a beautiful smile spread over her soft and half-averted face she held out her hand to me, and then my heart beat more wildly than ever.

Caressing the slender fingers between both my hands, I said, " Do not turn from me, Miss Guise. Oh, let me look into your eyes !"

She then turned to me with a half-startled expression, and I could see the white lids with their long black lashes were quivering perceptibly.

" Dear Miss Guise," I was beginning, " or will you permit me to say dearest—dearest Henriette——"

" Here she is in the library, of all places in the world !" exclaimed a merry and impetuous voice close by us, and a young lady in her travelling-dress burst suddenly upon us, threw her arms round the neck of Henriette, and kissed her on both cheeks, in mingled affection and fun.

" Blanche !"

" How scared you look, cousin !"

" You came upon me so suddenly," said Henriette.

" I hope I have not been de trop, and interrupted a plea-sant tête-à-tête ?"

" Not at all, Blanche dearest," replied Henriette, with a somewhat conscious look nevertheless. " You have just come in time for dinner."

" And though a gentleman was most attentive to me in the train, and insisted on giving me a lunch at York, I have caught *such* an appetite, by the way !"

" Glad to hear it," said the General, who had followed her. " In our menu to-day we are to have trout potted in Madeira, and the haunch of a stag shot in the park. We can also let you have a roasted teal," he added, with a mischievous glance at me.

" I am so glad to see you all again! Give me one more kiss, you dear, dear old thing !" exclaimed the young lady, as she embraced in succession her uncle and aunt, and then, approaching me, held up her soft Greuze-like face and ruby lips in a manner that was very bewildering, even to a man who had been on the point of making a declaration to another; for a subtle smile shone around them, and danced within her eyes.

" Blanche," said the General, " allow me to introduce Captain Rudkin of the Rifle Brigade — my niece, Miss Bingham."

" You have just said so in time ; for a moment I thought he was my cousin Jack."

" Poor Jack is broiling up-country at Allahabad."

" I wish the General had delayed his introduction for a moment or two," said I, with a smile and a bow, while it flashed on my mind that the implied compliment was unfair to Henriette.

" So delighted to see you, Captain Rudkin ! I have heard so much about you, that you seem quite like an old friend."

" Indeed !   How, Miss Bingham ?" I inquired.

"From Henriette's letters."

Poor Henriette coloured painfully, while Miss Bingham divested herself of her hat, veil, and seal-skin jacket, saying laughingly the while—

" And you have Colonel Stapleton here and Bob Howard, too.   So glad you have some gentlemen, auntie ! I was not born to blush unseen—bloom, I mean—or waste my sweetness on my own sex."

I now saw how remarkable was the face of the girl who had dropped so suddenly among us, and at a time so critical for Henriette and me. In expression it could be bright or cloudy, laughing, thoughtful, waggish, or petulant, all manner of things in rapid succession ; yet somehow always flashing and brilliant—a girl to take a man's senses by storm.

Though far from being regular, her features, taken altogether, were indeed lovely ; her hair of that brilliant chestnut tint which becomes golden in the sunshine ; her laughing eyes were somewhat of the same hue, a soft hazel, with dark eyebrows and lashes ; and though a little more petite than Henriette, her neck, hands, and ears—her whole figure was perfect.

The luxuriance of her hair was as wonderful as its fascinating colour, which was indeed that given by painters to their Venuses and other ideal beauties. With a great wealth of animal spirits, the girl, then in all the bloom of eighteen, though her extreme fairness of complexion and expression made her seem more girlish, had a charming subtlety of manner, and was well calculated to excite love in men, envy in women, and admiration in both; for with beauty, dress, and style she had all the desire to please.

As she withdrew with her aunt and cousin to dress for dinner, our eyes involuntarily followed her. Those of the white-haired General expressed pleasure and affection, as she was his favourite niece, and little could we then foresee the havoc her perilous beauty was to make among us in the time to come.

" She is charming !" I observed.

" Yes," said he enthusiastically, " and good as she is beautiful, though in truth she is *fairer than a fairy !*"

Was I already forgetting the interruption her sudden arrival had caused ?

CHAPTER V.

" LOVE NOT."

THE drawing-room at Thorsgill Hall was filled with the soft but brilliant light of many wax candles. As usual in such apartments, mirrors on all sides reflected and reproduced in endless perspective the draperies, the guests, and also the General's Indian objects of vertu, which were scattered over all the tables and consoles ; and there, seated on an ottoman, under the chandelier, which poured a flood of light upon her golden hair, her snow-white neck, and tapered arms, our new arrival, by her excessive animation, made herself the centre of attraction.

When seated side by side, the contrast between the cousins was wonderful. Though the daughters of two sisters, the girls were as different in appearance and character as day is from night, as winter from summer ; yet they had one great gift in common : each in her own style could charm her own sex as well as ours. It was an unconscious power of fascination, which may exist irrespective of beauty, of sweetness, even of virtue ; but, in this instance, these girls were as pure as they were beautiful and good in the highest degree.

The power I mean is most difficult of definition, and is that which a writer has termed " so delicate a mixture of many gifts and qualities that it is difficult to decide on the proportions of each." Yet times there were when the clear eyes of Blanche seemed to say, " I know that I *am* beautiful, and what men love and admire."

There was something magnetic in the girl's smile and touch, and she had a marvellous power and trick of the eyes.

Remembering—for she could never forget it—the little scene that was about to take so serious a turn in the oriel of the library, Henriette, when her glance caught mine, coloured perceptibly more than once, as if conscious of what might yet take place in time.

She was perfectly quiet and subdued in bearing, while in that of her cousin, though not less lady-like, there were waggery combined with pride, the desire to please and the power to dazzle, with plenty of self-possession and self-will, all of which one would easily pardon in a glowing little beauty, so rich in sunny colouring, with such glorious golden hair, and eyes so singular in hue that they defy analysis or description —for though we thought them light hazel, times there were when they seemed almost golden too; and with such charms and vivacity of manner, her little wild speeches were never misconstrued, and often received with laughter.

"Well, Henriette," we heard her say, in concluding some topic with her cousin, "it is my character; and don't be shocked, when I tell you that I would rather be wicked than weak, a knave than a fool, a hammer than an anvil."

"A most decided young woman, certainly," commented Stapleton in a low voice, while tugging at his moustache as usual.

"But I think her just the sort of girl to make a fellow cheerful and enchanted with himself, and with herself more especially," urged the young barrister.

"Too much one of the period, for my taste," replied Stapleton, who for some inscrutable reason did not seem, just then, to like her. "I believe that, for all the softness of her beauty and flourish of yellow hair, she has no more nerves than a locomotive."

"And, Blanche, how about your plunger friend?" asked Henriette with a bright smile.

"Oh, I left Brighton just in time to prevent him from

making a greater donkey of himself than he has been made by nature," replied Blanche, while laughing heartily behind her fan.

" In what way ?"

" He was awfully in love with me, no doubt, and kept us all —the Appleton girls and me—in music, bouquets, tickets for everything, and almost in gloves ; he lost so many bets—the good-natured fellow never seemed to tire of making them and losing them—for all of which I fear I was very ungrateful. There was a ball given by the Hussars just before I left, and I can't tell you how many stupid soft things he said between the figures of the quadrilles and in the crush of the supper-room, amid the overpowering and rather mixed odours of jockey-club and frangipanni, lobster-salad and hot-house plants, fruit and cold chicken. But his tender utterances were all in vain ; I was bound for distant India—he for the stern military duties of Knightsbridge Barracks ; so there was an end of it, and we were not fated to become a West-end Darby and Joan."

While she was running on in this fashion—one which led me to infer that it would be difficult to attempt the utterance of " stupid soft things " to her—the General, with his feet planted on the hearthrug and his back to the white marble chimney-piece, though there were flowers only, and not a fire, in the grate, was boring Stapleton with some episode of Chillianwallah ; the Howard sisters were performing a sweetly insipid duet at the piano ; their brother was conversing with our hostess, a handsome old lady with a white lace cap over her silver hair, and a complexion nearly as delicate now as in her youth, though wrinkled ; and I lingered indecisively near the cousins.

As the evening drew on, I began to detect a slight constraint in the manner of Henriette towards me, and on Blanche beckoning to me with her fan, and saying, "Come here, Captain Rudkin—are you afraid of me, that you have barely addressed me to-night ?" the former rose and joined the singers, while I took her place upon the central ottoman.

How brilliantly beautiful the girl looked in the full blaze of the light that shone on her flashing hair and heaving bust! She wore a dress of lavender-blue silk cut high upon the shoulders, but low in the front, with the finest lace of Malines round her delicate bosom and at the ends of her loose open sleeves. On each white arm was a bracelet of that delicate work and brilliant gold that comes from Delhi; a necklet of the same was round her perfect neck, and she wore a brooch and earrings formed of tiger's claws, all set in the same bright ductile Indian gold—" Mamma's present on her last birthday," as she afterwards told me.

All that a poet, all that a painter ever dreamed of in their happiest moments of inspiration, were in her smiles, in her eyes and lips. Would the storms of grief or passion ever furrow that delicate little face?

God alone knew.

She looked up like a little queen as she lay back in the deep soft ottoman, fanning herself slowly and leisurely, and eyeing me the while, somewhat critically I thought, over the top of her fan; but she lost no time in plunging into conversation, for topics were easily found.

India, which she had left in her childhood; Calcutta, whither she was going; where was my regiment cantoned? She talked away with singular volubility and grace of the last book which had made a sensation, the belle of the last season, or tenor or picture that had become famous; where she had been, and people she had met; the Brighton harriers, and all manner of things, investing them with an interest, the greatest art of conversation in any woman, and she was but a girl. Her transitions were always abrupt, however; thus, when we were talking of the then recent war in the Crimea, she suddenly said,

" My cousin Henriette is very pretty. Don't you think so?"

" Pretty—she is simply lovely."

" You admire her, then?"

" Of course; but who could fail to do so?"

Yet at that moment—traitor that I was !—I was already almost surmising in my heart, "How can a man love any woman but a fair one ?" And then, as I gazed into the face of Blanche Bingham, I recalled the words of a writer who says, that the charming activity of soul and spiritual energy "which give animation, grace, and living light to the animal form, is after all the real source of woman's beauty." The eyes of Henriette were handsome, dark, and thoughtful, but they did not possess the sunny light that shone in those of Blanche.

"And you leave for India—when ?" she asked me, after a little pause.

"In the second month of the year, probably. I have to take a detachment of troops."

"How delightful, if we were all going together !"

"Delightful, indeed !"

"But we go out overland. I do dote upon soldiers, though I don't think mamma would permit me to marry one."

"Why ?" I asked, surprised by the sudden turn our short conversation had taken ; one rather perilous too with such a companion.

"Because she approves highly of the Civil Service, and all people who know India say that there the red coats have no chance whatever compared with the black."

"Fortunately my uniform is a green one."

"Yes, of course, you are in the Rifles."

"And green is the colour of constancy," said I insinuatingly.

"And also of extreme verdure," she added, with half-closed eyes. Then, after a pause : "If I ever marry," she said, with her head a little on one side, and her eyelids cast down demurely, "which, perhaps, I never shall——"

"A strange doubt for a young lady—you especially. ʼ

"Why me especially ?"

"Can you ask me, with all those mirrors around us ?"

"I mean, that if I do, there is *one* kind of marriage I shall never make."

"May I inquire what it is?" I asked, becoming amused by the strange humour of the girl.

"That which is habitually termed by parents and guardians a 'prudent' marriage, which leads to a life of dull and respectable routine, with some elderly commissioner, or used-up planter, or a Calcutta merchant, with as many ailments as he has rupees; such a husband as match-making mammas prefer to a poor but handsome young man, with all the cardinal virtues and a great many more. I don't think I could pass through life without an episode or two, and dwindle down into a respectable old lady; one, perhaps, irreproachable as Mrs. Hannah More. Heavens! what would such a starched dame think if she saw me after the Brighton harriers, rushing my horse at a five-barred gate, or a breast-high hedge, as Jackey Appleton and I did the other day! I must love the man that I shall marry, and shall choose for myself, too."

"Happy, indeed, must the man be you approve of," said I in a lower tone than we had yet used.

"Now, Captain Rudkin," said she, turning her eyes full upon me, "we have had hunting, literature, art, music, and many other things under discussion, so do not let us degenerate into flirtation."

"In the present instance I should dread doing so; but why?"

"It sometimes paves the way for real love-making, and that is—is——"

"What?"

"Very pleasant with some people, very tiresome with others, and occasionally treasonable."

Full of fun and mischief, her eyes of golden hazel were cast on Henriette as she said this; and I felt my colour rise, for during the past hour, in which I had been absorbed in Blanche, I had not been quite unconscious that the dark eyebrows of her cousin—brows that almost met over her straight and delicately-cut nose—had worn a cloudy expression more than once.

Impelled by the tenderness I felt, by courtesy, and a fear that I had offended her by a neglect that was all unusual, I approached her ; but though her lips smiled gaily, the grave and somewhat hard expression of her eyes was distinctly perceptible to me, who had watched their changes so often and so earnestly ; yet Henriette had great command over herself, and I had still every anxiety to resume the thread of that little conversation which Blanche's sudden arrival had so awkwardly interrupted.

" This room is insufferably close," she said, in reply to some general remark of mine.

" The conservatory is lighted," I hinted, and drew back the curtain that fell before the entrance thereto. " May I offer you my arm ?"

" No, thanks, pray don't trouble," she replied hurriedly, and passed in, followed by young Howard.

I felt that I *had* piqued her unintentionally ; she was a little jealous ; and with this conviction a thrill of pleasure passed through my breast ; yet it seemed to me, that in the art of flirting, in the use of the eyes and little occasional touches with the hand, I had made more progress with Blanche in one hour than I had done with Henriette Guise in two months. The instinct of love is acute (if she did indeed love me), and perceptive of the slightest coldness in manner, in tone, in a glance, or the merest inflection of the voice ; for there is a sympathy that lovers alone can feel and know, and of which the unobservant or the uninitiated can know nothing.

A little space served to make matters more cloudy still ; for when Henriette re-entered the room Blanche had spread her ample blue-silk dress over the piano-stool, and with her white fingers rambling over the keys, her handsome head, her golden hair shining like an aureole round it, thrown well back, her seductive eyes upturned and bent on *me*, with no small *empressement*, while I officiated in the capacity of leaf-

turner, she sang a then somewhat hackneyed fashionable
song :—

> "Love not ! love not ! the thing you love may *change :*
> The rosy lip may cease to smile on you :
> The kindly beaming eye grow cold and strange ;
> The heart still warmly beat, but not be true."

The quiet dark eyes of her cousin regarded us, I thought,
with something of disdain.

Was this chosen song to be prophetic, or did Blanche sing
it, so pointedly and winningly, merely in her usual spirit of
waggish raillery?

When it was ended, a movement on the part of our hostess
indicated that the ladies were about to leave us.

" And now good night, dearest uncle," said Blanche, turning
up her bright face for his kiss, and taking his old face between
two hands that were as white as the leaves of the camellia.
" Of course you are all bound for the smoking-room, where,
amid the fumes of the 'fragrant weed '—isn't that the phrase
Captain Rudkin?—you will be discussing everything, from
breach-loaders to ballet girls, and from the winner of the
Derby to the newest thing in neck-ties."

As her aunt said again, her " tongue did indeed run on."
After that we heard her voice, laughing and humming " Love
not," as she passed upstairs to the corridors where the bed-
rooms were.

It seemed to me, amid after thoughts in the smoking-room,
that Blanche's soft hand had lingered a moment in mine, as
the girl made some playful remark ; and that when I turned
to look for Henriette, she was *gone.*

CHAPTER VI.

IN THE PICTURE GALLERY.

NEXT day I was up and abroad before any of our party, and
sauntered on the terrace before the house, enjoying a cigar

and the sunshine of a glorious and breezy September morning,
and marvelling whether I should be fortunate enough to meet
Henriette Guise alone once more.

The dewy masses of dark green ivy that covered the walls
of the hall were literally alive with twittering sparrows ; the
lark was soaring high in the blue welkin ; the ruddy morning
sun threw the shadows of the trees far across the grassy
sward, and brought out in strong light the quaint façade of the
mansion, with all its abutments, towers, pinnacles, and oriels,
the walls of old red brick, while the cornices, mullions and
transoms were of white stone, carved and polished.

Which of all those shining windows, I surmised, may light
the room of Henriette, when perhaps at this moment her white
cheek is resting on the pillow.

In the background, high over the Hall, on the slope of a
hill, but close by, were the ruins of an older edifice, its prede-
cessor ; a castle of more stirring times than ours, built by the
Geoffrey Dormer of King Stephen's days, as Henriette informed me, in the vaulted hall of which, for many hundred
winters, the red yule log had blazed in the bottle-chimney,
throwing a warm glow on many successive generations of
happy English faces ; on the green holly-bush and its scarlet
berries ; on the smoking haunch and the wassail bowl ; but
now, where whilom shouts and laughter rang, there is nothing
heard but the whistle of the bat and the rustle of the long
reedy grass as it waves on the cold hearthstone.

And more than once, when rambling there with Henriette,
she had shown me a great beam over the great entrance, and
above the shield charged with ten billets and the demi-lion of
the Dormers ; a great oak beam, where once swung the *panier
de mort*—an iron basket for hurling a torrent of stones on the
heads of invading Scots or other enemies—till the destruction
of the pile by David II., before the battle of Neville's Cross.

At one of the sunlit oriels, the central window of which
opened down to a flight of steps that led to the terrace, I saw
the fl..ter of a lady's dress, and hastening forward met—not

Henriette, but Blanche Bingham ; and I began to think there was some fatality in this.

"Good morning, Captain Rudkin," said she, playfully waving her hand, after kissing it, toward me. "I too am early abroad ; but I cannot forget my school-girl hours and habits."

How bright, pure, and marvellously fair the girl looked, fresh from her bed and bath, as she stood in the glare of the sunlight, clad in a white morning dress trimmed with blue ribbons ! She did indeed seem bewitching and kissable, with her scarlet mobile lips, dimpled cheeks, and laughing eyes, which, like all her features and her busy little tongue, were in full play ; for she was always on excellent terms with herself, and possessed so much individuality of character that those who once knew her could never forget her.

Though so young, and, to all appearance, artless, with her golden hair, her blush-rose cheeks, and pretty waggish ways, Blanche Bingham was nevertheless mistress of all the various modes by which the most experienced woman of the world can let a man see that he is agreeable to her ; and somehow she was permitted to make audacious little speeches, such as her cousin Henriette and other girls would not have ventured to utter, her soft beauty and mercurial spirits finding ready pardon for that which the ill-natured might have termed flippancy.

"This is the window of the picture gallery," said she, "let us promenade till breakfast-time."

"If you can find amusement in my society."

"Oh, I am sure I shall. I begin to like you very much, Captain Rudkin."

"How can you flatter me so ?" I asked, both puzzled to find the order of conversation becoming inverted.

"But really, I find no one here worth talking to but you. Aunt Dormer is always full of advice or stories of her old ayahs, the Dorcas meetings, the vicar's last sermon ; and such things don't interest me. Dear uncle Dormer always talks, if not of the county pack, bullocks and mangel-wurzel, grouse and hunting, of Anglo-Indian shop and Chillianwallah."

" There is Mr. Howard——"

" He is somewhat muffy (I am not at school now,) and always takes antibilious pills, and wears goloshes in wet weather."

" Stapleton, then ?" I suggested, laughing outright.

She coloured at the mention of *his* name, why, I knew not then, and replied :

" The gallant Colonel is too much occupied by the contemplation of himself to think of me, and I care not for him."

(These words were to come back to me at a future time and in another land.)

" I love my cousin Henriette, but she has grown quite *triste;* as we dressed our hair together this morning, I could not extract a word from her, even about *you ;* but when you know me better, Captain Rudkin, you will find that I am very difficult to please."

" Then how flattered I should be by your frankly admitting that you began to ' like ' me !"

"Not at all; perhaps I shall tire of you too."

" I thought that you longed to come to Thorsgill Hall ?"

" I was very happy at Brighton ; but relations must be humoured, and I am longing now to be with mamma in India."

" Quite natural ; but are you weary of England ?"

" I cannot say. Aunt tells me that the balls there are delightful ; only forty ladies perhaps present, the half of them married, and as many as four hundred gentleman all contending for their hands as partners."

" The Overland Route will soon change all that."

" What a premium Henriette and I shall be at in the Land of the Sun !" she exclaimed, with a little ringing laugh ; and I now began to perceive that if a phrenologist had passed his hand among her wealth of shining hair, he would find her organ of love of admiration pretty strongly developed.

At that moment a door was opened by a footman, and Henriette, with Stapleton, joined us. Handsome indeed she looked, in a pink morning dress trimmed with white lace—a wife for any man to be proud of, and over whose household she would infallibly shed grace and brilliance.

Her greeting to me was, I felt, somewhat coldly polite. Could she have thought that Blanche and I were there by appointment already?

In one point only had the cousins a little resemblance. Blanche, though her hair was golden, had eyebrows that were nearly as dark as those of Henriette, but more delicately pencilled ; and though both girls had been under the care of a West-end "professor of deportment," they possessed in all their actions a natural grace that she could never have imparted to them.

"I trust we—aw—don't intrude ?" said Stapleton, in his usual blandly insincere and rather offensive tone.

" What leads you to think so ?" asked Blanche curtly, but with a smile.

" Because," replied the Colonel, laughing, and applying his strong white hand to his tawny moustache, and, by a blundering attempt at a joke, giving his question more point, " the picture gallery and the library are so often the places for scenes and dénoûments in novels and dramas. In the first place, we have our own ancestors, or some ' other fellow's ' ancestors, looking down upon us sternly or serenely, as the case may be——"

" By the way," interrupted Blanche, with one of her merriest smiles, " surely I interrupted some very special conversation in the library on the evening of my arrival ?"

" You interrupted a very pleasant tête-à-tête, that was all," said I, on perceiving a distinct shade of annoyance cross the face of her cousin—a shade perceptible to myself alone.

" And our subject was perhaps less curious than the discussion we overheard between you and Captain Rudkin last night," said Henriette, with one of her quiet smiles.

"About marriage ; oh, yes, it was quite a serious affair."

"I thought your ideas, or your speeches at least, a little wild, Blanche," said her aunt, who had just joined us.

"Concerning the man I would *not* marry? Oh, dear aunt, how I should like to see in a dream, or in a mirror the happy man whom I am in future to honour, and of course disobey —as I shall be sure to do— while turning the domestic tread-mill, when all the excitement of the shower of old shoes and the wedding tour is over. Now, if I always acted properly as a young lady——"

"Do you not *do* so, Blanche?" asked Mrs. Dormer.

"Ah, don't chide me, dear auntie. I mean that if I did so, I should not converse about marriage to gentlemen ; but I fear I shall never be wise or saintly."

We now turned to inspect some of the pictures.

"That is Chillianwallah, of course," said Stapleton, with a glance at me, "and these are the 14th Light Dragoons advancing to the charge, supported by Dormer's Brigade."

"And this is a fox hunt in Langley Dale, with the General in at the death," said Blanche, pointing to a large oil-painting exhibiting a vast sweep of purple moorland, in the centre of which was a confused mob of struggling hounds killing their fox, groups of red-coated horsemen in the distance, and one close at hand presented a good likeness of our host on his favourite hunter.

She now proceeded to quiz the family portraits, and tell droll anecdotes about each. There were Dormers in wigs and breastplates, who had fought at Edgehill and Newbury ; dames in long stomachers and high toupees, with fans, apples, or pomander balls in their long lean fingers ; powdered belles who had made havoc among the beaux of former days ; and some there were who were dressed as shepherds and shepherdesses à la Watteau ; and on each and all she had some witty remark to make, considering that, as they were her own ancestors, she was free to do so.

"Here is my great grandfather, Sir Philip Dormer, who

fought at Dettingen, Minden, or somewhere, tending his sheep with crook, in a brocaded suit and brigadier wig, with Thorsgill Hall in the middle distance, a stream in the foreground :

> ' By the side of a murmuring brook
>   An elderly gentleman sat ;
>   On the top of his head was his wig,
>   On the top of his wig was his hat.' "

"Of whom is this the portrait ?" I asked. " Surely this proud and sad, yet lovely woman must have had a story ?"

"Happy women rarely have," replied Henriette. " Our grandfather brought it from Sicily, where he had been serving with the army under Sir John Stuart, the Count of Maida."

It was a full length, as dark as a Hans Holbein, yet as softly painted as a Titian, representing a lady in a long brocaded dress, covered with seed pearls, cut low and square to show a magnificent bosom. Her face very beautiful but very pale ; and the dark brown eyes had a gaze in them that followed from whatever point you viewed them. Her hair, a reddish auburn, fell in a mass behind her head, which was haughtily turned to the left, while her gathered skirt was held by her right hand, on the wrist of which sat a hooded falcon.

"You surmise correctly, Captain Rudkin," said Henriette, coming close to me ; " she had a story—a strange but not a sad one."

"Who was she ?" I asked, glad of an excuse for conversing with Henriette and gazing into her deep dark eyes.

"Camilla de Turinge, a rich and handsome lady of Messina ; we have all her history in a little manuscript book in the library."

"Please, cousin, don't produce the manuscript, or I should think I am at school again," said Blanche, "but tell us all about it."

"The book has it," began Henriette, her dark eyes filling with animation as she spoke, "that Roland, brother of Pedro,

King of Sicily, to whom he had given command of a squadron
of galleys to oppose the fleet of Robert, King of Naples, was
defeated at sea, and taken into captivity; from which his
brother in a spirit of resentment, failed to redeem him or pay
his ransom, which amounted to twelve thousand florins; so
he bade fair to remain a prisoner for life; and in bitterness he
spoke of this to Camilla de Turinge.

"'Take courage, Don Roland,' said she; 'when youth,
health, and hope are combined, what is there in this world
that we may not attain?'

"'True, with love and happiness perhaps; but I am a
hopeless prisoner.'

"'You shall be free on one condition.'

"'Oh, name it!' he exclaimed.

"Then the beautiful Messinian, after much circumlocution,
gave Roland to understand that he should have his ransom
money on condition he espoused her——"

"Shocking, to purchase a husband?" exclaimed Blanche.
"I should like to be loved for myself, and myself alone, even
as King Cophetua loved the beggar maid. Had she fallen in
love with him, Henriette?"

"Yes; for this Roland was one of the handsomest men in
the Two Sicilies; and seeing no other means of escaping from
a life of bondage, he promised her marriage as soon as he
could visit Messina. On payment of her twelve thousand
florins, Roland obtained his freedom, his sword and armour,
and at once put to sea, resolving to return no more, as he had
no intention of fulfilling his promise; and in justification
alleged the great disparity of their ranks in life, though
Camilla—who was determined to have justice done her——pro-
duced their mutual bond, the terms of which Don Pedro
ordered his brother to fulfil to the letter."

"I have no patience with this woman!" exclaimed Blanche;
"how could she be so odiously spiritless?"

"Wait a little, cousin. Accompanied by many great lords
and ladies, clad in gorgeous apparel, Roland set out for the

stately villa of his intended, who received them dressed in her richest attire ; and then, kneeling, he entreated that she would forgive his past duplicity, and let their engagement be fulfilled.

" ' Stay, sir,' said she ; ' I wished, in my ambition, to have a husband of royal blood, though, sooth to say, I did love and pity you ; but you have degraded yourself from your rank by breaking a plighted troth, and from that moment I have sworn never to be yours. Keep your ransom-money, and re-serve that dishonoured hand for another. You are free to go—adieu !'

"And snatching up her skirt (just as we see it in the picture), as if the touch of Roland were pollution, she swept from the room, leaving him overwhelmed with confusion and rage. After this she retired into a convent at Palermo, wherein grandpapa's regiment was quartered after the battle of Maida, and there he obtained this portrait."

" Captain Rudkin, you have been looking at me for the last ten minutes in most attentive silence," said Blanche, when her cousin ended : " now pray what do you think of me ?"

" Think !" I repeated, in some perplexity.

" That I am a very eccentric and unusual young lady ; is such the case ?"

" Unusual certainly," said I, gazing into the laughing eyes.

" Then you must tell me how and wherefore at breakfast, for there sounds the gong, and I shall take your arm."

And thus I was in a manner, made prisoner.

A single week after this saw a strange change in me, for my mind began to waver between the fair and the dark cousin. However anxious I may have been to seek a secret interview with Henriette, and to return to the subject of my suit, though perhaps she did not avoid me, she never, from the epoch of Blanche's arrival, permitted herself to be left alone with me. At times I conceived the idea of writing to her on the subject of the hopes that had been growing so dear to me ; but then the mere circumstance of finding her apparently too much occupied with Stapleton would pique me, and I relinquished the idea. We had often been much alone before, but never were so now.

Why was this?

Was it that she knew I had admired and learned to love her; but that she could not or would not accept me, and yet expected a regular proposal for the mere luxury of declining it?

I was most unjust to Henriette; but a long time was to elapse, and terrible events were to happen, ere I learned the light in which she viewed me then.

CHAPTER VII.

DRIFTING.

IN our limited circle at Thorsgill Hall it was impossible from the mere circumstance of propinquity, to remain insensible to the attractions of such a pretty girl as Blanche Bingham, who, as she had a decided penchant for the army, being one who made no secret of her "doting on the military," and who seemed to dress for me, sing for me, talk for me, as if systematically to pique Jocelyn Stapleton, who had been her admirer during her short season in London.

This on the one hand. On the other the reputed wealth and ambitious views of Henriette's parents, and hence the convictions that my prospects were hopeless with her, made me perhaps seek in Blanche a counterfoil, and a perilous one she proved; one whose eyes were for ever to haunt me in the time to come. A scrap of conversation which one day I was in a manner compelled to overhear, decided me in my plans for the future.

On the terrace beneath my window the cousins were conversing merrily, while gathering in a china vase the fading leaves of the monthly roses, that were trained over a wooden frame between the projecting oriels; and as they did so, my own name fell more than once on my ear.

I was writing at an open window, and the abstract question

of my right to listen was rendered faint by the intensity of my curiosity to hear what they said or thought of me.

"And so his name is Lancelot?" said Blanche.

"Yes."

"I saw it in the *Army List*; and I saw, too, that he had purchased his lieutenancy." (It seemed odd for a young lady to remark this, and take an interest in my funds.) "And it is he you wrote of so often as your admirer, Henriette?"

"I never said so much, Blanche."

"I inferred it from many things you wrote."

"I have quite forgotten what I wrote."

"And he has been here two months?"

"Two whole months and more."

"And has never proposed!"

"Never, Blanche; and no proposal was certainly expected by me."

"Why, Henriette dear, you are blushing scarlet; but then you are very fond of him—I can see that."

"You must neither say nor think so."

"Of course; but it does not matter what I say to you. Now tell me, would you accept him if he did propose?"

(How intently I listened for the reply!)

"Most certainly *not*—"

These three important words alone fell on my ear, for the conclusion of the sentence was lost as they turned the corner of the terrace. I drew a long breath—half a sigh, perhaps—and proceeded leisurely, yet not without an emotion of great pique, to manipulate and light a cigar.

"How fortunate," thought I, "that when her ideas are so decided, I did not commit myself, as on so many occasions I had so fully resolved to do! Yet the girl is beautiful, and I was pretty far gone with her before the other attraction came. However, I think I shall start to-morrow for town or for Tilbury Fort."

But I did neither; and feeling sure that I had judged the character of Miss Guise rightly, I abandoned myself to the attraction of the golden-haired counterfoil, and soon learned to be tolerably indifferent even to any attentions Stapleton might pay her. I felt horribly piqued, nevertheless, and at first somewhat sore at heart.

The women who have usually most power over that organ in the male world are not generally beauties, but they must possess some mysterious trick of manner or some secret magnetic influence : and, in the instance of Blanche Bingham, both were inherent, together with natural charms of the highest order ; and with a girl so frank and free, our acquaintance ripened, as she once phrased it, " with wonderful rapidity."

She and I were often on such perilous ground as I had never been with Henriette—half love-making, half banter, for her whole style of conversation was eminently calculated to lure a man into close flirtation, and thence to downright love-making.

"Oh, it must be a terrible mistake to fall in love with the wrong person, as that Lady Camilla did. I wonder if I shall ever do so," said she one evening, when we were seated in the same oriel of the drawing-room, where I had sat with Henriette on the occasion when the *Gazette* came, and my mind was then filled by her image only. "Aunt Dormer says young ladies should not talk of love to gentlemen," she continued, as from some passage in a novel we had fallen upon the subject ; "and so we must talk of something else."

" True ; for indeed it is perilous work."

" How ?"

"With you," said I, lowering my voice, as I gazed on the masses of her shining hair.

" Perhaps it is," said she, looking up at me with one of her coy and wonderful smiles.

" Do you know what the German Wieland, who was a great disciple of Cupid, said of Love ?"

" No."

" That its metaphysical effects began with the first sigh, and ended with the first kiss."

"Oh, that could never be ; and I don't think your friend Wieland knew anything about it. I don't think, moreover, that the great mass of you men know much concerning the refinements of love, that which is sentimental being so much an effort of the mere imagination."

It was rather bewildering work to hear the pretty casuist running on in this way, and eyeing me the while in a manner she had over the top of her fan. After a minute's silence she again looked up and said :

"You seem to make me a study ; you think me a horrible puzzle—an enigma, in fact."

"Pardon me, but I know your character perfectly."

"Indeed," said she, laughing, and showing a row of closely-set little teeth, that glittered like pearls in the sunshine ; "then you know more of me than I do of myself, and are cleverer than I thought."

"Thank you ; but nevertheless, I do."

"From what do you gather it? You have known me only for a fortnight."

"I gathered much of your characteristics from the last letter you wrote Mrs. Dormer from Brighton."

"Did auntie read my rantipole letter to *you* ?" she asked, with dilated eyes.

"Yes, and to us all at breakfast."

"And the passage about Colonel Stapleton ?" she exclaimed, colouring as she did so.

"Yes."

"How *could* she !"

I perceived a shade of keen annoyance cross her little face while she looked down and toyed with an opal ring, which looked suspiciously like one I had seen on the Colonel's hand; and this action I recalled at a future time, when all our circumstances had changed and become truly terrible.

"And from that letter you judge of me?"

"Well, it seemed a fair epitome of——"

"The conceits of a vain silly girl, who loves fun and folly, and has no desire to be thought a wallflower at any time, and who defies the envious eyes of all passé female detectives and envious rivals."

"What a singular account of yourself, Miss Bingham! Rivals you can have none; and must have ever many, many friends."

"People may have many acquaintances in this world, but few friends."

"Are you going to be misanthropical now?" I asked, laughing at her strange humour.

"When you really do know me, Captain Rudkin, you will find that I can be all manner of things in an hour."

And she smiled and laughed as she spoke, this strange fairy-like creature, who was beginning to see how her hoyden-ish gaiety of manner, her indescribable eyes, and the sunny masses of her silken hair had bewildered and charmed me.

The General, Howard, and Stapleton were now left to beat the moors or follow the harriers without me. I had invention enough to find excuses for remaining at the Hall, resolved to make the most of what remained of my leave of absence, only some seven short weeks now, and devoted myself to Blanche and Blanche only. In a party even so small as ours there was not privacy for any one, and few opportunities for love-making unless two strolled away together, and thus attracted attention. Yet we occasionally braved this; and times there were when I walked with her in the chase or the garden, the lawn or the avenue, when, her hand being on my arm, I held it in mine as it lay there, and she neither withdrew it nor made remark thereon. On this I had never ventured with Henriette; and aware of this, the impulse to take it became habitual, and I was fast drifted into deliberate love-making, which somehow she seemed to expect; for the girl was naturally prone to flirtation, and how few men could have looked into those eyes of hers and not felt, by their smile and their general expression, that the owner thereof thought him worth winning!

As yet I went no farther, not even when we rambled on the terrace, ostensibly to look at the moon.

For, despite the encouragement she gave me, I had a wholesome dread of her spirit of raillery, and surmised that perhaps I might only be making "a donkey" of myself, as she wrote her Guardsman was so nearly doing at Brighton. Thus, while her rare beauty attracted me on one hand, I feared that she might never be serious, and that if I addressed her gravely or passionately I might only excite her too ready ridicule ; and I knew that a lover once laughed at may deem his cause for ever lost.

Was it possible that the girl had conceived a fancy for me, that she was so pitiless in the rivalry of her almost equally beautiful, but less impulsive cousin ? And if so, why did she perplex me by wearing that opal ring which I suspected to have been once Colonel Stapleton's ?

So completely did Blanche attract me, and so completely had I abandoned myself to the charm of her society, that without any emotion of regret I found myself visiting with her many a spot, to the beauties of which I had been first intro- duced by Henriette, who soon found herself de trop where she had once been principal ; but the memory of her reply rankled in my heart, and more than once the dinner gong was thundered for us in vain, to the indignation of the General, whose punctuality was most military in its tenor. And so, on and on, I found myself as if attracted by a magnetic power beyond my own control, swiftly drifting into love with this fair hoyden, for such, in sooth, she was.

CHAPTER VIII.

"OVER BANK, BUSH, AND SCAUR."

A CRISIS in our affairs was brought about by a chain of little circumstances and an adventure, the end of which we could not have foreseen.

One evening when the General, Stapleton and the barrister, with old Bagshaw and the other keepers, had gone after the birds to the heathy wastes of Hindon Edge, the ladies proposed an expedition to visit the woods and ruins of Egliston Abbey.

Blanche Bingham and I proposed to ride, while the other four of our party were to occupy the carriage, which was soon brought round to the door, together with our horses.

What a picture Blanche was in her blue riding-habit, with her fair hair done up tightly in a coil, thus thrusting her smart hat rather forward, but jauntily over her forehead ; her little hands encased in tight and well-fitting gauntlet gloves ; a gold-mounted switch grasped in one, her ample skirt upheld by the other !

" You evidently consider me an object of interest," said she smilingly—but she was always smiling—as she came tripping down the perron, after I had handed her aunt, cousin, and the other two ladies into the carriage ; " now, what is the result of your inspection ?"

" Admiration, to be frank," said I.

" Every man in your regiment might have his mind occupied in the same lucrative way, for all that I value admiration," she continued, with a proud little pout, " that of one man being quite as valuable as that of another."

" Ah, do not say so !"

" What would you have me do ? I am used to it," said the saucy little beauty ; " and now, Captain Rudkin, help me to mount, and then please to give one glance at my bridle, as I never believe in grooms."

The pleasing task of swinging her light lithe figure into the saddle of her chestnut was soon accomplished—too soon, indeed, as it was one over which I was quite prepared to linger. She gathered up her reins, and her horse, which seemed disposed to swerve round and prove restive, she speedily reduced to obedience by the firmness of her hand on the bridle, and by one smart little touch with her switch.

How erectly and splendidly she sat her horse! but then it was impossible for this girl to do any action ungracefully.

"I am glad you ain't timorous, Miss Bingham," said a groom, touching his hat.

"I seldom am; but why now?"

"Because the chestnut don't look particularly steady to-day. Shorten your reins, miss, and keep him well in hand."

The carriage had already started and was bowling down the avenue, and we followed, but so leisurely that it was soon a quarter of a mile before us. Blanche was prattling gaily as usual, but found that her horse ere long caused her serious interruptions, and began to prove uncommonly restive, thus infecting with the same unruly spirit one of the General's tall roan hunters, on which I was mounted.

Frequently I leaned forward, patted the neck of the chestnut, whose skin was like satin, talked to him, and tried to coax him into a better mood; but all seemed unavailing. His quivering ears were often thrown back, his head was bent low, almost pulling the reins out of her delicate hands, and she told me that the strain was making her dear tender arms ache, and his mouth "seemed as hard as wood." Anon the chestnut began to stamp violently, with low angry snorts, and turn his ears back from time to time.

"I fear he seems bent on mischief," said I anxiously.

"Don't be alarmed for me," replied my companion; "if he is bent on making a scene, fortunately I am a very good horsewoman. I wish you had seen Jacky Appleton and me after the Brighton harriers."

"The brute seems fresh."

"He has been nearly three weeks in the stable, the groom told me."

The evening was one of sunshine, but the clouds were gathered in great dun masses, that darkened in some places to purple, making the woods and moorlands seem almost black ; and between these masses the rays fell in radiating flakes of golden light on farm and hamlet, copse and field, on church tower and cottage roof. The carriage was stopped from time to time at certain points, to enable the Miss Howards to examine certain features of the landscape ; and we took especial care to rein up at the same time and look about us too, so that we might preserve our relative distance ; for, sooth to say, though Henriette Guise more than once looked back after us, we were much more occupied with each other than with agricultural matters, archæology, or the objects of nature. But sometimes now we rode in silence, a silence, however, that was not without its eloquence, for glances could be exchanged that were full of deep and tender meaning.

Thus after a time we discovered that we had lost sight of the carriage altogether, and found that we had taken a different way. When last we saw it, the party had halted where the road went over an eminence, at a point whence the stately ruin and round towers of Barnard Castle, and the long wooded vista of the valley of the Tees, could be seen ; but we remembered that the roof had been closed by the footman.

Reflecting on this made us look about, and we found that, unnoticed by us during our mutual absorption, the sunlight had faded away ; that the whole sky was now veiled in masses of heavy cloud ; a low wind was soughing, as the Scots say, among the wayside trees ; the dark river seemed to brawl more hoarsely over its bed of rock ; the birds were flying low in a scared manner; the grey smoke from cottages hidden amongst the luxuriant coppices, which previously had ascended high in air, was now blown away at a right angle from the chimneys.

There was every sign of a wild night, and as a hint thereof some raindrops, that felt warm rather than cold, were beginning to plash on the dusty roadway, causing us mutually to reflect that we were several miles from home.

"This is not the way to Egliston Woods or the Abbey Bridge," said Blanche.

"And I fear that we shall see neither to-night," I replied, looking at my watch; "the time is a quarter-past six; and the sun has set."

Before Blanche could make a response, I had the sensation of being surrounded by fire, wrapped in it, as it were, the glare being blinding; and then a peal, like the salvo of fifty great guns discharged at once, reverberated over our heads.

"A thunderstorm! Take care, Miss Bingham; for God's sake, Blanche, be wary!"

I had no time to utter more.

Almost ere the first thunder-peal had died away there followed a second and a third, and when the latter burst, her startled chestnut reared wildly up, and then sprang forward with a bound. On each occasion the light girl nearly lost her seat, but stuck to her saddle bravely. For a moment the chestnut stood still, but trembling violently in every nerve and fibre. I urged my horse forward to take it by the bridle; but ere I could do so, the chestnut bolted away at full and furious speed, with neck outstretched, his ears laid close back on his sleek small head, and the bit wedged as if in a vice between his firm-set teeth.

With a trembling heart I followed at full speed, but failed to get near the wild brute that seemed so suddenly to become possessed by a devil, and to be bearing his rider away to destruction, amid the darkness that was fast coming on.

The blinding rain, which the thunder-peals seemed to have let loose from the sky, was borne full in our faces by the gusty wind ; but with all my strength and skill, and all the speed my hunter could exert, I followed her chestnut, which, after striking off the main road, took a way across a line of country which I knew to be full of quarries, lime-kilns, deep-cuttings and hollows, watercourses, loose stone fences, and other dangers which I shuddered to think of.

My own horse seemed now to become infected by a mad racing spirit ; each made the other worse in this fierce career, which I could not abandon, even had I been disposed to do so, and away they tore together.

No cry of terror escaped the brave girl, who bent all her energies to keep her seat and to guide a horse that was beyond her guidance now ; and like one in a dream—a nightmare—I followed her, with no sound in my ears but the rush of the hoofs, the hiss of the falling rain, an occasional shout of fear, pity, or dismay from a wayfarer ; and with her skirt flapping wildly before me, all sodden though it was, she was borne away, away, " over bank, bush, and scaur," into the wrack and obscurity of the stormy night, I knew not whither.

CHAPTER IX.

A NIGHT OF ALARM.

DRIVEN homeward in hot haste, the carriage with its four occupants returned to Thorsgill Hall. Mrs. Dormer asked of the lodge-keeper if we had arrived ; but he assured her that no one had passed down the avenue since our departure.

Then came the dog-cart from the moors, with the General and his two guests drenched, and all impatient for dry clothing and brandy. On being told that we were out in this sudden storm, he made light of it, never doubting but that we had taken shelter somewhere, and would most probably send a messenger for the carriage.

The dinner passed over in all its cumbrous Anglo-Indian state without the absentees ; episodes of the day's sport were discussed with vivacity ; but when nine o'clock was struck by all the clocks in the house, glances of surprise, and then of uneasiness, were exchanged.

Stapleton looked intensely annoyed, though what particular interest he could have in the affair it was difficult to divine. The General went again and again to the windows, and looked out into the blackness of the night—that wild, weird, and dreary September night—when the rain was pouring down in torrents, literally washing the walls of the Hall, and when the wind was bellowing among the old trees of the Chase.

" Blanche's horse looked very restive this evening," said Henriette ; " I trust those dreadful thunder-peals may not have frightened it."

" Heavens above !" said her uncle anxiously, "don't hint of such a thing. Ten o'clock now," he added, looking at his watch ; " what *can* have happened ? This absence is certainly out of the ordinary course of things. They have been away nearly seven hours already."

Stapleton thought it was very like an elopement, though of course he did not venture to say so ; and this idea grew stronger in his mind when midnight came, and the natural alarm of the household increased. He had no suggestions to offer, so he tugged his moustache viciously, and maintained an ominous silence.

" We have heard nothing of Chillianwallah to-night, however," thought he.

" The storm without is still dreadful !" said Henriette, as she withdrew the curtain of a window for a moment ; " listen to the rain, how it comes pouring down ! Is it not strange this terror should have come upon us to-night, uncle ?"

" Why, what night is it ?" he asked curtly.

" The anniversary of that on which the noisy company have

been usually heard in the north wing, and then there is always a storm, the housekeeper told me."

" North-country superstition and folly ! How can you talk of such things gravely ? They *must* have ridden for shelter somewhere !" suggested the General emphatically, for the fiftieth time.

" But why not have ridden *home ?*" asked Colonel Stapleton.

"True, true ; it is most mysterious—unaccountable. I wish Henriette had not spoken about the chestnut being restless," said Mrs. Dormer, now positively white with alarm.

" But I know Blanche to be a fearless and able rider," observed her husband, to soothe her.

Midnight passed. The ladies retired to wonder, surmise, and fill each other with fresh alarms ; the men lingered in the smoking-room, but did not think of bed. The darkness of night departed, and with it the storm. The day dawned and the morning came in serenely, showing the white mist curling up in the golden sheen from the vale of the Tees and many a grassy hollow, and showing also the trees considerably stripped and shorn of all their faded leaves by the violence of the wind ; and now mounted servants were sent forth to make inquiries. Two of these came speedily back with the tidings that just about sunset, or a little after it, a lady and gentleman answering to the description of those lost or absent, and both mounted, had been seen tearing at frightful speed along the road near Barnard Castle—that their horses had evidently run off with them, terrified, probably, by the thunder ; and that the course taken by them was due north.

Here was a clue to follow up without a moment's delay.

The General, his two friends, and a mounted groom started at once to make further inquiries, and rode fast in the direction indicated. From cottagers, toll-keepers, and workers hedging and ditching by the wayside, additional information was readily obtained ; and in one place Blanche's riding-switch was found, in another her hat and veil near a dry-stone wall, a little breach in the top of which seemed to indicate that a horse had crossed there without completely clearing it in the flying leap. The stones, too, had been freshly dislodged.

"How dreadful is this doubt and suspense !" exclaimed the old General, in a voice hoarse with emotion, as in imagination he pictured his beautiful young niece maimed or in agony, perhaps disfigured, crippled for life, it might be killed outright ; and how could such terrible tidings ever be broken to her parents in India !

But if such a catastrophe had occurred, news must have come ere this to Thorsgill Hall, was his next idea ; and then a cry of absolute alarm escaped the old man when he saw in a ploughed field, distant some twenty miles from home, the chestnut horse of Blanche, with saddle reversed and bridle trailing, and, more than all, unable to move, having a leg broken above the off fore-fetlock !

All this seemed to point to some dreadful occurrence. Meanwhile, where was she—that fairy-like creature with the golden hair—where her companion, and where his horse? Its hoof-marks were distinctly traceable to a certain part of the field. There were also found the marks of a man's foot, and of her smaller boot with its high instep and little brass heel, in the soft wet soil ; and after that all traces were lost.

"My God !" moaned the old gentleman, looking upward, "what can have happened ?"

Stapleton tugged at his moustache more vigorously than ever. He was greatly perplexed and really more alarmed now, for all these circumstances showed him that his secret idea of an elopement was no longer tenable.

Rapidly and sadly General Dormer rode homeward intent on telegraphing, and on reaching Thorsgill Hall found— that which we must reserve for a future chapter.

CHAPTER X.

WHAT HAPPENED.

MEANWHILE, during this time of suspense and alarm, where were we?

Miss Bingham's horse, having got the bridle-bit between his teeth was completely beyond her control. The scared animal felt his own strength and mastery, and, wild with terror, rushed onward with unabated speed. My efforts to overtake him only seemed to make him worse, yet I could not for a single moment draw my reins, lest I should lose sight of his rider in the dark; thus, wherever he bore her, I was compelled to follow. On one or two occasions, I got fairly abreast of him, going neck and neck, but could not, owing to the nature of the ground we traversed, reach her bridle.

"Oh, Captain Rudkin, Captain Rudkin!" she exclaimed, with a catching sob; "if I lose my seat, I shall certainly be killed!"

Anon her normal state of frolic broke out even here.

"I nearly came a cropper—nasty, that—over it like a bird, though—awkward drop—no crossing or looking before you leap here," she would say, with something between a sob and a laugh in her throat, as we flew over some stone fence or hedge, that suddenly came before us in the gloom, and when we were landed safely on the other side of it.

The pace was frightful; but more than once a gleam of lightning showed us the description of country we were crossing. Fortunately, much of it was now pasture land. The lights of Barnard Castle, with those of all its busy thread-mills, had disappeared in the obscurity behind us; and I was in total ignorance of the direction we were forced to take, with all the haphazard excitement of the hunting-field exaggerated a hundredfold.

Once Blanche was on the point of freeing her left foot from the stirrup, taking her right knee from the horn of the saddle,

5—2

and throwing herself off—a perilous expedient, the idea of which she relinquished when I called to her to keep in the saddle as long as her horse could keep his feet.

I thought of the poor girl's extreme beauty, and trembled lest aught should happen to mar it. Would I then love her the less? Ah, no. But how dreadful it was to surmise if that fair face should be destroyed. Many other thoughts occurred to me, difficult to describe now or to disentangle, as they seemed—if such can be the case—to flash upon my mind simultaneously.

After crossing a vast number of fields and pastures, causing many a covey of partridges to whirr up wildly from their places of shelter, clearing brooks and hedgerows, having left the perils I first mentioned far behind, we struck once more upon the highway, and as an ascent rose before us, I was not without hope that the devilish chestnut might become blown; but just then a flash of lightning seemed to cross our very path. Again the thunder burst overhead, to rumble away in the distance, and again her horse uttered a snort of terror and drove on with mad and headlong speed as before.

Lights were now visible before us, their reflection glimmering in the gathering pools of water. We passed some rows of houses, the outlines of which seemed all blurred to view in the slanting rain; but I recognised the little town of Brough, in the wild district of Stainmoor, with its ruined castle and ancient church, the clock of which was striking the hour of seven; and now I found that we must have galloped many miles.

Brough soon vanished behind us; but fortunately the way was clear and free in front, the toll-bars were all open as yet, no vehicles were in the way, and no one was abroad who could avoid being out in such a storm.

Blanche was becoming giddy, and beginning to feel that she could not much longer keep her seat. She was not fainting, however, for she was quite conscious; but her over-taxed muscles were relaxing, and she felt certain that if anything caused her horse to swerve, start, or take an unusual leap, she would be thrown from her saddle—it might be, to be dragged to death in the stirrup.

A few miles farther on would, I knew, bring us to Appleby on the Eden, in Westmoreland ; but fortunately we were not taken so far. Just where another road crossed at right angles that which we were pursuing, a black gap in the dry stone wall seemed to open before us. It was a field gateway that proved to be open ; and beyond lay a great space of deep moist fallow-land, which had been recently ploughed ; and over this her still half-frantic horse strove—but strove in vain —to continue at the same speed.

His strength and courage bore him on a little way—some hundred yards or so—and then his pace began to slacken quickly ; he breathed and laboured heavily—so did mine, especially when I began to shorten my reins to check him fairly. Anon the chestnut plunged heavily down on his head, while a fierce snort, as if of pain, escaped him ; but he rose again, partly in obedience to the bridle-hand of his rider. Once more the animal sank forward, but partly on his off side, while Blanche, gathering all her energies at that instant for a last effort, lightly and adroitly sprang from her saddle, to fall half fainting among the soft wet furrows of the field.

Pulling up my now breathless horse, I instantly alighted, threw the reins over my left arm, and approaching, lifted her tenderly up, and all wet, sodden, and weary as she was, she felt for a minute or two the impossibility of keeping her head, which was now bare, from resting on my shoulder, while one or two almost hysterical sobs escaped her.

The delight of the moment was certainly chilled in more ways than one—by my natural alarm lest she might ultimately suffer, and by the unpleasant accessory of the falling rain ; but I thanked Heaven in my heart that she was safe—safe from bruise, or maim, or injury ; and next moment, in a burst of anger, I administered four or five heavy lashes with my whip upon her panting horse, which never moved, but lay

gathered in a heap, as it were, amid the furrows. When I
thought over all the obstacles we had cleared in the dark, our
mutual escape seemed miraculous.

I looked round me in utter bewilderment. What was to be
done now ?

The wind had died away, but the rain was continuing to fall,
and more heavily than ever ; not a star was to be seen, and
darkness alone was visible. To remain, then, a moment
longer than was necessary in a ploughed field at such a time
and season was impossible. Blanche, however, was equal to
the occasion, and promptly said she would make an effort to
walk. She gathered her heavy skirt over one arm, laid the
other upon mine ere I could offer it, and we proceeded vaguely
in search of that which seemed hopeless—shelter.

My chief idea was to reach some country inn, where a
vehicle could be procured, or where I could leave her in
safety while I rode back to the Hall to report our little catastrophe to the General. That we should neither return until
we did so together on the morrow, did not occur to me, amid
all my surmises.

My heart was yet full of anxiety for what she was suffering;
and I was sincerely thankful when, after a time, the barking
of a large dog, and then the appearance of two or three lights,
shimmering and seeming blurred through the rain, announced
our vicinity to some habitation ; for in that district of high
rugged prominences and large tracts of low peat moss, of land
covered with oak, alder, ash, and hazel, mansions and cottages are not sown so thickly as in Surrey or Middlesex.

We had quitted the field, and found a beaten pathway,
which we pursued for some time, till among some clumps of
trees and through the blackness of the night there suddenly
appeared the blacker mass of a large house, in the basement
story of which the lights we had seen were shining.

No ray of light appeared elsewhere. In front of the mansion was a *porte-cochère* of stately aspect. Under its arches,
I half led and half supported my dripping and sinking com-

panion, and while my horse's hoofs clanked heavily enough on the pavement beneath them to have roused even sleepers, I applied my hand vigorously to an iron knob I discovered, and the notes of a large bell responded sonorously in the distance.

After considerable delay, which rendered me so impatient that I rang again and again, footsteps were heard, and then a ray of light streamed brightly out through a large keyhole. One half of the large folding-door was opened ; the ghostly depth of a long and darkened entrance-hall was seen beyond, and in the immediate foreground an old man, who looked like a gardener—and afterwards proved to be such—appeared with an upheld candle flaring in his hand, and with something of angry inquiry expressed in his weather-beaten face, while behind him were two female domestics, who eyed us with more surprise and distrust than commiseration.

Without waiting to question them or be questioned, for time pressed, I gave the old man the bridle of my horse, and led Blanche Bingham right into the hall of this—to us as yet —unknown mansion.

" We have had an accident—a runaway horse—you see the plight this young lady is in," said I hurriedly, in explanation ; " she must have instant change and shelter, for which I shall reward you well, good people ; and meantime have the goodness to take my card—if the rain has left me one—to your master."

CHAPTER XI.

" THE SITUATION HAD ITS CHARM."

WE had not, as in old romances, lighted upon the residence of robbers or coiners or madmen, of ghosts or ogres, but a snug old English household, where the delicacy of Blanche, together with her evidently helpless condition, readily excited the sympathy of these people, who instantly saw that she was a lady of position ; and one of them, who, by her black-silk dress, lace cap, portly aspect, and comely visage, appeared to be a matronly old housekeeper, informed me that, save one or two rooms, the whole house was shut up, the furniture shrouded in brown holland, but the lustres in linen bags, as the family was absent ; but that nevertheless we were welcome, and should be instantly attended to, while the gardener took my horse round to the stable-yard.

While Blanche Bingham was led away by one of the servants, the housekeeper ushered me into a cosy room, in the grate of which—most welcome sight!—a jovial fire was blazing up the chimney. This apartment was ample in its dimensions, and its decorations, which were rich, were of the style of the second George's era. The walls were divided into compartments by moulded panels, on which were painted landscapes, ruins, allegories and armorial bearings, all so highly varnished that the surface of the now almost black wainscot glittered in the firelight.

Beneath the heavy surbase or chair-belt were other devices, and at intervals there rose from it heavily-fluted pilasters supporting the gilded cornice and ceiling, which was also divided into dark panelling. The furniture, however, was modern, and the draperies of the windows were deep crimson; and so ruddy was the blaze of the fire in the low old-fashioned grate, that it quite eclipsed the light of two tall candles on the table, and four others which were now placed in the crystal girandoles on the mantelpiece, over which, on a high prancing white horse, was the portrait of an officer of the Marquis of Granby's days, in a Kevenhuller hat and enormous jack-boots.

Opposite hung a full-length painting of a smart-looking young fellow in Rifle uniform, with his sword under his left arm, a shako in his left hand, and the smoke of some imaginary battle rolling darkly in the distance.

" By Jove, that is a face I should know !" said I, pointing to it ; " 1 find myself among friends here."

It was the young squire, the old dame told me, now far away in the Indies among the Turks and heathens.

"Tom Prior of ours—I know him well," said I, scanning the familiar features of a brother officer; "and is this his father's house?"

"Yes, sir—Stoke Priory; but the old squire and my lady are now in Paris."

The nursery was above this room, she went on to say, in a communicative manner that would soon have become garrulous, but I was in no mood to listen to her; there Master Tom used to make such a racket! But there had been no little ones there since then, and that was years ago. She seemed a kind old north-country woman, that I could well imagine how she must have spoiled and petted "Master Tom," now one of the most self-possessed and confident young fellows in the P. C.'s Own Rifle Brigade; but though Stoke Priory bears rather an important place in our story, as we were never under its roof again, suffice it to say that, though taking its name from some wooden priory of the Saxon times, it was a great square ungainly-looking mansion of the prosaic days of George II., when taste was at its lowest ebb in Britain.

On learning that I was a guest of General Dormer at Thorsgill Hall, and that the young lady whom I had brought hither in a plight so miserable was his niece, the attentions of the good woman were redoubled; but I was startled to find that no messenger could be sent to the Hall for the carriage that night. The only man about the place was Giles Stocks, the gardener, and he was too old; so there was nothing for it but to wait patiently till morning, or ride back myself through the pelting storm; but the temptation to remain with *her* proved too great, and so I stayed.

Meantime I was accommodated with dry clothing, as some of Tom Prior's wardrobe was still extant in his old rooms. Some refreshments were spread for us, with warm coffee for the young lady and brandy for me; and at last we were left together and—alone—to look into each other's faces and endeavour to recall some of the tender expressions which, in my regard and terror for her, had escaped me, the former in spite of myself, during our wild career through the darkness.

Somehow it seemed like a dream and scarcely a reality to me that she was seated there beside me, in a loose white morning wrapper, over the dry clothing provided for her in haste, but which—though a world too wide for her—showed much more than we usually saw of her milk-white neck and arms ; her little feet in slippers planted cosily on the fender ; her head reclined back in a crimson-velvet chair, with all the wealth of her golden hair, unloosened to dry, hanging in a rippling shower behind it, or curling over her shoulders.

Every way how charming and piquante she looked.

" Such an adventure this is !" said she, with a little laugh that was almost hysterical ; " they will think that we are lost altogether, Captain Rudkin."

"At the Hall ?" I asked, scarcely knowing what to say.

"Yes, where else could I mean?   Oh, it's all like an adventure in some old story-book.   But we can in no way help our being here.   The circumstances were all beyond our own control."

"And might have ended tragically—fearfully so," said I.

In the glare of the fire her fair face and dress of white came strongly out from the dark background of the sombrely-pannelled and redly-curtained room.   Her lips were half parted with a smile at our whole situation, which certainly had its *charm*, to me especially.

As I gazed upon her I almost began to fancy that we were never to part.   Our perfect isolation was suggestive of thoughts that were alike perplexing and alluring ; and—dreamer that I was then !—I loved to imagine that we had been actually married that morning ; had the benediction and the usual shower of old slippers.   Was this the beginning of the honeymoon ?   Was this cosily-wainscoted room ours in some lone country inn, whither we had come to be secluded

from all the world? Was this the—no, no! It was indeed
but a momentary dream, and home to-morrow we should
have to go, with our strange explanations, to Thorsgill Hall;
while of the natural terror and suspense of those we had left
there, I felt for the time quite oblivious, as I drew close to her
side.

Nine o'clock struck sonorously from a great old-fashioned
clock on the echoing stone staircase.

I had fully displayed by word and deed, by expression of
eye and tone of voice, so deep an interest in her escape and
in all she had suffered—a manifestation all unchecked—that
I could not fail to feel encouraged to go farther; thus before
the hour I have mentioned had struck, I had told her—in
those broken accents which cannot be committed to paper
without exciting ridicule, even that of those who would dearly
dote on hearing such poured into their own ears—that I loved
her, loved her dearly, and more than all, I had amply won
her permission to do so.

Her face was very near mine; how it happened I never
knew, but in another moment out lips were pressed together;
and from that instant it was all over with me. I fondly
trusted it was the first kiss she had ever received from any
man save her doating old father; and thus began the most
delicious idyl of my life.

One promise she made me give, which, circumstanced as
we both were, seemed natural enough—that our engagement
should as yet remain unknown to her relations at Thorsgill
Hall. To this I acceded, and to what proposition of hers
would not I have done so then?

We were indeed joyously happy though India was still
before us, and we could not foresee our destiny, our *kismet*,
as the natives call it there.

After some minutes' silence she said, while colouring
deeply, on returning as it were from poetry to plain prose :—

"Oh, such a brute that chestnut is! I thought, by his jerk-
ing at the reins and shaking the bit, he had a mind to be off
with me; and so he was."

"There were more than the chestnut in that mood, though in a different fashion," said I, while drawing her dear head caressingly on my shoulder.

"My arms," she continued, pulling up a sleeve in a way that was very bewildering, "oh, how weary they are with tugging at the reins! and see my poor little hands, how red!"

"And yet how pretty they are in their present pinkness!" I exclaimed, while kissing them with an emotion that bordered on idolatry. "My darling, my darling! I swore to save you——"

"Or perish in the attempt, as the novels have it."

"I have succeeded to a certain extent."

"And a rare scrape we are in!"

At that time, how far off the world, acquaintances, friends relations and everything seemed from us! Even by me Henriette Guise was as completely forgotten as though she had never existed, until Blanche, after a little pause, said suddenly and coyly.

"And you do not—I mean did not—love my cousin Henriette?"

"Oh, no, not at all," I replied, but with some secret compunction nevertheless, as a pale, soft, and sweet face, with its dark deep eyes so full of sentiment, reflection, and penetration now came before me. "What has led you to ask this?"

"Her letters, and more than once your own manner."

"Ah, no, no; I have admired her certainly—as who would not?—·but no word of love has ever escaped me."

And this alone was true.

"Escaped you?" she queried. "Were you then so cautious?"

"Admiration is not love," said I. "I admired her; but, oh, Blanche, I *love* you, and all my future life is merged in yours."

My lips were close to her ear; her face was nestling in my neck, and I stroked half fatuously the moist masses of her golden hair that streamed over me.

"Blanche, Blanche, you will always love me? It is delightful to hear you repeat it."

"The situation is so sudden, I scarcely know what I am saying, Lancelot."

"Call me Lance," I urged.

"Dearest Lance, then."

"And you love me?"

"Oh, how often am to tell you that I do!"

"Bless you for saying so!"

"I fear that you will prove very exacting. But now I must leave you, dear delightful Lance, for there is that tiresome old clock wheezing and striking again—eleven, actually eleven —and we are in a strange house!"

She rang for her candlestick and attendant, and the entrance of the old housekeeper, nathless her genial and bustling manner, looking rather sleepy in her lace cap and silk gown, brought us back to the prosy world once more; and it became evident, from some blundering remarks which escaped her, that she was puzzled to know whether or not we were married, till suddenly she saw there was no plain hoop on *the* particular finger where, ere long, I hoped to place one; and with one of her merriest silver laughs at the doubt, Blanche Bingham bade me "Good night."

The door closed, and she was gone, leaving me in that mood of happiness on which it is useless to elaborate.

CHAPTER XII.

ACCEPTED.

How I got through the night I never knew; but I suppose I must have slept, and without even a dream of what had occurred since we cantered down the avenue of Thorsgill Hall.

With the first blush of dawn a sense of my new happiness rushed upon me—the conviction that Blanche loved me, and was mine as far as avowed love and solemn promises could make her. With momentary self-reproach I now began to think of Henriette Guise and her haunting face, and what she may, nay must, have expected from me, and the point to which our intercourse for two months past had evidently been leading up; but this emotion, a passing one, was quickly dismissed and forgotten, so absorbed was I in the complete success of my love affair with her more sparkling and, in some respects, more attractive cousin.

Though every incident of the past night was strongly and vividly impressed upon my mind, my new position seemed somewhat like a dream, the truth of which would not be realised until I met Blanche again and held her hands in mine.

I sprang from bed and looked out upon the landscape. The sun was high in the heavens; the storm had passed away, and the whole aspect of nature was serene and calm, though a silvery mist yet lingered on the summits of the green hills that rise opposite Appleby. Stoke Priory stands on somewhat high ground; thus the view from it embraces a vast extent of country, dotted by farmhouses and small villages covered with blue slate and whitened with whitewash, irregularly shaped fields spreading up the mountain sides, and almost invariably divided by stone walls—genuine Westmoreland scenery.

From the green shady valleys the mist, occasioned by the rain overnight, was curling slowly upward in the sunshine, and as morning was advancing, I thought that betimes a messenger should be despatched to our friends at the Hall.

Giles Stocks and another yokel now came to me, while I was dressing, with information that they had found the chestnut lying in the fallow field, in a wretched plight, and had been compelled to leave it, as it lashed out viciously with its hind legs whenever they approached. They thought at first that it would not rise, "because some horses were main obstinate after a fall, and won't do so till it suits their fancy," till they found that the poor beast's off leg was broken, and that there was nothing for it now but to give it a bullet through the head, or a good stroke with an axe.

Of course I could have neither done without the permission of General Dormer.

I knew how much the quiet jog-trot life at Thorsgill would be startled from its propriety by the whole episode of last night, and without further delay wrote the General a hurried note, telling him of all that had occurred—all, at least, save the sweet element that Blanche and I had infused in the adventure—and begged, as there was no vehicle to be had in our vicinity, that the carriage might be sent for us. Then I proceeded to make the best toilet I could achieve prior to meeting my intended again.

It was on his returning, in a great state of distress and perplexity, that the General found my mounted messenger awaiting him, and discovered also, to his surprise, that had he prosecuted his inquiries but a little way beyond the field where his chestnut lay, he might have come upon Blanche and me, seated over our coffee and eggs, in the same cosy room where we had passed the evening so delightfully and auspiciously, and where we now sat hand in hand, awaiting— yet not impatiently—the arrival of the carriage.

Though Blanche was, for her years, somewhat of a practical girl with all her *espièglerie* of manner, she dearly loved aught that savoured of romance, and in this adventure of ours there was a strong *soupçon* of it, so she liked the situation and yielded to it completely.

"But now, dearest Lance," she began confidentially and in a low earnest voice, "our engagement—is it not delicious to speak of it?" she asked parenthetically, while blushing— "must be, as I said last night, kept secret."

"May I not tell even the General—your good old uncle?"

"Neither him nor aunt Dormer as yet, I think."

"As you will, darling; I trust to your discretion."

"And to time, Lance love; to time and the influence you may have with my papa. I am sure mamma could no more resist you than I have done; and my remembrance of her is, that she was very kind, tender, and affectionate."

"Could your mother be otherwise?"

"You have no need to flatter me *now*."

"But why all this fear and caution?" I asked.

"You are a captain, to be sure, darling; but I know too well, from all aunt Dormer tells me, that collector or commissioner would sound better than even colonel in the ears of papa, who is terribly commercial in his views."

I winced a little at all this, and recalled the General's hints about the wealth, ambition, and "views" of Henriette's family, and deemed my chances there would have been small indeed—an heiress, watched by a dragon of a mamma.

"You have glorious hair, Blanche," said I, after a pause, as I toyed with it.

"All my own, too, and not, according to the usual story, cut off my head during an illness and made up for me to wear when well again. See!" and with her quick little fingers she undid a coil of wondrous length, that fell far below her waist.

"Dearest, dearest Blanche, you are indeed a fairy-like creature!"

"Stop, Lance darling—don't; there comes the carriage, with aunt in it. Oh, I hope she did not *see* you!"

In two minutes afterwards the General and Mrs. Dormer

arrived, with little Poplin, the lady's maid, carrying suitable habiliments for Miss Bingham, who was warmly embraced by them in turn; and it was a joyous sight to see the golden hair I so much admired mingling with the silver locks of her old uncle, as he clasped her again and again to his breast, with her fair face nestling in his neck.

The warm-hearted old man actually shed tears, and from his great affection for her I augured happily of his influence on our mutual future.

The chestnut was sentenced to be shot, an event over which Blanche, who had frequently ridden the horse, and almost daily had fed him with apples from her own pretty hand, shed " some natural tears," till she remembered that " it was a wicked brute, and might have cost us both our lives." " Yet don't we owe it a debt of gratitude, after all, dearest Lance ?" she whispered coyly to me, when driving home merrily in the carriage.

With the plan we had formed for our future arrangements, and that our engagement was to be a secret for a time, we found ere long a serious difficulty in addressing each other with sufficient formality in the presence of others; and that something had occurred between us, Henriette Guise could not mistake. The flirting manner of Blanche had completely disappeared; she had become graver, and I more tender. A certain brilliant and happy expression shone in her eyes whenever they met mine; while my bearing, in spite of myself, must have revealed that delightful consciousness of proprietary, which a successful and accepted suitor often finds it so difficult to conceal. My passing love for Henriette had been a silent one, and so no one could accuse me of having behaved ill.

One feature in our circle at the Hall puzzled me. It was an unmistakable tone and air of irritation, if not disdain, in the manner of Colonel Stapleton whenever our little episode was referred to, as it was most naturally for some days after

6

its occurrence.   To use a uommon phrase, he evidently "felt sore" on the subject.

"What the deuce can it be to him?" thought I.   "Is the fellow in love with her too, and have I supplanted him?"

Remembering the ring, so suspiciously like one of his, which I had seen Blanche wearing when first she came to the Hall, I was half inclined to think so.   I had not, how-ever, the bad taste to ask about that jewel; but lost no time in presenting her with one of mine, a fine rose-diamond, and received from her dear hand another, which was necessarily so tiny that I had to get it enlarged.

CHAPTER XIII.

A MEMORY OF THE CRIMEA.

BLANCHE usually wore several rings, but no one save her cousin, with whom she was as familiar as a sister, detected, or recognised, the strange one which now she wore con-stantly with scrupulous fidelity on her *engaged* finger; and Henriette's expression of face changed visibly, though she sought to conceal it by a smile, when she took Blanche's hand in hers, and turned the jewel round, as if to assure her-self, one wet day when we were all gathered near the fire in the library, idling over books and portfolios of prints, before "tiffin," as the General called luncheon.

"What a beautiful diamond!" she said in a low voice that Blanche alone heard; "you have not been in the habit of wearing it hitherto."

"No, not until I came here," was the evasive reply.

"It has a story, then!"

"A story which I shall tell you some day," said Blanche; adding hurriedly and somewhat awkwardly, to change the subject, "Dear Henriette, how pale and weary you look!"

" Perhaps I feel so," replied her cousin, while her proud lip quivered a little.

" How—why ?"

" One gets weary of everything in this world, at times."

" Don't say so, at your years and mine ; how absurd of you, Henriette !"

" But think of that night of terror, and the effect it had upon us all," said Henriette, raising her voice a little.

" Are you, or were you ever weary of life, Captain Rudkin ?" asked Blanche, looking up with a bright expression of eye, which I thought I alone could read ; but which, however, Stapleton detected.

" Your question is a strange one," said I ; but I did feel weary of life sometimes, when in the Crimea."

" Just after Chillianwallah—" the General was beginning, to the great alarm of us all, when Stapleton said abruptly.

" By the way, Rudkin, you were among the first who went there ?"

" I had the honour to be."

" And yet you were *not* at the Alma ?" he continued, in a somewhat marked tone.

" True, I was not. You have been studying ' Hart,' I presume ?"

" No ; but how were you absent ?"

" Because I had a bullet in my body."

(" Lancelot dearest !" almost escaped Blanche.)

" *Before* Alma ?" again queried the Colonel, in the same unpleasant tone.

" Precisely ; I had the honour to be the first officer wounded in the war."

" Where ?"

" At Bulganack, which was a mere prelude—a tuning of fiddles, as it were—before the more glorious passage of the Alma river. I was then in the cavalry, and had I been more prudent, I might have been in the cavalry still," I added in an explanatory tone to Blanche, who said eagerly,

6—2

" Do tell us all about it ; your wound, I mean."

" The story of my mishap will include that of another—something of love and a sister of charity, the episode of whose life was more interesting than mine ; and as young ladies have tired of music, the gentlemen of knocking the balls about at the billiard-table, and getting through a wet forenoon by the medium of Cavendish in the smoking-room and stables, I may as well try to kill an hour for you all."

The Colonel, who was neither bright nor brilliant, but whom a phrenologist would have said to possess two qualities, extreme reticence and powerful concentration—useful gifts when combined with that which he, with all his bravery, did not possess, an honest heart—twitched his moustache impatiently at my preamble ; which seemed greatly to whet the curiosity of the ladies, who all listened attentively while I related the following episode, which occurred in the then recent war in the Crimea.

As you all know, it was on the 14th of September that the allied army landed in the Crimea, near the lake of Kamishlu, some miles north of the Bulganack river. All got safely on shore except a boat-load of Zouaves, who were run down by a steam transport, and sent floundering to the bottom, with hairy knapsacks, blankets, red breeches, and all. Leaping mid-leg deep into the surf, Guardsmen and Highlanders, Rifles, Lancers, and Hussars, quitted their boats and scrambled to the beach, were all were formed rapidly by troops or companies into regiments and brigades on the open shore, which there was overhung by cliffs more than a hundred feet in height.

Though a cavalry force, always ludicrously slender, had been reduced at Varna by disease to little more than a thousand sabres, the disembarkation of their horses—all saddled, bridled, and accoutred—was a task of no small difficulty and danger.

I shall briefly skip over the miserable night of rain which we passed, without a tent to cover us, on that bleak and open beach, exposed to the chill blasts from the Euxine ; each soldier sleeping as-best he could, with his musket beside him, save the muffled outposts, who had their arms " reversed ;" each trooper standing by his horse in the ranks. As the pitiless rain came pouring down in one unceasing torrent, my poor charger shook his ears from time to time, and his mane too, as if to protest against the cruelty of the colonel, of the Horse Guards, or of his rider, in subjecting him to all this discomfort and annoyance ; while I, muffled in my cloak, which was soon soaked with water, with my head resting on a holster-flap, and an arm twisted in a stirrup-leather, strove to snatch the proverbial " forty winks " before the trumpets sounded to advance, and the working parties began to dig graves for those unfortunates who had perished in the night of cholera ; for thus grimly did the angels of suffering and death inaugurate our useless war in the Crimea.

Amid the sodden corpses—sodden with the rain of that most miserable night—we saw on her knees a little French sister of charity, whose pale face, as she prayed, with her eyes closed, and her white fingers telling the beads of her black rosary, impressed me strongly by the character of its beauty, sweetness, and resignation ; and as I checked my horse for a moment to observe her, I could little foresee how much I was yet to know of Sister Louise Marie, for so she was named.

The atmosphere of the morning was calm and serene, but mist was curling in the sunshine from the wet bivouac where sixty thousand men had passed the night. Far away on our right, the dark smoke from the funnels of the allied fleet rose like mighty columns high into the blue sky of the Euxine. The music of the many regimental bands rang pleasantly out upon the softened air ; and while advancing, we became sensible of an agreeable odour that pervaded it, as the feet of the marching men trod down the leaves of the wild lavender, and certain aromatic herbs which grew over all the ground traversed by the army.

As we began to move towards Sebastopol, I had the good luck, with a few troopers of my regiment, to be exploring for water with the gallant Nolan, when we came suddenly upon a Russian convoy of no less than eighty waggons laden with flour. This was our *first* view of the enemy, and so our excitement was keen and high. With a hearty British hurrah, we routed the Cossack guard *sabre à la main*, cut down half a dozen of them, and brought the prizes safely into camp.

I was with the advanced guard, which consisted of the 11th Hussars, and ours, the 13th Light Dragoons. We moved in columns of troops at deploying distance, and in our rear followed a party of Rifles, extended in skirmishing order for though broken and undulating, the country was open, and so far as we could see, destitute of trees. Every officer and soldier had three days' rations of salt pork and biscuit in his haversack. These had been issued to us before we left the shipping.

The time was a keenly exciting one. We knew that a Russian army was somewhere between us and Sebastopol, the point for which we were bound ; but *where* we knew not exactly, and full of irrepressible surmises and suggestions, some of the officers and men were talking in the ranks, when suddenly that strict disciplinarian, Lord Cardigan, who rode at the head of the 11th said, " Silence—and eyes front ! There are Cossack vedettes in sight."

I swept the horizon with my telescope, and could discern on the summit of a green ridge, defined darkly and distinctly against the sky, the figures of ten or twelve Cossacks, riding at equi-distance, with their knees up to their holsters, so short were their stirrups ; their backs bent, and their heads cased in round fur caps, thrust so far forward as to be almost between the ears of their shaggy ponies. They were scarcely visible, when they wheeled about and vanished to the rear with their lance-heads flashing in the sun.

" These vedettes, from their number, seem to indicate the presence of a large force," said the Earl to Captain Nolan.

"So every moment I expect to see the flying artillery come up," responded the latter, his eyes sparkling and the blood mantling in his cheek, as hotly as it did on the fatal day when he fell in the death-ride at Balaclava.

No cannon, however, appeared, and under a now burning sun the forward march went on. We were half afraid to eat our salt rations, as no water was to be had ; the springs had been dried up a month before, and the verdure had almost disappeared, for the heat was a hundred degrees in the shade. I turned in my saddle and looked rearward, to where our scarlet columns of infantry, so firm and compact, came on with colours flying and bayonets glittering in the sun.

Along all this line of march were men lying here and there behind them, their red coats dotting the route we had come. Many of these were victims in the first stages of cholera, the ghastly scourge that had followed us from Varna. They lay with their jackets torn open, their stocks unclasped, their parched tongues protruding, their distorted faces blackening in the sunshine, while the army marched on and onward still, and while the Alpine vulture from the marble rocks of Kamishlu looked expectantly on the banquet that was to come.

The greatest number of these victims who fell by the way-side under disease or fatigue seemed to belong to the Household Brigade, and with the aid of my field-glass I could see the same sister of charity, in her black dress and quaint white hood, on her knees busy among those unfortunate fellows, who were fated never to march more in this world, consoling them, and, so far as her means permitted, supplying their wants.

Ere long a cheer rent the air, when we came in sight of a cool stream rippling pleasantly between grassy banks and groves of wild olive and pomegranate trees, turpentine and caper bushes. It was a lovely evening then, and the setting sun was wreathed in clouds of gold and amber. The infantry halted, piled arms, and, breaking their ranks, rushed forward to slake the thirst that maddened them—the Highland Brigade alone waited for the command of Sir Colin Campbell, who halted them at some distance from the stream, that they might fill their canteens in an orderly manner ; while, less fortunate, we, the 13th Light Dragoons, with the 11th Hussars, wearing then their blue jackets and scarlet pelisses, all elaborately braided with gold, in attendance upon old Lord Raglan, had to ride far on in advance of the First Division of infantry to reconnoitre, as fresh groups of Cossacks had been visible with their lances glinting on the brow of a neighbouring hill.

An alarm was now sent to the rear, whither I was despatched with an order, in consequence of which, making a dreadful clatter with their limbers, spare wheels, buckets, rammers, sponges, and forge waggons, the flying artillery went thundering to the front.

Just where the road from Sebastopol to the landing place at Eupatoria crosses the river called the Bulganack, it traverses a number of grassy slopes and undulations ; and over these, after splashing through the stream, the Hussars and ours rode boldly ; but it was not until we had surmounted the last of them that we became suddenly aware of more than two thousand Russian cavalry advancing in line to meet us, with their skirmishers in front in extended order, and with carbines unslung.

On a signal from Lord Raglan, his orderly trumpeter sounded a halt, and we all reined up, and each man looked with a grim smile in his comrade's face, so much as to say, " The time has come !"

" Forward skirmishers," cried Lord Cardigan; "the Brigade will form line to the front."

On the flank of each squadron the brass trumpets rang shrilly out as we deployed into line, and the men selected for skirmishing darted out at full speed, unslinging their carbines as they went, and dressing from the flanks as strictly as they would have done in Maidstone barrack-yard, for even when under fire the lessons of the drill-sergeant are rarely forgotten.

In rear of this formidable line of Russian cavalry rose another swelling eminence, beyond which were distinctly visible the glittering tips of a long line of bayonets ; for there concealed and quietly waiting till we should be lured within range of musketry, were the six battalions of the 17th Infantry Division, each a thousand strong, with two batteries of artillery, and no less than nine sotnias of Cossacks ; so the little force which formed the British advance guard was thus suddenly placed in a perilous and dreadful dilemma. In short, it was menaced with total capture or destruction.

" What the deuce is to be done ?" asked the Quartermaster General, who was the first to discover the whole situation. " How are we to avoid an action, and yet with honour cover the retreat of the 11th and 13th Dragoons ?"

But now the 8th Hussars and the 17th Lancers, with all their bannerets fluttering, and our nine-pounder field batteries were sweeping up to support us ; and the Muscovite infantry, fearing that a much greater force was among the hollows in our rear, and that consequently they might fall into the same snare they had prepared for us, remained quietly behind the eminence, while the skirmishers on each side opened that desultory fire which with dragoons is usually so ineffective ; but as there was every prospect of our being charged by the heavy cavalry, we were ordered to fall back by alternate squadrons ; and the moment this retrograde movement began the Russian artillery came rumbling out of the hollow at a gallop. The guns were wheeled round, the limbers cast off in a trice, and a cannonade was instantly opened on us.

Then gap after gap appeared in the ranks of the 11th and 13th, as rider and horse went floundering down, shot dead or to roll about in mortal agony, for cannon-shot wounds are usually fatal ; and as we fell back in this regular but protracted order, the round bullets ploughed and ripped up the turf about our horses' hoofs,

A cornet who carried our regimental standard was unhorsed by a nine-pound shot, which disembowelled the animal he rode ; he lay half under it, unable to release himself, and, as we continued to retire, there was every prospect of his falling into the hands of the butcherly Russians.

"Poor Tom Dacres !" said the squadron leader ; "he is done for."

"And the standard will be taken !" exclaimed the Colonel, who was perhaps more concerned for the honour of the regiment than for Dacres' safety ; "those devils are already within pistol range of it. It is lost."

"It is not," said I, as a sudden burst of enthusiasm seized me, and I was anxious to rescue Dacres, who was one of the best fellows in the regiment, and, moreover, was "the only son of his mother, and she was a widow," far, far away in fenny Lincolnshire. "I shall retake it, even if in their hands."

"Dare you attempt this ?"

"No."

"What then, Rudkin ?"

"I shall *do* it, Colonel, and that is better than attempting. Who will follow me to the rear ?"

The whole squadron would have volunteered, but I quickly selected three brave fellows, and wheeling round our horses we galloped back to where, pale, half stunned, and half breathless, poor Dacres lay on his back, with both his legs and the standard too under his dead horse, which in its last agony had rolled over him just as he had freed his feet from the stirrups. Without dismounting we dragged him up by our hands and the standard with him ; but shot after shot whistled about us, and ere I had time to think of it, one of these killed my horse under me, and another struck me in the chest just as I left the saddle, and I fell, but staggered up, only to fall again, while the idea flashed upon me and took utterance on my lips : "O God, am I to fall already—to die so soon ?"

It was, though momentary, a bitter conviction, in the prime of health and life to leave so suddenly this pleasant world. to be among the first to perish in our new career of glory, after escaping the charnel-nouse at Varna, or a grave in the Vale of Aladdyn. A blindness, that was momentary too, came upon me, and when I looked again from the ground where I lay, I could see the three dragoons who had followed me (one bearing the recovered standard) rejoining the Brigade. There was a fourth, who was afoot, and whom I knew to be Dacres, safe, while I had all the bitterness of being helpless and abandoned, for as I afterwards learned, they believed I had been killed.

But little time was left me for reflection, as I was almost immediately surrounded by a crowd of ferocious-looking Russian dragoons, clad in coarse green uniforms braided with yellow, and wearing glazed helmets, under the peaks of which but little more of face than their red snub noses and massive black beards was visible. Blow after blow was dealt me, chiefly about the shako and on the plates of my epaulettes, till, choking in blood, I fell again on the turf, and for some time was quite insensible.

When I recovered, the moon was shining brightly in a cloudless sky, and all around me the scenery was as visible as it would have been at noonday. Scared doubtless by the din of the recent cannonading and carbine firing, the birds were still twittering about in the caper bushes and laurels on the bank of the Bulganack, the current of which I could see shining and rippling as it flowed away towards the Euxine. Our advanced guard of cavalry, together with the staff and flying artillery, had fallen back upon the camp, and I was left lying there alone on the ground where the *first* passage of arms had taken place between our troops and those of Russia —a passage now forgotten amid the greater splendour of the Alma ; yet not altogether was I alone, for near me lay the bodies of those who had fallen. They were already stripped by the Tartar peasantry, and lay gleaming, white, still, and ghastly under the steady radiance of the moon.

Two dead horses, Dacre's charger and mine, lay near me, but denuded of all their dragoon trappings.

How I had escaped the plunderers I know not ; but only my epaulettes, sash, and sword were gone. The pain in my chest was most oppressive. I thought I was dying now, and felt quite resigned ; more than I should *now*, for then I had no one in whom——

(I checked the speech that was about to follow, as my eyes involuntarily met those of Blanche, which were full of the tenderest commiseration.)

I lay still and with eyes closed, for at that dread moment the border land of shadows—the land of the Great Uncertainty—seemed terribly near indeed.

"Hélas, mort sur le champ d'honneur !" said a soft voice near me.

My head was tenderly raised, as if the speaker wished to test whether I was really gone, and on looking up, I saw bending over me on her knees the sweet sad face of Sister Louise Marie, the little French sœur de charité, who was already so well known to our troops at Varna by her innumerable acts of goodness, kindness, benevolence, and Christian bravery.

Her little face seemed very white, and whiter still her great quaint hood in the moonlight ; but blood again choked me, my eyes closed, and though the pain of my wound resembled something like a red-hot sword rankling in my breast, I became a second time unconscious.

When once more I came back to the world, the sun was shining brightly ; the pain in my chest was greatly alleviated, for somehow, unknown to me, the ball had been extracted by Doctor Thompson of the 44th—the glorious " surgeon of the Alma "—he who remained voluntarily with that terrible *grey acre* of Russian wounded, and perished with the most of them. A soft pad secured by a bandage had stopped further hæmorrhage. Again my head was gently lifted up, a cooling drink was given me, and this after a time enabled me to look around.

I was lying on a species of pallet or camp bed, on the clay

floor of a Tartar cottage; an edifice usually excavated out of the slope of a steep hill or bank, in proportion to the accommodation required. This saves the expense of a back wall, and the angles are filled up by baked mud. The roof which thus projects out of the hill is quite flat and supported by posts, thus forming a pleasant verandah. Through the open windows of such an edifice as this, and beyond these posts, which were covered with vine-leaves and flowering creepers, I could see, stretching in distance far away, and steeped in the light of a sunny noon, the rocky vale through which the Bulganack wanders to the Black Sea.

In one corner of this rude apartment, which was almost destitute of furniture, as the place had been looted by Russian foragers, crouched a Tartar woman, wearing a white fereedje, grinding corn with a handmill ; her dark glittering eyes fixed on me from time to time with vague wonder   In another, on a low divan and quite motionless, was seated the sister of charity, reading intently a little book, red-edged, with a cross on the boards ; a Breviary to all appearance.

The pure and regular profile of her little face, which was familiar to me now, was fully displayed, as the hood of her head-dress was folded back ; and as she sat in the blaze of sunshine that streamed through the unglazed window, I could see that her face, though young and beautiful—so beautiful that her grim attire of black serge, over which flowed the cape of her unshapely white coif, failed to mar it—though very peaceful and divine in its expression, yet bore traces of care that had been premature, and suffering that had been great ; though there were times when she could seem happy, merry, and cheerful ; for with her the bitterness of all the past had gone out of her life.

Her eyes were dark, and their lashes long and black, though her hair was of the richest brown. On the marriage finger of the left hand I afterwards detected two wedding rings, which I thought singular, as the religious wear but *one;* so Sister Louise Marie had evidently a story.

Slight though the mere motion was of turning on my pillow it arrested her attention ; and hurrying to my bedside she knelt down with a cup of Crimskoi wine-and-water.

"Where am I, mademoiselle ?" I asked faintly.

"You must not call me mademoiselle, as if I were a great lady or a waiting-maid," she replied, smiling.

"What then ?"

"Your sister."

"Sister Louise Marie ?"

"Ah, you know me then?" she exclaimed, with a still brighter smile.

"Know you ! ah, who in Bulgaria and in the Valley of the Plague did not know you? You are an angel on earth !"

"Hush ! you go too far. Would that I merited such a character ! But you must not speak--more than all, if you are going to be impious ; and I, monsieur, who am to be your nurse, must control you."

"My nurse—you ?"

Then she told, with many a pretty little French gesticulation of manner, that with the aid of two soldiers, less severely wounded than myself, she had conveyed me to a cottage at Bulganack, where the ball had been easily extracted ; and that she had been left there in charge of me and six other sick and wounded soldiers—four British and two French ; and then, lest I should talk too much, she left me for a time, after playfully putting her small soft hands upon my eyelids, and saying,

"Tenez-vous bien tranquille—fermez les yeux " (Be still, and close your eyes).

Though alleviated, as I have said, the pain of my wound was still great. There seemed to be a load crushing down my chest with every respiration ; but hope now began to gather prayerfully in my heart that I should yet get well, and forget my chances of being helplessly murdered by Tartar shepherds, Greek robbers, or prowling Cossacks. As the faces of my comrades came in succession before me, I longed to be in the saddle, and once again among them ; but ere that could be, I knew that, alas, many must fall never to rise again, as it was evident that a general action was inevitable ere a few days elapsed.

Without further aid from the surgeon, who had simply given his directions to her, I was left entirely to the care of Sister Louise Marie ; and certainly no real sister, no wife or mother, could have nursed me more tenderly ; though doubtless she was quite as heedful of the unfortunates who occupied the adjacent huts.

Though very subdued in manner, she was full of pretty and engaging ways.

"Call me your little sister," she would sometimes say.

And more than once, when I was half asleep, she dipped a finger in a little font which she had hung near my bed and crossed me on the forehead with holy water.

"Sister Louise, you treat me quite as if I were a child," said I ; "what a tender mother you would be !"

She became, if possible, more pale than usual when I said this. A little spasm crossed her face, and her eyelids drooped as she folded her hands upon her breast—hands that, notwithstanding all the menial work she did for us, were as white as your own, Miss Bingham ; and looking up to heaven, she said in a voice that was inexpressibly touching :

"I have been both wife and mother, monsieur, in the days when I never thought to be a sister of charity."

"A wife—a mother—you ?" I repeated with surprise, as her face seemed so young and girlish.

"Why do these words surprise you, mon ami ?"

"Because I could not have supposed all this."

"I am alone in the world now ; I have none to care for save those who suffer, and you are one of them."

"In your tender hands, dear Sister Louise, my sufferings are fast passing away—a few weeks more must see me well and strong ; but were I to live a thousand years I shall never, never forget you."

She looked at me and smiled sadly at my earnestness ; and now I knew that she *had* a story to tell ; but it proved a very simple one.

"What was your husband, may I ask, Sister Louise?" said I, after a pause.

"A soldier like yourself—an officer of the 10th Regiment of Chasseurs à Pied."

"And his name?" I asked, to lure her on. "Louis-René Morin."

Her voice trembled as she repeated the name of one who was doubtless so dear to her once, but only a sad and beloved memory now, though she had nearly learned to veil all emotion under a calm and usually cheerful exterior.

"And your child?"

"I had—two."

Then "the iron seemed to enter her soul ;" and while her lips moved as if she was muttering some silent prayer, her thick black eyelashes became moist and matted with the large tears that welled up unbidden.

"And they——"

"Are in heaven now, monsieur mon frère," she replied hastily ; and again her soft dark eyes were cast upwards with an expression alike beautiful and divine.

"See, mon ami, see," said she, as her tremulous little hands drew out of her bosom what seemed to me at first a bunch of charms attached to a blue-silk ribbon ; but which proved to be little consecrated medals, a tiny crucifix, and a gold locket containing three locks of hair. Two of these were fair, one being golden, the other quite flaxen ; and no doubt with all her cultivated air of resignation, this locket was the most precious reliquary she possessed, as it held all that remained on earth of the little tendrils that had crept and twined themselves around the mother's heart ; though she consoled herself that they were in heaven, and praying there for poor lonely *maman* in her weeds as a sister of charity.

"Tell me how all these sorrows came to pass?" said I, taking her hand caressingly in mine.

"My story may be compressed into a few sentences," said she; and while fixing her eyes downward on the clay floor of the Tartar hut, instead of looking at me, she began thus, or rather somewhat in this fashion.

CHAPTER XIV.

THE SISTER OF CHARITY.

I AM now twenty-four years of age. When, in my mere girlhood, I became a happy wife ; oh, can it be that but six years have passed since then—six years that seem as ages now !—and since I had a little boy who called me mother, a cherub with rosy cheeks and golden curls, who was just beginning to lisp and prattle, when my second great sorrow came—a child sent me to replace the loss of my first little René, whose hair was so flaxen and silky.

O mon Dieu ! I can see them both yet—the last more plainly than the first—more vividly even as when I held him up to receive his father's kiss—the farewell kiss of my Louis, so handsome, brave, and tender, as he marched in haste with his regiment from Avignon to Paris, where there was soon to be enacted that terrible *coup d'état;* for the 10th Chasseurs à Pied proved to be one of those corps on whom the Emperor, then Prince President of the Republic, mainly relied for support against the citizens.

For two years we had lived in happiness at Avignon, and then time softened to me the blow I had suffered in the loss of my first little baby. We were not in the barracks at the Papal Palace, but—though our means were limited—rented a pretty

7

cottage on a green slope, at the base of which, between vineyards and rose gardens, flowed the Rhone.

In memory I can see it yet, that secluded abode, half-
buried amid honeysuckle and jasmine, with its charming little
flower-garden, where Louis' comrades, who had served with
him under Canrobert in Africa, often came to smoke, play
chess or dominoes, accompany me at the piano, or play with
my little boy, for the Chasseurs were as kind-hearted and
happy fellows as they were brave ; and in fancy, too, I can see
dear, quaint old Avignon, with all its embattled walls and
towers, and the belfry of the Cordeliers, where Petrarch first
saw Laura ; the sterile rocks of Vaucluse, Mont Ventoux, ever
beautiful with vegetation though its head is veiled in snow,
and the undulating hills all green with vineyards and groves
of olive and mulberry trees—a scene on which my eyes shall
never look again, nor should I desire to do so, now that all
whom I loved are gone.

My heart seemed to go with the Chasseurs as the echoes of
their drums died away on the Paris road. The regiment, I
have said, marched hurriedly and in haste, and I was left alone
with my child and full of keen anxiety, for whispers came of
terrible things that were expected in Paris ; but no sure
tidings reached me. No letters came ; the telegraph wires
were cut in many places ; in others the rails were torn up ;
the newspapers dared not print much intelligence ; the mails
were most uncertain ; so we, in that remote province, knew
little or nothing of what was being done elsewhere, till long
after it was past and over.

As the days stole slowly on and became weeks, how
anxiously I reckoned them and longed for my dear Louis !
and how I missed his happy comrades—merry Jules Perreau,
who won his epaulettes when fighting with the 64th against
Abou Maza in Africa ; Emile de Castellain, who had the
deadly encounter with two Sheiks in the terrible Djerma Pass,
and slew them both ; and who, though a great, brawny, and
bearded captain, was the very slave of a pretty wife, whose

little white feet he would have worshipped, had she commanded him to do so ; and then there was handsome François
Guérin, who led his company so bravely at Narah, where the
fierce Arabs had their nests like eagles among the rocks, and
who died of fever in the Vale of Aladdyn, raving alternately in
prayer to the Blessed Virgin, and in fancied love speeches to
Mademoiselle Pompon, the dancer at the Porte St. Martin.
Alas, how sad it was !

I nursed and laid them all in their graves at Varna—horrible
Varna !

Time, I have said, passed on, but there came no tidings
from Paris—no letters from my husband ; but one night—oh,
I shall never forget it !—I heard the sound of shrieks, of male-
dictions and musketry, near my cottage, where cowering I lay
abed, with little Louis nestling in my breast. After a time
these terrible noises passed away, and all became ominously
still ; but I had heard that the people were full of wrath
against the troops of the Republic ; and that the troops hated
and despised the citizens, and that hence many fugitives and
deserters were tracked and murdered on the highways.

I feared that something dreadful must have taken place in
my vicinity ; that my husband might be returning to me and
—but no—no! I thrust the idea aside, as not to be dwelt upon.

Peeping forth fearfully in the early morning, while all Avignon lay sunk in purple shadow, and the Rhone looked so
deep and blue, I saw at the bottom of our little garden the
body of a man in uniform.

It was not the light green and gold of the Chasseurs, but
dark blue embroidered with oak-leaves, the costume of a
French general. He was not, as I at first surmised, dead ; but
sorely exhausted from wounds, bruises, and toil. He had, no
doubt, been assailed by some of the turbulent peasantry, and
would be so again if discovered by them. I roused him, and,
assisting him with my little strength, laid him on the only bed'
my cottage contained. I bathed and bound up his wounds,
in suspecting the source of which I had been right.

He was a fugitive from Paris, seeking to escape from France; for, after he was able to speak, so he told me, and of the terrible events which had recently taken place there. He related that the Prince President, aided by St. Arnaud and Fleury, had resolved to coerce the Constitutionists, and with this view had swept into prison at Paris every statesman and general who was in any way eminent for public spirit and ability ; that he, General Baron Loisel, would have shared the same fate had he not successfully found concealment. Louis Napoleon was then declared Dictator of France, and the selected regiments were marched into the streets by General Canrobert, who commenced an indiscriminate massacre to strike terror into the Parisians, two thousand of whom were shot on the Boulevards, though barricades were thrown up and resistance offered by many armed men.

The 10th Chasseurs à Pied—how my heart leaped at their name !—had thrice stormed a barricade which he with all who adhered to him had thrown up in the Boulevard Poissonnière, using in its construction omnibuses overturned and filled with stones, beds, pianos, and other furniture from the adjacent houses: thrice it was stormed, and twice retaken. With his own hand he (Baron Loisel) had sabred or shot down four of the officers of the Chasseurs ; but the barrier was carried at last, and all its defenders fled for shelter into the nearest houses. Then the Chasseurs poured volleys of musketry through the shutters of the closed windows, compelling all who were therein to lie flat on the floor.

The house in which he had sought refuge was forcibly entered, the door being blown open by musket-balls, and every human being in it was bayoneted, save himself, regardless of their prayers and screams for mercy. He lay secure and unseen under a shop-counter till darkness fell, after which he made his escape from the city, and was on his way to the frontier when assailed at night by some armed peasantry, who, in pursuance of their feud with the army, had fired on him in mere wantonness because he was in uniform.

So there had been fighting in Paris, the 10th had been severely engaged, and at least four of their officers had fallen, and by the hand of this man ! All this gave me cause for much and terrible reflection.

Perhaps this man's weapon had reached the heart of my husband, in whose very bed I was now nursing and restoring him that he might continue his flight to Switzerland, though errors and alarms had brought him to Avignon out of his direct route. He further told me that a very hopeless exile was before him, unless his old comrade St. Arnaud, to whom he wrote without delay, stood his friend with Louis Napoleon.

None of his wounds were very severe, so he recovered rapidly.

One night, when he was convalescent, little Louis in his night-dress was kneeling on my knee, with his rosy dimpled hands clasped before him, and I was teaching him to beg of God that when he died he might join his baby brother René, who had gone to heaven before him. After a pause the child turned to where the Baron, seated in a chair, was regarding us with mingled interest and emotion.

" I shall pray for you too, monsieur," said Louis.

" Why for me, child ?" he asked.

" Because you are a soldier, like my father."

And after he had lisped a few words after me, the Baron rose and said :

" What is his name, madame ?"

" Louis, Monsieur."

On this his eyes filled with tears, and taking the wondering child in his arms, he kissed him, and said: " I too have a Louis, a little fellow just his age, whom I have left in Paris, and never more may see, unless St. Arnaud befriends me ; and there too I have a young wife, who doubtless mourns for me as dead."

We had now a kind of common sympathy between us, though there were times when a foreboding seized me, and I could not help shuddering. Oh, could it be possible that my Louis was one of the four officers who had fallen by *his* hand?

One morning a messenger reached my cottage bearing a letter, the contents of which filled my patient with joy. It was from St. Arnaud, and enclosed the full pardon of Louis Napoleon; so the Baron prepared to return at once to Paris, where he promised gratefully and faithfully to search for my husband, of whom I heard nothing for two months.

A fortnight more passed away in aching and grinding anxiety, and then a letter came to me from the General. It was brief and said:

"I have found your husband; come to him without delay."

He had found my dear, dear Louis; but how?—dead or alive, wounded or in captivity? The letter was painfully, tantalisingly curt; but there was not a moment to be lost now. Collecting all the little money I had, I took my child in my arms, and locking the door of our beloved cottage near the Rhone, with its roof and walls a leafy mass of climbing roses, creeper, jasmine, and vine, all blended together and alive with little singing birds, without visiting poor baby's grave at St. Pierre, I set out for Paris, with a heart swollen by one great and absorbing anxiety—my husband's fate.

I had often to travel afoot, for I was too poor to take the rail always; but heaven supported me, otherwise I know not how I should have got over the vast distance which lies between Avignon and the capital, when my forebodings proved to be fearfully correct.

Baron Loisel, true to his promise, had searched and found my husband, lying severely wounded in a common hospital of the city—wounded by four balls fired from *his* revolver at the barricade in the Boulevard Poissonnière—and had conveyed him to his own house in a fashionable suburb, and there I found him—but oh, how changed!—carefully attended by the best surgeons in Paris, surrounded by every remedy, luxury, and appliance that the grateful Baron could provide ; but, alas, he was sinking fast.

Why dwell on this ?

His wounds were mortal ; he did not live twelve hours after I saw him, and just as the Angelus bells were ringing out upon the air, he expired with his head upon my breast, and clasping our child's hand in his own. I felt as if it was all a maddening dream—a nightmare from which I must awake to find myself in our dear cottage again, and that the sound I heard was not the hum of Paris, but the murmur of the Rhone.

Half my life seemed to have left me, and to have gone with him into the darkness of eternity, when I sat beside his premature grave in Père la Chaise, that wilderness of crosses, flowers, and obelisks ; but I strove to pluck up courage, for my child yet was with me—left but for a time only. My trials and miseries were not yet over.

My little Louis sickened and died ; I laid him beside his father, and then I was alone, and without an object in the world—most terribly alone. There seemed nothing worth living for now, and never more would I return to Avignon, where every object must remind me poignantly of those I had lost. But " blessed are they that mourn, for they shall be comforted ;" so in time there came peace to my heart, with a great love of charity to all who were in sorrow or suffering.

I adopted the habit I now wear—and so am here.

The girl's face—for in truth she was but little more than a girl—was full of holy beauty as she ended her simple story ; but it spoke of the sadness of the unforgotten past, blended with a divine hope for the future, and in her long-lashed eyes and on her lips there seemed to hover the very spirit of the words she had quoted.

Thus it was that she wore *two* plain rings ; the first her husband's wedding gift, the second as a religieuse.

I quitted Bulganack when convalescent ; but instead of
going to the hospital at Scutari, or idling about Pera, I rejoined my regiment in the camp of the Light Brigade, or all
that remained of it after Balaclava ; and when *next* I saw
Sister Louise Marie, she had found her true home—one that
was far beyond the grave.

One morning, after a fearful storm of snow and biting wind
I had breakfasted on some half-ground coffee, boiled in a
camp-kettle lid, and instantly mounted, as I had to ride on
duty to the French camp.

As I passed the huts and tall poplar trees of Balaclava on
my left, the rear of the Turkish defences and batteries, and
Lord Raglan's head-quarters (a large farm-house with some
vineyards), and then rode in a north-westerly direction towards the right flank of the French army, the cold blast that
swept over the snowy waste from the Black Sea was beyond
conception bitter and paralysing, though I was well provided
against it, in a thick pilot coat, a furred hood, and long Crimean boots, together with some of those cosy cuffs, com-
forters, and muffatees which the kind girls of England sent
us, and every way looking as unlike a smart Light Dragoon
as possible ; and strange to say, notwithstanding the intensity
of the cold, wherever the ground was bare, the bulbous roots,
especially the purple crocus and snowdrop, were sprouting.

On the sheltered or lee side of an old ruined wall in a lonely
place, I saw a dark object lying amid the snow, and on drawing nearer, discovered it to be a woman—a sister of charity,
either torpid with cold or frozen dead. Springing from my
horse, I found the latter to be the case, and more than all,
as I drew back her hood, that this victim to her Christian
duties and the horror of our winter camp was poor little
Louise Marie, who had nursed me so tenderly at Bulganack
—she who had ever been so cheerful and hopeful, so placid
and sweetly content.

I was deeply moved, familiar as we were then with death
and suffering, on making this painful and startling discovery.

Her eyes were closed, or very nearly so ; thus she must have passed away in a species of sleep or torpor, the result of exhaustion and cold, and darkly the long black lashes lay on her cheeks, now paler than marble, pale as the snowflakes that rested on her dress. Her small white hands, that had never wearied in the performance of kind offices to the sick or suffering, were now, as I had often seen them, crossed upon her breast. One grasped her rosary, and her little bunch of relics which I had seen at Bulganack, with the locket that contained her children's hair ; the other held a little basket in which were some medicines with which she had no doubt been going on one of her errands of mercy, when her delicate nature had succumbed to those severities she was so ill-calculated to endure ; and so she had perished thus miserably and helplessly in the night, though eighty thousand Frenchmen were almost within hail of the place where she lay.

I galloped to their camp, and returned with a few of the 6th Zouaves ; and these rough fellows, all bronzed and bearded, were deeply moved, some of them to tears, as they dug her last bed in the snow-covered ground. Muffling her in my cloak—other coffin or shroud there was none—we buried her in the habit of her order, and all her little relics with her ; and as they covered her up, a corporal, a stately man, on the breast of whose tattered jacket were the medals he had won under Canrobert at Mascara and Oran, uncovered his now grizzled head to the winter blast, and read with reverence from his missal the prayers for the dead. Each man then raised his right hand in salute and we separated in haste, for already a rocket soaring high in the grey leaden atmosphere announced that a simultaneous cannonade was to be opened on Sebastopol from all points at once.

That soldiers should be buried in heaps, and lie over each other in ghastly tiers after a battle, seemed only the natural order of events ; but somehow, of all our graves in the Crimea the last home of that little French sister of charity, within sound of the adverse batteries at Sebastopol, seemed to me the most uncouth.   Her miserable fate made a deep impression upon me even then, though King Death was ever at our elbows, and we recked but little of him.

> "So the long-drawn days had ended
>   Of the lonely loveless life
> Of a bride—the bride of heaven—
>   Always bride, but never wife."

More than once, when relating this brief memory of the Crimea, I had been interrupted by pretty little expressions of well-bred commiseration from the ladies, and when stealing a glance at Blanche, I had detected tears in her dear eyes at certain parts of it, but more particularly at that passage where I had been unhorsed and shot down ; and this manifestation of tenderness intensely gratified me, though her manner was as gay as ever.

"I thank you for your story, dearest Lance," she whispered as she passed me, adding aloud, "you have certainly whiled away an hour of a wet day, after we had become ennuyed with music and ourselves, the racing game, and cockamaroo to boot."

"Thus it was, Colonel, in consequence of the bullet which led to my acquaintance with the French sister of charity, that I was *not* at the Alma," said I, with some point to Stapleton, who, having been anxious for billiards, had listened to me with an impatience which he did not care much to disguise ; but his long moustaches found him some occupation the while ; and at "tiffin," the General, as I fully expected, told us that after Chillianwallah some such adventure as mine had occurred to Rummun Singh, the subahdar major of his regiment, the difference being that his nurse was not a sister of charity, but a deuced pretty Nautch girl, who had missed her *troupe*, and been strolling near the field.

I did not quite see the resemblance ; but the worthy old General's associations of ideas were often singular, as they all tended to India in general, and the famous field in particular.

CHAPTER XV.

DAY DREAMS.

A TIME is coming when I shall have to record more startling events than friendly gatherings round the library fire, flirting speeches, or love-making ; for we—the actors, at least, in this little life-drama—were all bound for India, where a perilous time indeed was before us.

Such is the inconstancy of our nature, and so selfish is the human heart at times, that in the absorption of my new passion for Blanche Bingham, I was quite oblivious of any pain my attentions might inflict on her cousin, the gentle Henriette, whom I had at one time been so solicitous to please.

If—as at one time I had hoped and flattered myself—she had been beginning to love me, during the months of our past pleasant intimacy at Thorsgill Hall, she must now have become painfully sensible of considerable neglect, in the omission of attentions which she had been wont to receive from me, and not quite as a matter of course ; for a heart that loves is subtle in discovering this, " and women," says a female writer, " being perhaps less humanised than men, retain many of the simple forms of animal instincts still ; and, somehow, instinct seldomer makes mistakes than pure reason in this kind of matter."

Is it unreasoning egotism to admit that, in the exultation of my new proprietary and successful love affair, I actually felt as if I had something to revenge upon her for the petty episode in the conservatory with Colonel Stapleton, and furthermore for the fragment of the conversation overheard when the cousins were gathering the rose-leaves ?

And there were times, when I was hovering about or conversing with my fair *fiancée,* that I have found her quiet dark eyes regarding us with something of sadness, if not disdain, in their expression; and then only did a sentiment of reproach occur to me, though saying in my heart the while— for Blanche had fairly taken it by storm—" Thank Heaven I did not go too far, and so commit myself !"

I, who had so many miserable doubts concerning the future with Henriette, had not, or seemed to have none so far as her more volatile cousin was concerned. I had taken a leap in the dark and proposed blindly, trusting to Fate and those Parcæ the Horse Guards, and, like Micawber, that "something would turn up" for me in India.

I was full of happiness certainly ; but true it is "that seldom can one reap joy in this world, without entailing sorrow on another ;" and though I foresaw it not then, Henriette's hour of retribution was to come, when I was to suffer for the vanity in which I was indulging then.

So deeply did the passion for Blanche inspire me, that my life seemed only to date from the time she came to Thorsgill Hall, but a few weeks back. Beyond that period, all seemed a chaos, a cloudy and unprofitable waste; and though I looked forward with dread to the temporary separation which was inevitable, I longed with impatience to bridge it over, if possible, by activity—to rejoin, to embark and to sail for India, where alone I could win her, and where I trusted that some kind spirit would smile upon our fortunes ; "for," as she once whispered to me, "I would not have our marriage spoken of as a ' bread-and-cheese one,' dearest Lance."

But in my perfect assurance of her love, I had no doubt of everything being possible ; and even schemed in my heart that, if her family objected on the plea of funds, and that I was only a captain of Rifles, I should persuade Blanche to marry, and march up country in spite of them. I was too absorbed to see a difficulty in anything. Would she prefer love in camp and quarters—a barrack or a bungalow to a palace at Garden Reach ; and being carried in a palanquin, slung on two bamboo poles, to a handsome carriage and pair in Chowringhee?

Time ere long would show.

" Such a pity it is that those girls are going away so far as India," said Howard, one day when their departure began to be spoken of.

" Yes," replied Stapleton, "and 'as blooming candidates for matrimonial preferment.' They will not be in Calcutta a month before both are engaged, and all the more readily that they don't require to shake the pagoda tree."

How was it that the Colonel's tone always jarred upon my ear? Where was now my former jealousy of this personage, who, it seemed to me, since the advent of Blanche's arrival, had addicted himself more than ever to dangling about Miss Guise? Yet I began to perceive, after a time, that our tall tawny-haired friend was covertly unpleasant in his manner when I was by the side of my intended.

" The deuce !" thought I ; "does the fellow mean to rival me with both? Henriette was somewhat of an attraction to him before ; can she be less so now?"

Stapleton was undoubtedly a well-bred man ; hence a tone of half compliment, half banter, and covert insouciance, which he adopted at times when he conversed with Blanche seemed to me very inexplicable, unless it could be that he felt secretly irritated by the mode in which he was mentioned in her letter from Brighton. This bearing galled and annoyed me the more that I had no acknowledged right to resent it, and I knew him to be a blasé man of the world ; hence I was not sorry when he announced one morning that his presence was required in town, when he would be a week at "the Rag," previous to rejoining at Chatham. He took his departure by the up-train, and I saw him no more till we met in Bengal, under very different circumstances.

Now our happy little circle at Thorsgill Hall—my visit which was indeed one of those events in life described by Moore as a green spot in the waste of memory—was about to be broken up, and perhaps, small though it was, never to meet all together again.

India was before most of us—India with its vastness of empire and extent; and happy it was for us that we could not lift the veil of the future, that hid the horrors of the coming mutiny.

The Howards left us for London, and then came a night when I heard, with an indifference that at one time would have astonished me, that Henriette Guise was to leave us on the morrow to visit Mrs. Appleton, her future chaperone. This sudden announcement took all at the Hall by surprise —all, at least, save one, though I obtained a clue to it ere long.

"Why would she not wait for her cousin Blanche, that they might travel together?" asked her uncle and aunt. But Henriette, though she shed abundance of tears at a leave-taking that would too probably be a final one in this world, was quietly and resolutely determined to quit Thorsgill Hall. Mrs. Poplin did the requisite packing, and the preparations for her departure were soon complete; but ere it took place we had a somewhat startling episode.

CHAPTER XVI.

CONTAINING SOMETHING OF THE "OLD, OLD STORY."

SOME of the incidents connected with this flying visit to Thorsgill Hall may seem trivial ; but they became nevertheless full of importance in the time to come—at least to the author of these pages.

On the night before her departure, Henriette Guise excelled herself in her toilet, though " all her things " were packed up. How charmingly her dark hair was smoothed and dressed around her graceful head ! Indian bracelets, the last gifts of General Dormer, glittered on her white arms ; and round and white her shoulders came out of the maize-coloured dress that fitted her to perfection, while the blush-rose hat nestled over her left ear looked as fresh and sweet as herself. Well might aunt Dormer—I had already mentally adopted her as a relation—say, " Darling, you are looking your very best to-night !"

And, sooth to say, she was doing so. She was unusually gay. I thought the girl was glad to be going, and I could not help reflecting how nearly it had been that she and I might not have been parting thus ; and so my thoughts went back to that sunny evening when we were seated in the bay window of the library, and when I was on the very verge of a proposal, encouraged by the confiding manner in which she replaced her hand in mine, after suddenly withdrawing it.

For some time past she had generally evaded me ; or perhaps it might have been that I had become indifferent to her movements, so completely was I absorbed in those of another ; but on this night—the last, too probably, we should ever spend together—she was unusually frank and friendly with me.

As I turned from her and gazed on Blanche, nestling with girlish grace and childlike affection close by the old General, over whose face smiles seemed to ripple at some of the things she was saying to him, the thought occurred to me, was I acting fairly to him in contracting a secret engagement with his niece, while under his own roof, and without his knowledge? But it was Blanche herself who had sealed my lips, and pledged me to secrecy for a time.

The General and his wife—a kind old couple indeed—doted on these two beautiful girls ; all the more that their own little ones had all passed away in childhood, and found their graves at various up-country stations in the Punjaub and elsewhere.

Suddenly the old man left Blanche's side, and crossed the drawing-room to where Henriette was seated on the sofa with me, talking of such commonplace matters as the requirements for the overland route. He took her white face caressingly between his brown hands, and kissing her tenderly on the forehead, said,

"This is the last night you may be in Thorsgill Hall for years to come, my dear, dear girl ; and though whatever we are doing for the *last* time has generally something of sadness in it, let me hear you sing again ; just once again, Henriette."

"With pleasure, dearest uncle ; but what shall it be?"

"Anything you please."

"Something merry?"

"Well, I would rather not ; for though that wag, Blanche, has been making me laugh, I am far from feeling merry when I know that your place here will be vacant to-morrow, and I feel by anticipation how lonely the old house will be without you all."

"Then I shall sing you something very, very sad," she replied, smiling brightly, as she seated herself at the piano.

I rose to be of service, as usual, but she simply bowed and said,

"Thanks, no ; I do not require music, as I shall sing from memory."

On this I retired to my seat, and Henriette at once commenced a little lyrical piece, the accompaniment to which was
very beautiful. It seemed a very singular song for a young
girl to sing, and her mode of execution, with the sweetness of
the melody, rather than the words, actually moved me ; but
there was always a seductive cadence in the voice of Henriette Guise.

At first I suspected that it was some composition of her
own ; but she assured me afterwards that it was from the
pen of an unknown or forgotten Scottish writer, and now I
can only recall two of the verses :

> "Oh, would that the wind that is sweeping now
>   O'er the restless and weary wave
> Were swaying the leaves of the cypress-bough
>   O'er the calm of my early grave !
> And my heart, with its pulses of fire and life,
>   Oh, would it were still as stone !
> I am weary, weary of all the strife
>   And the selfish world I have known.

> "I only sigh for a bright quiet spot
>   In the churchyard by the stream,
> Whereon the morning sunbeams float,
>   And the stars at midnight dream ;
> Where only Nature's sounds may wake
>   The sacred and silent air,
> And only her beautiful things may break
>   Through the long grass waving there."

Her voice seemed to become a little tremulous as she concluded, but she left the piano with one of her brightest
smiles, and said :

"How silent you all are ! A song is often a signal for
general conversation. I fear that I have made you quite
melancholy, and this may be ominous to one having a long
journey before her."

8

"Good heavens, where did you pick up that grave-digger's ditty, Henriette?" asked Blanche. "It sounded like some horrible dirge."

"Yet, my dear girl, you sang it very sweetly," said the General, playfully pinching the chin of the performer, who soon after rose to retire.

"Good night, Captain Rudkin," said she, with a gaiety of manner that was far from flattering ; "or rather, I should say good-bye," she added, "as I leave this place so early that I shall not see you to-morrow."

"So soon ?" I stammered.

"Yes, very early. I must, if possible, catch the 'Flying Scotchman' at Darlington ; and too probably we shall never meet again, though we *may* hear of each other."

"Good-bye, then ; but not for ever, I hope," said I, smiling too, while I thought, considering my future relations with Blanche in Calcutta, of the certainty we should have of seeing each other a good deal, for then I must become by alliance a cousin also.

Her hand, so soft and shapely, touched mine for a moment. Sweet was her manner and calm her smile, as with a farewell bow she withdrew, accompanied by her aunt and uncle, who had some matters on which to confer with her, or some final arrangements to make ; and so I was left alone with Blanche, while the song and inscrutable bearing of Henriette seemed, I knew not why, to haunt me reproachfully.

This emotion was very fleeting, for another little hand, quite as soft and shapely, stole into mine, a bright face came nestling close to my cheek, and Blanche said in her most winning tone :

"Lance, will you always love me as you do now?"

"Why do you ask me such a question, Blanche ?" said I softly, while looking into her dear confiding eyes, after one quick glance to see that the curtains of the drawing-room arch were still close.

"Forgive me, darling; but I am so happy that I tremble——"

"Tremble, Blanche—for what?"

"The future; I cannot help it. I love you and Henriette,
too, all the more that you are so good without being a bit
stupid."

"Blanche!"

"Well—because stupidity and goodness so often go together; but, O Lance, I do love you!"

Sweet are the lips that tell us—not in words alone—how
dear we are; yet words are precious too—most precious to
remember.

"And now good-night, my own one," she whispered. "I
must follow my cousin—good-night."

In the intoxication of such whispers, and with the fond-
lings of these dear hands, what was the departure of Henriette to me?

Blanche disappeared, and I was left for a time to revel in
my own happy thoughts.

CHAPTER XVII.

THE COUSINS.

" TEARS, cousin," said Blanche, on perceiving that the former had been weeping when she joined her in her dressing-room; "but it is natural—you are leaving us, Henriette."

"Aunt is so dear—uncle so kind—and I may never see them more," she replied hurriedly, and not without a little air of annoyance.

Of late there had not been much of the mutual confidence that had hitherto existed between the cousins ; but on this night, as it was the last they could spend together at Thorsgill Hall before their departure to India, after Mrs. Poplin had been dismissed, Blanche, while caressing in her lap a little black-and-tan terrier I had given her, with silver collar and bell—a creature so tiny that it could pass through a stirrup-iron—sat in her dressing-robe by Henriette's bed-room fire, chatting with all her usual gaiety ; while the latter with her nimble white fingers coiled up the silky masses of her dark hair for the night.

One might readily have thought that beauty such as theirs, though so different in its character, did not require much enhancement ; yet upon the toilette-table, which, like its great oval mirror, was gracefully draped in rose-coloured silk and white lace, lay innumerable pieces of jewellery, cut-glass bottles full of mysterious essences and compounds, and all the etcetera that Rimmel and the best shops in Bond Street can furnish—requirements which, if absolutely necessary, were quite enough to have made my barrack-room and bungalow prospects vanish in thin smoke.

It is scarcely etiquette, I fear, to report conversations or private confidences between young ladies when in, or nearly in, their night-dresses, when their back hair is all undone, and their pretty feet, half slippered, are planted on the warm fender, and the merits or demerits of their male friends are under review, together with matches, engagements, lovers, honeymoons, and everything save cats, poodles, and parrots ; but without some such breach of etiquette, how is Chapter XVII. to be written, or my story told ?

"Accept that pearl spray for your dark hair, Henriette," said Blanche ; "it does not suit mine."

"Thanks, dear cousin," replied Henriette, laying the jewel, the effect of which she had been trying, back into its case ; "but I cannot think of depriving you of it."

"Why?"

"It is so valuable."

"I have plenty of other ornaments—enough and to spare ; moreover, pearls don't suit me. You remember that Rudkin admired you with it on the first night you wore it, as you told me, so do pray keep it."

"A thousand thanks, dear Blanche," said Henriette, putting her arms round her cousin's neck from behind, and kissing the crown of her head. "Yes, he *did* admire its effect," she continued, replacing the spray for a moment amid her dark hair, and glancing at her side face coquettishly in the mirror.

"So he told me," said Blanche, as she ran her fairy fingers through the rippling masses of her golden hair ; "and then Colonel Stapleton—— "

"I was so glad when *he* went away," interrupted Henriette. "I am seldom deceived in my first impressions of men, and to me there always seemed something sinister and insincere about it—yet he can be very taking in manner, I grant you ; however, his sudden attentions bored rather than flattered me."

"Sudden, were they ?"

"Somewhat so."

"I thought he was rather given to ignoring ladies—rejoicing in the freedom of bachelorhood, and turning up his single blessed nose at matrimony."

"I never thought he had any views in that way, at least so far as I was concerned," said Henriette frankly; "and then there was poor simple Mr. Howard—I think he was a silent admirer of us both."

"Too silent for my taste," said Blanche, tossing up the terrier to catch it again in her lap.

"But he was quiet and gentle—very like his mother, I think."

"Yes, very like, so far as want of beard and whiskers go."

"Blanche, what odd things you say! Captain Rudkin seems hopelessly smitten with you."

"Perhaps," replied the other carelessly; "but it is useless, you know, cousin."

Henriette eyed her keenly for a moment, but Blanche was smiling into the fire. Then turning suddenly, as if struck by some association of ideas, she asked:

"What *is* the cause of this sudden determination of yours to visit Brighton?"

"Determination?" repeated Henriette, who coloured quickly, as Blanche could detect in the mirror.

"Yes, cousin."

"What other cause could I have but a wish to see the Appletons?"

"But won't you see enough of them, as we go all out together overland?"

"Mrs. Appleton is so motherly—so kind."

"Not more so than aunt Dormer, surely?"

"Oh, no, she could never be so."

"Come now, Henriette dear—you cannot hoodwink me."

"I do not think of doing so," replied poor Henriette, blushing more deeply now.

"The truth is—if you will confess it—that this old country house has grown weary to you, intolerable, since the occurrence of a certain event."

" To what event do you refer ?" asked Henriette, while her short upper lip quivered and her face resumed its general paleness of complexion.

" Cannot you guess ?"

" Indeed I cannot."

" I mean the departure of Stapleton," said Blanche, though this perhaps was not the reply she had at first intended, for she was in a mischievous mood to-night.

" What is Colonel Stapleton to me ?" asked Henriette, with an emotion of relief, yet with a haughty toss of her little head. " A minute ago did I not express my satisfaction that he had gone ?"

" That might only be a cloak," laughed Blanche.

" Cousin," replied Henriette innocently, " I would conceal nothing from *you*."

" Had you never a fancy for Lancelot Rudkin—or he for you ?"

All things considered, the question was perhaps a cruel one ; but, with all her good qualities, Blanche could at times be rather pitiless in her rivalries, even though the yearning heart of her addressed might be, for all she knew, torn by neglect and disappointment—and it was a large and tender heart which beat under the soft white bosom of her she spoke to now.

" Oh, no," said Henriette, turning fully round and displaying two lovely dimpled elbows, as she coiled away the last wreath of her hair and stuck in a long pin. " What have you ever seen in me to make you think so ?"

" Only an admission you nearly made on that day when we were gathering the rose-leaves."

" You labour under some very strange misapprehension or mistake."

" And then there was that little tableau in the library window."

" I repeat that you are quite mistaken, dear cousin," said Henriette, now assuming the offensive ; he is *your* admirer, and you know he is."

"Mine?" exclaimed Blanche, laughing.

"Yes ; and if you are not engaged, you ought to be."

"Ought to be ! what do you mean ?"

Henriette made no reply, so Blanche smiled a saucy con-scious smile, and immediately changed the subject.

"I wonder if Jacky Appleton's curate still adores even her shadow, as he used to do, at Brighton. It isn't much use his doing so, however. If my Plunger is there, I shall make you welcome to the reversion of him."

"Thanks, Blanche. How can I appreciate your genero-sity ?" asked Henriette, who was too gentle to feel long annoyed, and was now laughing merrily.

"By being civil to the poor fellow. Though he is an heir to an old baronetcy, I don't think I could endure him now."

"Why *now*, more especially ?"

"I cannot say."

"Is it love of change, or change of love ?"

"Both perhaps ; and now, good-night. The carriage will be at the door for you betimes to-morrow, uncle says, so once again, dear cousin, good-night ;" and with a kiss on each cheek Blanche Bingham swept away to her own room leaving Henriette, who was not fated to have much repose for that night.

During the foregoing conversation she had checked with difficulty more than once an indignant feeling, that made large tears gather under her white eyelids, or a flush to cross her cheek. She felt instinctively that there had been some-thing unkind in the tone and bearing of her volatile cousin, and Henriette regretted this, and strove to thrust the convic-tion aside ; for though she had plenty of proper spirit, she was gentle and soft-hearted by nature ; she sincerely loved her bright little cousin, and now they were about to be separated for a time.

She did not complete her undressing ; but sat thoughtfully gazing into the changing embers of the fire long after Blanche

had deposited her tiny dog in a dainty mother-of-pearl
basket lined with silk, laid her head on the laced pillow, and
gone off into the land of pleasant dreams.

CHAPTER XVIII.

A CATASTROPHE OCCURS.

MEANWHILE, all unconscious that I was the subject of such an
interesting discussion between such rosy lips, I was lingering
alone, over a havanna, in the billiard-room, rying a succession of hazardous strokes and cannons for mere practice,
haunted the while by the strange and melancholy song
Henriette had sung. I had been for some time left entirely
to my own reflections ; the General had long been abed, as
he kept what he called "Indian hours," and, to the great disgust of the butler and housemaids, was always up and abroad,
or in every one's way, daily " by gun fire."

In all my cogitations the idea of Henriette mingled
strangely with that of Blanche, and I felt that which a writer
has described as " the indefinable instinct of something yet
to come."

Her approaching departure brought the reality of my own
more vividly before me. It was pretty close at hand now,
and by anticipation I felt all the cruel wrench the separation
from Blanche would be, and the blank in my life that must
follow till I rejoined her in Calcutta.

" A good stroke that," thought I approvingly, as I pocketed
the red ball ; " but I suppose when I am mated at Garden
Reach, when the Lord Bishop of Calcutta has uttered the
necessary benediction, and Paterfamilias has added " Bless

you, my children!" much of this sort of thing will he at an end. No more backing the red, making books on the Calcutta Derby or the Sonepore Plate ; no more picnics for the ladies of the station, or champagne suppers in the mess-room ; no more flirtations at the band-stand, or hog-spearing, or tiger-potting, or betting on who'll pull the longest straw from the roof of the bungalow or any other absurdity. Of course, I shall become tremendously domestic—begin to have an idea of the smartest things in bonnets and holland riding-habits—shall look after the ice-club, perhaps even the ayahs, maho-gany-coloured, lean and bony, in scarlet and yellow raiment—that is, if they have anything to wheel in perambulators under a sunshade—perambulators, ye gods ! Farewell, a long farewell to all my—What the deuce *is* the matter ?" I ex-claimed aloud, as my mental soliloquy was suddenly brought to an end by an alarming cry that came to my ear.

"Fire ! fire ! The house is on fire !"

It was the shrill voice of a woman evidently in great terror, so I rushed from the room.

The butler, or some one else, was now clanging at the deep and sonorous house bell, which hung in a species of square turret above the centre of the mansion, an edifice rather quad-rangular in design ; and the din of this at such an hour brought the scared inmates from their various rooms in hot haste, all more or less attired, as some—the female portion especially—had been abed.

The lamp in the great central staircase, which luckily was all of stone and massively built, was yet burning, and by its light I saw Blanche and Mrs. Poplin in their night dresses, with shawls thrown hastily about them, rushing down in terror and bewilderment—the former bearing Tiny in his mother-of-pearl basket.

"Oh, Lancelot, Lancelot! the rooms below ours are on fire !" said she, as she swept past me to seek her aunt.

"Thank heaven you are safe, dear Blanche !" I exclaimed

in my excitement, heedless of who might detect our familiarity or want of ceremony.

" But Henriette—Henriette !"

" Where is she ?" I asked hurriedly.

" In her room—in her room still, sir !" screamed Poplin ; " the door was locked, and I could not make her hear us."

I rushed up the stone staircase towards the corridor off which I knew that the sleeping-rooms of the cousins opened. It was lined with ancient wainscot panelling and floored entirely with wood. The smoke was rolling from it in volumes as the fire from below reached it, and I could see the little jets of red flame already spirting up through the joints of the planking.

At the extreme end of the corridor I could also see the figure of Henriette as she stood silent and terror-stricken at the door of her room, which she dared not leave, lest the floor of the passage should give way beneath her. She stretched her arms towards me imploringly in mute appeal—or, if she spoke, the clang of the house bell, the crackling of the flames as they spread fast in the wainscoted rooms below, and the mingled cries of alarm from the household, drowning what she said.

Her retreat was cut off !

I could see no means of approaching her, save at the risk of falling into the flaming gulf below, as the crackling boards must fail to sustain my weight. My blood curdled.

I had seen the corpse of a woman who had been scorched to death in a blazing hut at Varna ; I remembered its loathsome aspect—the hair gone, the hands shrunk up like freakish knots, its contorted attitude, blackened, lean, shrivelled, horrible ! The memory of it at that moment made me shudder, as I went plunging down the staircase to the terrace outside to see if by any means I could reach the fatal room in which Miss Guise was now completely imprisoned.

Three of the lower rooms in that wing of the hall were now filled with fire and smoke, and zig-zag rents were already apparent in the old brick walls. The flames were just bursting from the windows ; the ancient lozenge-shaped panes quickly passed away, and the mullions, with their stone tracery, were defined in black outline against the red light within. From amid the ivy that clung to the old walls the twittering birds were scared in flocks by the flames and general uproar which had so suddenly startled the serenity of the autumn night. The carved stonework of the hall, its coats of arms, half shrouded among dark-green leaves, the gurgoyles along the roof or cornice, looking like griffins or chimeras grinning amid the smoke, and all its other architectural features, stood boldly out in the red and glowing glare. As the wind got in, showers of brands and sparks began to rain over all the terrace, and after a time, when the flame reached the roof, the molten lead began to drop through the open mouths of the gurgoyles just mentioned, rendering it perilous work to be near them.

At the window of her room was Henriette Guise, wild with natural terror now.

"Help me—save me ! Do not let me perish, dearest uncle ! Help me, Captain Rudkin ! I am too young to die—too wicked perhaps " (poor innocent Henriette). " Help me —help me !"

Her cries and her situation made my heart thrill. I had no means of reaching her, and hence returned to the staircase again. Mrs. Dormer was lying there in a helpless swoon, and old Mrs. Jellipott, the housekeeper, on seeing her mistress thus, went off in the same fashion, but not so quietly, as she lay in her night dress uttering a series of shrill screams at regular intervals, while beating a tattoo with her heels, quite unheeded by the scared domestics, male and female.

General Dormer, whose heart had never failed him, even at Chillianwallah, wrung his hands in the extremity of his misery.

"Aid me to save my girl if you can, Lance Rudkin," he cried. " I am old and stiff now, but with God's help we may —nay, we must—do something."

Silently I rushed up the great staircase again ; there was less smoke in the corridor ; but now the flames were shooting through an open gap in the wooden flooring close to where it joined the stone pavement of the landing-place. This flaming aperture which separated me from Henriette's room was, as yet, only some four or five feet broad.

Repeatedly I was driven back by the smoke, which was overpowering, until I placed a wetted handkerchief across my mouth ; then, aided by a tall and sturdy footman, I tore from its hinges a door to bridge over the gap, and thus passed it. The moment I did so more of the flooring fell in, and with it my temporary bridge ; more fiercely than ever the flames shot up and my retreat, like that of her I sought to save, was also cut off; but I had reached her room, and she threw herself half-fainting on my arm as I shut the door to exclude the sparks and smoke.

Not a moment was to be lost, and I turned to the still opened window, against which two ladders, brought from the stable-yard and lashed together had been planted by the gardener and grooms.

The window-sill was fully twenty-four feet from the ground the descent would have been easy, but between us and escape there was an unthought-of barrier. The antique windows in this wing of the house were all mullioned, and the space between each of these shafts would not have permitted even a child to pass !

"We are lost ; and I have destroyed you !" said Henriette in a low gasping voice, as her head drooped on my shoulder, and she closed her eyes while for a moment the memory of her melancholy song flashed upon me.

Was it really ominous of evil, and to prove prophetic ?

Lovely indeed did the girl look in her pale beauty and half disrobed for the night, just as she had fallen asleep near the fire amid her meditations, her black hair all dishevelled and streaming in soft masses over her white shoulders.

I felt, while gazing upon her, that some reparation from me was indeed owing. It seemed hard that she should perish so miserably, and almost in sight of Blanche too. At all hazards I had come to save her, and if I failed—though so happy in the success of my love—I could but die with her.

I deposited Henriette in a chair, and looked wildly about for some means of escaping from the terrible trap in which we were so suddenly placed, and where we had scarcely a moment for delay or reflection, for death was close indeed ; the flames were already crackling in the room beneath, and the heat of them became awfully apparent ; but in such dilemmas instinct is often stronger than reason.

Death was in the rear and no escape in front ! Were Henriette and I to die thus, and together after all? A death so fearful too, and so suddenly brought upon us ! But half-an-hour ago all was so quiet and peaceful—this catastrophe as unthought of as the deluge.

In the vague hope of gaining the roof I looked to the ceiling, but it was too lofty to be reached, even had I the means of breaking through it. The room was wainscoted ; I sounded the panels on every side with a poker and found the solid wall everywhere. I struck at the mullions of the windows with the same implement till it bent and broke in two, and my arm tingled to the shoulder with the futile strokes.

In the room there was a small settle, a kind of sofa, of oak, antique and richly carved. Seizing this, to use as a species of battering ram, I dashed it against the mullions of the window in fierce succession and with breathless haste. Despair and anxiety for her who was watching me with imploring eyes imbued me with a strength I was all unaware of possessing or being able to exert.

At the third stroke I dashed out one of the mullions, thus beating two apertures into one. A burst of applause came from below, where some of the servants and labourers on the estate were gathered in an anxious and excited group. Grateful was the sensation of the cool night wind as it blew on my flushed face when I passed out upon the ladder, and lifting Henriette after me, began slowly and carefully the difficult task of descending—difficult while thus laden.

We had barely left the window ere flames shot through it, and a storm of sparks flew over us as the floor of the room fell in, and the fire from below burst up.

Our peril had been greater even than I thought, and we had not escaped it a moment too soon.

" Saved, saved, and by *you !*" murmured Henriette, as she hung half fainting in my right arm while I steadied myself with my left hand, and fortunately for us both the girl's weight was light.

" Bravo, captain ! Hooray !" cried the grooms and gardeners who stood beneath, their upturned faces shining in the ruddy glare.

" Hold the ladder steady, my men," said I, feeling that the task I had yet to accomplish was somewhat arduous ; but in less than half a minute the ground was reached safely, and my charge consigned to the care of her uncle and Blanche.

" Now, my lads," cried I, " follow me with axes and fire-buckets ; let us do what we can to save the old house."

In a country district, and especially so excluded and remote as that occupied by Thorsgill Hall, fire-engines were not to be thought of, and had not the great stone staircase intervened to cut off the flames from the rest of the building, it must have perished, notwithstanding all our willing efforts with water in stable-buckets passed from hand to hand, and all our exertions in cutting down wooden partitions here and there.

The " ghost's wing " alone was destroyed by the catastrophe.

Of course no one knew the origin of this fire, which might

have ended so fatally, and also have destroyed the whole of the fine old ancestral mansion, which had been the home of the Dormers for many generations, so of course nobody was to blame. With a hearty adjective the jolly old General said he " didn't care now that his Henriette was safe." But there were some rumours of a knight of the shoulder-knot having been flirting with a pretty housemaid — old Bagshaw the keeper's daughter—and exchanging marks of their mutual esteem, till scared by the sudden and stealthy approach of the wary and rigid Mrs. Jelipott, and that hence a lighted candle had been hidden near some inflammable material, and so forth. The cause was soon forgotten in the magnitude of the effect, and of the terrible risk run by Henriette, whom I had saved, but only to encounter greater perils elsewhere perhaps.

Boundless was the gratitude of her uncle and aunt, and I felt assured of having, at least, their warmest consent to my engagement with Blanche, had I been permitted by her to reveal our mutual secret ; but dearer to me were the praises of her, and on this occasion she ventured to say more than she could otherwise have done.

" Oh, it was a terrible half-hour, Lance darling," she whispered in my ear ; " but how heroic, how romantic too, was the rescue of poor dear Henriette !"

" Greater romances and more heroism appear in the newspapers every day, Blanche," said I.

" But I hope she didn't kiss you in the midst of her gratitude."

' Why ?" I asked, laughing.

" Because I should be so jealous ! And as for your kisses, they are no longer your own."

" Whose then ?"

" Can you ask me ?—mine, of course, every one," and laughingly patting my cheek she hastened to rejoin her cousin.

Once more the household—all save some grooms and labourers, who watched or worked in the ruined wing—subsided for the remainder of the night, or rather morning. Mrs. Dormer and Mrs. Jelipott had each a dose of sal voatile, and the General a jorum of " brandy-pawnee, for, man alive, but this affair was worse than Chillianwallan." After my recent Crimean experiences, and such a devil of a hurly-burly and excitement, I was too much of a soldier to turn-in. I also took from the butler a stiff glass of brandy-and-water as a nightcap, and had my "forty winks" on a sofa in the billiard-room, where I dozed and dreamt, not of her I loved, or of her I had saved, but, oddly enough, of the cavalry charge at Bulganack, and the Sister of Charity who nursed me in the Tartar cottage—poor little Louise Marie ; and this association of ideas was caused by some sensations of pain in the old bullet-wound, the result of my exertions in beating-out the mullion of the window, or bearing Henriette down the ladder.

By the events of the night all the household at the hall were completely upset ; yet, to our great surprise, Henriette Guise was still resolute in her intention to leave us.

CHAPTER XIX.

HENRIETTE'S DEPARTURE.

WHATEVER may happen in a house—robbery, fire, or even death—people, being civilized, must as usual meet at break-fast, luncheon, and dinner ; so we duly assembled at the first-named repast when the gong clanged, anxious to compare our notes on the recent event, and looking all more or less worried and weary. The General certainly was the most lively of the party, though regretting the loss of a hookah given to him by the Rajah of Chutneypore, a pair of pistols presented by the Governor-General, and some other Indian *impedimenta.*

Henriette had an aspect both haggard and wan ; indeed, she was a few shades paler than was her wont, and answered me with difficulty when I made the usual well-bred and ex-pected, but nevertheless sincere and earnest, inquiries about her health.

Her aunt entreated and the General ordered her to remain at the Hall, as her nerves were evidently shaken by the dread-ful fright she had undergone ; but no—no—she had promised to visit Mrs. Appleton, and was resolved to start that very day for Brighton, and no power could detain her. She was —for her—almost angrily energetic on this point. Her ward-robe had luckily escaped the destruction of everything else in her room, by having been, after it was packed, placed in the entrance-hall over-night.

Breakfast done, the General had a consultation to hold with his steward concerning the late accident ; Blanche had another to make with Mrs. Poplin about their mutual losses in the conflagration ; and I was left to smoke a solitary cigar in the library while idling over the morning papers.

I was occupied thus when suddenly by my side I found Henriette Guise in her hat and otter-skin jacket, attired for her journey, and somewhat nervously striving to button an obstinate glove on her slender and shapely hand.

"Allow me, Miss Guise," said I, starting up. "And so you are still resolved to desert us?"

"Yes; the carriage will be at the door in another minute, Captain Rudkin."

"How much we shall all miss you!"

"I am so glad to see you for a moment alone, Captain Rudkin, before I go."

"Why *alone ?*" I asked, struck by a nervous peculiarity in her manner, and retaining in mine the hand on which I had just buttoned the straw-coloured kid glove.

"That I may once again thank you, but coherently, for saving me as you did last night; I must have perished else. Thank you, if I can in words," she added, with a tremulousness of voice which I naturally attributed to the terror she had undergone. "Thus I am glad to see you alone, as I said; for Blanche—Blanche, as you are aware, makes so light of everything."

Her curved lip was quivering with emotion, for she was an affectionate and impulsive girl, and there were very unmistakable tears welling up in her beautiful dark eyes.

"You are still nervous and highly excited—why go to-day?" I urged. "To-morrow will find you stronger and more composed. Surely I have earned some right to entreat!"

But she only smiled and shook her head.

As I gazed on her softly-featured face and in her eyes, the brightness of which was mellowed by the fringes of their long dark lashes, for a moment, but a moment only, something of former emotions came back to me with a force of which I was scarcely aware at the time, and of which Blanche might not have approved. But I was only a sincere friend now, and

9—2

remembering that fact, Henriette looked down, and strove to become to all appearance cold, collected, and composed.

She had a smart little hat with a single feather; it was placed jauntily well over her forehead, and her veil was twisted round it. Her gloves fitted her hands to perfection; and her toilette, so far as collar, cuffs, and studs went, was complete in its good taste. At each of her small and closely set ears there dangled a single pearl. The intense blackness of her soft silky hair, with her eyebrows and eyelashes, as contrasted with the pale white purity of her complexion, struck me as very singular in their degree. It was a face that one never could forget.

It seemed that her eyes looked brighter and her lips paler than I had ever seen them before.

As we looked at each other for a few seconds in nervous silence, I felt the conviction forced upon me that the girl had a greater regard for me than I could ever have flattered myself to have been the case. I read it in her eyes by an expression that is indescribable; I saw it in her manner, and the idea filled me with perplexity.

"Often," as Scott says, "how easy it is for the tongue to betray what the heart would gladly conceal:" so thus, when Henriette spoke again, there was a chord—a little tremor—in her sweet voice that touched me deeply, not then perhaps so much as when I thought of it afterwards. Her little hand was placed upon my arm now, and I felt that, mechanically and unknown to herself, its grasp was tightening there.

"To you I owe my life—my rescue from a fate that is too terrible to contemplate. I have indeed no words wherewith to thank you, dear Captain Rudkin, but I shall never forget you, be assured of that."

I pressed her hand in silence, and she resumed with an effort, her eyes downcast the while:

"I know not what I may have said or admitted in my great terror, for all that passed last night seems like a hazy dream to me now, but—but think not the less of me, Captain Rudkin, if I did so."

"You said nothing, Miss Guise—nothing that I can remember," I replied in all sincerity and with some surprise, for a fear was evidently haunting her that some secret of her heart had escaped her during her great dismay, and my assurance seemed to give her infinite relief.

"We have had a pleasant autumn visit here, Captain Rudkin, and had many happy days that may never come again; but there is the carriage at the door, and now, good-bye— good-bye for ever, too probably !"

"Do not say for ever; we shall meet again, I trust."

I stooped, and was in the act of kissing her gloved hand, when the playful voice of Blanche said :

"Are you actually about to part so coldly and frigidly with a mere shake of the hand ?"

Urged thus I obeyed the hint, and touched the pale cheek of Henriette with my lips. In a moment more she had rushed downstairs.

I felt that, under all the circumstances, the playful and impulsive Blanche should not have urged me—supposed to be a mere friend—to salute her cousin thus; but following her down the perron, I led her to the carriage, into which she sprang lightly and in haste, as if it was a place for concealment. A tall footman closed the door, the General waved his hand from the window, I lifted my hat, and she was gone.

From an oriel of the drawing-room Blanche was blowing kisses after the carriage as it bowled down the avenue, and I proceeded to join her.

I now saw that I had been rendered utterly oblivious of the many indescribable and unteachable signs by which a man learns that a woman loves him, and so careless of that which once I would have perilled all to win, I had grown pleased— heavens, pleased !—to think that Henriette was going away.

Servants are more acute observers than we give them credit for being.

"Poor thing!" I heard Mrs. Poplin say to Mrs. Jellipot, as I passed through the softly-carpeted hall; she is just breaking her 'art about that conceited Captain Rudkin, when she might have had that 'andsome Colonel Stapleton, who seemed so fond of her."

"And couldn't the captain see it?"

"No, not he."

"Why, Poplin?"

"Why? Bless you, ma'am, he sees nothing in this world but Miss Blanche and her golden 'air; and talking of her makes me think that young ladies can do many a thing that a poor servant daren't do."

Were these gossips indeed right? I did not wish to think so, and so hurried upstairs lest I should hear more. If all this were really the case, whence came the decisive nature of the reply to her cousin, which I had so accidentally overheard—the firm words "certainly *not*"?

I was sorely puzzled altogether. "We wonder if any man that walks the earth is worthy of the whole devotion of a woman's heart?" questions the author of "General Bounce;" and some such surmise flashed through my mind as I thought over all the past night and morning. It filled me with pity and friendship for Henriette; for I must have been something more or something less than man if much that was mysterious in the girl's manner and face had not deeply impressed and affected me.

But this was for a little time only; Blanche soon obliterated it.

And when her cousin was swept away from us down the long and stately avenue that led towards the little railway station at Winston, the little church and parsonage of which, from the summit of a wooded hill, look down upon the Tees—swept away, I say, in the Dormers' stately coach, with its gay hammercloth and florid panels, charged with the demi-lion and ten billets, *azure* and *or*, its portly white-wigged coachman, its powdered valet and high-stepping bays—I never knew till long, long after how bitter were the tears the girl shed behind her veil in a corner of it, and which the old General, who accompanied her, thought were the natural result of grief for her departure.

CHAPTER XX.

"CALL ME YOUR LITTLE WIFE."

BLANCHE and I were left for one more week together; but the day of parting came soon—too soon, indeed—a day the memory of which was fated to haunt me long, even amid wild and stirring scenes; and in a fortnight from that time she was to sail from Southampton with the Appletons, on her departure for India, thus anticipating mine by several weeks.

At noon, by a secret arrangement, we met in the garden at a time when none were likely to miss us. Aunt Dormer was closeted with Mrs. Jellipott, on household matters intent; the General was busy with Bagshaw the keeper and Mr. Tim Snaffel, a little lean old huntsman, with a long body and bandy legs, about the dosing of some favourite harriers, with syrup of buckthorn and vegetable broth, for a breaking-out somewhere; so *he* was also, luckily for us, out of the way.

How well I can recall the place and time, even in minor details, of this last meeting—a meeting of which the brilliant goldfinch twittering in an old pear-tree, the woodcock and the deer in their lair among the fern, were the only witnesses; a parting all the more tender that our final one would of necessity be formal and cold, as far as acting went, in the presence of others.

The tints of autumn had deepened in the shady avenue and far-spreading chase; in the garden, the gaudy dahlias that bordered the walks had been already marred in beauty by the frost of early morning, in the last chill hour before the dawn, the crisped leaves lay thick under the bared hedge-rows, and the whole aspect of Nature enhanced the sadness of our last meeting and parting ; and we could but thank Heaven that we were both leaving pleasant Thorsgill about the same time, and hence that one would not be long com-pelled to lament, amid the same scenes, the absence of the other.

I was first at our trysting-place, and on seeing Blanche approach I hastened to meet her ; but there was little need of that, for in a moment her soft arms were round my neck, and her face—fair as a dream of Eden—was nestled on my breast, and I led her into an arbour.

The dialogue of parting lovers is usually somewhat hack-neyed ; yet in the words and ways of Blanche Bingham there were some little mannerisms peculiarly her own.

"Oh, this is indeed love !" she murmured, as she laid her head on my breast ; "this is indeed love at last," she added lower. "I have flirted with many, had my fancies too, per-haps, but I never thought to love any man as I do you, Lance."

"So it is with me, darling," said I, while playing dreamily with her marvellous hair ; "the love of you fills up every illu-sion of the heart, which we are told may find many a resting-place, but only once a home."

"I wonder if all lovers think the same as we do" said she, after a pause.

"Doubtless, Blanche ; yet how strange it seems that we, who are all in all to each other now, but a few weeks ago knew not of each other's existence! Fate has thrown us together, and Fate must not separate us."

"While living, Lance darling ; but there is our journey to India—that long, long journey to be performed apart, separate —and I love you so," she sobbed. "Oh, that papa were here ? Could not Uncle Dormer—but no, no, it is not to be thought of ! We must be patient, and wait—wait—and I shall ever think of you as my lover-husband ; so call me your little wife, Lance," she whispered, with an engaging caress.

"You are indeed my dearest little wife !" I rejoined, in the same breathless voice.

Blanche could—to use a common phrase—turn the old General round her pretty fingers, as indeed she did every one else at the Hall ; yet she shrank nervously from intrusting him with our secret.

"You must never hint of engagement in your letters here," she said, with her bright hazel eyes full of tears for me to kiss away ; "nor must you write to papa about it, or to cousin Henriette——"

"She would be the *last* person——" I began.

"Or to any one else till you can see dear mamma at Cal· cutta, and bring her round, as I know you will, to listen favourably to you, to us both ; and I shall write you often, as often as I can, from Southampton, from Marseilles and the Point de Galle ; but of you, darling ?——"

"Of me you can only hear at long uncertain intervals, and through others."

And so, with aching hearts, we made our little arrangements for the sad interval of our separation.

The birds continued to twitter around us ; the faded leaves drifted away on the wind ; the shadows began to fall eastward ; but we still sat there, often in dreamy silence, a silence more eloquent than words could be, the silence of two souls joined in one, entranced, forgetful of the passing time and of all but ourselves.

To me there seemed to be but one woman in the world now, one heart worth living for—the heart that was pressed to me, and which appeared to throb for me alone. "It is so strange," exclaims a brilliant writer ; "we see a million of faces, we hear a million of voices, we meet a million of women with flowers in their breasts and light in their eyes, and they do not touch us. Then we see *one*, and she holds us for life and death, and plays with us idly often—idly as a child with a toy. She is not nobler, better, or more beautiful than all those we passed, and yet the world is empty to us without her." But why dwell longer on all this? We were soon brought back to this practical and workaday world by Mr. Vintage, the butler, who after having set some bottles of the General's most favourite and particular claret to air before the fire in honour of my departure, thundered the warning gong for dinner on the terrace.

We started at the odious sound.

Again her dear arms went round my neck, and our lips met for the last time in a long, long kiss.

Those who saw us quietly and decorously seated at the last meal we were to take together—the tall footmen with their silver entrée dishes, and old Vintage in his amplitude of white vest and black coat, with his peculiar claret and moselle—could little imagine the recent scene in the arbour, or the emotions that were welling up in our hearts, while the great épergne, with all its flowers, towered between us.

At last the fatal hour came ; and I saw the fair face of Blanche grow very pale as the sound of the carriage-wheels and of the horses' hoofs rasped on the ground before the entrance to the Hall ; and then Mr. Vintage, announcing that my baggage was in the rumble, stood respectfully with the door open to bow me out.

The General shook my hand warmly ; Mrs. Dormer kissed me twice, as a mother might do ; Blanche's hand I only took lingeringly in mine, and kissed it, to all appearance as frigidly as Sir Charles Grandison would have done, and in another moment we were apart—the little face, with its tresses of mar-vellous hair and soft eyes of golden hazel, had gone from me, perhaps for ever.

We shall see.

As the easily-hung carriage went rolling down the avenue, the scene of many a happy ramble, the evening seemed some-how to grow suddenly darker to my fancy. In thinking over the past it appeared to me full of omissions. I counted over a thousand things I ought to have said, a thousand caresses I might have given; yet the time we were together seemed pretty well filled up in both ways; but the imagination of love is ever active, and often self-tormenting.

How was I to kill the time that must intervene between this evening and the day of embarkation? What if I should be ordered to remain with the dépôt, instead of going to India? But that idea was too intolerable to be entertained. What was I to say in the first letter I could write to her with safety? In what terms would I break our tender secret to Mrs. Bingham at Garden Reach; and what manner of woman was she—gentle and kind, or haughty and cold? It seemed impossible that the mother of my bright, merry Blanche could be either of the last; and then there must be papa Bingham to encounter.

All these points and many more I thought of while the monotonous train, "with its drowsy hum," bore me on; now pausing at stately York, with its castle and minster towering high in air; now at Peterborough, with its cathedral and lonely castle mound; past stations filled with glittering lights and bustle; anon roaring through dark tunnels, or darting out of their gloom into the radiance of the moon, when fields and hedgerows, paddocks of rich grass-land or freshly-ploughed fallow, wayside streams and pools of shining water, seemed all flying past in circles on either side.

Queen Mab was not with me that night; and from a short sleep I was roused to find I was quietly gliding into the great station at King's Cross.

Once more I was in Babylon. It was but a few hours ago that I had been seated with Blanche in the arbour; and already a confused infinity of time seemed to have elapsed since we parted.

CHAPTER XXI.

TILBURY FORT.

BACK again to old Tilbury, opposite Gravesend—or Knaves-
end, as a traveller once suggested it should be called. I had
bid farewell to "mufti"; no more leave now, nor did I care to
have it till in "the Land of the Sun," as *she* once named it.

All the world knows Tilbury, with its two relics, which are,
or used to be, kept in the canteen—Queen Bess's chair and
De Ruyter's cannon-ball; the chair in which she rested and
imbibed a tankard of home-brewed after haranguing her
troops in the adjacent camp; and the rusty six-pound shot
fired from the Dutch admiral's ship when the colours of their
high mightinesses struck terror along the shores of the Med-
way, while worthy Mr. Pepys was imploring our seamen to
fight, and King Charles was flirting with the maids of honour
at Whitehall.

Though flat and gloomy, it is a quaint place, old Tilbury;
but the present regular fortification was only engrafted by Sir
Martin Beck, engineer to Charles II., on the old block-house
of bluff Harry's time, after it had been burnt by the Dutch.

The bastions are faced with brick, and have a moat and
double ditch; and within them is the spacious barrack-yard,
where many a time and oft I have "handled" a musketry
squad, and for many a tiresome hour taught aiming drill at
black spots painted on the barrack wall.

My chief chum, Joe Lonsdale of ours, had gone on leave of
absence, which my rejoining had enabled him to obtain;
thus, being in sole command of a depôt nearly two hundred
strong, left me little leisure time on my hands.

I was back to military duty once again; but how changed
in some respects seemed all professional interests for a time
to me! Amid the monotony of life in Tilbury Fort—for it is

a monotonous, gloomy, and Dutch-looking place--how I longed to see again that fairy face, and hear the tones of that playful voice which memory brought so distinctly to my ear, assuring me—as her letters did—that she loved me still! Dreamer that I was! For a regular lover is a man of one thought only, and hence for a time is somewhat akin to a fool in the estimation of many.

Our orders from the Commandant at Chatham were to get all the new recruits for India ' licked into shape,' as the phrase is, without delay; and while daily I worked hard with a musketry squad, my mind was ever elsewhere—ever sighing over the happy past while nervously fearful of the future; for if her family declined to permit her to share a captain's bunga low, the time to come might prove gloomy enough for us both.

Jewellery of all kinds—bracelets, necklets, rings, and those thousand pretty trifles now framed by taste and invention for pleasing women and luring men's money away—I longed to send, even to the dilapidation of my Indian outfit! but, situated as we were, it was impossible to have done so without exciting comment at Thorsgill Hall, and letting in an unnecessary light upon our secret relations. These mementos, however, I consoled myself by forwarding to Southampton.

How happily, in my day-dreams, I rehearsed all that had passed between us on that eventful evening at Stoke Priory, and our tender parting in the arbour! In imagination I seemed to see her again and again, to feel her little hand steal softly into mine, with the tender kisses of the time that was, alas, no more; and often in the night, when I might have enjoyed the jovial society of my comrades, or a sound sleep after a hard day's drill, I have mused and pondered till the morning drums beat réveille in the echoing barrack yard, announc· ing, as it seemed, that I had yet before me another day of separation from Blanche Bingham.

That on which she was to sail from Southampton arrived, and I had flattered myself that I might procure one day's leave to see her depart; but by the dictum of inexorable Fate

I found myself in orders for a garrison court-martial, and so could but write an answer to her last letter, dated from the hotel of Mrs. Appleton, under whose wing, as chaperone, she and Henriette Guise were together now.

I had previously sent her many presents of books, music, and other unostentatious trifles to the Hall, and the receipt of these she acknowledged by letters, which in tenor were all that I could have wished.

Love missives are usually voted stupid, save by those who are most interested in them ; yet with what avidity do we find these additions to the literature of the country devoured when they are 'aired' by some special pleader in the Divorce Court or a breach-of-promise case, and when all the pretty nothings, so pleasing to those who recognise the pet phrases, are held up to coarse ridicule or empty laughter !

Little did the worthy bugle-major who acted as postman at the Fort know how my heart quickened at his approach, and how both heart and eye dwelt on every word of the dear letters he brought me. Apart from all love, it is always pleasing to receive a girl's letter ; for even mild " Dear sir," traced by her pretty penmanship, seems so different from the same prefix to "amount of account rendered," from some cold-blooded limb of law—a legal Shylock waiting for his pound of flesh.

Though the last I should receive in England, most welcome was her letter to me, as water to one who was athirst in the desert, or rain to the flowers drooping and the grass-blades withering in the sun of an arid season ; but there were two paragraphs in it which gave me occasion for a little thought.

" Colonel Stapleton paid us a farewell visit. He is looking exceedingly well, but Jacky Appleton (who has thrown over her mild curate) thinks his long moustaches will be a greater source of amusement to him than of terror to an enemy."

(" Stapleton coming to the front again," thought I.)

" I can see you in fancy, my dearest Lance, in that dull barrack-room, which you have so often described to me at Thorsgill ; and all the love of my heart seems to go with this to you ! Oh, need I say how I miss the days and hours we spent at dear old uncle Dormer's ? Yes, yes ; separation is indeed, as your last delightful letter said, a living death. If I could but lay my poor little head on your breast as in the happy past times ! But consider my departure from South- ampton as only the beginning of our joyous ending.

"And only think, darling, how delightful ! My quondam admirer, our Brighton friend, the Plunger, is actually going out with our party overland. He has succeeded to his baron- etcy, and is now Sir Harry Calvert, of Something Hall, somewhere. He is to be an extra aide-de-camp on the staff of the Governor-General, I believe, but am uncertain. One thing I am sure of ; he is rather disposed to be troublesome " (" the devil he is !" was my comment) " and attentive ; but you know, dearest, that I loathe all mankind save you."

She concluded by promising to write to me from every point at which the steamer touched in the Mediterranean and Red Sea ; and placing her letter next my heart, I buckled on my sword, and went to the court-martial in a mood of mind that proved very beneficial to the prisoner we had to try, a certain obstreperous Dan O'Regan of ours, who, when tipsy, had been defying to mortal combat, and threatening " to desthroy," the sentinel at the Water-gate, when "confined to barracks."

Now I knew she was on the high seas, and fairly en route for her luxurious home at Garden Reach ; so I turned reso- lutely to the inevitable, and became more reconciled to the many duties I had to perform.

Blanche and Henriette were gone; but I had not heard the last of Stapleton, a personage of whose insouciance I have more than once complained.

About this time I received a letter from my brother officer, Joe Lonsdale of ours, one of those handsome and pleasant

fellows that all married woman like and spinsters dote upon.
He was enjoying his freedom in London, and now he pressed
me to " leave Tilbury on the wild shores of Essex, and come
to town, were it only for a single night!"   Among other temp-
tations held forth by Joe was "a glorious ballet at the ——
Theatre." ("I have cut all that sort of thing now, my boy,"
thought I.) " The manager is, or was, backed by Calvert of
the Guards, who wished him to engage permanently a certain
danseuse, and he has given me his box, as he is gone to
India. (Calvert? this was no doubt Blanche's quondam admirer.)   "In the refreshment-room there is a most popular
barmaid, to whom I shall introduce you, and whom, when she
looks nice, I chuck under the chin. 'It isn't immorality, but
only habit,' as a writer says ; but do come up, were it only for
a day, Rudkin.
' " I met Stapleton at Hounslow Barracks, where Vignolles
had been giving a squad of jolly girls four o'clock tea in his
quarters, with the adjutant's wife and her inferior half (as she
not inaptly named that gallant officer) to play propriety for
the occasion. We all went to a ball somewhere after, and
such fun we had, Lance! I proposed to two of them, and I
hope our letters of readiness will soon come, for I am in a
deuced scrape. Perhaps you will act the irate parent, and
telegraph for me ; but were I cousin to the tom-cat at the
Horse Guards, I would use his interest to effect an exchange,
as I don't want to go to India at all." (Poor Joe little foresaw
what was before him there !)
   " Next day I dined with Stapleton at the Rag. It was his
farewell feed, as he goes out with the first Indian drafts in the
Jumna, so we shall soon follow. Some pleasant fellows were
present—Vignolles of the Hussars ; Hicks of the 19th, who
got as tight as a drum ; Jones of the 43rd, and others.
   " The Colonel, though a model of propriety, got slightly
'screwed,' to say the least of it. He told us—when he became communicative—of his visit to ' Old Chillianwallah,' as
he named General Dormer, and of a flirtation he had with a

girl at his place—a lovely girl with golden hair, whose minia-
ture he showed us. Do you know her? He said she was
like the heroine of a certain novel, of whom it was owned
that 'all she did, even that which seemed almost childish,
was done with that unspeakable grace which makes trifles
charming.'"

I put down Joe's letter. "Golden hair"? Could it be
that Stapleton had possessed himself surreptitiously of that
which even I had not—a likeness of my intended?

"Can the fellow be such a beastly snob as to hint such a
thing?" I exclaimed.

The description of her manner was alarmingly like that of
Blanche; yet it might apply to a thousand girls. It is impossible not to admit that this passage in Joe Lonsdale's
letter about Stapleton annoyed me, and for many hours of
the night I lingered over a cigar, making theories and building up many improbable fancies; and finally came to the
conclusion that on such rambling statements as these it might
be rash to start for town, or Chatham, or wherever the
Colonel was, and "collar" him concerning a miniature to
which he had not given a name, and might prove to be only
that of some dancing-girl, to be had for a shilling or two at
the nearest stationer's; and still less did I think of the whole
affair when I got her first letter, posted at Gibraltar, full of
those endearing little phrases which were so characteristic of
her manner, so playful, or, as the French would term it,
caressante et folâtre. In a fortnight from that date she expected to be at Aden, and nearly half the world would be
between us then.

"Oh, that I had the magic carpet of the Arabian story,
that I might come to you at will, darling Lance; or the enchanted telescope of the fairy tale, that I might see you!"
she concluded. "How much do time and distance destroy
our happiness; those 'grim giants' that beset human life,
and to whom all its annoyances are due!"

I was proud of my regiment—as what soldier is not? All

the Line are Light Infantry or Riflemen now; but *we* were
the first, the original and genuine article! Though now
named the Prince Consort's Own Rifle Brigade, consisting of
three battalions, we were originally the old 95th Regiment,
raised on the 25th of August, 1800, by General Coote Man-
ningham, who was succeeded nine years after, as colonel, by
Sir David Dundas, author of the then famous *Eighteen
Manœuvres;* and in subsequent years the corps saw all the
hard service of the war so gallantly waged between Britain
and France, and it has fought in every part of the world, from
the bombardment of Copenhagen and the disaster at Monte
Video down to Inkermann and the fall of Sebastopol. We
had now twenty-one great battles enumerated among our
honours, and more were yet to be won in India.

After her letter from Gibraltar, I looked in vain for another
from Blanche; but none came to me; and her unkind silence
was unaccountable.

From each place where the P. and O. liner touched she
had written regularly to her Aunt Dormer, as the good-
natured General duly informed me : I was thus *au fait*, to a
certain extent, concerning her movements; thus illness had
not prevented her writing to me. Fickleness—that horrid
idea never occurred to me. Could her subsequent letters to
Tilbury have miscarried? Had Mrs. Appleton discovered the
correspondence through some indiscretion of Blanche, or by
some gossiping communications made to her own girls, and
in virtue of her position as chaperone interfered with her
epistles, or forbidden them until she duly handed over her
charge at Garden Reach?

This seemed the most probable idea; and as the drowning will cling to straws, I hastened to adopt it. Then I strove
to console myself with the hope that when she reached home,
and was free from Mrs. Appleton's control, she would have
ample facilities for writing to me, though I could have none
for replying. But a time came when a letter from Calcutta
must have reached me had it been written; but none ever

came, and a horrible perplexity began to seize and haunt me.

In the first agony of my suspense I was on the point of writing on the subject to Mrs. Dormer or the General, but remembering the wishes and injunctions of Blanche, I thrust aside the idea ; yet my heart went fondly back to the dear old Hall, with all its oriels, ivy, and clustering roses, amid which I knew the birds were nestling and twittering in the sunshine.

I felt now that I had no object in life but to get away from Tilbury, and counted the days that must intervene before our transport, the Punniar, came to anchor in the river.

Three months had now elapsed since I had last heard of Blanche, save through the family at Thorsgill Hall ; and still between me and my men on parade, between me and my daily avocations, between me and my wits, there seemed to float a fairy-like figure, with golden hazel eyes, masses of sunny hair, and a face with a sweet waggish smile, that told of the happy time at Thorsgill, when everything in Nature and in all our surroundings seemed but as so many links in the chain of love that bound us together.

Alone in my gloomy barrack-room—and feeling at times most terribly alone—I conned and dreamed over all the sweet past, or revelled in the anticipation of the future that was to come. I thought with tenderness over all my sunny fairy's pretty ways and little sayings—her thorough individuality—and recalled all the dear old pet-phrases that were to be uttered again.

India ! The mighty sea was to be traversed, all Africa to be gone round, and the Bay of Bengal to be ploughed by the Punniar, before we should be reunited. It seemed in-tolerable—incredible. Yet this cold and wearisome delay had to be borne !

With all this canker in my heart, I had, fortunately, the routine of military life to go through : there were drills and parades to undergo ; guards and pickets to command ; "officer for the day" to see the men's bread and beef weighed out at seven A.M. ; rooms to inspect, prisoners to visit ; tattoo reports to collect, day reports to write, and all the petty business of the soldier's workaday world in time of peace to do.

At last jolly Joe Lonsdale rejoined from London, and aided me with a will in the occupation of getting through the time. We had always billiards after mess. Dancing I eschewed, much to the surprise of several "bits of muslin," as Joe called them, who had been specially wont to look for me on such occasions. So the nights were, as I have said, devoted to pool and pyramids, varied with a little hazard, devilled bones, and champagne ; and I have often, I am sorry to say, passed in through the old Elizabethan gate of Tilbury with a light pocket and a lighter head, seeing two sentries where the corporal of the guard had posted only one, and when the "Queen's morning drums" were beating in the barrack-square.

CHAPTER XXII.

THE PUNNIAR.

THORSGILL HALL, I have said, was a childless home, as all the little ones of General Dormer had found their graves at various stations up-country ; all save one, Jack Dormer, who had grown to manhood, and was now one of the smartest lieutenants in our Rifle Brigade. Jack, I knew, was quartered at Dumdum, and consequently could have informed me of his cousin's movements had I written to him and frankly sought his confidence ; but the idea of doing so occurred too late, as the "route" for India arrived unexpectedly upon us, and the Punniar came to anchor off Tilbury, to receive on board twenty officers and four hundred men from that fort and from Chatham, for various corps in Bengal—two hundred being for the Rifle Brigade alone—with women, according to the then existing regulations, in proportion of twelve to one hundred rank and file.

We had to complete the Indian outfits for ourselves and our men in hot haste, and the day of embarkation came, before which we had to leave our P.P.C. cards for all our friends and the staff. For these enigmatical letters, Joe Lonsdale, a habitual joker, substituted D.I.O., signifying, "Damme, I'm off."

It was a gloomy February morning when the bugle sounded the "assembly." The hour was six, and the sun was yet far below the horizon ; a grey mist hung heavily over the river, shrouding the shores of Kent and Essex ; and the leafless trees, the brick bastions, the grass-embankments, and the guns in the embrasures, like everything else, were dripping with moisture.

Gravesend—famous in those days for its asparagus and its rascally watermen—was completely hidden from view ; but we heard the drums waking the echoes of its streets, half silent and empty at that early hour, as the detachments from Chatham came cheering and marching down to the place of embarkation for a ship of which the loose topsails, with blue peter at the foremast head, alone were visible above the haze.

The barrack windows in Tilbury were crowded with soldiers in their shirt-sleeves, cheering our fellows as they fell in under the eye of the Fort Adjutant. All were in heavy marching order, with great coats and kettles strapped to their knapsacks. On the dark-green Rifle uniform of a few their Turkish and Crimean medals showed to great advantage ; and we had a crop of others yet to win in the sunny land for which we were departing.

Save a few who had wives and little ones to leave behind them, all were heedlessly merry, and not a few were half tipsy ; but on an occasion of this kind—with young soldiers especially—discipline is always somewhat relaxed till they are all safe on board ship, after which of necessity the reins are pulled tight together.

Despite the oppressive gloom of the morning, I felt in the highest possible spirits. When again we trod dry land, Blanche, I thought, could not be far from me ; and already in fond anticipation I saw the Punniar steaming up the waters of the Hooghly.

Amid the busy whirl about me my heart was full of thoughts —thoughts of her ; " but let the heart watch—sad sentinel, weary of its post !"

Military embarkations in time of peace are all pretty much alike ; the soldiers and 'heir tearful wives, or sweethearts, all looking somewhat pale in the early morning, and, as I have said, a few tipsy—" overwhelmed," as Lonsdale phrased it, " by strong beer and violent blubbering "—the music of the band, half drowned by noisy cheers while playing " The girl I left behind me," varied by " Good-bye, sweetheart, good-bye."

As we had only a short march through the Water Gate in the centre of the curtain-wall to the side of the river, we were without music, and my detachment went off to the ship in two large boats, which were pulled by fatigue parties of their comrades.

One band as it marched through Gravesend played "Love not." As the cadence, brought by the morning wind across the rippling river, fell upon my ear, it stirred rather a sad emotion in my heart for a little time, as I saw in memory Blanche Bingham seated at the piano in Thorsgill, when she sang that very song with such piquancy and point in her manner, her handsome head thrown back, her seducing eyes fixed on me, and the coils of her hair gleaming in the waxen lights ; and most unpleasantly there mingled with this reminiscence a consciousness of the ominous silence that had ensued—the curtain that seemed to have fallen between my love and me.

The troops, with all their baggage and sea necessaries packed and cased, were all on board at last ; the capstan was manned by soldiers and seamen, who tramped merrily round with the bars, beating time with their feet as they hove short on the anchor ; while with their farewell cheers, to which we responded, the boats' crews that had brought us off shot away into the rising mist shoreward to each side of the river.

As a rule, soldiers don't reflect much, and it is fortunate for them that they are so constituted. When the colours are uncased and flying, when the cartridges are cast loose in the pouches, when the line of skirmishers is thrown out, and the cavalry and flying artillery go thundering to the front, when every face is flushed and every eye lit up, when we " stiffen the sinews and summon up the blood," would it do to consider the sombre crape that was to be worn, the tears that were to be shed, and the darkness of death that ere long must fall on many a happy home?

" Not a lady going out with us, married or single," said

Joe Lonsdale. "I have been all over the main deck, through the cuddy, and everywhere—not a vestige of a petticoat to be seen."

"Better without them at sea, are we not?" growled a crusty looking old Major of the Line, who was in command of us all. "What do you want with them?"

Joe eyed him half superciliously and sang :—

> "When we're far from the lips of those that we love,
>   We make love to the lips that are near.

A good regimental maxim, Major ; a way we usually have in the army."

"Not unknown in the navy too, I suspect," added the Captain of the transport, with a knowing wink.

"Think you and I met at Sandhurst," said a tall officer of Lancers to me.

"Ten years ago?"

"Exactly. You remember me—Home of the 9th.

"Perfectly ; we were then going through that course of careful training——"

"Which seems necessary to make a young fellow fit food for the demon of war," interrupted Lonsdale : "a victim of the villanous saltpetre. Have a weed, old fellow?"

"Thanks! I have been twice in India, Rudkin, since those days when we studied Straith together, with gunnery, 'and how to scale a fortress or a nunnery,' as Byron has it."

A summons to breakfast in the cuddy cut short the banter that was beginning on the poop, and ere that welcome meal was over the screw of the Punniar was lashing the muddy current of the Thames to foam, as she cleft her way down the river ; and ere long Sheerness, with its docks and hulks, and the low flat Isle of Sheppey, with its pastures and oozy marshes were all on our starboard beam.

A little time more and the increasing roll of the great Indian steamer announced that we were beyond the Nore light, and that the pilot in charge, beside the men at the wheel, was keeping a sharp eye upon those long narrow sandbanks which lie in parallel ranges in the estuary of the stately Thames. He left us at Deal, and then our last link with the shore-- with dear old England—was broken.

Ere this the Major commanding had issued his final orders for the voyage, according to H.M. Regulations.

We—the officers of each detachment—had to see that our men were experienced in the mode of tying, untying, and stretching their hammocks, and that their bedding, knapsacks, accoutrements, &c., were all disposed in the places allotted to them ; that their sea necessaries were served out and their haversacks numbered. A guard under an officer was mounted, as we had more than three subalterns on board, and a captain of the day was in orders.

The troops were divided into watches, like the ship's company ; but for deck duty only. It was a fine afternoon when we took our last farewell of the rugged Start on the coast of Devonshire. In the red sunset this bold ridge, which slopes abruptly into the sea, crowned in its entire length by splintered crags, worn and torn by the Atlantic storms, and all shaggy with moss, looked quaintly grim and stern. During the first few weeks of our outward voyage we had incessant squalls and rain. The latter served one good purpose, in addition to the steam hose and swabbing ; it thoroughly cleansed the ship's deck, her guns, bulwarks, and lower rigging, from a great quantity of iron rust that pervaded everything, in consequence of a vast quantity of old shot, shell, and bar-iron having been put on board at Woolwich to serve as ballast.

In crossing the Line the etiquette necessarily observed on board of a transport repressed much of the rough folly in which Jack is, or rather was, wont to indulge in honour of Neptune and his queen ; but as we approached the Cape, we had alternate storms and calms, and during one of the latter I shot more than one enormous albatross with my short rifle.

Whether it was to avenge "the bird of fear," I do not pretend to say; but next day about the same time, when I had been displaying my accuracy of aim, and just as the strange flat Table Mountain, with its summit veiled in mist, begun to rise upon our portbow, a sudden squall struck the Punniar and carried away the foremast, with the maintop-mast, of course, and the flying jib-boom, while we were nearly swamped by the weather-roll. One large boat was blown fairly off the booms, and never recovered, and one of our engines was in some way injured by the terrible concussion.

These sudden disasters necessitated our running into Cape Town to refit, and caused an unexpected delay of many, many weeks, during which I chafed sorely, amid the hearty satisfaction with which my brother officers betook them to shore-life and sporting with their double-barrels among the innumerable wild animals with which the region abounds, and I remember that among these Lonsdale brought down by a single shot a beautiful khoo, or African buffalo, in a kloof of the mountains, and Home of the Lancers was equally successful in potting a bos cafer, with its gigantic horns.

Once again, however, we were at sea, and drank "Sweethearts and wives," on a Saturday night, just as the Lion's Head melted into the deep, and the land of the Hottentots was left behind us.

The tedium of our voyage was varied by parades when the weather permitted, rigging wind sales to ventilate the orlop deck, such sails being always in charge of the sergeant of the watch, getting the hammocks up for stowage in the nettings, seeing the men messed, and so forth.

Salt water is said to be an admirable specific against the tender passion; but on this occasion I did not find it so. I have known men boast that their hearts grew lighter with change of scene, which is natural enough, and paradoxically lighter still as the distance increased between them and some beloved object ; but the latter was never the case with me.

My friend Lonsdale was the king of good fellows, and perhaps my groomsman to be ; but he was so heedless and rackety that I shrunk from making him a confidant as yet ; and often in the lone hours of the night, when I was officer of deck-watch, and my men, muffled in their great coats, were clustered under the lee of the boats, the bulwarks, or the break of the poop, while the great steamer sped silently and surely on her way up the mighty Bay of Bengal, her screw leaving a long and snowy wake in the seething waves astern, her canvas bellying out upon the breeze, the heavens cloudless and starry, the waves around us like silver, the dark cordage towering aloft taut to windward, in graceful bights and bends to leeward, the smoky pennant from the black funnel rolling far away over our watery track ;—often, I say, in such quiet hours as these, the image of the girl to whom I was hastening came before me with a strange distinctness, while I built airy castles, of which she was the sole empress and chatelaine, with flowers climbing the walls, birds singing in every window, and sunshine over everything.

Then those tender eyes would seem to look into mine again and that wondrous hair to sweep softly over my face, when even the sharp spoon-drift of the sea was unfelt, till, like a very boy, I yearned for her—yearned in the heart of a man who had fought his way through the embrasures of the Redan to the hell of strife that reigned within it.

I expected to be in quarters at Dumdum for some time. This would afford me ample opportunities for visiting the Binghams, and I thought over every means by which I might ingratiate myself with the family, and studied every point, even as to whether I should first present myself in uniform or mufti.

She had assured me that I should easily win over " mamma;" and I prayed heaven that it might be so. It was pleasant to dream over all the probabilities and eventualities, through the medium of a mild havanna amid the soft atmosphere of the Indian night, ere the ship's bell clanged to change the watch.

The procession to church, the bells, the benediction, the bride's bonnet, and then her travelling costume (what would it be in India ?) the breakfast, and the regimental band. Then there would be six bridesmaids of course—all the crême de la crême of Chowringhee, Garden Reach, or whatever was the " swell" place ; nothing visible of them but their heads and snowy shoulders amid a sea of white tulle, or would it be Dacca muslin ? Was it my duty or that of the groomsman to insert my regulation sword, in the true Indian fashion, in the crusted wedding cake, for the first cut thereof? And so on, and so on, the bright and pleasant phantasmagoria was woven, while the stately punniar sped on her way with her living freight, while the screw revolved without ceasing, while the wind hummed through the rigging aloft, while the waves ran merrily past in silver sheen, and sometimes the lights of Madras, Pondicherry, or Pullicat were visible as we glided along the coast of CoromandeL

CHAPTER XXIII.

CHANDPAUL GHAUT.

WE lost sight of the land for a little time, and encountered a heavy headwind after passing the low headland named Point Palmyras; but next morning saw us off the Sandheads, where we received on board the pilot who was to conduct us up the Hooghly, which we were now entering under half steam with a fair wind, and we were all on deck betimes to " sniff" the land of our exile, and exchange congratulations that we were so soon to leave our floating prison, and already, in anticipation, our men were cheerily beginning to pack and strap their knapsacks below.

On our starboard bow there loomed dimly a low flat cluster of islands, the soil of which is merely stiff black mud, amid the salt ooze of which the alligators revel, and the Java fern, the Buckra palm, and the samphire grasses grow. This is the Ganga Saugor of poor Leyden's beautiful poem, and which he anathematises as the place where human victims were exposed by the superstitious Hindoos :—

"On sea-girt Saugor's desert isle,
    Mantled with thickets dark and dun,
May never moon or starlight smile,
    Nor ever beam the summer sun."

Poets have sung fluently of the beauty of the Ganges, but this deltoid of the mighty river, in addition to being both dangerous and difficult for navigation, owing to its numerous sand-banks, which are constantly shifting their relative positions, has shores that are totally devoid of interest, most desolate and unlovely, though always hailed with delight after the long voyage from Europe; and merrily we ran along them, with sail, steam, and tide, till we came to anchor for a brief space at Kedgeree, on the western bank of the stream—a town in a swampy and unhealthy place, presenting to the eye a dismal and unbroken line of dense black wood and thicket.

To me the Hooghly looked swollen and brown; the sky was black and lowering; and the shore on either side, as the stream narrowed, seemed fitting abodes for the grim Fever King. However, as we drew nearer the city of palaces the clouds dispersed; the sun shone out hotly and fiercely, glowing on the land, which seemed to quiver and vibrate in its sheen, and on the river, which at times appeared to become a prismatic tide of flowing diamonds, rubies, and topazes; and now a stout awning was rigged on the poop of the Punniar.

Fruit-boats with black and almost naked steersmen and paddlers were now coming thick about the ship; and I could perceive that as the banks narrowed, they increased in beauty and fertility.

As we bore on, the scenery became indeed lovely; rich and deep were the hues of the Indian foliage on the banks of the stream, which in some places were too densely wooded to permit the erection of houses; but the "holy river" itself teemed with busy life.

The shipping of every nation in the world was there, and boliahs, dingies, and countless other boats shot to and fro, filled with jabbering natives, clad only with the scanty cummerbund or middle-cloth. They literally swarmed about us as the Punniar cleft on her way; and now dwelling-houses of perfectly European aspect began to appear among the native villages, as each successive reach of the river was traversed; and these increased in number, in stateliness, beauty, and design, till ere long the river narrowed to the breadth of the Thames at Tilbury, and then Fort William appeared in all its strength and majesty.

Built in the form of an octagon, with many extensive outworks, it is laid out in squares, interspersed with groves of trees, and contains bomb-proof barracks for ten thousand soldiers. It is the chief defence of Calcutta; six hundred pieces of cannon are required to arm its walls, which were meant by Lord Clive to be, in case of dire extremity, the last stronghold of Britain in Bengal.

The " City of Palaces "—with its Black Town and European Town, its extensive esplanade before the fort, its numerous *ghauts* or stately flights of broad steps leading down to the river ; its magnificent edifices and stately streets, where carriages, phaetons, buggies, and palanquins are for ever passing to and fro, the black coachmen and valets attired in muslin with white turbans ; its Parsees, Jews, Sepoys, and so forth—has been so often and so ably described, that I shall not detain the reader from my own narrative by "talking guide-book."

" That is Garden Reach," said Home of the Lancers, at a certain bend of the river ; "somehow, this place always reminds me of the Thames at Kew or Putney. The esplanade is, as you will ere long see, the great promenade of Calcutta, and there in the early morning, or in the evening, all the beauty and fashion of the place are to be seen mounted or in carriages. I was quartered here two years, and know every stone of the place. Beyond the fort, which you see is of vast extent, lies the Chowringhee Road, on which are some very handsome houses ; they have all colonnaded fronts, flat roofs, and beautiful gardens."

Eagerly did I survey the quarters he indicated from the lower rigging of the steamer, particularly the neighbourhood of the East India Company's splendid Botanical Garden, which is three hundred acres in extent ; for I knew that in one of those stately mansions, plastered with snow-white chunam, which rivals the finest marble of Carrara, *she* must be residing.

But now the steam was let off, and with a roar, as the iron cable rushed through the hawse-hole, the anchor was "let go ; for we were close in by Chandpaul Ghaut, where we were to disembark when the order to do so was issued.

The Fort-Major, attended by an officer of the medical staff, came on board to inspect the troops and hear the "report" of our commanding officer, and to make the necessary arrangements for the landing of the various drafts ; and at the same time there came on board a horde of natives, offering fruit or essences for sale, and clamouring for employment as porters, valets, grooms, grass-cutters, or water-carriers.

As we had come to anchor quite close to the ghaut, with a powerful warp sent out astern, I could perceive on the summit of it a group of young men, some in undress uniform, and others in plain clothes, watching our arrival with some interest, and scanning the deck with opera-glasses as if in search of some one.

"This interest is usually manifested on the arrival of a vessel, or used to be before the Overland Route made it so easy to come out here," said Home ; "young fellows, and old fellows too come to see the fair fresh faces from England, especially if ladies are expected ; but so far as the Punniar is concerned they will be disappointed, as Lonsdale was when he came on board at Tilbury."

With the usual amount of banter which seems inseparable from both services, many old friends and acquaintances now began to greet and welcome each other, though not a few looked vaguely about, unable to see a familiar face.

Among those on the steps of the ghaut were two smart and good-looking young fellows in the dark-green braided and frogged patrol-jackets of our corps, with handsome and expensive pith helmets, having blue veils twisted round them. Each had a cigar in his mouth—a Chinsurah cheroot, of course ; but they had cultivated so much beard and moustache of late that I did not at first recognize them till Lonsdale shouted—

"How are you, Tom ?   Jack, how goes it ?"

"Welcome to Calcutta, Lonsdale," cried the first ; "glad to see you again, Rudkin."

"By Jove—Jack Dormer and Tom Prior !" I responded, waving my forage-cap.

"Still the Damon and Pythias of the Rifle Brigade," said Lonsdale, "enjoying their post-prandial weeds—a soothing luxury which their classical prototypes never knew."

"They could have the Falernian tipple, though," said Dormer.

"Which I don't envy them—prefer iced Clicquot or sparkling Moselle."

"No girls—no ladies on board, I see, Lonsdale?"

"Not one, Jack, worse luck; not a bit of book-muslin!"

"How many of ours are with you, Rudkin?" asked Tom Prior.

"Two sergeants and 198 rank and file."

"Glad to hear it—we'll need every man of them if this row goes on."

"What row, Prior?"

"About the greased cartridges."

By this time a communication had been established between the ship and the ghaut; our two brothers of the Brigade came on board, and warmly we shook each other by the hand. Despite India, Dormer and Prior were still healthy and vigorous-looking young Englishmen, with short crisp hair, bushy moustaches, ruddy complexions, and clear penetrating eyes. The former was a fair man with a square open forehead; the latter, whose portrait I had seen in his father's house on that eventful night when the chestnut horse ran away, was very dark, with a good-natured mouth that seemed prone to laughter.

Other officers were now streaming on board, so a cross-fire of brief questions and replies rang on all sides.

"Welcome back, Jones, to the land of the pagoda-tree!" cried a tall Horse Artilleryman.

"Hope you have been shaking it successfully, Smith."

"No, but Brown of ours has to some purpose."

"What is the latest *gup* [*i.e.* gossip] about him?"

"Married a rich wife, and come in for a pot of money. She is a half caste though."

11

" Oh, the devil she is !"

" How is old Potter of ours ?" asked the line officer ; " has
he got any liver left ?"

" Poor Potter got a sunstroke on the march to Allahabad,
and has gone home invalided," replied Tom Prior.   "I say,
Home, have you heard of Ellerslie of your corps ?"

" Not since we sailed ; how could I ?"

" His story is quite romantic."

" In what way, Prior ?"

" He was engaged to a girl near Maidstone, but got his
lower jaw blown away when at musketry practice."

" Horrible !   Poor fellow !"

" He wrote to absolve his fair one from her vows of troth
and all that sort of thing, as he was now so disfigured that he
feared she could never look upon him without shuddering ;
but his darling proved a regular brick ! She wrote back, that
if an inch of him came home she would marry it ; and married
they were—an awfully jolly girl too ; and now she feeds him
with Liebig's extract, and so forth, through a silver tube."

("Just what my Blanche would do," thought I.)

" By Jove, I would rather have had my brains blown out !"
was the earnest response of Home.

" I thought Baird of ours would have been here to welcome
us," said an officer of the 72nd Highlanders.

" He is on duty," said Dormer, "and, as of old, is under the
firm belief that every woman he passes on the course, or
meets at a ball, is plotting nefariously against his single
blessedness."

" Yet he has a looking-glass in his bungalow, I suppose."

" Is Rivington of the 1st Bengal at head-quarters ?" asked
some one in the uniform of John Company's service.

" He died a month ago of jungle fever."

" Macleod ?"

" Gone on sick leave to the hills."

" How's Tompkins of the 2nd Cavalry ?"

" Oh, Tompkins is as jolly as ever ; smokes his thirty

cheroots a day, plays billiards as of old, and bets on every-thing, from the planters' plate to the longest straw out of the bungalow roof ; takes his hock, sherry, and champagne like a cherub."

And so on and on the friendly banter went, till I drew Dormer apart, to have my curiosity, now irrepressible, satisfied.

" Your cousins have reached Calcutta and are well, I hope, Jack ?" said I.

"Yes, all right."

" Both well in every way ?"

" Both quite well, thanks, and exceedingly jolly."

It was delightful to talk of *her* to one who must have seen her recently—only that morning, perhaps. I was about to ask one other question, though I scarcely knew how to form it, when Jack said,

" You must provide yourself with a kitmutgar, syces, a punkahwallah, and ever so many servants to loaf about your compound. The first will employ the rest for you—all as great rascals as himself no doubt. Have seven of them, and christen them after the days of the week. Here is one, who seems just the sort of nigger you want," he added, as a native clad in spotless white stuff, with a muslin turban of portentous dimensions twisted round his head, came forward salaaming and bowing very low.

He was a small undersized man, with a skin like mahogany, a lean, withered, and sapless-like frame, and black, piercing, and to my mind unpleasantly stealthy eyes.

" Qui hy—here, you—what is your deuced name ?" asked Dormer.

" Rao Sing, sahibs."

" A Hindoo, of course—*sing* means a lion. He doesn't look much like one, does he, Rudkin ?"

"You have certificates, of course ?" I queried.

" Yes, captain sahib," he replied, producing a packet from his breast.

"These papers," said Jack, "are seldom worth a rush. They are transferred from one fellow to another, and are often sold by those who have obtained masters to those who are in search of them; hence a description of the holder should always be appended, to prevent these Rum Johnnies from imposing upon us."

I may here mention that this is the name for those native servants out of place, who dabble in a little English, and haunt the ghauts in search of employment when strangers arrive.

As Dormer looked over the papers, he burst into a fit of laughter at one which ran thus :

"I hereby do certify that the bearer of this document served at Dumdum as kitmutgar for six months, and that there is not a greater rascal in all British India.

"PRICE JONES,
"Capt. B. H. Artillery."

"Very good certificate, captain sahib," whined the proprietor in perfect ignorance of this not uncommon practical joke.

Another ran thus :

"I hereby certify that the bearer, Rao Sing, served me as kitmutgar for a year at Agra, during which he made a small fortune out of me by peculation, and out of all my tradesmen by *dustoorie*."

"JOCELYN S. STAPLETON.
"Colonel B.N.I."

Dustoorie, a great source of expense to Europeans in the East, means the invariable custom among their domestics of getting a bonus on every article they purchase ; the merchant is thus compelled to pay it without a murmur, and add the sum he loses, in self-defence, to the proper value of the article sold, and it was to this my acquaintance the Colonel referred.

These papers were probably practical jokes, as the man had other testimonials of undoubtedly good character.

"You are a gem, Rao Sing—you'll do," said Dormer. "I think you may as well engage him, Rudkin."

On my doing so, he folded his brown paws together, bowed and salaamed again and again, in that slimy and snaky way peculiar to the Hindostanees, stealthy cunning glittering in his eyes the while.

"Kya hookm, captain sahib?" he asked, meaning "What order have you to give?"

On which I turned him over to my servant, Dan O'Regan, that together they might look after my baggage; and Dan, a genuine bog-trotter, who had never been in India before, viewed with singular distrust, comicality, and aversion "the haythen naggur" who was to be his future compatriot.

CHAPTER XXIV.

THE MARCH TO DUMDUM.

NEXT morning, ere the sun was above the somewhat level scenery, and when his light was tipping with red the church spires, the battlements of Fort William, and the roof of the Tirhetta Bazaar, the troops were all on shore in marching order, and those destined for the barracks at Dumdum—to wit, my detachment of Rifles, and some of the East India Company's European Artillery—began their way to that place.

It lies only seven miles from Calcutta, and brief though that journey, there are circumstances connected with it which I may never forget.

"Well," thought I, "my men once 'handed over' to the colonel and adjutant at head-quarters, I will get a horse from Prior or some one, and scamper back in the direction of Chowringhee, after the Binghams."

Rao Sing, my kitmutgar, had now provided me with the usual staff of dingy-looking native servants, who went with O'Regan in the baggage-waggon, and he eyed with astonishment their sole garment—the cummerbund.

"Bedad, the haythen craturs haven't rags enough on them to tie up a dacent-sized currant-bush!"

We took the route through the streets for Dumdum. Fort William towered high up on our right; we crossed the site of the old Mahratta Ditch, and where Omichunds Gardens lay in the year of Plassy; and so on through the streets of that stately city, which British enterprise has raised on the ground where once stood the petty Indian village of Govindpoor.

So full was I of anxiety to pay my projected visit, that the fun of Lonsdale intensely bored me, and little that we passed proved of interest, yet every group and object was new. Now it was the handsome English carriage of some dweller in Chowringhee—the Park Lane of Calcutta—preceded by men bearing silver maces to clear the way ; or a *carhancy*, the hackney carriage of the country, filled by half a dozen natives, whose skins were rancid with ghee ; palanquins on poles, or a smart buggy, in which some officer or civilian was driving to pay his morning calls ; *boxwallahs*, or native hawkers, clad in spotless white muslin, preceded by porters bearing the goods on their heads, and surrounded by naked little children, with only amulets tied round their brown necks.

Now it might be a fakir or religious mendicant. with no other covering than his beard and matted elf-locks, his face painted red or yellow, the eye of Siva on his brow, his beads in one lean bony hand, the other held forth to beg an anna from the passing Feringhees. Most of the people we passed were black, many half-naked, or clad in tawdry silks, tattered brocades, and white cotton, all suggestive of anything but oriental splendour.

Here and there were pretty mosques, houses of Grecian architecture, white with chunam. In time we left the great city behind us, and proceeded between orchards and gardens along the road that led to Dumdum. There Jack Dormer met us, mounted on one of those ugly horses peculiar to the Bengal breed, about fifteen hands high. He came flying along at full speed, with the blue veil of his pith helmet floating behind him.

"Good-morning," said he, reining up ; "Prior is coming with the band to play you in—he'll meet us about a mile on this side of the barracks. We must get you and Lonsdale a mount. Prior has a fine Arab horse he means to part with," added Jack, as he joined me in rear of my party, which Lonsdale, as subaltern, was leading. "How many niggers has Rao Sing engaged for you?"

"Seven, I believe."

"Ah, he believes in odd numbers, like the Rajah of Cuddelore, who had a wife for every day in the year. I'm in deuced low spirits this morning, Lance."

" How—why ?"

" I've lost a hundred and fifty gold mohurs by backing the wrong horse for the Governor-General's Plate at our last races ; so my good old governor at Thorsgill Hall must stump out again, unless my uncle Bingham will do the liberal thing ; but I have bled him pretty well of late."

" He is very wealthy ?"   I began, as a leading question.

" Wealthy !   I believe you, my boy—rich as Crœsus !   He made a pretty pot of money out of Indian bonds, the opium department, and in many other ways."

" He lives somewhere between Garden Reach and the Chowringhee Road, I believe ?"

" Exactly—in a house as big as a barrack, where every native servant has half-a-dozen more to help him to do nothing, and they seem equal in number to the slaves of the lamp in the palace of Aladdin ?"

" You'll introduce me, won't you ?"

" Of course, Rudkin : most happy indeed !"

" Does your cousin Blanche—I mean Miss Bingham—ever mention *me* ?" I asked after a pause.

" No, not that I can remember."

" How cautious the dear girl is !" thought I.

" Does Miss Guise do so ?"

" No ; I suppose her mind is too full of her engagement."

" To whom ?" I asked, with the faintest emotion of pique.

" Colonel Stapleton."

" Whew !   Stapleton of the Bengal Army ?"

" The same."

" Have the ladies never referred to the pleasant time we all spent together at Thorsgill Hall ?" I asked anxiously.

" Never, to me at least."

" When did you see them last ?"

" I had a glorious canter with Henriette on the course yesterday morning, just before I rode down to Chandpaul Ghaut. Blanche, of course, I have not seen since—since—"

"When ?"

"Since her marriage."

Her marriage!

The men were marching "at ease," singing, talking, and laughing, and at that moment, as Jack was intent on lighting a refractory cigar, he could not see the expression which I felt come over my face. No voice was left me to ask more questions ; so after a few whiffs, Jack Dormer, all unconscious of the stab he had given me, began speaking again.

"Did you not hear that she was married ?"

"You forget that we came round the Cape, and were detained by disasters in Table Bay," said I, huskily.

"She hooked a baronet who came out with her and the Appletons overland. I must introduce you there too—nice girls—give good balls, and all that sort of thing."

"And this baronet, Jack ?"

"Sir Harry Calvert : he was in the Guards as Captain—he got into a line regiment as lieutenant-colonel, and he is now up-country on the staff. He was an old admirer—met her at Brighton—her first love, she assured me, just as I was beginning to get spoony on her myself. Not that I believed her, for women never do marry their first loves, except in novels. Perhaps his little bit of title attracted her ; she is as mad as a hatter about him, though why a hatter should be particularly so, I can't tell. Before they left Calcutta, you should have seen her placing her little kid-gloved hand and slender wrist so confidingly on 'dearest Harry's' arm, airing all her happiness with that bearing so peculiar to brides, you know."

"How the deuce should I know? never was hooked in my life?" said I, in a voice that sounded strange to myself.

"And hanging on every word he says : only, I fear this cooing and billing won't last long up-country."

"A deuced lucky hit for our staff-baronet," said Lonsdale,

who had now fallen to the rear and joined us ; " I know he lost a pot of money on that girl and her theatre in the Strand. He's just the man to make old Bingham's sacks or lacs of rupees fly, when the worthy owner thereof is in a warmer place than Kamptee, between which and the other hot place —you know the Indian saw—there seems only a sheet of paper."

" You forget, Master Joe Lonsdale, that you are speaking of my uncle," said Dormer, half angrily. " Can I give you any more news of these fair daughters of Britannia ?"

" I don't think so," said I, faintly.

In the lives of all of us there are some days so full of pain, of mortification, and sadness, that it would seem as if no joy in the time to come can efface them from the recollection ; and such a day was this to me while marching along that Indian highway. I listened to Jack Dormer's barrack-room and Chowringhee gossip with that vague and sickly smile we all put on when we seek to conceal our emotions from others.

" Is not this story of—of Miss Bingham's marriage one of your usual jokes, Jack ?" I asked after a long pause.

" Joke !" said he, with real astonishment ; " not at all ; they had not been here a month when it took place. Uncle Bingham played the heavy father to perfection, and Blanche did indeed look lovely. It was quite a swell affair—I will show you the notice of it in the *Bengal Hurkaru.*"

Blanche married, and Henriette engaged—and to Stapleton ! It was some time before I could at all realize these two facts. Had pique with me caused the latter state of affairs ? I had not vanity enough left in me now to flatter myself that it was ; yet I had been given fully to understand that her first and general impressions of him had been most unfavourable. As if he half divined my thoughts, Jack Dormer said,

" Local *gup* avers that my cousin Henriette refused three excellent offers before she accepted Stapleton ; and even now

I don't think somehow she is very fond of him, while he is the most cool lover I ever saw."

" I never knew an engaged man who, just about a week before he was to be turned off, didn't wish himself out of the scrape," said Lonsdale; " and from all I know of Calvert in London, he never seemed much of a marrying man. Perhaps he has sown all his wild oats, has reaped a crop of repent-ance, and his melancholy remains have made a resolution to be virtuous."

" Sir Harry *is* getting rather grizzled now ; so be assured that he will keep all moustached popinjays at a respectful distance from la belle Blanche," added Dormer, laughing.

" There comes a time of life when every man should settle and marry," said Lonsdale, with an air of reflection that scemed comical in him; " and I agree with the late William Cobbett, M.P., and ex-sergeant-major, that one's wife should have good teeth, chew her food well, and plant her feet firmly on the ground when she walks ; and then she'll do."

" How silent you have become, Rudkin!" said Dormer, pre-senting his case to me ; " have a cigar?"

" Thanks."

I took it, for this was one of those occasions when the habit of smoking becomes a consolatory process, yet it failed me then. I was filled with rage, disappointment, and all the bitterness of wounded love and shattered self-esteem. Love at times took the form of contempt and loathing ; then anon I prayed in my heart that whatever became of me, she at least might be happy ; and then would come dull dogged in-difference with but one desire—to avoid her in this world.

Yet that most natural desire now was not fated to be gratified.

While I was in a state of irritation, the brass band of the regiment, with Tom Prior and the adjutant, who was anxious to see what my new recruits were like, came suddenly in sight at a turn of the road.

" Eyes front—keep to your fours ; silence, men !" cried I, in a voice so firm and stern that Dormer said,

" Hallo, Rudkin, what the devil's up ?   Has a Brahminee cobra stung you ?"

My reply, whatever it was, the crash of the bugles, trombones, and cornets thoroughly succeeded in drowning, and amid the ringing music I was not ill pleased to be left for a time to my own conflicting thoughts.   Thirst oppressed me, and at a wayside hotel I imbibed a stiff glass of brandy-pawnee, at an hour so unusual that on any other occasion it might at least have made me giddy ; but it strung my nerves, and through the medium thereof I began to *face* the calamity that had befallen me ; for such it seemed to me *then*.

Was the old axiom of "a fair face and a false heart" true? And was my ideal woman but a very common piece of human clay after all?   Prior to our embarkation at Tilbury, I had suffered all the grinding torture and suspense her silence induced, an agony which to one who loves truly and keenly is intolerable ; I dared not admit even to myself, as day by day the weeks and months rolled on, that cherished hopes began to fade.   As we steamed up the Hooghly, I had been in a state of almost delirious happiness at the certain prospect of meeting Blanche within an hour or two after our long separation ; and *this* was the news I heard !

I looked back with anger now to those dreamy hours of affection and anxiety, when I had welcomed every sunset with the knowledge that one day more of our time of probation was past ! how every time the log line was thrown I welcomed the distance that was shortening between Blanche and myself, hailing the waves that ran past me and were left astern in the sunshine.

I resolved, if possible, to forget her, and hoped that change of scene would enable me to do so : and certainly change and total separation seldom fail to achieve that end ; but as yet it was bitter to feel the conviction that I had gone from out her life as completely as if I had never existed.

Nothing remained of her now to me but a lock of that wonderful golden hair, a relic I resolved to destroy.

"Well, well ; it is all over now, and we are parted for ever, in this world at least !" thought I.

But it was not to be so. People may lose sight of each other for a time, but they don't part " for ever " in this age of steam by land and sea so readily and hopelessly as they did in the days of our forefathers.

CHAPTER XXV.

WHAT I LIT MY PIPE WITH.

"THIS is my bunk," said Dormer, with whom I had promised to breakfast, as he ushered me into his quarters, after I had —early though the hour—duly " reported" myself to the commandant at Dumdum, to the lieutenant-colonel of my battalion, and seen my detachment " told off " to their various companies by the adjutant and sergeant-major.

Like others in that famous barracks, Jack's abode was not very luxurious. In one corner of the room was a charpoy, or bed ; in another were any number of bottles, some full, others empty ; elsewhere were hog-spears, guns, a regulation rifle, some Indian arms, among them a handsome tulwar taken in a skirmish from the chief of a hill-tribe. A hookah an overland and a buffalo trunk, a bamboo chair covered by a tiger-skin, in the head of which was the orifice made by a ball from Jack's breech-loader ; a couple of Landseer's dogs framed in light-coloured wood, a cane-bottomed chair or two, and a plain toon wooden table, made up the appurtenances and ornaments of the " den," as he not inaptly termed it ; but to these I must add a somewhat tattered punkah over- head, a bare floor, very much discoloured by stains of ink, and a board or two on which some orders or regulations were pasted.

Outside, the shadows were deep and dark under the bright fierce light of the uprisen and unclouded sun. The barracks of Dumdum are situated in a very swampy district, for where they are not environed by jungles and paddy-fields, they are so by a salt-water lake; and as an officer has written, the place "has been especially selected as the head-quarters, of the artillery, because it is the dampest place in India, and therefore considered eminently adapted to the purpose of carrying on experiments in gunpowder; and moreover, on account of its morning fogs, a very fitting place for practising at a long range against invisible targets."

To these disadvantages may be added, that it is, or was, a "half batta station," as officers quartered so near the Presidency are allowed less pay than those living at a distance; so young subalterns were compelled to add economy to their other military studies.

"Khoda Bux!" shouted Dormer, making a lash on the toonwood table with his riding switch; "kitmutgar, qui hy, is the punkahwallah asleep?"

"Sahib, yes," said his native servant with a low salaam.

"Then rouse him with that bamboo stick; the lazy devil is always chewing opium, or smoking bang from his cocoa-nut hubble-bubble."

The order was promptly obeyed, and after hearing sundry whacks bestowed upon a pair of bare brown shoulders, thereby eliciting shrill outcries, the cord outside the room was pulled and the frayed and shabby punkah overhead began to sway slowly to and fro.

"Breakfast now, Khoda—and look sharp about it; set covers for five," said Dormer, as we were joined by Lonsdale, Prior, Jones of the Horse Artillery, and a staff-surgeon, Doctor Gargill, who was a Scotchman of course.

Notwithstanding the morning march of seven miles from Calcutta, I had no great appetite for breakfast, especially the thoroughly Indian one laid before us by Khoda Bux: rice, with green chillies, cayenne, butter and fish, fried cockup, *à la mode des Indes*, all mashed up together, with cold beef and red tamarind chutney from Madras ; so while my companions all hearty and jolly young fellows, did ample justice to those things, I contented myself with a great cup of cold tea well dashed with brandy.

"Rudkin," said Jack, "if you begin Indian life this way you'll kill yourself. Do get up an appetite ; but if you won't eat look at that old copy of the *Hurkaru,* you'll find all about my cousin's marriage there."

This was ill-calculated to achieve what Jack recommended ; but I turned over the paper and found the paragraph referred to ; it ran thus :—

" The festivities of the last few days in Mr. Bingham's princely mansion have terminated in the solemnisation of the nuptials between Lieutenant-Colonel Sir Harry Calvert, Bart., with Miss Blanche Bingham at the cathedral, which was filled on the occasion by a brilliant company. The gallant bride-goom, attended by Colonel J. S. Stapleton, B.N.I., entered the sacred edifice shortly after eleven o'clock, accompanied by the bride, who looked very lovely in her crêpe du Chine dress, trimmed with deep Brussels lace, and her veil, which was of the same, relieved with orange flowers, pearls, and diamonds. The bridesmaids—six belles of Chowringhee—wore white silk dresses trimmed with pink rosebuds ; but none looked more beautiful than the bride's own cousin, Miss Guise. The ceremony was performed by the Lord Bishop," &c.

" Where is Stapleton just now ?" I asked, as I tore up the paper and proceeded to light my pipe with it.

" The Colonel is at Agra, giving evidence before a general court-martial," said Doctor Gargill ; " discontents are increasing fast among the Company's troops ; and if much more of this thing goes on we'll have something else to do than studying the *Army List* or the thermometer, or making up a betting book over a bottle of bitter, next to iced champagne, the greatest luxury in an Indian cantonment."

What those discontents were to which the doctor referred I cared not then to inquire ; though I was to hear enough of them in the coming time.

" Anything in the shape of fluid is better than your Scotch whisky, doctor," said Lonsdale, " for that I consider slow poison."

" Slow, indeed," retorted Gargill ; " I have drunk it every day for twenty years, and am not dead yet ; and what does Captain Osburne tell us ? That of all the wines that were sent to Runjeet Sing by the Governor-General, consisting of port, claret, hock, champagne, &c., the Scotch *whisky* was the wine he liked best."

" You'll be recommending boiled bagpipes next," said Dormer ; and as Gargill began to look irritated, to change the subject he turned to Prior : " Is it true, Tom, what Jones has been saying, that you have become so frightfully spoony on one of the Appleton girls."

" Well, I must confess to a weakness for Jacky," replied Prior, laughing ; " but I have not yet made up my mind to propose."

" Why, she is both handsome and lively."

" Would she accept me ?"

" Would she !" exclaimed Jack, as he lay back in a bamboo chair, and puffed at a long cheroot ; " don't you know that girls in their teens—like older girls past their thirties—will accept anybody?"

" This is complimentary to the ladies in general, and to me in particular, Jack."

The lightness of heart displayed by those around me made my own feel heavier by very contrast ; but I had to rouse myself, for now as a captain I had various duties to perform that had not fallen to my share before. I had to receive over my company from the officer who had been in charge of it, and I had the arms, accoutrements, books, and pay-accounts of the men to examine with care and attention ; and yet amid these duties there was the ever-recurring question in my mind, Was this world the same that it was before I knew Blanche? It scarcely seemed so ; yet I resolved—hard though the task—to do as I had done before I saw her fair and faithless face—to throw myself with ardour into my profession. There was plenty to do, and there was much to learn ; and I could but hope that, as my sword-belt wore my coat, so would the memory of this sting wear away.

Therefore to my duty—to the task of looking after my soldiers in the new land to which we had come—I turned mechanically, but with a sick heart, from which ambition and enthusiasm had for the time alike died out. I had my place in life to fulfil, like those who return from the grave when they have buried their dead ; but the duties I once loved so well seemed dull drudgery now ; nevertheless, they helped me to get through the day.

In my fantastic reveries I was more than once "rowed" by the colonel for sundry petty mistakes, and should certainly have been so by the adjutant ; but I was his senior officer now, and only underwent a serious expostulation for losing my distance at open column, for missing my covering and marching on the camp colour in such a fashion that it passed through the centre of a subdivision when we were "right in front," and other enormities.

But often the memory of the past haunted me in the lone hours of the hot Indian night, when all was still but the howling jackals in the adjacent swamp, and nothing stirred save these, the mosquitoes, and the sentries, who hourly clanged the metal ghurrie to indicate the time.

"What the deuce is the matter with you, Lance?" Lonsdale would sometimes say. "In all my life I never saw a man so altered as you."

One night, feeling dull and low-spirited, I went over to Dormer's quarters after mess.

12

"Enter, master," said Khoda Bux, bowing and salaaming; "Dormer Sahib at home."

I found Jack jolly and lively as usual, and after imbibing sundry glasses of brandy-pawnee, and smoking more cheroots than were good for me, I was seized by one of those absurd fits of confidence that men often have at such times, and had a desire to speak of Blanche. I had never even inquired where she and her husband were, but I asked him now.

"They are up-country at Allahabad, where Calvert is on the staff," replied Dormer.

Then, after a little circumlocution, I told him all the story of our engagement, and of her deliberate perfidy, to which honest Jack listened with genuine indignation.

"Don't bother about it, old fellow," said he, after a pause; "you'll forget it in time. I was thrown over myself once for a cursed fellow in the Civil Service—thought of shooting myself or some one else, or of volunteering against the hill-tribes; but now I am as jolly as a sand-boy; and when I see how matrimony has spoiled my once ideal, I look back with wonder to the

"Hubble, bubble,
Toil and trouble"

the whole affair gave me. Love at Blanche's age is simply a farce. Be assured, Rudkin, that the real love, which is calculated to rouse romance or despair, which is deep, strong, and lasting, is not the love for a school-girl, but for a ripe woman between her twenties and thirties."

And Jack perhaps was right.

"This," said he, "accounts for what was a puzzle to me—your ill-concealed repugnance to visit the Binghams after asking for an introduction, or even for going near Chowringhee at all."

"Believe me, Dormer, I would rather have been dead in

my coffin, with that girl's tears falling on my face—a widow
—than alive with the fierce and wild emotions I feel at
times."

"Events have proved that her tears would soon have been
dried," said he, with a sly smile.

"You don't know, Jack, how I doted on the girl."

"Very likely ; but a baronet in hand is worth two captains
in the bush."

"But hang it, Jack," said I, annoyed by his banter, "I was
solemnly engaged to her."

"Blanche could never be very solemn at any time ; and
even if one is so, I don't think it makes much difference on
the Overland Route sometimes, and it was often worse when
girls had to come round the Cape. You may consider
yourself deuced lucky. She might have changed her mind
when it was too late. It will be all the same a hundred years hence ; and what's the odds so long as you are
happy ?"

Thinking he would console me with such sage reflections
as these, Jack reclined back in his bamboo easy chair, one
leg over an arm thereof, the other placed on the toonwood
table, with his glass of brandy-and-water on one side of him,
a pile of cigar ashes on the other, and looking the very picture of a handsome, saucy, and perfectly contented young
Englishman.

"You'll come with me and see my cousin Henriette?"
said he.

"Excuse me, Jack—I am rather sore about the sex just
now," I replied, feeling after *all* that had passed, it would be
impossible for me to meet Miss Guise with pleasure again.
Dormer eyed me with a curious smile, and said :

"This is an age of progression, old fellow—steam, tele-
graphy, science, and all that sort of thing, including table-
turning and paper collars ; so hearts are won and lost, broken
and mended again, with a celerity that would have appalled
our powdered grandparents. So a day will come when you

may sing with Tommy Moore, and laugh at the time referred to :

> 'My only books
> Were woman's looks,
> And folly all they taught me.'"

"Two in the morning," said I, looking at my watch, as the metal ghurrie was clanged at the main guard ; "time to turn in."

"Egad ! yes. Don't think me inhospitable ; but we have to be up betimes for an hour's recreation, named light-infantry exercise, among the fog and wet grass of this most dismal hole Dumdum, where in summer the vapour is exactly like that which comes from a wet blanket before a blazing fire. Qui hy ! Khoda Bux, have coffee ready for us at gun-fire, and woe to you if you fail, unhappy pagan !"

After sharing my secret with Jack Dormer—though his consolations were somewhat offhand and extremely common-place— I began to feel lighter in heart, and daily less " sore " on the subject of Blanche Bingham.

CHAPTER XXVI.

ON THE COURSE AT CALCUTTA.

ON an evening soon after this confidence had been reposed
in Dormer, he, Lonsdale, and I ordered our horses for the
purpose of having a turn on the course at Calcutta, where
the fashionables and idlers ride or drive from six o'clock till
darkness sets in—seeing and being seen.

At a little distance from the barracks we crossed a stream,
near which there is—or was—a Hindoo temple, consisting of
four horse-shoe arches, to which flights of steps ascended.
The roof was shaped like an inverted pear, of pure white
marble, and under it was a bronzed four-armed idol on a
pedestal of red stone.

On the steps nearest the stream, a tiny tributary of the
great river, was a charming-looking little Hindoo maiden, clad
in one of those indescribable, and to all appearance shapeless,
garments generally worn by the native women, and which
appear to be always of one piece. To me it seemed brilliant
scarlet cotton. Her long black hair was all unbound, and
she was chanting some monotonous evening prayer, while
from one of those plaited baskets that are made at Pullicat
she was casting, with an action full of inimitable grace,
flowers of various colours into the stream—votive offerings
doubtless to be borne into the "Nile of Hindostan"—the
holy Ganga or river, which the Hindoos are taught to believe
is the eldest daughter of the great mountain Himavata, and
as it issues from the root of the Bujputra tree, flows directly
from heaven. For in costume or customs, in manners and
superstition, the natives of Hindostan are unchanged since
the days of Alexander of Macedon.

"Is she about to bathe?" asked Lonsdale, checking his

horse for a moment and adjusting his eye-glass, doubtless to aid his powers of vision.

"Not at all," replied Dormer; "you are still in a state of griffinage. She is simply saying the last of the three prayers which the Hindoos must say daily—in the morning, at noon, and in the evening—always with their faces turned to the east. Their votive offerings generally consist of fruits, flowers, rice, and incense or spices made at the temples."

"Such a charming picture the whole thing makes—the temple, the stream, and the girl," said I, "together with that little grove of baubool-trees behind the edifice."

These trees—the *acacia Arabica*—are singularly graceful, and bear a yellow flower, shedding a delightful perfume which scents the air for a great distance; and I turned away and rode on with my companions, all unconscious of the part this little Hindoo maiden was yet to play in my narrative.

In due time we reached the spacious course or esplanade which lies between the Chowringhee Road and the great citadel of Fort William, and at the extreme end of which stands the Government House, erected by the Marquis of Wellesley, a structure every way worthy of the ruler of an empire so vast as that of India. It consists of a centre with four wings, and over the colossal arches or gates that lead to it are placed sphinxes, and on two are the royal arms and those of the East India Company.

On the level plain before it were crowds of Europeans and natives, enjoying the cool air of the evening, and there were every variety and shade of beauty and every description of vehicle, from the stately coach-and-four to the palanquins and hackeries of Hindostan. Equestrians were very numerous. Many of these were ladies; but many more were officers of Horse Artillery, the Bengal Light Cavalry, in silver-grey uniforms, faced with orange and laced with silver, or in the blue undress surtout of the Line, with gilt shoulder-scales and scarlet sash.

Of course we proceeded to inspect and criticise the ladies.

"I say, Joe, do you see that fair one in the brown-holland riding-habit trimmed with red braid?" asked Dormer.

"On the piebald—the horse for luck?"

"Yes—so now is your time to wish."

"Well, what about her? She isn't young—nor pretty either."

"She has four lacs of rupees in Bank of Bengal shares, and other interests; think of that; four lacs, Joe!"

"Sacks I could understand, but lacs are beyond me. 'What's the demmed total?' as Mantalini says."

"A lac is ten thousand pounds sterling."

"Forty thousand pounds—by Jove! I'll have her—that is, if you can get me introduced."

"Of course I can; she is always tiffing or dining and so forth at the Binghams', or Mrs. Appleton's, in Chowringhee. I suppose *you* don't care about trying your hand, Lance?"

"No—thanks, Dormer."

"Rudkin is evidently above all mercenary considerations," said Lonsdale, who was no doubt sure of success, for it was extraordinary the progress he could make with women when he chose to be insinuating, exactly because he did not care a doit about any one in particular. His practised manner was reduced to a method; risks he often ran, but no repulse ever broke Joe's heart, or affected his uncommon flow of spirits.

Unluckily for this matrimonial scheme between him and Dormer, before it could be put in operation the order came for our battalion to change its quarters.

"Ah, there is a lovely girl!" exclaimed Joe with admiration; "if *she* had only a lac or so of rupees!"

"And so she has—she's my cousin Henriette, by Jove!" said Dormer; "and attended only by a European groom

Here she usually has a staff of fellows—a regular *suwarri*—about her."

Lonsdale was introduced in form ; me she instantly recognised, and gave me a brilliant smile.

"Very warm this evening," I ventured to say.

To this original remark she assented cordially, adding :

"What do you think of India ?"

"I have been in India before for a year with the Light Cavalry," said I.

"Calcutta, then ?"

"Really, I can scarcely judge as yet," said I, feeling somewhat confused in my manner.

"Have you left cards on any one yet ?"

"On none."

"Why? How odd !"

"Hard duty at Dumdum——," I was beginning.

"Smoking cheroots, drinking brandy-pawnee in his shirt-sleeves, lolling in the verandah, studying the *Army List* or thermometer, and trying to get through the day somehow—these are the hard duties he has to undergo at Dumdum," said Dormer ; "will you believe it, cousin Henriette, he has become a veritable hermit—a misanthrope ?"

"No, I will not believe it," said she smiling, yet scanning my face closely the while.

"Have you heard from the dear old people at Thorsgill Hall lately ?" asked Dormer.

"Yes—by the last mail."

"They are well, I hope ?" said I.

"Yes—and aunt Dormer says the burned wing is quite repaired now, and the ghosts are scared for ever," she replied, with a quick blushing glance at me. "I read the announcement of your arrival with troops on board the Punniar in the papers. Why have you never called with cousin Jack to see me ?"

"Pardon me, but I shall hasten to do myself this pleasure to-morrow."

" Too late."

" How so ? I have offended you ?"

" Oh no, indeed no ; but I take the river steamer to-morrow for up-country with Jacky Appleton. I go to Allahabad —to—to—visit friends there."

As I looked into the soft sweet face—yet it was a marked one and full of character too—memory went back to the time of our peculiar parting at Thorsgill Hall. She was quite collected now, and another bright smile spread over her features as she said :

" We have met once more after all, Captain Rudkin."

" Yes ; you bade me farewell, adding, I remember, 'for ever, too probably ;' but I told you that we should meet again."

(I certainly did ; but thought it would be under different circumstances.)

" The moment I learn that you are back from Allahabad, I shall do myself the honour of visiting you with your cousin," said I ; and after a little conversation on general subjects, in which Lonsdale, who was enchanted by her beauty, bore a part, we separated.

She was going, I knew, to visit her cousin Blanche, to whose marriage, or even her existence, she had never made the slightest reference ; neither did I, for somehow we both felt it to be an awkward subject.

" How flushed you look, Rudkin !" observed Lonsdale, as we rode homeward after evening gunfire.

" It is not quite the season for the prickly heat in Calcutta," said I evasively.

" But it is always the season here for plenty of *gup* among the *Ditchers*, as the residents of Calcutta are called," Jack remarked. " Will you believe it, Rudkin, that if you dance twice consecutively with the same girl, it is considered equal to an engagement ?"

"But the Overland Route will alter all that."

I wondered when the cousins met what Henriette Guise would say of me to Blanche, and whether the mention of my name would yet stir a chord of secret tenderness in her heart. Whether it did so or not mattered little or nothing now. The face and voice of Henriette brought all the vanished past more vividly before me, and reflection banished sleep long after I had cast myself upon my charpoy, or native bed of wattled tape, after Rao Sing had whisked the chowry, an implement like an horse's tail tied to a red drumstick, and drawn the muslin curtains close for the same purpose, to exclude those worse than all the plagues of Egypt — the mosquitoes.

On comparing notes next day on parade, I found that Joe Lonsdale had been thinking all night long of Henriette, whom he declared to be "the sweetest girl he had ever met in his life," and that he was quite prepared to "enter stakes" against Stapleton.

CHAPTER XXVII.

THE BEWITCHED SEPOY.

ONE afternoon, a little subsequent to my chance meeting with Henriette Guise, I was strolling along the road that lies between the rice and paddy fields, and when passing near the little temple in the baubool grove, saw there the same young girl whom I had seen before. With many genuflections that were full of wonderful grace, she was now fanning the bronze idol; while a Hindoo fakir—a hideous old man, with his lean and shrunken body smeared with grease and ashes, his elf-locks matted with the same unpleasant condiments, the eye of Siva painted on his brow, a brass lotah hanging at his girdle, and his sole attire a cummerbund—was solemnly anointing the god with ghee; and on his knees before it, offering rice, fruit, and flowers, in obedience to those laws compiled by Menou 1280 years before the Christian era, was a tall and powerfully-built grenadier of the 2nd Bengal Native Infantry, praying very devoutedly.

I drew a little nearer, but not so close as to intrude upon these strange devotions, as some of the ceremonies of the *pooja* were about to be performed. A mat was spread before the shrine, on which were placed a bell of metal to be rung, a conch shell on which to blow; and a censer filled with benzoin, sugar, and other articles, was lighted, wherewith to offer incense to the god. While the fakir, after using both the bell and the conch, gave the *tiluk*, or mark on the forehead of the idol, then dipping his right thumb in sandal-wood ashes, he continued to mutter his prayers and ashlocks, or verses, in honour of his imaginary deity, and to throw more benzoin and ral into the burning censer, the girl began to dance before the shrine; but the grenadier remained rapt in his devotion.

The girl had no music but the sound of her own soft voice,

as she sang in a low and monotonous cadence.   Then, as her
light and certainly scanty dress became inflated by the wind
and by her whirling movements, though there was nothing
of the Nautch dancing in her measures, never did a lovely
little female form seem more completely or lusciously
to swim, as it were, in the air, which her bare and outstretched taper arms and tiny hands seemed as if seeking
to embrace.

Her long unbound tresses floated wildly around her, at
times almost hiding her small face, and so absorbed was she
and her companions also that they did not perceive that I was
looking on ; and that now another Sepoy—a subadar, in his
raggie, or undress jacket—a native captain of the same regiment as the devotee, had drawn near the shrine, but made
no genuflection, or shewed any intention of joining in what
was going forward.

His keen black glittering orbs were fixed solely on the girl,
whose extreme beauty attracted his attention acutely ; but
suddenly his figure caught her eye.

Then her features seemed to become convulsed with terror
and horror ; her eyes glared wildly as she parted and threw
back her hair with her hands ; and shrinking, crouching down
beside the pedestal of the idol, she pointed silently to the
subadar.   The fakir set down his censer, and uttered a
shrill cry of dismay, on hearing which the grenadier sprang
to his feet.

His dark face seemed to grow darker with sudden rage and
hatred, while the veins in his forehead swelled and his eyes
sparkled with fire ; and shouting something—I know not what
—in which the word *jadoo* (magic) occurred more than once,
he drew his bayonet and rushed on the subadar, who drew
his sword and stood on his defence, like a man who quite
expected the attack.

Here was a serious case of insubordination, and of drawing
a weapon upon a superior officer.   I also drew, and hastened
forward to interfere ; but I was too late.   The grenadier had

eluded the point of his adversary's sword, and plunged the
bayonet into his side. In doing so, however, a stone caught
his foot; he fell heavily forward, and ere he could rise the
foot of the bleeding subadar was planted on his breast, and
he was on the point of being run through the heart, as the
wounded officer raised the hilt upward at arm's length, pointing the blade downward for that purpose.

With a wild cry the dancing girl sprang forward and threw
herself upon the body of the grenadier, and sought with her
own slender and sylph-like form to shield him from the death
that was impending. One arm was around him, and one,
like her eyes, uplifted imploringly to the face of the dark and
now certainly ferocious-looking subadar.

"Spare him—spare him!" she said in Hindostanee, and
then her voice died away; but though her lips were silent,
her beautiful eyes were full of eloquence, and the soul of a
woman beamed in her expression, though her face was almost
childish. She was by far the fairest of her race I had ever
seen, and in her complexion she had an olive lustre that was
almost Spanish. Her forehead was broad and low; her mouth
was, though full and pouting, small and beautiful, and the
little upper lip that quivered now with terror revealed the
whiteness of her teeth. Her hair, black of course, but glossy,
voluminous, and silky, covered all her shoulders and the face
and breast of her father, for which I afterwards learned the
prostrate grenadier to be.

The infuriated subadar was merciless, and swearing by
Siva, the god of terror, who dwells amid the eternal snow of
the Himalayas, that he would have vengeance, was about to
pin the grenadier to the earth with his sword, when I parried
the downward thrust by mine and grasped his hand. On perceiving that I was a European officer he instantly saluted me,
and placing his left hand on his wound showed it to me
covered with blood, as if mutely asserting that he was right
in what he was about to do.

The girl now clung to me, embracing my knees, kissing my

hand, and entreating me to protect her father, who looked sullenly on, but keeping the drawn bayonet still in his hand, as if for his own defence.

"This is rank mutiny," said I in Hindostanee ; "how dared you, grenadier, to draw upon the subadar ?"

"Because he has wronged me, captain sahib," replied the Sepoy ; "and but for the devilish spells he has cast upon me I should not have been under his foot."

"Would you have killed him ?" I asked.

"Yes, sahib !" hissed the Sepoy through his set teeth, which glistened white under his black moustache.

"And wherefore ?"

"To break the charm."

I did not understand what all this meant ; but turning to the native captain, I said :

"Subadar, do you know this man ?"

"Yes, sahib, his name is Gunga Ram," replied the subadar, who was now getting faint, and whose wound I stanched by placing my handkerchief folded as a pad upon it, and binding it there with his own sash.

"Surrender your bayonet," said I sternly to the Sepoy, who immediately gave me the weapon. I then pointed with my sword to the barracks, saying, "You must march there before us as a prisoner—proceed instantly."

The man salaamed, and obeying without a murmur, went straight to the main guard house.

In due time he was arraigned before a general court-martial in full dress uniform, minus his belt, shako, and shoes, for drawing upon his superior officer and attempting to murder Kureem Sing, subadar of the 2nd Bengal Native Infantry. I was the principal witness in this trial, at which the following strange revelations were made :

The subadar and Gunga Ram had long been at feud, and the former, as superior, had of course many opportunities of galling and tormenting the latter, who had crowned their enmity by refusing to give him his daughter Azuma, the girl whom I had seen at the wayside temple, and whose uncle, Kalidasa Ram, was the fakir, a religious mendicant and priest. There are regular sets of dancing girls attached to all the great Hindoo temples, dedicated to that purpose by their parents; but the scene of this outrage was simply a wayside shrine.

From the moment of Gunga's refusal a change came over his whole constitution. From being a tall, hardy, and gallant soldier, he became weak, timid, and quite irresolute. He lost flesh daily; even his stature he asserted was diminishing while hourly he felt the process of decay was becoming worse and worse. In vain did the medical officers assure him that all this was pure fancy. The conviction preyed upon his mind, inducing the most morbid melancholy, and life—with certain death drawing nearer and nearer—became intolerable.

He had but one enemy in the world, the sudadar, who was his evil genius, and of whose magic spells he believed himself to be the victim. He was assured that Kureem Sing had been frequently seen near the stream in which the girl cast the votive flowers. It is a common belief with the Hindoos, that if you wish to get rid of an enemy, you have only to fashion a waxen or clay figure as much like him or her as possible, subject it to certain magical incantations, and melt it, if wax, before the fire; if of clay, place it in a running stream, and as the model melts or wastes, so surely will your enemy pine and die of some mysterious and indescribable disease; hence Gunga Ram was certain that he was the helpless victim of *jadoo*, or magic, and that nothing but the death of the subadar would break the spell.

In vain had his brother the fakir given him a certain charm, or *mantra*, which he showed the court. It was bound about his right arm, and consisted of a dingy scrap of paper, on which some words in Arabic were written.

He reverently replaced it, exclaiming:

"O Om, thou divine spirit, remember me;

This strange superstition is mentioned in the history of Scotland so far back as the tenth century, when the illness of King Duff, as Buchanan records, was found to proceed from a wax model which a woman was melting before a fire at Forres ; and the same superstition, known as the *corp-cree*, still exists in the Highlands. A marked instance of it occurred among the Sepoys in the case of Bucktawur Sing, of the 15th or 30th (I forget which) Regiment of the Bengal Army, just before the desperate mutiny at Nuseerabad in Rajpootana.

It proved a difficult matter to deal with mentally ; but one fact was plain before the court—that insubordination and attempted murder must be summarily punished ; so Gunga Ram was sentenced to be confined for life in the common prison at Calcutta.

Three days before his removal, when visiting the barrack cells in my capacity as captain of the day, I saw the unfortunate Gunga Ram lying on his charpoy, greatly depressed in spirit. He knew me, and thanked me for preserving a life which he assured me could not last long now, adding that as he was degraded and had lost his position as a high-caste Brahmin by what he had undergone, he did not regret to die but for the sake of his daughter Azuma, who would be left helpless in the world, and at the mercy of the subadar perhaps.

I bade him cheer up and be of good heart ; that his sentence might be commuted after a time, and that I would endeavour to get some kind *mehm sahib*, or European lady, to take charge of Azuma.

In English so broken and absurd, that to repeat it verbatim would be useless, the poor fellow said :

" Captain sahib, you pledge me your word that you will be kind to my girl ?"

" I do."

" I served at Maharajahpore, Moodkee, and Ferozeshuhur where I was thrice wounded," said he, pointing to his medals.

" I thank you, captain sahib, and shall go to prison—or to the holy Ganges—death—with peace and comfort now."

He placed my hand upon his head in token of gratitude, and then I left him.

He was taken from the barracks to prison under an escort, consisting of a *naick*, or corporal, and six, commanded by his enemy the subadar, and from this time Gunga passes out of my story, though, Azuma has to play a rather prominent part in it.

On that same evening " letters of readiness " came for the battalion from head-quarters ; hence we knew that we must soon be on the move, though we knew not exactly for where. All was surmise in the mess-room.

CHAPTER XXVIII.

AZUMA.

WEARY, after a hard morning drill amid the mists that so often pervade the marshy locality of Dumdum, I had discussed a pretty solid tiffin, and was roused from what is commonly called "a lie down," or siesta, by Dan O'Regan announcing that a person wished to see me.

" Who or what is he ?"

" Sure it's one of them haythen naygurs, sir," replied Dan ; "he calls himself a praste—but, oh, to the Lord, that I may never see such another !"

Dan had been in such a perpetual state of perplexity and wonder at all the sights and scenes around us since we left the Punniar, that his surprise now was nothing new ; so I said briefly :

" Show him up."

Considering the object of my visitor, I thought it a fortunate circumstance that I was quite alone. Dormer had ridden into Calcutta, to attend one of those auction-marts which then used to be a sort of lounge for the idle ; Prior, having sat too long at mess the night before, had inadvertently lit his pipe with a letter of credit, and hiring one of those hack-carriages known as "Dum-dumers," had also driven to the city about it in some perplexity ; while Lonsdale had gone by river to Barrackpore, a large cantonment or military village on the east side of the Hooghly.

Somewhat to my surprise, O'Regan ushered in the Hindoo fakir, Kalidasa Ram, whom I had last seen at the court-martial, as naked, as greasy, and as filthy as ever. He approached me bowing and salaaming, and coming so close that I was glad to place my table between him and myself ; for the whole room was now pervaded by the odour of the rancid ghee with which his limbs were smeared, while some strange devices, half hidden by his long beard, were done on his bare breast in yellow chalk.

I thought of desiring Rao Sing to burn some pastiles in a *dhooie-kalsin*, one of those clay vessels for the purpose of fumigation.

The conversation that ensued was in Hindostanee.

Whether it was the result of superstition, fear, or real bad health induced by both, no one could tell, but the poor grenadier, Gunga Ram, was, as my visitor informed me, dead ; all the specifics in the *dawah khana* (medicine chest) of the doctor sahib could not lengthen his days.

"Well," said I, somewhat impatiently, as my visitor's personal aspect disgusted me, "what have I to do with this ?"

"Much," he replied, putting down his pilgrim's staff, and placing the palms of his lean dark hands together ; "much."

"The deuce I have ! In what way ?"

"Rudkin sahib—captain sahib—hear me," said the fakir,

in whose sunken eyes a strange leering light was beginning to twinkle; "you remember the girl Azuma?"

"I do perfectly."

"And that she was beautiful to look upon?"

"Very," said I, beginning to be puzzled by the old man's manner and expression of face.

"You did much to protect her father from the punishment his imprudence brought upon him; and for that, the pretty Azuma is more than grateful."

"Did she send you to say so?" I asked impatiently.

"No; but he implored you to protect and befriend her, which perhaps, captain sahib, you have forgotten. But I— her kinsman—am her lawful protector, who can bestow her as I please; for she has no other friend in the world but me and Brahma—unless I add the captain sahib."

"Well?" I asked, staring at him as he paused.

I am going a long pilgrimage, even to Ganga Dwara—the Gate of the Ganges—and the great fair of Hurdwar, in the kingdom of Delhi."

"I wish you a pleasant journey; but what is all this to me?" I asked, as he filled his mouth with betel-nut and chunam.

"Little, I know; but it matters much to Azuma; she will be left quite alone, and the sahib must remember how fair she is Could not the sahib watch over her until some mehm sahib requires an ayah?"

"I! What the mischief *can* the old fellow mean?" was my next thought.

"She is beautiful; she dances, she sings, and tells wonderful tales of the genii, and of the powers of Vishnu, Siva, and Brahma; she gladdens the eyes of all who see her," he added, grinning horribly.

"I grant you all this, and will see if any of the ladies of the regiment can protect her."

"I must make an offering to the great shrine of Vishnu at the end of my journey," he continued, drawing nearer me, his eyes gleaming stealthily, his lean hands outstretched, his smeared body tainting the air and causing me to recoil, while sinking his voice, he added, "I must offer a silver lotus to Vishnu; I can beg my way to Hurdwar; but the sacred lotus will cost me a hundred and fifty rupees. If the captain sahib will give me that sum, Azuma shall remain as hostage for it."

He paused for a reply, cringing and salaaming.

"I shall certainly not make any such arrangement; Joupaugal!—Away, fool!" said I angrily.

"I am no fool," he replied meekly.

"A very decided knave, then! Do you actually propose to sell the girl as if she were goods in a bazaar—and to me?"

"If not to you I shall to some one else, who will be less scrupulous—perhaps to the subadar, Kureem Sing."

"Think of how great a horror she must have of that man, whom she deems her father's destroyer. She is so beautiful —do have some pity," I urged.

"I would rather have the rupees. How can I go to Hurd-war without the sacred lotus?"

"Begone, I say, or I shall summon a file of the guard and have you expelled from the barracks."

He came back twice again at intervals of half an hour, threatening to bestow her on the temple of the monkey god; and being really anxious to save or serve the girl, while also remembering that I had pledged my word to her dying father, I gave the old wretch the money, and told him to fetch her at once. In the meantime I went in search of some of the ladies of the regiment; but found that they were all gone with a carriage party to the Botanical Gardens in the city.

On returning to my quarters I found the fakir already there with the poor little girl, whom he had tricked out with silver bangles on her slender wrists, the flowers and perfume of jasmine in her glossy hair, and over her head a pink scarf of Dacca muslin, edged with slender silver lace.

She knelt down very humbly and kissed my hand.

To reassure her, I told her to cheer up, and that I hoped very soon to find her a kind mistress—perhaps before night-fall—among the mehm sahibs. She seemed then to take courage, and looked up at me with smiles of gratitude ; while the fakir,—having pocketed his rupees, shouldered a wallet, which I perceived to be filled with those little cakes known as *chupatties*, the rapid and mysterious distribution of which over all India was beginning to excite much attention and speculation about this time,—exclaimed, " Wah ! wah !" (Well done !), and salaamed his odious person out of the room.

The rancid ghee had departed, and the fragrance of the jasmine flowers was pleasant in its place.

" I have neither father nor mother—sister nor brother—you will be kind to me, sahib?" said the poor girl, looking up at me with an imploring expression in her soft dark oriental eyes, while the horrible fakir was fraternising with some Hindoo Sepoys ere he left the barrack-gate.

" Kind to you—who could fail to be so ?"

I kissed the falling tears from the poor little—well, they were rather brown—cheeks. It was done in a brotherly way, of course, and quite platonically ; but the tears being so kissed away, there might be a strong temptation to continue the process after they were gone. So I put her in the care of Dan O'Regan's wife till some of our ladies returned.

Though any such transaction as that with the fakir was expressly forbidden by the East India Company, I had scarcely completed the strange investment of my spare rupees when the adjutant dropped in to mention that the battalion would move up-country in a day or two, and that as some serious commotions were expected, every officer was to reduce his establishment of native servants, male or female, as much as possible.

What was I to do now with Azuma ? After the orders just mentioned, it would have been worse than useless to speak to any of the ladies of the corps concerning her, and Miss Guise, who alone could have assisted me, was at Allahabad.

She could not remain in my quarters, as she would not be there an hour before Dormer, Joe Lonsdale, Prior, or some other equally enterprising spirits discovered her ; so what plan could I fall upon ?

"I am always in some infernal scrape," thought I, as I sighed and lit a cigar, wishing the while that the fakir was at the bottom of his sacred Ganges, with his lotus—a flower, strangely enough, holy alike to the ancient Egyptians and the modern Hindoos.

CHAPTER XXIX.

THE PALANQUIN.

THE "letters of readiness" which the battalion received were rapidly followed by the "route," and of all the places in India, so far as I was concerned, it was for—Allahabad ! "What strange events, what unexpected meetings and sudden separations are sailors liable to !" says Captain Marryat ; but so it is too with soldiers ; and here we were ordered up-country, to where she—*they* were !

"We are actually to march for Allahabad," I repeated for the third time to Dormer, as we idled in the mess-room.

"Yes ; what is there so wonderful in that ?" he asked.

"It is terrible, Jack."

"How so ? The distance, do you mean ?—about four hundred and sixty miles, as the crow flies."

"*She* is there, and, of course, her devilish husband too I shall be meeting her daily in those deuced cantonments.

My bungalow may actually be next to his. What shall I do, Jack?"

"Don't think of such things, especially at this perilous time."

"Perilous—how."

"When disturbances are daily expected among the native troops."

"I forgot ; but then I must——"

"You must meet Blanche, and her husband too, as any gentleman should," said Jack, with more decision of manner than he usually adopted, "and as if nothing had ever passed between you and her. Depend upon it, she will affect to forget, if she has not already forgotten, all about it. A woman always flatters herself that she has never but once been in love, and that is with the hero for the time."

"What a horrid idea, Jack! This is rank heresy."

"Fact though, my dear boy," said Jack. "Pass the brandy-bottle ; thanks. Once you're up-country, she'll perhaps make as great a fuss with you as she does with her Maltese spaniel. Calvert gave her one of these curs as they came out overland." (*Vide* little Tiny, cashiered, thought I.) "Don't make a silly show of wearing the willow, old fellow. It is no use, once you're thrown over."

"Will you believe it Jack, that before this artful girl came to Thorsgill Hall I was on the point of proposing to your cousin Henriette?"

"The deuce you were ! You have a great desire to become a member of the family. Henriette is by far the finer girl of the two."

"It is like fatality, this move to Allahabad?" I began again. "There, probably, I shall see her every day ; and how can I face her, or rather how can she face me?"

"What sort of a station is Allahabad?" asked Lonsdale, who now came into the room.

"Oh, a delightful one," replied Dormer ; "healthy, although humid, and the permanent station of the Sudder-commission.

There every man ' falls in love with his pretty wife over again, or his neighbour's, if he prefers her,' as Fanny Fern has it ; so it will be just the place for you, Joe."

When I went back to my quarters, I heard something very different from the light-hearted banter of my comrades in the mess-bungalow.   Kneeling on a carpet, with her face to the east, Azuma was concluding her morning prayer in Hindostanee, and was saying very devoutly and softly :

"God is One ; Creator of all that is ; a perfect sphere, without beginning and without end !   Fire is the superior of the Brahmin ; but Vishnu is superior to fire.   Unveil, O Thou who givest sustenance to the world, that face of the true sun, which is now hidden by a ray of golden light, so that we may see the truth and know our whole duty !"

Such was the conclusion of the poor girl's prayer to her imaginary deity, " the great lord of the lotus."

As she arose to greet me, I found that her dark eyes were swimming in tears, and she told me that she had heard of the " route " up-country from Rao Sing.

"And what of that ?" I asked, taking her child-like hands in mine.   "You cannot regret leaving this place, where that odious subadar, Kureem Sing, is quartered ?"

"Oh, no," said she.   "Then you are not intending to leave me behind !"

"Far from it ; you shall have a palanquin for yourself.   I know two ladies at Allahabad, and there you shall go with me to them.   Are you happy now ?"

"Oh, yes, yes, yes !" replied the girl, her eyes becoming more than ever radiant with smiles and tears, as she nestled with inimitable grace on the floor close beside my feet, and placing her elbows on my knees, and her chin in her hands, gazed up at me with gratitude.   Next to that emotion the great passion of the girl's heart was a boundless love and regard for the memory of her father, the old soldier of the 2nd Grenadiers.   I had saved him from the sword of that sorcerer, the subadar—I, a Feringhee officer, one of the

Ghora-logue, or white people ; consequently I was a species
of demi-god in her eyes.

I soon found that, flattered by my notice and kindness, the
girl's manner became caressing, and certainly full of peril for
her as time passed on.

At first her face was always suffused with blushes when I
addressed her, and her humid eyes were cast down ; but as
she became accustomed to me, her confusion passed away,
and softly and pleadingly they always looked into mine.

" Yes, Azuma," said I, "when at Allahabad I hope to find
a young lady whose ayah you must be ; a lady with eyes as
dark and as beautiful as your own," I added, thinking of
Henriette Guise.

" Oh, do not put poor Azuma away !" pleaded the little
Hindoo ; " she will fan you when you are hot and weary, and
watch you when you go to sleep."

I feared there was not much chance of my sleeping if the
conversation went on thus, for she added :

" When last I lit my love-lamp, and set it on the holy river,
it floated bravely down, when those of twenty other girls at
the ghaut went out or sunk."

" And what then ?"

" On that evening I saw *you*."

Here was an alarming inference, and most alluringly drawn,
with all that wonderful sweetness and subtlety of manner
peculiar to all the women of the East, especially the Indo-
Britons or Eurasians.

It was fortunate for her that my kitmutgar, Rao Sing, was
a Hindoo ; otherwise the poor girl might have starved ; as
the edibles prepared for her by Dan and his wife, whose
special care " the bit cratur" as she called her was, were
deemed by Azuma polluted and unfit for food by the laws of
her religion. And most simple were her tastes ; a little boiled
rice on a lotus-leaf, fruit of any kind, the great oriental
delicacy of *tyer* or clouted cream, the gelatinous *nouga*, which,
like the luscious toddy, is procured from the Palmyra palm,

and eaten with sugar—these, and such as these, with a chupattie and clarified butter, sufficed her as food ; for the laws of Menou forbid his followers to eat of anything that has ever had animal life.

Times there were when she would sing to me long stanzas in honour of Krishnu, under his name of Rama, and of his loves with the milkmaids of Madhura ; and there was a novelty in this strange friendship that made me *forget* much of the past.

At last came the day when we were to march. I was roused from dreamless slumber by the bugles sounding " the warning " in the barrack-square, and by the voice of Rao Sing saying :

" Salaam, sahib ; master want to be washed—bath ready."

Then I sprang into the brick-built trough so named, and the jars of water, which had been standing all night in the shady cool verandah, were soused over me, the greatest of Indian luxuries. A wing of a chicken on a piece of toast, and a tumbler of cold sangaree (negus) at the mess-bunga-low, sufficed for breakfast, and I repaired to the parade-ground, where the battalion was falling in, and the sergeants " proving " the companies.

This was one of those steamy mornings peculiar to that locality, especially at that particular season ; but when the sun rose and attained some height, the full fierceness of his glare was dreadful when reflected from the walls of white-washed masonry around us ; and though, like the other officers, I wore a sun-helmet, while the men had only puggerees, I felt as if my eyes would be scorched in their sockets before the column got in motion, headed by the European band of the 2nd Bengal Grenadiers, which, with the usual military courtesy, played us to the station of the first section of the Great East-Indian Railway, which at that time went no farther than, viâ Burdwan, to Rajmahal on the Ganges.

" Good-bye, Rudkin," said Jones of the Bengal Horse Artillery, as we marched out of Dumdum ; " you are deuced

lucky to be leaving this hole, where for so many hours daily
we of the scientific corps have to imbibe fog and gunpowder
smoke, while wading about after field-battery bullocks in the
wet grass, and, supposing that we are at gun-practice, firing
John Company's cannon-shot at invisible targets, when we
would rather be flirting in the Botanical or out with the Calcutta hounds."

I had seen my little friend off in her palanquin, and in
charge of Rao Sing, borne by four bearers, who, like all
others in the East, uttered dismal sounds as they trotted
along, to the cadence of their own bare feet, in this fashion :
" Hih, hah—huh, hah ! hih, hah—huh, hah !"

A special train conveyed the regiment through Burdwan,
an extensive coal district, to the ancient city of Rajmahal,
which stands on the western bank of the Ganges, at the base
of a range of undulating hills. The modern or European
town consisted then of one street, composed of stone houses,
generally two stories in height. There the line of railway,
which it was intended to carry up the whole valley of the
Ganges, terminated, and we had to take the river steamers,
or other boats, for the remainder of the journey.

The battalion, with its baggage, women, children, and servants, European and native, proved too numerous a multitude
for one boat, and so we required three, and this number increased in proportion as we ascended the river. I was fortunately in the same craft with my friends Dormer, Prior, and
Lonsdale. On this watery way we practised with our rifles
and revolvers at the claret and champagne bottles as they were
thrown overboard, and occasionally had whiffs upon the air
that were the reverse of " the sweet south that breathes upon
a bank of violets," when the dead bodies of Hindoos, with
vultures perching on them, floated past : and once we came
with a terrible shock upon something more odious still—the
enormously swollen carcass of a dead elephant, in a great
state of decomposition, rolling down the current.

As I had fully foreseen, the closed palanquin occupied by

my protégée soon excited the comments and curiosity of the ladies of the regiment, particularly of the adjutant's wife, who was a great gossip; and the result was, that when we came to Bhoglipoor, a large Mahomedan town in a district covered with forests and thickets, amid which the wild elephant roams untamed, Jack Dormer took me to task on the subject, with a somewhat comical expression of face.

"Rudkin, that confounded palanquin of yours is a source of serious speculation to all the ladies of the battalion," said he, laughing.

"Let them speculate as they please, if they won't take the contents off my hands," I replied with irritation.

"The wife of the adjutant alone compliments you."

"How—for what?"

"For showing some desire to settle in life."

"In what way?

"Providing yourself with an ayah before you have a wife and family—like having a coachman without the carriage and pair."

"Let the palanquin alone, Jack. Tell the ladies who are making themselves so busy, that a writer who knew India well has written, that 'there are three things of which you must never ask the contents—a subaltern's bungalow, a lady's chit, and a governor-general's cranium.'"

"True; but you are a captain."

"Yes; but we are all subalterns under the rank of major."

"By Jove! I never knew that before."

"Any military dictionary will tell you so."

Rumour spread fast that the veiled occupant of the palanquin was a young girl of great beauty; and when we reached Patna, passing through a fleet of "opium clippers" and budgerows or passage-boats, a magnificent and walled city, having many mosques and temples, Prior and Lonsdale began on the subject once more.

"I fear," said Tom, "that all the ladies of the battalion would put you in Coventry, but you are deemed the best round-dancer in the corps, so they can't spare you ; moreover, that palanquin, or its supposed occupant, is a dreadful aggravation to the unwedded vestals——"

"Who have failed in the matrimonial market here, and yet won't go home as 'returned goods,'" said I.

"Exactly ; you comprehend, my friend."

"Yes ; but I shall not be interfered with."

"Of course not."

"My intentions are the best in the world ; and this is the reward of philanthropy !" said I, angrily.

On this they shouted with laughter.

"Now, don't be a humbug, Lance," said Lonsdale ; "it looks more like philandering, as the adjutant's wife maintains it to be."

"Before that worthy lady expresses an opinion, I wish she would reflect whether her opinion is worth having."

But they were bent on teazing me.

"Don't put yourself on a highly moral pedestal, Rudkin," said Jack Dormer ; "the idea of a fellow travelling about the world with a girl in a palanquin, and thinking that people won't speak of it !"

"Of course," added Tom Prior, "the wonderfully strong yet tender feelings of Mrs. Grundy are inexpressibly shocked."

I applied a few mild adjectives to the name of the good lady in question.

"Had she been a Hindoo of fifty—but one of fifteen !"

"I am the victim of circumstances, Dormer," said I. "How could I foresee the order about reducing the number of native servants to the lowest minimum ?"

"What *do* you mean ?" they all asked together.

I then told them the story of the friendless girl, the promise I had given to her father, and of the fakir from whose cupidity I was anxious to save her, and then the banter to some extent ceased.

"It is quite a dilemma, Jack," said I ; "but it would be utter inhumanity to cast the poor thing adrift here."

"Of course. She's so pretty, too; it is not to be thought of!"

"And to gratify the evil-minded and self-righteous, who go about thanking God that they are not as others are!"

To all this they agreed with me, and that, on reaching a large station like Allahabad, something might be done for her easily.

It was a grilling April now; the season of mango-fish and the prickly-heat; the curse of the young European in India: where in some places, when sleeping under "a Bengal blanket," as our soldiers call the sun, the mercury in the thermometer stands at the fever point, and those who cannot afford iced drinks are reduced to bitter beer, cold tea, and grumbling at the clerk of the weather.

A little soured by the remarks that had been made to me, by the somewhat cold manner of some of the ladies on the poop, and having other things to occupy my mind, I did not, like Dormer, Prior, Lonsdale, and others, enjoy myself, as youth only can enjoy itself, and find everything funny, sunny, and glorious at Benares, where our river-boats tarried for a time.

All the cabin-passengers went on shore to see the sights of that place, the holy city of the Hindoos, and one so strictly oriental in character, that it differs widely from all the other cities of Hindostan.

Through her half-opened veil I saw the poor girl Azuma, screening her fine eyes with her well-shaped little hand, and gazing with longing and eagerness at the wonderful combination of the beautiful and the grotesque, all piled confusedly together within that stupendous wall which there spreads along the river's bank. The long, handsome, and lofty ghauts, crowded by gaily-attired natives, the closely-packed houses, the lofty temples, the still more lofty minarets, and the luxuriant foliage fringing the parapets, and even the flat roofs, of many of the mansions; and the whole city was steeped in the purple light of a setting sun.

Seeing the eagerness of the girl's look, "Azuma," said I, "should you like to be taken on shore?"

"Yes; oh, yes!" she exclaimed, with clasped hands.

"Well, I shall escort you."

Desiring Rao Sing to summon the bearers, while I put on my sword and sun-helmet, her palanquin was landed at the foot of one of the stately ghauts, at a place where the water was so clear, and the downward reflection of everything so sharp and well-defined, that the eye almost failed to detect the white steps which were real and those which were reflection.

Through the narrow streets, which are crowded by a population of more than half a million, we threaded our way, till we came to a dâk-bungalow, or house for travellers, commanding a pleasant view of the great mosque, built by Aurungzebe, on the side of the Hindoo temple of Mahadura. It was kept by a European, and there I ordered dinner; and amused as a child would have been with all the sights and scenes around her, the Hindoo girl sat on a divan at a window overlooking the esplanade before the mosque.

The *tatty*, or window-screen, composed of the roots of sweet-scented grass, well drenched with water, was partially lifted up, and the cool atmosphere of the room was delightful.

Our dinner over—mine was quite an Indo-European repast, hers was simply rice and fruit—I lit a cigar, had a bottle of St. Julien, and proceeded to enjoy the luxury of total idleness; while the Hindoo, seated by my knee, in her favourite position, on a *morah*, or ratten footstool, excited by the many objects around her connected with her peculiar faith—the great number of pagodas, dedicated to the almost countless gods of the Hindoo mythology—prattled away (poor little pagan!) of the world to come, while I listened with a good-natured smile, and made concentric rings of smoke in the air.

Her father had been a high-caste Brahmin, and to them alone is taught the language of the Shasters, those volumes which contain the philosophy of the Hindoos ; and from him she had learned all about Yama, the future abode of the good, the approach to which is through delightful paths, under the shadow of fragrant trees, by the side of streams covered with the lotus—paths where showers of flowers fall upon them as they pass, and where the air resounds with the songs of angels.

Then, while her dark eyes grew round and startled in expression by the eagerness and fervour of her thoughts, while clasping my hand in hers, she prattled away of the passage to the *other* place, through dark and dismal paths, where the wicked trod over sharp stones, amid showers of hot ashes and burning coal, and where the air was loaded by the wails and shrieks of horrible apparitions. And while she spoke of these things, with an earnestness and grace peculiarly oriental and her own, I could not help recalling the remark of the Abbé Dupanloup, how necessary it was that *some* belief should exist in the human heart.

In her manner there was much that reminded me of a Maltese girl, who, at Valetta, insisted on enlightening me on the legends of the saints.

While conversing there, or rather while dreamily listening to my protégée, we were suddenly startled by vociferous shouts of " Rama, Rama !" and a multitude of those religious beggars, fakirs or pilgrims, who infest Benares and make it their head-quarters, poured past in all their disgusting squalor, dirt, and scantiness of costume, on their way to some pagoda.

" Look, look, sahib !" she exclaimed, and pointed with her hand, and I saw the horrid fakir, Kalidasa Ram, like all the rest, distributing from his wallet those mysterious chupatties, or tiny cakes, to the hordes of natives who accompanied them. What could this mean, or of what was it the symbol?

I asked Azuma if it had aught to do with the Hindoo faith; but she shook her head, and replied that she never heard of such a thing before ; and that, so far from distributing anything, these fakirs looked instead for alms and offerings, invoking curses on the heads of all who withheld them, thinking to gain that from terror which they failed to get from religion or charity.

So the evening stole on ; the shadows were deepening in the narrow streets of Benares ; red as blood, the last light of the sun lingered on the minarets of the mosque of Aurungzebe, which rise to the height of two hundred and thirty feet above the river ; the bottle of St. Julien was empty ; my third cheroot was ended ; and the head of Azuma began to droop wearily on her hand. I summoned her attendants, and we proceeded back to the ghaut, getting on board the river-boat amid the sudden darkness that always follows sunset in India ; but I heard a " cheeky" young subaltern of "ours " say to some one :

" By jingo, here comes Rudkin, on guard over the palanquin !"

But those who made light of the matter little knew how much this attractive girl's future troubled me.

After reaching Mirzapore, with its ghauts and glittering temples, its flaming iron-works and busy carpet manufactories, and passing through fleets of cotton boats in the snaky windings of the river between high banks, I knew that next morning would find us at—Allahabad.

"And now, Heaven help me," thought I, "I am about to see again this fairy-like creature who has so cruelly deceived me. Her husband is on the staff--my senior officer too—and perhaps to him I may have to present myself.

CHAPTER XXX.

THE MORNING VISIT.

DULY next morning we found ourselves close to the famous and ancient city of Allahabad, with its great fortress, which was founded by the Emperor Ackbar on the site of the older Hindoo town of Prayag, which signifies a junction, for there is the confluence of the Jumna with the Ganges. The water of the latter was then low, and near the stately fort of Ackbar —which I. shall have to describe at a subsequent time—were visible a number of sand-banks, the resort of legions of alligators, which we could see basking amid the ooze in the sunshine.

We landed while the sun was below the horizon, yet his coming radiance tipped redly the summit of the Bundelcund bank of the Jumna, which is rocky, and rises in towering cliffs crowned by Hindoo pagodas and mouldering hill-forts. From the city and fortress of Allah we had to march a considerable distance to reach the cantonments into which we were played by the European band of the 6th Bengal Native Infantry. The air on this occasion was, I remember, " The Laird of Cockpen," adopted out of compliment to the Governor-General, the Marquis of Dalhousie, whose patrimony in Scotland was a place of that name.

In India it is—or in my time was—the custom, on marching into or arriving at a station, for an officer to call on all the married ladies.

" So, Rudkin, we must get their names," said Dormer, " and call upon every one, even before we get the mess established."

" On Lady Calvert, too—I ?"

" You—of course ; the visit will create quite a sensation in her breast, I have no doubt ; I like sensations, though I hate a scene."

" There will be no scene, Jack—be assured of that," I replied, knowing well that if I omitted to call on her, and her only, the circumstance must excite remark in the entire cantonments, and that she would have scored it down to pique, jealousy, revenge, or some other similar sentiment, which now I was far from feeling, and certainly had no desire to display, even had I felt it.

The officers of the 6th had breakfast awaiting us in their mess-bungalow, and the moment that meal was over Dormer and I set forth to visit his cousins.

" Better get it over at once, Rudkin," said he.

The residence of Sir Harry Calvert was a fine stately mansion outside the cantonments, and surrounded by beautiful gardens. In architecture it was somewhat Grecian, with a noble portico of fluted pillars ; a broad cornice finished its third story, and thereon, like enormous and bloated herons, with stupendous beaks and pouches, sat some of those birds called adjutants in India, only moving now and then to inflict sharp punishment on any smaller animal of the winged creation that came near them.

A verandah surrounded the house, and between the pillars of it were large green blinds of split bamboo, to exclude the glare of the sun at noon ; but now, at half-past eight, the morning was pleasant, fresh, and invigorating.

" Mehm Sahib—hye !—Mehm Sahib Calvert in ?" I asked of the durwan whom we found dozing in the verandah.

" Yes, and missy Beebee," replied the official, a fat old Hindostanee in an enormous white turban.

" He means Henriette, of course," said Jack, as we gave him our cards and entered a marble vestibule, where a fountain—a jet—filled with gold and silver fish, was plashing pleasantly from one basin to another below.

We were ushered into a double drawing-room of perfectly European aspect, so far as mirrors, console-table, glass-

shades, and many framed engravings could make it. I felt a
little bewildered at first. Would Blanche—I could never
think of her as Lady Calvert—on seeing me grow pale, change
colour, cling to a chair, or what?

Unchanged in all her fair beauty, save that she looked a
little paler, the result of the climate doubtless—she rose from
a plaited cane sofa, on which she had been lying, fanning
herself, well powdered, and with all her beautiful hair floating
about her for coolness.

Henriette started from the piano as we were announced,
and unmistakably her lovely face looked paler, whiter than
usual, and there was a troubled expression in her fine eyes.

Dormer kissed both his charming cousins in a cousinly way,
and Blanche, so far from exhibiting the smallest emotion,
greeted me frankly with full-open eyes that never flinched,
though she *did* speak nervously and rapidly.

"Welcome to Allahabad! When did you arrive?" she
asked, making great use of her fan, a miracle of Chinese
carving.

"I little thought we should ever meet again," said I, in a
voice that faltered in spite of myself, and of her terribly re-
assuring manner. I felt, too, somewhat sad.

"Here you will find me in full performance of all the duties
of domestic life, and fulfilling all those offices that accrue to
the representative British matron in India," said she, with
something of her old playful manner, which seemed most
heartless now.

Apparently Dormer felt this, for he asked sharply,

"Where's Calvert?"

"Breakfasting with the commandant."

I was not sorry to hear this; it would have proved rather
too much to have met him just then. She poured questions upon us, without waiting or seeming to care for the
answer.

"When did you arrive?—oh, this morning, I remember.
Had you a pleasant voyage out? Did you not find Dumdum

a horrid place? Will you remain with your corps or get on the staff? Did any ladies come out with you? Any marriages likely to take place?" etc.

Such were the commonplaces asked me, while I looked wonderingly in her eyes, and on her lips and hair, which I had been wont to cover with kisses in the past time that seemed now a hundred years ago.

"I am glad, indeed, to see you," she said during a pause; "it seems such an age since we parted at dear Thorsgill Hall. We had quite a flirtation there, you must remember?"

"I am not likely to *forget*," said I very quietly, while my eyes wandered unconsciously to those of Henriette, who had scarcely spoken; but how truly did her words on the morning of our parting at Thorsgill come back to me, when she said "that Blanche made light of everything!"

A flirtation! And this was the creature for whom I had worn out my heart and wasted its best affection.

The words cured me, however. "Better," says a writer, "ah, better for the old love to be buried deep in the earth, with a headstone setting forth its extent and constancy, than for it thus to walk again like an apparition through the chambers of the soul, where it has become a stranger, and its presence is as unwelcome as unexpected."

"You have just come too late for my cousin's fancy ball," said Henriette, breaking another awkward pause; "we had it last week."

"And a delightful one it was!" added Blanche.

"In what character did you go, Lady Calvert?" I asked.

"I went as Queen Elizabeth."

"And there would be an Earl of Leicester, of course?"

"Yes—Colonel Stapleton. By the way, he remains with us, having got a staff appointment, through Sir Harry."

"*He* ought to have been Leicester," said Dormer.

"He was on duty at the fort."

"And you, Miss Guise?"

" I went as Mary Queen of Scots," said Henriette, colouring
a little. " Do you think it was very vain of me ?"

"Far from it ; a charming Mary you must have made. There
would no doubt be a Bothwell or a Chastelard ?"

" I had neither," replied Henriette ; " Jacky Appleton was
my attendant as Mary Seton."

" I am quite anxious to see this celebrated namesake of
mine," said Jack Dormer.

" She has gone shopping in the carriage to Allahabad," replied Lady Calvert ; and then she added, " I have a reception
to-night, and hope you will both do me the pleasure of coming,
and then you shall see her."

Jack expressed his delight and mine, and we bowed ourselves out.   The durwan gave us our swords in the vestibule,
and we issued into the cloudless sunshine.

"What a heaven life would be but for its memories !"
thought I, mentally quoting some author — I know not
whom.   And this was the girl who had come between me
and my wits — between me and Henriette—the folds of
whose dress, the waves of whose golden hair, and whose
smiles and accents had been more to me than life, or death,
or heaven.

All had passed like a dream, but I still seemed to hear the
sound of her voice in my ear as we passed through the cantonments in search of our compounds and bungalows, where
our servants, European and native, would be putting all our
" traps " in order.

The lines occupied by the 6th Bengal Infantry, a corps with
dark-green facings, and locally known as the *Gowan-ka-Pultan*, from the name of the Scotsman who raised them in the
year 1759, some of the 3rd Oude Irregulars, and of the Ferozepore Regiment of Sikhs, were, as usual, in such cantonments, streets of little bungalows or huts, built of bamboos,
thatched with straw and plastered over with mud, baked hard
and dry in the sunshine.   On the flanks of those streets was
a better species of similar edifices for the subahdars and other

native officers ; and in all these huts there was one apartment, the zenana, occupied by the females of the family, into which no man, no matter what his rank, dared to penetrate, save the sepoy himself.

Through these streets of huts an incredible number of natives were always swarming, wrangling with the sutlers, or offering for sale rice, shawls, pipe-sticks, tobacco, *bhang*, and jewellery ; and there, too, were indecent Nautch girls, half or wholly naked fakirs, fortune-tellers, jugglers with swords, baskets, balls, and spinning-tops, tumblers' and snake-charmers with their flutes.

There, too, were the sepoys, lithe, but bony and awkward, busy in every direction, with their various modes of cooking, each according to rules of his faith, Hindoo or Mohammedan, but chiefly making pilaff, though many were content to dine on a piece of common bread steeped in pure cold water.

It was on this day that I first became conscious that the sepoys were beginning to eye furtively and sullenly the European officers, and to avoid, if possible, according them the usual salute when passing.

CHAPTER XXXI.

BLANCHE'S RECEPTION,

WE dined with the 6th in their mess-bungalow, which, like such places in general, was all windows, draughts, and open doors, with a huge tattered punkah swaying overhead. I then hastened to my quarters to make an elaborate toilette and don my full uniform, as I had been assured at mess that I should find " the commandant, the staff, and the entire garrison, the collector, judge, the cream of the Civil Service, and everybody that was anybody, at Lady Calvert's."

" How will all this new and strange intercourse end?" thought I, while hooking on my elaborately braided jacket, with its Crimean medals and clasps, adjusting my crimson sash and silver-mounted belt to a nicety, and making a most careful parting behind, by the use of a pair of ivory-handled hair-brushes.

As I passed through the outer room of my bungalow, I came suddenly upon Azuma, who was coquettishly arranging her muslin costume, wreathing the masses of her dark per-fumed hair, and playing with her ankle ornaments, as I paused for a minute to observe her, for her passion for jewellery was truly oriental, and I had rather foolishly fostered it as we came up-country. She greeted me with one of her brightest smiles, but said, for perhaps I had a pre-occupied expres-sion :

" My lord sahib looks weary and ill ; stay, and poor Azuma shall nurse you so nicely, so gently."

But I put her little brown hand aside with impatience, as I thought of another hand which never again should rest in mine, then the smile on her face died away.

"I am going to the house of a great mehm sahib, Azuma," said I kindly; "but I shall not forget you when I am there."

She took my hand between hers and kissed it.

"Perhaps she may want an ayah, and how fortunate that will be for you!"

Her countenance fell again. She threw up her arms and turned away. What she meant I had no time to inquire; but in India a European is always forcibly impressed by what a traveller terms "the luxuriant use of the arms made by women in conversation, whether they are walking or sitting and even when the tones of the voice are by no means animated."

I found Calvert's house a blaze of light, and the punkahs all at work, as the heat was excessive. Dormer, Lonsdale, Prior, and many more of "ours" were present; their dark green Rifle uniforms standing boldly out among the light dresses of the ladies, the silver-grey of the Light Cavalry, and the scarlet of the Staff and 6th Bengal. Both drawing-rooms were crowded, and so many of the artillery, engineers, dragoons, and others hovered about our hostess, that some time elapsed before I got near her.

"Who is that in the sugar-loaf hat?" asked Lonsdale of Captain Birch, the Fort-adjutant.

"A parsee—Peeroo Mull—the great banker in Allahabad; a good friend to know I can assure you."

"By Jove, he might pass for the twin-brother of Ali Baba; but here comes a swell with no end of diamonds.'

"His Highness the Rajah of Chutneypore, escorted by Innes of the Engineers," replied the adjutant.

"He looks as stolid and as grand as if he had just walked out of Madame Tussaud's," was the off-hand comment of Lonsdale, as the Rajah, a dark, little, and, to my idea, cunning-looking personage, passed towards the head of the room, the gay crowd parting courteously before him. From head to foot he was literally covered with jewels; his turban, his body-dress—a shapeless kind of garment—and his sandals were all blazing with diamonds.

"Who are those that Dormer is making himself so agreeable to—three pretty girls?" asked Lonsdale.

"Oh, those are Armenians—each is said to carry a lac of rupees on her own person in jewels," replied Birch.

They were all fair and handsome, though black-haired. The head-dress of each was a tiara of leaf-gold, with long pendants behind, the front being a mass of precious stones.

Our English ladies were all gaily and exquisitely dressed ; but their principal charms were not in their costume. Amid the throng many black servants in white jackets and turbans were handing about fast-melting ices and sparkling champagne, on massive silver salvers, under the direction of the khansaman, or native butler. At last I got near Blanche, who held out her hand to me, with a brighter smile than before ; for, amid the ever-shifting throng of her guests, she was more self-possessed than before.

"So glad you have come early ; I must introduce you to my—to Harry. Sir Harry—Captain Rudkin, an old European friend."

We bowed as she passed on to speak to some one else. Calvert, a tall and good-looking man, about five-and-thirty, or perhaps forty, was in staff uniform. He was already getting grizzled and rather bald. I was spiteful enough to be glad to see that, and hope ere long his head would shine like a billiard ball. Moreover, I thought he had a dissipated look, and recalled a passage in Joe Lonsdale's letter from London to me at Tilbury.

He was talking to me of India and the growing discontent among the Company's troops ; and while I replied mechanically, my eyes were following Blanche. Her hair, as golden and luxuriant as ever, was slightly blown about by the punkah overhead ; but her cheeks, once ever like the rose-leaf, had again resumed something of that tinge amid the heat of her crowded rooms. She was simply clad in Dacca muslin, with

the prettiest of Delhi bracelets on her snowy wrists, and delicate gloves on her hands. Fairer she seemed than ever, and
my heart throbbed. but was *not* to be lost again.

" Oh, Mr. Prior," I heard her say to Tom, "you are *so* like
your portrait !"

" My portrait ?" he repeated, with a bewildered air.

" Yes—a full length."

" Ah, at Stoke Priory ; you have been there, then ?"

" One night ; I shall not likely forget it."

" Nor shall I," was my thought, as I turned away with
something like disgust growing in my heart to find that she
could callously and smilingly recur to that occasion, and pass
on laughingly to join Colonel Stapleton, who at that moment
was ushered in. Her words and bearing were indeed rapidly
curing me ; yet I could not keep my gaze from following her,
and this she soon discovered ; so I resolved to visit her
as seldom as possible, if ever again, and cursed the fate that
had sent our battalion to Allahabad.

"Have some champagne and be jolly," urged Dormer, in an
earnest whisper ; "this sort of thing won't do, Rudkin."

" I can't help it, Jack," said I ; "you can never know the
havoc that fair little creature has made with me. I wish I had
never, never met her ; and yet, when I think of the days of
sweet companionship at Thorsgill Hall, surely she must have
loved me *then !*"

" Very probably she fancied she did."

" What sort of man is her husband—clever ?"

" Well, he seems to have all the sense never made use of
by Solomon," was Jack's response.

" Miss Appleton, Captain Rudkin and my cousin, Mr.
Dormer, of the Rifles," said Henriette, introducing us to a
very pretty girl, having a gay manner, which won her the
credit of being one of the greatest flirts at the station, with the
reputation for saying the strangest things in the world, and,
if *gup* was to be believed, of doing them too. So an animated
conversation began between her and Dormer forthwith ;

while I seated myself beside Henriette, whom I thought it strange that, save to utter one or two commonplace remarks, Stapleton never approached during the whole evening. Hence I was half inclined to deem Jack's story of their engagement a false rumour. All the more so, that I caught her quiet dark eyes regarding me sometimes with kind and melancholy interest, convincing me that she knew our story.

"Lady Calvert," I heard Miss Appleton say, "you did not join our riding-party this morning."

"I was engaged."

"But it was a promise," said Miss Appleton.

"Sometimes, my dear Jacky, promises are like those wonderful chupatties that are in circulation—made to be broken."

So it was, indeed, with her; and her promise to me was as significant of future treachery as those same chupatties were to be.

"Blanche," resumed Miss Appleton behind her fan, laughing. "I wish you had seen Brown of the Oude Irregulars this morning on his grey Arab."

"What sort of an air has he in the saddle?"

"Oh, don't ask, pray!"

"Why?"

"Because it beats that of an infantry adjutant. Oh, what have I said!" she suddenly exclaimed, and looked with coquettish entreaty at Dormer. "I do hope you are not an adjutant, Mr. Dormer?"

Jack hastened to assure her that he had not the honour to be so useful a person; and now, as the company were beginning to disperse, and some to make whispered arrangements for meeting at the band-stand next evening, he and I rose to take our departure.

As we bade our hostess farewell, she said laughingly, while leaning on Stapleton's arm and furiously flirting her fan:

"Your friend Mr. Lonsdale tells me he is quite smitten with my youngest Armenian friend."

" Oh, cousin, Lonsdale is always in love with some one."

" And love, as Madame de Staël says—for so I read at
school—is but an episode in a man's life.   Good-night, Captain Rudkin. We shall perhaps meet at the band to-morrow;"
and she sailed off towards the Rajah, whose palkee, formed
of the richest materials, preceded by fifty torch-bearers and
followed by as many more, was now announced as being at
the portico.

" She looked at me, Jack, as she made that trite quotation,"
said I, as we descended the brilliantly lighted stair; " she has
no more heart than a Hindoo idol !"

" Not half so much as a Hindoo ʹgirl, certainly," he responded, with a wink that provoked me, all the more as, until
he said this, I had utterly forgotten all about Azuma, and lost
the best of opportunities for getting her placed somewhere.
However, if I had forgotten her, *others* had not.

Several ladies who were whispering together in the vestibule
suddenly ceased as Dormer and I passed out on our way to
the cantonments; and next morning at parade I learned that
gossip had already been busy about me.   There were at the
station two Presbyterian spinsters, who, like most Scots folks
out of Scotland, had left their kirk behind them, but not
their malevolence ; mature damsels, with uncommonly tight
opinions and loose tongues, who had been asserting that the
poor girl whom her hard destiny had cast on my hands was
a *gholaum*, a slave, or something of that kind.

Ignorant of all this as yet, on returning to my bungalow, to
my surprise I found Azuma lingering in the verandah and
gazing at the moon. The sight of Blanche had made me
gloomy.

" Why are you here at this strange hour ?" said I.   " Go to
your charpoy."

" I waited to see you return," she replied, very kindly. " Is
my lord sahib sorry that he took me from Kalidasa the fakir?
If so, send me back to Dumdum."

" To the cruel subahdar Kureem Sing ?"

"No, no," said she, shuddering and covering her eyes; "but you shall have no trouble with the poor Hindoo girl; she will hide herself in the jungle if you bid her."

"No, Azuma, you shall stay where you are."

"Oh, I am happy—so happy!" and, kneeling by my side, she covered my hand with tears and kisses.

"Poor child," said I, raising her from the floor; "the dew is falling heavily, the verandah is quite damp, and you are chilled. Call Regan's wife to attend to you; and now good-night."

She kissed her little hand to me and retired with a grateful glance; her whole manner was plaintively sweet and touching.

"That girl is evidently getting a deuced deal too fond of me," thought I, as Rao Sing, looking very cross and sleepy, appeared with my night-light and the chowry; "but I shall not make such a fool of myself as to fall in love with her or any one else."

After one grand passion, it seems for a time difficult to love another; to man—woman, too, doubtless—they seem mere substitutes or illusions; even courtship becomes matter of fact; for the old, old story that is told with tremulous lips to a first, is easily repeated to a second or third.

CHAPTER XXXII.

A CONFIRMED FLIRT.

I DID not see Blanche again for a little time. The day after her reception I was on duty as " captain of the day." As such, I had to see all the cells opened and fresh bread served out to the prisoners, who were becoming unusually numerous among the sepoys, as frequent cases of insubordination were now occurring. From the prison I turned to where the white walls and green jalousies of Sir Harry Calvert's house were shining in the morning sun, and I scarcely know what I was thinking of, when the " orderly sergeant" told me that the cells were all reclosed.

At eight I went over to the mess bungalow, where I found several of " ours" reading the papers, or discussing their coffee and the personal appearance of the ladies we had met overnight ; and there was but one opinion about the " wonderful beauty of Lady Calvert," which under other circumstances might have been pleasant enough to hear. Among others, Lonsdale was there, and I questioned him about the minia-ture which Stapleton had exhibited for off-hand criticism at " the Rag," and asked him if he had seen any resemblance ; but he seemed unable to remember, or, more probably, was unwilling to say what he thought.

Visiting the guards and barrack-rooms after each meal occupied the rest of the day till " retreat," when I inspected the inlying picquet, and we all sat late at mess, as some strange rumours had come floating up country of a mutiny among the 2nd Grenadiers at Dumdum ; but as yet nothing was known for certainty.

On the following day I had occasion to visit the fort of Allahabad, where a company of " ours" was stationed, and re-

mained all night, being rather quizzed, I remember, about
occupying "a haunted bungalow," where a ghost in white
always came at twelve at night and blew out the lamp, which
in such places is often merely a crystal tumbler with a little
oil and floating wick.   Whether it came or not I cannot say ;
but when I awoke at gun-fire, and summoned Rao Sing to
bring me a cup of cold tea, the night-light was certainly *out*.

Apart from the presence of Blanche at the station, I think
I should have enjoyed soldiering at Allahabad very much ;
most of the officers were very pleasant, and the ladies
were all one could wish ; thus our occasional re-unions at the
band-stand, where the musicians of each corps played in succession, were always gay and well attended.

Daily, then, when Sir Harry was not present, and sometimes
even when he was so, she had always a crowd of the most
foolish fellows at the station hovering around her, in puggerees
or pith helmets and patrol raggies ; and with them she practised the old game of attraction and playing with the hearts of
others without endangering her own.   She was the loadstar,
the cynosure of all the subalterns in quarters, and they seemed
to vie with each other as to who would make the most silly
remark, or pay her the most exaggerated compliment.

Sometimes a revengeful devil seemed to whisper in my
ear :—

"Why not cut in and have a flirtation with her, and then
leave her disdainfully ?"

My old love would have found this perilous work—playing
with edged tools indeed ; and my soul shrank from the idea,
for " there are some hearts so constituted that they must possess *all* or nothing," says Florence Marryat truly.

The Rajah of Chutneypore was often there with a gay and
glittering *suwarrie* of armed followers, and his palkee was
always deposited by the side of that of Lady Calvert, whose
most valuable diamonds were of course alleged by good-
natured people to be his gifts.

Many times there were when I purposely avoided this

promenade, where I found myself on a footing so strange and unnatural with her ; and frequently rode to Mhow, Pertabgur, or Koosee, to kill time and keep out of the way.

At these band-stand promenades I became painfully sensible of one fact : that Henriette Guise was cold in her manner, though kind, but nothing more. She would not be cordial with me. Why was this? Was it caused by the memory of the past, or a fear of what might be again? Was it the whisper about Azuma, or her own engagement with Stapleton —if engagement there was ?

So far as the luckless Hindoo girl was concerned, I felt the inutility of attempting to explain to her how completely I had been the victim of circumstances in that matter ; and yet there were many reasons for which I was anxious to retain the good opinion of Miss Guise.

"It is the old story of 'much ado about nothing,'" said I one day to Dormer ; " and I wish I could assure your cousin that I am actuated only by pure pity—platonism—what you will."

"Platonism !" responded Jack, with one of his most know·ing glances. " *Mon camarade, c'est un mot dangereux !*"

The somewhat uncertain state of our Indian affairs was, I understood, the cause alone that delayed the marriage of Henriette ; but for my part I thought the blasé Colonel remarkably cool in his attentions.

Blanche never permitted me to pass her carriage or palkee without summoning me to her side by a wave of her fan, and engaging in some of her old waggish raillery ; but I thought it terrible to see that this creature, formed in so beautiful a mould, was just as much delighted with the attentions of any of the garrison as with those of the fool she had married ; and she would no doubt have had me on her staff too, but I shrank from *that* position with *her* after the past ; and since that time she was evidently fuller of flirtation, of vanity, and aplomb than ever.

"Cousin Jack," said she one day while the band of the 6th

15

were playing some of the melodies of the *Trovatore*, "don't you think my Harry the handsomest man in the cantonments ?"

"Not at all, Blanche," said Jack Dormer, bluntly ; "he's not so handsome as I am, and not half as much so as Rudkin there."

She flushed at this reply, and turning to Henriette :

"What is in your bottle, dear—Jockey Club or Frangipanni !"

"It is Stapleton's."

"Never mind, cousin ; he won't mind *me* having it. Do you ?" she added, looking up at the Colonel, who approached tugging his whiskers ; and as he made some wellbred reply, she sighed ; for this once pet of mine was a wellskilled artist in all manner of sighing, and she could give plaintive upward glances at him, exactly as she had been wont to do on me and others ; and now she lay languidly back in her handsome palkee, fanning herself and looking like the princess of a fairy tale, while the tawny and nearly naked bearers squatted close by, and stared with wonder at her white beauty.

"Is it true, Colonel," I heard her ask after a pause, "that old " (some one—I did not catch the name) "has gone to Calcutta ?"

"Yes," replied the Colonel in a low voice ; "he has disbanded his zenana, and gone in for morality—a pew in the cathedral and a wife at Chowringhee."

I certainly thought this a very free and easy mode of speaking to a lady ; but there came a day when I ceased to be surprised at anything. Rumour in the cantonments said that the Colonel spent a great deal of his time at Sir Harry's mansion ; that he tiffed there daily ; that the durwan knew pretty well that when the Colonel Sahib once passed in, he would not pass out in a hurry—so the Scotch spinsters averred—till driving time or the hour for the band-stand arrived ; but as there are no doors, and almost every aperture is open in

India, with ignorant native servants hovering everywhere, it is of course a "great country" for gossips, though they are usually not shocked at much.

On this day there was an undefinable something in the manner of Blanche that sorely jarred on my feelings, and as I lifted my sun-helmet and left her, on chancing to look back, the hollow-hearted beauty blew me a kiss from the points of her pretty fingers, and laughingly drew the white silk curtain of the palkee. There was a mockery in this that shocked me.

Repelled thus on one-hand, I was not without perils to face by counter-attraction on the other.

I had been nearly ten days at Allahabad without getting Azuma any employment. I had ventured to ask Blanche's interest; but she only looked at me quizzically and laughed while Henriette rose and left us.

"What the devil am I to do, Jack?" said I one day in great perplexity. "Shall I be saddled with this little Houri for life?"

But Dormer only threw himself back in his bamboo arm-chair and uttered a roar of laughter. He could little foresee the tragic end to this part of my story. On this last evening when I left Blanche and entered my bungalow to dress for mess, I found the girl on her knees, with her back to the setting sun, her face turned eastward as usual, and so greatly absorbed in her devotions as to be unaware of my approach; so I heard her praying to the goddess of destruction—to Kali, who was adored by the Thugs—to Kali, "the dark goddess with the iron mace"—Kali, "the flesh tearer"—that I might be protected amid the perils to come.

"What are those perils?" I asked when she had ended her evening prayer. "Do tell me," I added caressingly.

"Hush, Rao Sing!" she said, glancing hastily round, as if fearful of being overheard, and then shaking her head mournfully; and strange to say, no power of mine and no entreaty could draw the secret from her.

"You have been speaking to the mehm sahibs about me," said she, looking down as if to conceal the angry glitter in her eye ; but I saw her beautiful little bust heaving with suppressed emotion. "I hate them ! O, how I hate them !"

"Why ?" I asked, surprised by this sudden outburst.

"Are they not tyrants and lords rather than wives or loves to those slaves their Feringhee husbands ?"

I was half inclined to agree with her, being rather sore on the subject of the mehm sahibs just then,

"Believe me, Azuma, that I would net give a hair of your head for all the mehm sahibs in Allahabad."

"Will you swear this ?" she asked, with an expression in her black eyes as if seeking to read my soul.

"By what ?" I asked, thinking I was going too far.

"Kali !"

"Yes ; by Kali and jingo to boot."

If this satisfied her and dried her tears, what did it matter to me ? She now took my hands in hers and scanned my face attentively.

"You sorrow; you are grieving for some one. I can read it in your eyes," said she, a little reproachfully.

"Perhaps."

"For some one far, far away in the isle of the Feringhees ?"

"That I do not, be assured, Azuma."

"You regret something, then ?" she persisted.

"We have all something in life to regret ; save one so innocent as you, Azuma."

"Do not talk to me thus," she exclaimed impetuously, for by nature she was full of passion and wild and sudden impulse ; "yet you are my lord and master, and poor little Azuma is your slave, and loves you much—oh, you can never know how much, for you have no caste, and cannot meet her in the other world !"

She now threw her arm round my neck, and clung to me

wildly, imploring me to take her away from Allahabad—away to Calcutta or Bombay.

"This is utter madness, child," said I, becoming quite bewildered. "Why should I take you to either place; and how leave my regiment?"

"Oh, you know not what you say; it must soon leave you," she said in a sad low wailing voice, and sinking again on her knees, covered her face with her hands, and sobbed bitterly.

I was beginning to think her brain was turned, and was compelled to summon O'Regan's wife, as the bugles were already sounding for mess ; but the next day's dawk, or post, let in a terrible light on the secret that preyed on the heart of the Hindoo girl.

CHAPTER XXXIII.

STARTLING NEWS.

As if it were but yesterday, I remember when tidings came to us of the mutiny of Meerut and the revolt of the city and kingdom of Delhi.

Prior to this there had been mutterings of the coming storm at Dumdum, Umballa, and Sealkote, concerning the greased cartridges, which were merely an excuse for revolting, as after that took place the sepoys used them freely enough against us without fear of losing caste. At each of these three dépôts there was of necessity a good deal of preliminary drill to be gone through, to teach the men how to handle the rifle, which had been substituted for the old musket, and how to make up the greased cartridges.

While this tuition was in progress at Dumdum a sepoy of

the 2nd Grenadiers was taunted by a *classie*, or workman in the magazine, with having lost his caste, by biting cartridges greased with the fat of bullocks and cows.

The horrified Brahmin rushed at once to the barracks and spread the report of this among his comrades. The cartridges were by them distinctly seen to be greased. Fast spread the alarm among the Hindoos, and the Mohammedans, fearing that the fat of the pig—the accursed of the Prophet— might be also used, took up the alarm in common with them.

On the Inspector-General of Ordnance admitting that beef fat *was* used in the process, General Birch telegraphed to the three dépôts prohibiting the issue of any cartridges but such as were in a dry state ; still the discontent spread after the cause was removed ; so it is impossible to account for the terrible results, save on the theory of a premeditated plot, a mighty organised conspiracy.

Who, then, was the active agent in this ?

An idea seemed gradually to spread among all the people of Hindostan that, on the centenary of Clive's great victory at Plassy, the *raj*, or rule, of the East India Company would crumble to pieces under the united power of the sepoy troops; and as an emblem of their perfect unanimity, the chupatties, and in some instances the lotus flower, were passed from fort to fort and from cantonment to cantonment, pledging each regiment to stand by the other in the intended massacre of their officers and all Europeans.

Nowhere was the hatred of the latter more deep and strong than in the kingdom of Delhi, where the swaggering insolence of the Mohammedans was never very much concealed ; for the loss of empire inspired the tributary king and all his people with sullen animosity against us ; so, while feeling their weakness, they did but abide their time, though their blood was dreadfully inflamed by the final decision of Lord Dalhousie in 1849 that, on the death of the reigning king—an orthodox Soonee—his grandson should be recognised as heir, apparently upon the sole condition that he retired from the Palace at Delhi and took up his residence at Kootub.

To relate how we came to meddle in the affairs of Delhi, or annexed the kingdom of Oude, whose people are followers of Ali, is foreign from my story ; but the first result of the mischief-makers was the refusal on the part of the 19th Native Infantry, stationed at Berhampore, to use any cartridges at all. In consequence of this, Colonel Mitchell disarmed them in presence of a European regiment and a battery of guns. They were disbanded, and scattered themselves over the upper provinces, spreading discontent wherever they went, and inflaming the people.

Incited by a mutineer called Mungal Pandy, whose name afterwards became the sobriquet for all his comrades, the 34th Native Infantry revolted at Barrackpore, and were turned out of the service, to carry their grievances elsewhere. Matters grew worse and worse. The 7th Oude Irregular Infantry, on the 3rd of May, refused to use their cartridges, and left their parade in a tumultuous mob. By Sir Henry Lawrence, H.M. 32nd Foot and eight pieces of cannon were at once called out, when the sight of the gunners with their lighted matches proved too much for the mutineers, who flung away their rifles and fled in the wildest confusion.

But a more terrible scene was to come at Meerut, initiated by the 3rd Light Cavalry, eighty-five of whom were sentenced to ten years' imprisonment. On this there was a general revolt of all the native troops at the station. Colonel Finnis of the 11th was murdered by his own men ; the jail was forced, and all the felons and miscreants, mutineers and dacoits therein, were released and armed.

Joined by these reckless villains, the whole cantonments and adjacent dwelling-houses were by the mutineers given to the flames, and every European who fell into their hands was barbarously mutilated, then slain. This took place on the 9th of May,—the outbreak occurring at a time when our 6th Dragoon Guards and 60th Rifles were at church ; and before these troops could prevent it, the whole armed force from Meerut set off *en masse* for the city of Delhi, where all the native troops instantly mutinied. A general massacre of all Europeans ensued, with a barbarity truly Oriental, yet baffling all description, and forty-eight young girls—all ladies—were taken into the palace of Delhi, and after being most infamously used for many days by the leaders of the revolt, were stripped and turned into the street, to be destroyed by the Kindalas and lowest ruffians there ; one is said to have been crucified against the wall inside the Cashmere Gate.

On the day I refer to, Lonsdale and I were seated quietly tiffing in the mess-bungalow on chicken-cutlets with tomato sauce, washed down with foaming Bass. All was still in the parade-ground, where the sun was glaring outside, and where the sepoys, in their own lines, were cooking in a fashion peculiar to themselves ; for after bathing—an indispensable ceremony—each man kindles his own fire, around which he draws a circle, within which no man of an inferior caste dare pass. He then kneads his chupatties, of flour, rice, or dahl (peasemeal), and bakes them on an inverted vessel, pours on them melted ghee from a brass pot, and the simple repast is soon concluded.

All was going on with us as usual in Allahabad, when tidings of these terrible events were brought by the dawk boat up the river, and an emotion of utter *insecurity* pervaded the breast of every European there. Officers of all regiments at the station came crowding into our mess-bungalow.

And now the mysterious warnings of Azuma, her grief and her terror for me, showed that among my own native servants dark hints must have reached her ears that were unheard by me, and unknown to O'Regan or his wife, before whom they could freely converse in Hindostance. I had again and again urged her to speak and explain what she knew ; but terror always seemed to fetter her tongue, though of whom it could be I knew not, unless it were the horrible fakir, Kalidasa Ram who, I understood, had been seen more than once in the sepoy lines.

All remained quiet at Allahabad, though every post brought us fresh stories of horror ; now it was at Ferozepore, where H.M. 61st Foot succeeded in cutting up the mutineers and blowing many from the guns ; anon it was at Allyghur, Lucknow, Nuzeerabad, Bareilly, and many other places, whence we heard only of mutiny, murder, destruction of property and life under circumstances so cruel that one might have thought all the fiends of the lower regions had been vomited upward from Hindostan.

Of some premonitory symptoms of the coming storm I became personally cognizant however.

One morning, prior to our taking a ride round the city, I had breakfasted with that most heedless of all heedless fellows, Joe Lonsdale, whose natural flow of spirits even the growing dangers failed to effect ; but the dawk-wallah (or postman) had left at his quarters a number of letters, some of which had not a cheering influence upon that usually lively personage.

He opened them before me, and commented freely upon their contents. He had actually proposed for one of the Armenian " fifty thousand pounders," as he called them, and been refused.

" She is engaged, I now hear, to some devil of a fellow in the opium department," said Joe, while making up a cigarette. " Just my luck always ; but what are the odds, so long as I am happy ! Why did I not propose for the second sister ? I have squeezed her hand more than once under Calvert's table-cloth. I think she'd have had me, and that would still have kept the rupees in the family."

" Meaning you ?"

" Of course ; but it's too late now," he added, going on with the perusal of his correspondence. There was a dun, from the Agra or some other bank, for an instalment on a renewed bill. "A confounded nuisance," he ejaculated, "to have to pay so many rupees per month for what was spent long ago ; it is a burning shame ! What is this ?—an account from a *bunniah* (shopkeeper) in the city for bitter beer, champagne, and cheroots ; from another for glazed boots, white kids, and perfumes, with Gazepore rose-water ; another for ices, soda-and-brandy, a silver-mounted hookah ; another for jewellery for a lady."

"Who is she ?" I asked ; "the Armenian ?"

"No ; a little Eurasian girl I meet at the band-stand sometimes."

"Have you cash to settle all these, Joe ?"

"By no means."

"What is the total ?"

"I haven't the heart to inquire ; but if this row with the Pandies goes on, I shall pay them all off with a roll on the drum. A rising here is just the thing for me, Rudkin, in the present state of my exchequer, if my book fails on the Bangalore races."

"For Heaven's sake, Joe, don't talk so thoughtlessly," said I ; "the faces of the married men and of their wives are sad to contemplate in their gnawing anxiety."

"Then thank Heaven you have not a wife, or any little responsibilities either."

I was silent—when I thought of the two beautiful cousins, and how nearly I had been becoming the spouse of each in succession.

"I think I shall order some more of everything from these niggers ; they are becoming very importunate now, and moreover they decline to take the Company's paper."

"Which I am certain bodes evil."

"How ?"

"By showing that they have no faith in the stability of our rule."

"Perhaps ; but when you can't pay, a fresh order imparts commercial confidence ; so I'll have some more brandy, ices, wine, and cheroots; promise them all their balances at an early day, and to each wind up with something about the state of the thermometer and prospect of the indigo crop. Qui hy !" he added, shouting for his native servant ; " order the horses round—and now, Rudkin, we shall start for the bazaar."

We rode into the city, nine-tenths of the native houses of which consist of mud superstructures upon the remains of ancient splendour, the ruins of the days of the great Ackbar ; the only fine buildings in the place being the royal palace, now our government house, and the Serai and mausoleums of the Sultan Koshru and his mother. As we rode through the streets I was distinctly sensible of a lowering, obstinate, and sullen expression in the faces of nearly every man we passed ; and also, that though an edict had been issued prohibiting all who were not in the service from carrying or wearing arms in public, it seemed to be but partially obeyed, if at all, as every able-bodied passenger, whether Hindoo or Mohammedan, was accoutred with a musket, matchlock, and spear ; many had shields slung on their backs, and many had tulwars and khunjurs (*i.e.* swords and daggers), with pistols in their belt ; and all this display seemed indicative of approaching trouble.

If more evidence were wanting, we found it in the bazaar, where Lonsdale went to distribute his orders, and restore confidence in his creditors by running deeper in their debt. We perceived the greatest excitement prevailing there. Travelling fakirs had brought in exaggerated stories, which they exultingly related, of the outbreaks at Nowgong and the massacre at Jhansi, where fifty-five hapless Europeans, including ladies and children, were besieged in a little star-fort, were ultimately starved into surrendering, and were then destroyed by the native cavalry, who tied them in two rows, separating the men from the women. The former were first slaughtered before their wives and their children who clutched their mother's skirts, in which they buried their little frightened faces ; and then all were put to death by the sword and pistol. The sole difference between these dreadful murders and those which had been, or were being, enacted elsewhere was, that the unfortunate ladies were neither stripped nor subjected to any indignity. The first victim who was cut down was Captain Burgess, whose elbows were tied behind his back, and he was permitted to have a Prayer-book in his hands.

The relation of these things, which were told in a very scared manner and with bated breath by Peeroo Mull, the opulent native banker, made our blood boil to fever heat, and even Joe Lonsdale looked about the bazaar, as if he would like to have emptied his revolver (we never went abroad without one now) on some of the " niggers," who were swaggering with arms, in defiance of the issued order.

Although in more than one instance an itinerant fakir had received a hundred lashes on his meagre back at the triangles for denouncing war against us, outside the bazaar we came suddenly on one of these bigoted knaves, who was perched between the humps of a dromedary, preaching to a fast-gathering crowd ; and though we lingered a few minutes to observe and listen, he neither lowered his voice nor ceased his harangue ; yet he must have been aware that I, at least, knew the language in which he spoke, for this orator was no other than Kalidasa Ram, looking more lean and attenuated, his ribs seeming to start through his brown skin, more than ever smeared with ashes and ghee, and with the huge eye of Siva painted on his forehead, and with a sword and dagger stuck in his sole garment, a narrow and filthy cummerbund.

The listening crowd were Hindoos and Mohammedans, and, though hating and despising each other, they had one sympathy in common—their hatred of us.

Vishnu the Preserver had appeared, he told them, to several Brahmin sepoys in a dream at the same moment, though these sepoys were hundreds of leagues apart; and the four-armed god had told them that the days of the Ghora-logue (white people) were numbered; that the *raj* (rule) of the pale beasts would soon be over, and their curry-faced women must become the slaves and playthings of their conquerors. He assured the Mohammedans that Allah would bless any attempt they made to throw off the yoke of the infidel Feringhees, whose queen wished to make Christians of all Hindostan by the destruction of caste. Jan Bool, he continued, while he ground his teeth, and his eyes flashed with a glare like that of insanity, shall rend his raiment and cast ashes on his head; and the Koompanie, with their tea-trade and their ships, shall pass away, for the hundredth year had come. Then again should the widows of the Hindoo perform the Suttee and, the Thugs offer lives to Kali, their gods would be no longer called mere idols of brass and stone; no longer would their bread be polluted with the bone-dust of the sacred cow or the salt with its blood; neither should the sepoys of any creed be compelled to defile themselves by touching cartridges greased with the fat of the unclean pig.

Among the listening crowd, who were getting excited, I saw my rascal Rao Sing, with Jack Dormer's kitmutgar, Khoda Bux; and as "Dean! Dean!" (Faith! Faith!) began to be muttered on all sides, Lonsdale and I, deeming that we were somewhat in peril, and by our presence might provoke an outbreak, quitted and rode back to the cantonments to report what we had heard and seen.

On entering the mess-bungalow, we found a strong muster of officers belonging to the 6th, the staff, and our corps, who had invited them to "tiffin," as luncheon is always called in India.

"When are these horrors to end?" exclaimed our colonel, when we told him what Peeroo Mull had related of the dreadful events at Nowgong and Jhansi. "Will your Pandies here be staunch, do you think?" he asked the colonel of the 6th Native Infantry.

"As they have not yet mutinied, I think it scarcely fair to apply that sobriquet to them," replied the other stiffly. "I can swear by them. Remember the scene of yesterday morning; it was one which would not have disgraced the earlier days of the French Revolution."

What he referred to has now become a matter of history. On hearing that a suspicion of their loyalty was entertained by the Europeans at the station, they went to their officers in a body, and with tears in their eyes—crocodile tears they proved in the sequel—besought them to have faith in their honour. They then fraternized in the most brotherly manner; perfect confidence was restored; the regiment even offered to march against Delhi, and it was almost believed that had any mutineers approached us they would have been attacked by the 6th.

"I am glad to hear you are so confident, colonel," said I, "for we Europeans are but a handful; and if I thought all would remain quiet in Allahabad, I'd volunteer for service against the Pandies elsewhere."

"And so would I—and I—and I," said Dormer and others.

"We require every man here that we have," responded the colonel; "but I cannot help thinking that, notwithstanding the melodramatic scene of yesterday, those fellows of the 6th are doubtful. Many have passed me without saluting, and some have dared to make insulting remarks when Miss Guise and other ladies have passed them."

"There are a few black sheep everywhere," remarked Captain Birch; "but I am sure we may trust the battalion. My opinion of Indians is, that those in whom you put trust will be worthy of it; but those in whom you have no confidence hold themselves justified in deceiving you."

"My subahdar major," resumed the colonel of the 6th emphatically, "has sworn on the head of a Brahmin Jemidar—the most sacred oath a Hindoo can take—that he will answer for the faith of my entire battalion."

"We are wise, at all events, to spend so much of our time in revolver practice," said Lonsdale; "besides, I can't help thinking that His Highness of Chutneypore is up to some secret game."

"And so do I," added Dormer; "he was a daily dangler about Calvert's house, and now he never even enters the cantonment, though my cousin Blanche has more than once sent for him."

Stapleton, who was present and had not yet spoken, smiled quietly in his old disdainful way, and gave the inevitable tug to his long fair moustache and whiskers, which were blended together.

CHAPTER XXXIV.

A TERRIBLE REVELATION.

NOTWITHSTANDING the confident assertions of the colonel and officers of the sepoy regiment, we felt that we were all as it were on the brink of a volcano.

It is impossible to describe the agony of the *suspense* endured at this time by the Europeans in such stations as Allahabad, where as yet the native troops had *not* revolted, but still might rise at any favourable or capricious moment. No man could reckon upon the events of an hour ; no man laid his head on the pillow at night with the certainty that he would be a live man in the morning ; and in the morning none rose without a dread that we might never see the sun set ; for such was the fate of many : and worst of all were the anxieties of those who had wives and helpless little ones ; for all over India, even in those places which were apparently quiet, the sepoys of the Infantry and the sowars of the Light Cavalry were planning and arranging the most dreadful schemes to murder each other's officers, to seize on their wives and daughters, to make spoil of everything, and yet remain true " to their salt," as the treacherous wretches phrased it.

Instead of revolting in detail, had all India done so at once —as India yet may do, when the natives learn their own power—the vast peninsula must have been lost to us for a time, if not for ever.

How soon might the atrocities of Meerut, Delhi, Jhansi, and many other places, be enacted in those as yet quiet cantonments at Allahabad, was the surmise of us all. How soon might those we loved best on earth be stretched lifeless on the ground, or be barbarously mutilated e e they were hacked to piece. by those demons of Hindoos and Mohammedans, though the former had sworn to be true to us over the waters of the Ganges, and the latter on the Koran ! Parents, if they were to be destroyed, pondered on what might be the future fate of their helpless children, though, with a keen refinement of cruelty, these were usually destroyed first by the mutineers under the eyes of their parents, and the wife was subjected to every barbarity before the destruction of her husband.

In the evening of that day on which I had been in the city I did not go to mess, as Calvert had invited me to a male supper party, and to see a match at billiards played by Stapleton and Dormer, on which some heavy bets were pending. The heat was now something awful, so I had my charpoy removed into the verandah, and, stretching myself on it, I gradually dozed off to sleep, despite the boredom of mosquitoes, the fear lest a Brahminee cobra or some such reptile might come wriggling along the floor, or a huge centipede fall flop on my face from the straw roof of the edifice I had once pictured myself sharing with Blanche Bingham. I was beginning to hate India now and everything therein ; from the Governor-General down to Rao Sing, who, with his white turban, black-glowing eyes, brown face, and white grinning teeth, seemed always so provokingly cool and comfortable that I felt inclined to throw something at his head.

The occasional cantonment sounds, the hourly clang of the little gongs or ghurries, the cry of " All's well !" from our sentries passing from post to post, and dying away in the distance as darkness fell and the stars came out, the sepoy challenge " Hookam durr ?" and the answer " Perhind " (similar to our " Who comes there ?" and the reply, " Friend !"), alike failed to disturb me ; but I had a strange dream of Blanche, of whom I fancied myself in pursuit along an unknown path, in some far and foreign country ; but she always contrived to elude me, till once, just when about to overtake her, I thought a faintness came upon me, and then she drew my head caressingly upon her breast.

As I looked up lovingly upon her, her eyes of golden hazel

16

seemed to darken more and more, till her face became a strange mingled likeness of Henriette Guise and Azuma the Hindoo girl. I started and awoke, to find my head actually supported by the little brown arm of the latter ; and as I started up to keep my appointment with Calvert, she laid her finger on her mouth, and then glanced nervously around her.

"Sahib," she whispered, " I must speak now : if you go forth to-night, go armed."

"I am never otherwise, Azuma."

"But great danger is very near you," she whispered earnestly.

"Very probably; but what is this danger? Are the sepoys of the 6th—the Gowan-ka-Pultan—not true to their salt ?"

She shook her pretty little head mournfully.

"Danger is nearer you than them, and than you think."

Blanche's perfidy had made me very distrustful of every one, but I asked :

"What *do* you mean by these frequent hints and innuendoes of coming peril to me? Whence or from whom is it to come? Do speak, Azuma," I added caressingly.

"You do not know," she whispered, " how little the sepoys here are to be trusted, and with what consummate treachery they can hide the purpose they have in hand. Oh that you were safe beyond the Mahratta ditch !   It would matter little then what becomes of Azuma !"

How piquante and winning the little creature looked as she said this in her most touching manner !

"You have heard something, girl, that I know not, and that my friends know nothing of. What is this terrible secret that preys upon your mind ?"

But that I was never fated to learn ; her lips parted, and she was about to speak, when a face—the face, I felt certain, of Rao Sing, my kitmutgar—appeared within the green jalousie of a window overlooking the verandah. I could see the white teeth and eyeballs glistening between the spars, and the girl, fearing no doubt that she had been overheard, sprang from my side and disappeared. I entered my room hurriedly, with the intention of punishing the eavesdropper ; but Rao Sing—if he it was—had levanted by a window that was open on the other side.

Perplexed and annoyed by the communication but half made, and by the interruption, or watching, that savoured of both jealousy and treachery, I was nevertheless compelled to keep my appointment ; and taking my sword and revolver, passed along the sepoy lines, left the cantonments, and took my way to the house of Sir Harry Calvert, whom I found with several officers in the billiard-room, Birch, Innes, and others from the fort, smoking, laughing, and chatting gaily ; most of them were in their shirt-sleeves.

Stapleton, who had just left the ladies in the drawing-room, was in full uniform, which he proceeded to doff that he might play with greater ease ; and tossing his sash and gold-embroidered shoulder-belt with its cartridge-box to Sir Harry's kitmutgar, desired him to take it away.

Now it chanced that this servant was quite a new hand, a native belonging to a very wild race, the Kholees, who are often preferred, especially in Goojerat, for the service of the police, or as porters to gentlemen's houses. He was a very ignorant fellow, and consequently had rather hazy ideas of the relation existing between the Colonel and Miss Guise, as an Oriental has no conception whatever of the true position of a Christian woman—more than all, that of an English lady—as maid, wife, or widow ; so, in a blundering way, he took the sash and pouch-belt to her room, and there left them.

Through this mistake there occurred a discovery that led to some very painful events ; and others that occurred subsequently have quite blotted from my mind the playing of Stapleton and Jack Dormer, the bets that were made, and the number of gold mohurs and rupees that changed hands on the occasion as the night wore on.

Many had left the house, but a protracted game ensued between Sir Harry Calvert and Lonsdale, Dormer acting as marker. I had promised to wait for the two last named, that we might walk to our quarters together; and as the billiard-room had become oppressively hot, I wandered into the garden, pondering in the cool starlight on the peculiarity of my position—the guest of Blanche's husband, and longing to be far from Allahabad and at any other station in India, even those now desolated by mutiny and massacre. How strange it all seemed! and then thoughts that I could not thrust aside pressed themselves upon me.

I heard the languid, drawling voice of Calvert, the rollicking tones of Lonsdale and of others chatting gaily in the billiard-room, the tall windows of which came down to the floor of the verandah, and as the *tattys* or screens of scented grass matting were drawn aside, long bright flakes of steady light fell brightly athwart the flowery parterres. I could hear the click of the billiard balls, and the flap occasionally of the great birds' wings on the roof as these noises roused them; but now a very different sound stole out upon the soft air of the Indian night from other windows.

It was the voice of Henriette Guise, accompanying herself at the piano, as she sang one of those low and plaintive lyrics which I had often heard her perform at Thorsgill Hall. All the past came upon me, summoned by her sweetly modulated and familiar voice, and memory went back to the constraint and peculiarity of our farewell on the morning of her departure for Brighton, the tremor in her tones, the quiver of her lips, and the perplexing expression of her very beautiful eyes.

"Bah!" thought I bitterly; "as the fiancée of Colonel Stapleton she must have got over all that humbug now! The world is only a huge teetotum after all."

She seemed to be alone; the song was one she had often sung to *me* before Blanche came. Could she be thinking of that vanished time? Her voice gradually died away, but the subdued tinkling of the piano continued in a way that suggested she had become sunk in thought, and that the pretty white fingers, which had lingered in mine on that eventful evening in the library oriel, were wandering over the keys mechanically.

At last I heard the lid of the instrument closed, and then her shadow slowly passed the white silk window-curtains, as if she was retiring for the night ; but, lost in thought, I know not how long I lingered in the garden-seat on which I had cast myself, under a shady russa tree, the spreading foliage of which was covered with crimson and yellow flowers in their fullest bloom.

The players were still deep in their game, and I thought of joining them, when suddenly I heard the sound of voices near me, talking and laughing, but in subdued tones : they were those of Blanche and Stapleton, who I thought had gone to the cantonments long ago.

They were on the other side of one of those prickly-pear hedges which intersected the spacious garden in some places, and they seemed to be promenading to and fro.

" Oh Jocelyn," said she, " something startling is about to happen !"

" Startling, dear Blanche ?"

" Yes," she replied, and in fancy I could see her old bright smile, or it might be her pleading expression, playing about her face.

" What is it ? Speak !" said Stapleton impatiently.

" Poor Harry has to leave this, to inspect a troop of Horse Artillery."

" Where does the troop lie ?"

" At Chutneypore."

" Sorry it isn't the Cove of Cork, which is rather farther off. But we must be careful, Blanche ; in India, these silk curtains and tattys of woven grass, which do duty for doors and windows, and those swarms of native servants who are always gliding about stealthily and noiselessly with their bare feet, keen eyes, and open ears, surprising people in the most innocent acts of playfulness, and supposing there must be guilt in everything, may all serve to teach us caution."

"I most fear Henriette, with her quiet earnest eyes."

An expression of impatience escaped Stapleton, who added, "The dew is damp on that beautiful hair of yours ; we must go indoors."

But they lingered, however. Such were the terms on which they were. Oh, it was too terrible ! Fairer than a fairy, the old General was fond of calling her ; but he could little con- ceive that she was falser than a fiend. I remained as if para- lysed, and was compelled to hear more of this mingled flirta- tion and banter, and thereby found a key to much that had puzzled me in the past time. I disdained to eavesdrop, yet I, of all men, feared to stir lest my discovery should become known to them, and so perhaps overwhelm her with mortifi- cation and fear.

Keen observers though they were, as I have elsewhere said, Mesdames Poplin and Jellipot at Thorsgill Hall had not de- tected anything of this, though they seemed to know that Henriette Guise "was breaking her poor heart about that conceited Captain Rudkin."

She had deluded me, and now she was yet more cruelly deluding another, who, to do him justice, loved her only too well. Where was all this to end ? Oh for the old duelling days, thought I, and a brace of pistols at ten paces !

" A lovely hand yours is indeed, Blanche," he said in a low voice.

" Take care or I shall lose my marriage ring !"

" It certainly hangs loosely on your pretty finger."

Even then and there he could not repress his constitutional habit of sneering quietly.

"I wish Captain Rudkin had not come here up-country," said Blanche after a pause.

" Why ?"

" You know that I did use him ill."

" He seems to have deuced soon consoled himself, if report says true. Never mind Rudkin ; your flirtation with him I always laughed at ; but now, were it not for this accursed tie, which binds you to another——"

" You might have prevented its formation had you chosen—and—and——"

"What ?"

" You did not."

His reply was inaudible ; but he added,

" Were you free to-morrow, I would marry you, Blanche, without a month's delay."

" Easily said, when you know I am not likely to be—free !" she replied bitterly, as they passed indoors.

And this was the woman I had so loved, and for whom I had sacrificed another ! The cure was complete now, and yet it filled me with honest sorrow.

I sat for a time like one in a dream, and scarcely was able to realize the truth of what I had heard. The lights still streamed out from the windows of the billiard-room, and then I heard again the click of the balls and the voices of the players. " The woman who deliberates is lost," says Addison ; but here was a heartless flirt who never deliberated at all. But it seems impossible to account for the capricious fancies of some women, or the kind of men they will love. Here was Stapleton, selfish, cold, blandly insincere, cautious, and *blasé*, loved to all appearance beyond Calvert, who, though somewhat *blasé*, too, was generous, open, gallant, tender, and true to her ; and loved beyond me, who would have faced a battery of guns for her.

Something like a malediction escaped me, and, fearing they might return, I quitted the garden, and without waiting for Dormer or Lonsdale, hurried home to the cantonments, feeling sick at heart and crushed in spirit.

Had these two forgotten the mine beneath our feet—the volcano to which I have referred ?

Alas, it seemed so.

CHAPTER XXXV.

THE SLEEP OF AZUMA.

ANOTHER great shock awaited me ; but let me not anticipate. At the door of my bungalow, I was surprised to see my kit-mutgar, Rao Sing, hovering about.

"Waiting for captain sahib," said he, salaaming.

" Bring some brandy-pawnee and cigars into the verandah, place them on the tea-poy, and then you may leave me. Who the deuce is that on the sofa ?" I asked, on seeing by the star-light a white figure lying thereon at full length.

He told me it was Azuma ; that she had waited long in my outer room to see me, but was now sound asleep ; and begged me not to disturb her, as she had seemed very weary. All this did not seem strange, though her presence there was un-usual. Doubtless the poor girl had some fresh warning to give me of impending danger before retiring for the night.

Seating myself in the cool verandah, with the brandy-and-water beside me on the tea-poy, or little table, I lay back in my cane easy-chair, and fixing my eyes on the stars, gave way to reflections, which were only disturbed by hearing Dormer, with Joe Lonsdale, stumbling into the next bungalow, the latter hiccuping a good deal, and saying,

" Wish I had a couple of cousins here like you, Jack ! She *is* a stunning girl, though in a quiet way, Miss Guise ; I pre-fer her, by Jove ! to Lady Calvert, who carries too much sail for me. Horrid chinsurahs ; and I've been smoking like a factory chimney."

Even heedless Joe was not so short-sighted as I had been. How ingenious we are at self-torture, and how apt to muse on corroding thoughts ; to feed, as it were on our own hearts ! I had now the mortifying knowledge and conviction that she had never loved me at all, but had systematically and afore-thought come between Henriette and me, unless it were the case that "a woman who really loves the love of the time being will never admit, even to herself, that she has ever loved any one else."

And for this creature, who had seemed as bright as a sun-beam, pure as the snow that has newly fallen on the waving branch—this fruit of the Dead Sea, so beautiful to the eye, yet bitter to the taste—I had forsaken Henriette without a word of explanation. I had been *lured* away from her, and deliberately taught to treasure another in my inner heart ; another, the touch of whose hand and the glance of whose eye were both magnetic to me ; under whose window at the old hall I had often watched when all were abed—watched as a pilgrim might the light of his altar, as little Azuma did the idols of her temple.

When I recalled all the sweet intercourse of the past, all the tenderness I had lavished upon her, all our delicious little speeches and avowals of mutual regard, I was lost in wonder at the baseness of such a change as this.

Report said that Stapleton was engaged to Henriette Guise. I dared not inform the girl of all I knew ; yet how could I permit her to sacrifice herself to one so worthless ?

All thought of going to bed had left me, as I knew that in an hour or so the morning bugles would sound for parade. "Remembering the wondrous adaptability of the human heart, what matters the past ?" asks a writer. "Hearts are not like roses—that die, having once withered. No, rather, like the branch from which the flowers spring, they have power, when aided by the sunshine, to put forth fresh buds, so long as the parent tree lasts."

How full the world seemed of cross-purposes, thought I, while glancing at the recumbent figure of Azuma as the day-light came in, as it always does in the tropics, quickly, and remembering that the impulsive yet gentle Hindoo worshipped me as if I were a superior being. When I had last looked back, on leaving her on the preceding evening, I had seen her hands clasped in prayer—a prayer that was heard by no earthly ear—with her eyes full of tears, and I knew that these and the invocation were alike for me.

She was a singular contrast to Blanche Bingham certainly; but still there was a glorious beauty in her dark eyes, and much of child-like prettiness or subtlety of grace in all her little ways. Brilliant was her smile, with all its Indian warmth of expression. Charming indeed was all her beauty in its way, though I knew it would be so evanescent, that at forty she would be quite an old woman—perhaps a grandmother.

She slept so soundly that even the deep sullen boom of the morning gun, as it pealed over the sleeping cantonments, failed to make her stir or give the slightest start.

Her figure seemed graceful; yet there was a rigid kind of angularity in it that began to impress me with surprise. I tossed aside the end of my cigar and, entering the bungalow, lifted the *doopatta*, or large muslin veil, which completely enveloped her.

Horror! The poor girl had been murdered—most brutally murdered; and the "sound sleep," of which the slimy reptile Rao Sing had spoken, was the endless slumber of death.

She was drenched in blood, and all the floor below the cane sofa on which she lay was one large pool of the same crimson tint, and amid it lay a *khunjar*, or native dagger, which I knew belonged to Rao Sing, and which had been twice plunged in her heart, consequently no cry could have escaped her.

All her ornaments of which she was so fond—the *kutchi-kuppi* or gold pins of her silky hair, her gold *varaumalai* necklace, at which hung a row of pagoda coins, her ear-rings, and her *manili koppu* or bangles that were round her slender ankles—had all been rent from her with savage violence, after death, as our doctor, Gargill, who was promptly summoned, informed me; and by whom—whom could I suspect but Rao Sing, whom I had detected eavesdropping? His must have been the white teeth and eyeballs I had seen glistening through the green jalousies; he must have been the object of the poor girl's terror, and his must have been the hand that sealed her lips by death, lest she might reveal some secret—some terrible Indian plot which she had discovered.

The fellow had artfully enough disposed her body on the sofa, as if asleep, to deceive me, and with his spoil, including many gold mohurs, or sixteen rupee pieces, of mine, had quietly gone over to the sepoy lines, where all trace of him was lost and sure concealment given him ; for, as I have else-where mentioned, there are apartments in the dwellings of the native soldiers from which even the officer of the day is ex-cluded.

This unexpected horror drew me from my own corroding thoughts, from sorrow for and mortification at, the conduct of Lady Calvert. I could think quietly of her as Lady Calvert *now*, and I pondered sadly over the regard this impulsive Oriental girl had displayed for myself—a regard excited only by a little kindness and compassion.

Poor Azuma ! it was truly in an evil hour she linked her destiny, even for a month, with mine. I knew that all the love of this simple heart was lavished without return on me, and her death, and more th n all, the mode of it, filled me with grief and fury. It was, 1 thought, terribly significant that our lotus-eating life in Allahabad was at an end.

I meant to inter her remains, though most of the Hindoos either burn their dead or throw them into the Ganges or its tributaries. The funeral piles of the rich are mingled with sandal wood and fed by aromatic oils, while the poor are con-sumed with humble faggots. But my intentions were frus-trated by a noisy crowd of the 6th Bengal Infantry, led by Kalidasa Ram, who came to my bungalow when I was absent and carried her away for cremation in rear of the sepoy lines.

I offered fifty gold mohurs for the murderer's apprehension, but did so in vain ; for now " great events were on the gale,"

and the assassination of this unfortunate girl was only a
prelude to the greater horrors that were to ensue among us.

But the burning of the poor girl's remains, if it was a source
of intense repugnance to me, was no less so to honest Dan
O'Regan, a pious Catholic, who had said all the prayers for
the dead on his knees by the side of the " poor haythen cray-
thur," as he called her, " who was so sinless and so simple."

CHAPTER XXXVI.

STAPLETON'S CARTRIDGE-BOX.

As I afterwards learned, I was not the only one in the cantonments of Allahabad who passed a sleepless night.

After a laughing time of it with Jacky Appleton, a lively and
amusing girl, and marvelling much *where* her cousin Blanche
was, Henriette Guise had retired to her room, where, to her
surprise, and perhaps amusement, she found Stapleton's belt
and cartridge-box lying on her bed. She was puzzled to know
how they came to be there, and on expressing something of
this to her ayah, the latter proposed to put them out of the
room.

"It is some joke of the Colonel's, or more probably some
mistake," said Henriette with a smile that was not perhaps
altogether one of brightness; "but I suppose the day is
coming when I must get used to seeing such things about
me."

Seated before her mirror and lost in thought, or reflections
engendered by the song she had been singing to herself,
Henriette had her long black hair let down and brushed out
by the quick tawny fingers of the ayah ; then it was coiled up

for the night ; she was disrobed, and lay down on perhaps rather than *in* her bed, the nights were so warm now ; the lamp was adjusted, the mosquito curtains drawn, and then the ayah withdrew.

The song she had sung was still lingering in the ears and ·on the lips of Henriette, till suddenly she said to herself,

"Why think of it or of those days *now* ?　Let me put such thoughts aside and for ever ; it should be so."

Then as if to aid her to do this—whatever the memories were that she referred to—she looked from time to time at the gay staff-belt with its velvet and gold embroidered cartridge-box, and suddenly inspired by one of those impulses which are quite unaccountable, she slipped from her bed and took them in her hands.　As she did so the flap of the box unclosed, and instead of cartridges, which one might have expected to find there in such perilous times, there fell out a packet of letters and notes.

At that moment she caught sight of her own figure reflected in the tall pier-glass, looking so pure and pale in her laced and frilled night dress, her dark braided tresses and dark eyes, and her little "white feet glancing bare," that with something of a coquettish smile she thought, "Well, I am surely pretty ;" but another would have said she was simply lovely.

She then proceeded to gather up the Colonel's letters for the purpose of replacing them.　Many were open or without envelopes ; and to a girl of her well-bred mind and delicate nature, the idea of reading any of these documents would never have occurred ; but while arranging them she suddenly perceived that they were all in her cousin Blanche's handwriting, and were addressed—though without signatures—to Colonel Stapleton.

A hidden evil, the extent and nature of which she could not at first fathom, a cold foreboding of coming shame and sorrow, fell upon her shrinking and sensitive heart, and she sank for a moment on her knees, as many of the well-known " trifles light as air " began to take tangible shapes for her torment now.

" It is wrong even to think of reading one of them," she murmured ; " and yet—and yet, what secrets may be here !'"

In all there were twelve. Twelve ! Evidently they were not invitations, but pretty long epistles ; so what could they be about ? And how did these two come to correspond ? She was all unaware of this excessive intimacy. Tremblingly lest she might be tempted, she proceeded to replace them one by one in the strange and unusual receptacle from which they had dropped, and as she did so she could perceive, by the postmarks on those which still had envelopes, dates and names of places far apart, some in England and some in India.

What mystery was here ? Alas, it was soon to be solved.

As she took up the last, which had accidentally opened, her startled eyes saw that it commenced with terms of affection which no friendship could warrant. In great horror and dismay she pushed back the tresses from her white temples, as if seeking coolness, air, and then said resolutely aloud,

" I shall discover what is hidden here ; the temptation put before me is too great, too terrible, for the human heart to resist."

Then, with eyes swimming and almost blinded by tears, she read through the last of the fatal letters from Blanche, though every word stabbed her sensitive bosom with pain, even as a bayonet would have done ; and from it she learned but too surely and too sadly, the terms that existed between her flirting kinswoman and her intended, even before she came to Thorsgill Hall, so true it is that the treachery of the human heart is as boundless as the sea. She now remembered Stapleton's undisguised irritation at the episode of the storm, the wild night-ride that ended at Stoke Priory, and a hundred other things, that seemed either harmless or inexplicable, were plain enough now " as proofs of Holy Writ."

She threw herself on her bed and buried her sweet pale face in the pillow, lest the heavy sobs that convulsed her white shoulders and bosom might be overheard through the frail walls of the Indian house. Suddenly she started up and stood erect, her dark eyes flashing through their tears and her hands clenched tightly.

"She cruelly deceived poor Rudkin," she muttered; "so was she to be trusted in future? Has she made a shipwreck of his life, as she has made of mine? Yet I in turn deceived Stapleton, whom I accepted out of mere pique, when he—an insult !—proposed to me out of mere ennui, or more probably to cloak this cruel intrigue. What an escape I have had! A little time and this traitor, whom I was schooling myself to love, would have been my husband. O my God, what a hollow world this is !"

After a time an emotion of thankfulness blended with her sorrow and disgust ; then, as her indignation grew less, she became more composed, and throwing on a loose robe, she unlocked her escritoire, a handsome white-ivory box inlaid with Bombay silver work. With hasty and trembling fingers she drew off her betrothal ring, selected from among her jewellery some gifts of Stapleton's, bestowed upon her at Calcutta and Allahabad, and making up these and the letters too in *one* packet, she addressed it to Colonel Stapleton, and sealed it with a seal which she well knew he would recognise as her family crest, a coroneted swan ; and filled the while with wonder that Stapleton could be so madly careless of her erring cousin's honour—to say nothing of his own—as to make such a place as his cartridge-box the receptacle for their secrets, she placed the packet therein, and carefully closed the flap over it.

On her bed she lay sleepless in the silence of the night, thinking bitterly, at times madly, of the shame that might come upon Blanche, whom she really loved so much ; on the

insult to which she herself had been subjected ; of the lover
she had lost in me ; of her regard, such as it was, bestowed
on Stapleton, and by him despised ! And she could not but
think with pity of one who was ignorant of this terrible secret,
the suave, bland, good-looking fellow, with the parted hair, a
row of teeth like ivory, mild blue eyes, and fly-away whiskers,
who after sowing his wild oats while in the Guards, and spend-
ing a fortune on the danseuse of Lonsdale's letter, was content
now to soldier in earnest, and to broil as a domestic Bene-
dick in India, for the sake of the little flirt who had married
him solely for his baronetcy.

Yet Stapleton might not have been at first to blame in this
black business ; for Blanche, she knew, by her coquetry of
manner had a way of luring or insensibly compelling men to
make love to her.

" How true are one's first instincts !" she said.   In the
early days of our acquaintance I mistrusted, even disliked,
Stapleton ; and now—I hate him !"

Fortunately she did not feel in all this that any cherished idol
was shattered, or that the great passion of her life was crushed;
no light had gone out of it ; a flood of light had rather been
cast upon it.   But she did loathe herself for having trusted
Stapleton, and felt that their mock engagement—more than
ever a mockery now—had degraded her in her own eyes.

"Perhaps I shall get over all this in time," she thought; "but
oh, what am I to do to save Blanche ?   Kind Heaven, inspire
me, for the worse may be yet to come !"

Imploringly the dark eyes of the girl looked upward, beyond the ceiling where the dark punkah hung motionless and
still in the hot breathless night, for doubtless the treacherous
wallah was in the sepoy lines hatching mischief ; but she
knew that far beyond that ceiling was the blue starry sky, and
that the eyes of God were on her.

" Rudkin deserted me," she continued to mutter, "and
Blanche and Stapleton have both deceived me.   In whom
can I trust ?"

A gulf must for ever yawn between her past and future life; and with all her hair thrown back, and with hands placed upon her throbbing temples, she tried to look calmly at the bitter empty years that were to come—years in which she must mistrust every one—the arid desert she might have to journey over alone—all alone !

She felt it alike impossible to remain in Allahabad the guest of her cousin, and to leave her to this great peril by returning instantly, as she felt inclined to do, to her family at Calcutta ; and in her gentle heart she felt no genuine indignation at Blanche, but only terror and pity for her, so loved, so petted and admired.

Her night-lamp had gone out ; she was in darkness now, and she lay there praying, talking to herself, weeping with eyes wide open, and seeing, as one might in a dream, the red fire-flies flashing about outside the green closed jalousies, till the distant boom of the morning gun announced that day was at hand, and the hot and airless Indian night had passed away.

By this time she was almost in a fever with bitter thought ; but she could little dream that I shared her secret, and that I too, after a sleepless night, started at the boom of the same morning gun.

When I heard of all this affair of the cartridge-box afterwards, I cursed Stapleton in my heart. Yet why and wherefore? He was vain and weak, and this brilliant but artful and winning creature had, as the phrase is, " flung herself at him," as she had done at me, at Sir Harry Calvert, and others probably ; so he had yielded to the snare, for doubtless " the woman had tempted," as long ago in Eden.

When the usual time for rising—an early hour in India—came, Henriette was unable to leave her bed, and, in short, was very feverish and seriously indisposed. With all her usual impulsive manner and display of affection, Blanche kissed her and hung about her, doing various little kind offices ; but the tears which Henriette could with difficulty restrain, her coldness of manner and curt yet sad replies, her hard-set mouth and eyes, caused considerable perplexity to the little *intriguante*, who was far from guessing the cause even when Sir Harry knocked on the doorpost and said laughingly :

"Are Stapleton's pouch and belt in Miss Guise's room, Blanche ?"

"Yes, Harry; how on earth came they to be here ?" she replied, changing colour visibly, yet without a suspicion that anything was known.

"Oh, it seems that his new kitmutgar, a Kholee idiot, left it here last night. Stapleton requires them instantly, as he is field-officer of the day. I shall take them—thanks," he added, as Blanche handed out the required accoutrement. " By-by, darling," said Sir Harry, little knowing what he held in his hands ; " I too am going to parade—an awful bore !"

"Without kissing me once—fie, Harry !" said she, with one of her prettiest pouts, as she ran her child-like fingers through his long fair whiskers.

"And now I am off like a bird," said the tall and good-looking ex-Guardsman, as he stooped, kissed the little sharer of his dignities, and clattered away with his sword and spurs to join his friend Stapleton.

The caresses, the condolence, even the presence of Blanche, were intolerable to her cousin, who became inspired by an intense longing to get away from her house and to return home. She became seriously indisposed, and remained secluded in her room. A week slipped away thus.

To her satisfaction she was spared the annoyance of any visits from Colonel Stapleton, who must have heard of her illness, but ignored the circumstance. He never now came near the mansion of the Calverts, where he had been a daily visitor, and avoided even turning his horse's head in that direction if possible.

The increased weight of the appendage to his shoulder-belt had caused Stapleton to examine it, and the contents thereof

—the returned presents and Blanche's letters all sealed up *together*, and addressed to him in the handwriting of Miss Guise—at once informed him that she now knew all. With her, he felt certain that if she had read all the letters—which he never doubted she must have done—the matter was past all explanation; hence he never attempted to make one; and though feeling a little flattered by the rumours of her indisposition, he never sent to her even one card of inquiry. He cursed his kitmutgar, and resolved to horsewhip him; but he disappeared just about that time, and with him all the Colonel's silver plate vanished too.

Blanche knew not what to think of his studious and continued absence; as little did she know that the Colonel had carefully committed to the flames every scrap of her handwriting that he possessed; while to Sir Harry Calvert, though the cold conduct of Stapleton was inexplicable, he disdained to notice it, and they contented themselves with simply bowing to each other when on parade or duty. Henriette and he were supposed to have quarrelled.

"I've dangled after his wife too long, perhaps; too openly, certainly," was the reflection of the Colonel. "Perhaps Sir Harry was not the husband for her, and she was not the wife for Sir Harry; yet they have taken each other to have and to hold, for better or worse, et cetera; so I think I'll send in my papers and get away from this."

He did not know the nature of Henriette; thus he was not without natural alarm that, prompted by revenge and justice, she might lay bare this awkward secret, and cause a terrible *esclandre:* and well did he know that nowhere was gossip more doted on, especially by the self-righteous, than in India. Should this come to pass—

"The devil!" thought he; "to become the property of newspapers—the *Hurkaru,* and all the other prints of India and England."

Malice loves a shining light, even as the seemingly pious love self-glorification, while the great herd of the undiscovered go about thanking God that they are not as other men. Stapleton, whose constitutional hauteur and *insouciance* had won him many enemies, knew well how such a piece of scandal as "a row between him and Calvert" would be enjoyed. He knew how his past history would be ransacked, and already heard the dark innuendoes of those who "always expected something queer would happen," the cowards who stabbed in the dark, and others who said, "this will take his infernal pride down a peg;" but in his selfishness of spirit he never thought of *her* pride of heart and the perils of a lost position. He could abandon himself freely to a pleasant intrigue with a thorough-paced little flirt, but disliked the probable results.

For long had Stapleton partaken of Sir Harry's hospitality—his *recherché* dinners, with strange but tempting Indian dishes, his pickles hot as red cinders, his curries, green chillies, and stuffed mango nuts, his dry champagne and wonderful claret; of all till the finger-glasses came with variegated laurel-leaves in the Ghazepore rose-water; had ridden his horses and smoked his best cigars; and, as kind people would be sure to say, *this* was his return!

All the scandalous stories he had read, heard, or scoffed at and made light of in others, came scathingly back to his memory now. Was he to become a source of mockery too?

And she—but he never thought of her, and only felt the truth of the adage, "the trains of the devil are long, but they are sure to blow up at last."

CHAPTER XXXVII.

HOW THE SIXTH WERE "TRUE TO THEIR SALT."

NOTWITHSTANDING the terrors that reigned now in so many parts of India, Joe Lonsdale and Tom Prior, with Lady Calvert and other enterprising spirits, were actually organizing a fancy ball to soothe the drooping spirits of the ladies at the station, especially as all seemed to be so quiet in Allahabad, and that such perfect confidence was reposed by the officers of the 6th Bengal Native Infantry and other Indian corps in their men.

To this entertainment Joe proposed to go as a certain person who shall be nameless, and to that end had picturesquely provided himself with horns, a curling tail, and fiery trident tipped with glowing tinfoil ; and it was enacted by the managing committee that there should be no more Queens of Scots than three, and that any lady who came to the ball in question "not in fancy dress would not be admitted without a certificate that she was over her fiftieth year ; and no officer was to be present in uniform save the officer of the day." By these measures they thought to ensure a fair muster of picturesque costumes.

Unfortunately for the intended festivity, it was knocked on the head by our battalion receiving a sudden route for Lucknow, taking the Indian Railway to Calpee, thence to cross the Ganges at Cawnpore, and march the rest, a distance of some thirty *coss*, or sixty miles English ; and most unfortunately for ourselves—for me especially, as I was anxious to be away from Allahabad—Jack Dormer and I, as the first two officers on the roLster for duty, were left behind in charge of some convalescents with the women and children, who were unfitted for so hasty a movement.

This departure of the only European regiment from Allahabad had in the sequel a most fatal effect for us all.

Dormer and I had been made honorary members of the
mess of the 6th, as our own had departed.

On the evening of the 5th of June, dressed in an open
shell-jacket and a white vest—a free-and-easy costume for
the climate—and luckily having with me my sword and revolver in its case, I sauntered slowly towards the mess-bungalow, and could hear from a distance the notes of Blanche's
piano, and her voice floating through the open windows on
the soft and ambient air, bringing "the old time o'er me"
once again, but for a moment only ; and soon the distant
cadence was drowned by the drums and fifes under the mess-
house verandah announcing that dinner was served.

The ghurries had clanged seven in the evening, and the
unclouded sun, which had been glaring all day in his Oriental
fierceness, scorching, as it were, the cantonments, defying all
the coolness to be achieved by the libations of tatty-wetters,
punkahs, cold tea, or iced champagne, was now sinking westward beyond the windings of the Jumna.

Opposite me at the table was seated Stapleton, with his
immovable expression, or rather conventional smile on his
face while twirling his moustache. How little he knew that
I held the clue to his secret thoughts ; and how much his
voice grated on my ear as he talked and laughed with Birch,
the fort-adjutant ! Laughed ? Poor wretch, he little knew
where three hours hence would find him !

All the most trivial events of this evening of the 5th of June
are vividly impressed upon my mind.

I felt pre-occupied ; was it to be in my case, as in that of
so many men, that a woman was to influence by good or
evil—evil and falsehood in the present instance—all the future
of my career? "Adam," says a female novelist, "took his
first lesson (in deceit) from Eve ; but Eve took hers from the
the devil."

I was roused from my casuistic thoughts by Dormer saying,

"Pass the wine, Rudkin, and don't go to sleep. I have lost a pot of money—always my luck—upon that deuced billiard-match of Calvert's ; and after mine with Stapleton, I was just thinking of substituting German silver for my plate or leaving it at Peeroo Mull's, when my rascal Khoda Bux bolted with it."

"And my buggywallah has vanished with my trap and horse," said one of the 6th. " Look sharp there," he added, to one of the native servants, with an adjective ; "we require fresh wine."

"Sahib may dam him own eyes as much as he pleases," said the servant, insolently giving the speaker's chair a push, "but I will tank him not to dam mine."

"Leave the room, fellow," said the president, who was a young lieutenant.

The native grinned and withdrew immediately.

"Where the devil have all the *noukur-lague* gone ?" said Dormer, looking round ; and we now perceived that we were left to attend upon ourselves, and that the whole retinue of native servants had quitted the mess bungalow.

Before any one had time to reply, the scattered report of musketry was heard.

" What is that ?" demanded Dormer, starting up.

" Shots !"

"Shots, indeed !" exclaimed Stapleton, as two bullets whistled through the window past his head and sank into the wall beyond.

" It is a disturbance in the bazaar," said one.

" It is not," suggested another more correctly ; " the 6th are revolting ; this is the way these scoundrels are *true to their salt !*"

This proved to be the case ; we saw a tremendous commotion in their lines, along the front of which one sepoy appeared, as if engaged in a solitary game of football, with what

proved to be a bleeding head, just hewn from the shoulders of
a European drummer : and now, starting from the table, we
all rushed to secure our swords and other arms, revolvers,
and rifles.

This was exactly at half-past nine in the evening. It would
appear that some stragglers, among whom was Kureem Sing,
ex-subahdar of the disbanded 2nd Grenadiers, had reached the
cantonments about nightfall, and worked the men of the 6th,
after all their promises, to frenzy by falsehoods.

The Hindoos among them were warned to beware of the
Feringhee queen's insidious designs upon their sacred caste ;
the Mohammedans were adjured by their common faith and
the memory of the Prophet. They were desired to lose no
time in extirpating us all, as fresh troops were marching up
country to destroy all who refused to embrace Christianity.
Many were coming by water in the river budgerees ; others
from Agra, drawn by those screaming, fiery, and smoking
dragons, who travelled on the iron road with a swiftness sur-
passing the Ekkas of old.

After wavering for a time the sepoys became convinced by
the exhortations of these firebrands. The Mussulmans had
ever in secret a natural hatred of the Christians ; but with the
Hindoos caste has attained the culminating point of power
beyond what it possesses in any other land, as it is incorpo-
rated with their religion, and has rendered the supposed
possessors of it bigoted, fanatical, and uncompromising, as it
denies the possibility of conversion, and ignores all prosely-
tism with supreme contempt.

An indiscriminate fire of musketry was now opened on all
sides, and the work of death and pillage began. Nearly all
the ladies, the soldiers' wives, and the children had been
placed in the fort at Allahabad ; but there were three or four
who had left the cantonments and taken up their residence in
Sir Harry Calvert's mansion, and of those who were there,
Jack Dormer and I instantly thought.

"To the fort, to the fort !" was the cry on every hand.
"We have not a moment to lose."

"I must save my cousins," exclaimed Dormer; "who will follow me? Rudkin?"

"Of course," said I.

"And I," added Stapleton, who, whatever he lacked, did not lack the true instinctive courage of an English gentleman.

As we rushed through the cantonments towards the house of Calvert, a hailstorm of balls swept about us, and five officers of the 6th, together with nine young ensigns doing duty with that corps, were shot down in a few minutes, while five only made their escape to the fort. The first I saw hit was a poor lad of sixteen. He passed me rearward, running he knew not whither; he had his hand placed over the region of his heart; there was wildness in his eyes and agony in his face.

"O mother!" he cried, in a voice like a scream; he then fell and rolled over on his back, stone dead, with his unclosed eyes staring at the—to me at that time—most hateful Indian sky.

Dormer's servant, with Dan O'Regan and a number of our convalescents, came rushing after us from the hospital on the first alarm, throwing on their accoutrements and loading and capping their rifles as they ran; and, at the head of these, we made a stand at the gates of Calvert's house, and opened a sharp fire of musketry on all who approached. Luckily all the mutineers of the 6th did not come that way, as some found employment in plundering the bungalows before firing them, and others in forcing the jail to liberate all the thieves, *dacoits*, *kindalas* and pariahs, *shodas* and other infamous characters who were there, to the number of more than three thousand.

We had indeed not a moment to lose!

On the first sound of the firing Sir Harry had ordered out his carriage and horses to convey Blanche and her friends to the fort; but the native servants had all joined the mutineers; so while the gate was defended by O'Regan and his comrades, Dormer and I harnessed and traced the horses at the back of the mansion, where, accompanied by Miss Appleton, Blanche appeared in a piquante blue-silk hood and cashmere shawl.

How beautiful she looked in the extremity of her terror, as the sound of the musketry and the yells on all hands appalled her; for the horrors that had happened elsewhere were around us now. Her tears fell fast; but tears, like smiles, are often snares; faces are sometimes lies, and Lavater a fool.

"Thanks, thanks," she murmured, as I half lifted her into the carriage; "I deceived you once cruelly, Lancelot Rudkin," she whispered, with her white hand placed on my arm.

"Yes," said I, but quite coolly.

"You will forgive me for all that now?"

"I do; but there is another deceit for which I cannot forgive you."

"Name it."

"Ask your own heart."

She grew paler than even terror had made ner, and exclaimed, as I now assisted two other ladies in,

"Henriette, Henriette, why does she linger? We shall all perish if she keeps us waiting thus!"

Dormer hurried to his cousin's room, aware that she was ill in bed. But she was not there. Her couch was in disorder; the stains of bloody hands were upon the white coverlet, and the mosquito curtains were torn down. The young fellow's heart died within him.

"Henriette, Henriette!" he cried again and again; but there was no response.

She had been carried off by the native servants to perish miserably, and at that moment to look for her would be vain and ensure the destruction of all the rest. Can pen and ink portray the horror and great pity that filled his breast at that moment? He dared not tell of this to Blanche. He came rushing out, with a face as pale as a sheet of paper, and said hoarsely,

"She is dressing—away, away! I shall bring her off with me on Calvert's horse."

O'Regan was installed as driver with his rifle slung, and he drove the carriage at frantic speed along the road towards the city, where all was yet quiet, and where an artillery officer with two pieces of cannon held the bridge of the Jumna to prevent the advance of some mutineers who were expected from Benares.

Many other fugitives were now flying towards the fort, while we, the handful of Europeans, endeavoured to cover their retreat as well as we could. What a scene it was! Delicate English ladies and the humbler wives of our soldiers, who had but one community of feeling now, wild with terror, their children clutching their skirts and hiding therein their scared little faces; fathers and husbands looking in keen misery at both, and then turning with a scowl of fierce defiance at the revolters.

" Do not straggle, do not straggle! keep together, all Europeans and Indo-Britons!" cried Sir Harry Calvert, who towered above us all in stature. The *blasé* Guardsman of Regent Street and "the Row" was gone now, and in his place the resolute English officer remained.

We were closely pressed and often brought to a stand by nearly a hundred sepoys and other armed natives, led by Rao Sing, by Jack's kitmutgar, Khoda Bux, and by the now frantic fakir Kalidasa Ram, whose yells and gestures of exultation were as those of a tearing lunatic now; and whose name, singular to say, was that borne by the greatest of Hindoo poets, the author of the exquisite and tender " Sacontala," which has been rendered into English by Sir William Jones.

During one of these compulsory stands or temporary halts, Dormer, with teeth clenched and blood-shot eyes, informed me that his cousin had been carried off.

A terrible pang wrung my heart as he said this. In the rage and sorrow that filled me I could make no reply; but raised my hands and eyes upward, framing the while some unuttered vow of vengeance.

When I thought of her extreme beauty, her sweetness of disposition and delicacy of person and nature, and of all that she had so nearly been to me—when all that flashed upon me —I say, when I thought of her, helpless in the hands of demons such as these mutineers, my blood alternately boiled and curdled, and I could but hope—almost pray in my heart that they had slain her and—*at once.*

Though a mere ' handful,' we more than once faced about and rushed at the rascals with the charged bayonet, a movement which, notwithstanding their excess in numbers, never failed to scatter them. Carrying a large brass lotah filled with water thickly impregnated with *bhang,* the fakir Kalidasa Ram—escaping the balls of our best marksmen as if he had a charmed life—passed among them, giving each man a mouthful.

The effect of this drug is to madden rather than intoxicate, and its results soon became apparent, as it transformed them into literal demons, with all the energy of insanity and the recklessness of the drunkard. The secret and long-pent-up hatred of generations and of race, caste, creed, and colour were there. Their eye-balls gleamed and blazed ; their white teeth glistened as they ground them ; they hissed and hooted, yelled and shrieked in the madness of their rancour and loathing, the Mohammedan vying with the Hindoo, the Bheel, the Kholee, and the Khond, who worship the cattle goddess.

And to think that Henriette Guise was in the hands of such human demons !

" *Chulo—chulo ! Deen—deen !*" (" Come on ! Faith— faith!") cried the subahdar Kureem Sing, brandishing a tulwar. " Death to the Koompanie Bahadour, who seeks to defile us in this world and destroy us in that to come by making us Christians ! Death to the Feringhees and their queen, who greases the cartridges with the fat of the sacred cow !"

In a sudden rush made by a few whom these cries inspired with fresh courage, Sir Henry Calvert was cut off from us and surrounded by them, but displayed the greatest valour. Sword in hand he charged three or four of them, escaping their bullets, as luckily the *bhang* had the effect of making them shoot wildly. He was met, however, by the bayonets of two and the tulwar of Kureem Sing, whose left arm was protected by a round shield. His horse unluckily proved restive and unmanageable, and ere he could either strike or parry, a bayonet pierced his thigh and the blood spouted forth.

Wheeling his horse round, by a backhanded blow he clove the skull of one antagonist, and closing in with another, whose shako had fallen off, he seized him by the hair of the head and thrust his sword down his throat, but was now stabbed in the arm, and would inevitably have been cut down and destroyed but for me.

When I saw his deadly peril I thought of Blanche, and forgot her errors. This tall, empty-headed, yet gentlemanly "Rawdon Crawley" of a husband loved her well, and I thought that I would rescue him if I could for her sake, or rather for the memory of the vanished past ; hoping at the same time that some sepoy bullet might cut short Stapleton's career. Like many others of our genuine Britons, Sir Harry was one who could box, swim like a duck, fence to perfection, defend a wicket gallantly, a prime bowler, clear ever so many five-barred gates or ride a hurdle race ; and for such a stately fellow to be beset thus by "those beastly niggers, those infernal Pandies," as he freely called them, was an intolerable thing, so he defended himself like a paladin, till his sword-arm was wounded and the weapon fell from his hand.

Followed by four of ours, poor fellows who had quitted the sick-ward in the hospital to fight for their lives, I made a rush at Kureem Sing and those who adhered to him, and driving them back, rescued Sir Harry, whose horse was led off by the bridle, and who had no time to thank me ; for I was now surrounded in turn, and the three feeble fellows who remained with me were speedily beaten down and bayoneted.

"Save Captain Rudkin !" I heard a voice cry amid the horrid hurly-burly and darkness, for night was fairly in now ;

and a fine old staff-officer spurred his horse towards me alone, for the attempt to rescue me seemed too desperate, and in a minute or less all was over with us both. There was a wild yell, a rough shout ending in a shriek, and the old colonel was down under his horse's hoofs, his grey hairs were trampled in blood and dust, yet he struggled manfully with all his strength till three bayonets pinned him to the earth in death.

Far away in a drawing-room in happy England a lady is sitting under a glittering lustre, making a doll's frock for a little golden-haired girl that is nestling by her knee, and they are talking of papa—"of dear papa," whom they are soon to see—in blessed unconsciousness that he is lying on his face, pierced by three bayonet wounds, a ball through his head, and his brains oozing from the orifice.

Never more will poor papa kiss his little one or his "dear old woman," as he was wont to call the girl-wife who knew not that she was a widow.

In this conflict no man asked for mercy, for none expected it. Resolved to sell my life as dearly as I could, I rushed again upon Kureem Sing, who seemed the chief leader among our pursuers in that quarter. My sword—one of those rubbishy regulation weapons furnished by our army-clothiers—broke on his round shield; but passing the point of his weapon, I closed in, and, grasping his right wrist, dashed my hilt with the remaining fragment of the blade into his mouth with all the strength of arm I could exert, demolishing his entire front stock of grinders; but at that moment I was struck down by the butt end of a musket, which was applied with sufficient force fairly under the left ear to render me senseless for a time.

When I recovered the moon was shining; all around me were dead, and the shouts and shots sounded faint and distant now. Giddy and weak, I felt unable to walk, and, to seek concealment, crawled on my hands and knees, and hid among some tall, green, feathery jungle-grass that grew by the wayside, intending to remain there until I could gather sufficient strength and coherence of ideas to reach the fort at Allahabad. By this time the cantonments, Calvert's handsome house, and all the other buildings in the vicinity, were in flames of every hue and colour, varying according to the nature of the fuel that fed them. Skyward they rose in dancing and waving pinnacles, while vast volumes of sombre smoke rolled away sullenly on the night wind. I could hear the crackling and roar of the conflagration, mingling with the incessant and distant shouts of the mutineers, *Muro Feringheeun Ko !*" (" Kill the Europeans !")

Anon these shouts seemed to come nearer and nearer the place where I lay. Then came the sound of chains and the rumble of artillery. The shouts soon rose into frantic yells, and two field pieces came past, with the drag-ropes manned by sepoys, and followed by a naked rabble of the lowest wretches who frequent the market-place, and usually hang about all cantonments. Past me they swept at a run, like yelling fiends, and in spite of my peril a loud cry of despair escaped me when I saw a European women, with her black hair dishevelled, her dress torn to ribbons and grimed with dust and mud, bound helplessly by the hands and feet to the trail of one of the guns ; and this most helpless creature was —Henriette Guise !

Mechanically I struggled up, as if I would seek to follow her ; but again the light went out of my eyes, a death-like sickness of the heart came over me, and I fell senseless on my face amid the now dewy jungle-grass.

It would appear, as I have stated, that two guns, under an artillery officer, had been placed at the pontoon-bridge of the Jumma, to guard the passage of the river there. Two companies of the infamous 6th Bengal Native Infantry were also posted at the same place, for the same purpose, while one hundred and fifty sowars, or troopers of the 3rd Oude Irregulars held a garden which lay between the fort and the bridge.

When firing was heard in the cantonments, the two com-

panies of the 6th seized the cannon and fired them at the
artillery officer, who galloped to the garden for the Oude
cavalry, while the officers of the 6th were hustled, insulted,
and had several harmless shots fired at them ; but they were
allowed to escape into the fort, which some time subsequently
Sir Harry, with the remains of our party, reached in safety,
with Blanche and many others, but, unfortunately, not all the
European women in Allahabad.

Intent on recapturing the guns, Lieutenant Alexander, a
gallant young fellow, came galloping out of the garden with as
many troopers as would follow him ; but as he dashed along
the road a sepoy, from a place of concealment, shot him
through the heart.

Certain now that the game was over at the bridge, the
artillery officer fled to the fort, and put the commandant
there on his guard. The garrison consisted of seventy
European invalids from Chunar, in the Mirzapore district ;
the Ferozepore battalion of Sikhs, four hundred strong ;
eighty sepoys of the treacherous 6th, who held the main
gate ; and a company of volunteers, formed of all the
European civilians, clerks and so forth, in the city ; and
brave fellows they all proved themselves in the end.

The first step of the officer commanding was to disarm and
expel the detachment of the 6th, whose rifles were all found
to be loaded, capped, and ready for immediate mischief.

The mutineers, on being joined by the three thousand male-
factors whom they let loose from the gaol, now proceeded to
the general work of massacre and destruction, torture and
pillage, with hearty good will. Captain Birch, the garrison
adjutant, and Lieutenant Innes, the executive engineer, being
found in the streets, were both shot down ; and one officer of
the 6th was actually crucified to the ground with four bayonets,
and then had a fire kindled above his body ; but these and
many other horrors are matters of history now.

Three officers escaped, perfectly nude, into the fort by
swimming the Ganges ; the fourth, who made a similar

attempt, was Stapleton, and most miserable was his fate. In his haste he sprang in at a place where, among the tall reeds, some alligators, eighteen or twenty feet in length, were lurking for prey ; for to these ferocious and formidable brutes man and beast are equally acceptable, and when hungry they are said to swallow even stones and other substances incapable of nourishment, simply to prevent contraction of the intestines consequent on lack of food.

When the luckless Colonel took a header, and sprang in, he did not see that the enormous flat head of one of these monsters was close to him among the ooze, where they left their eggs to be hatched by the sun ; and ere his shuddering companions—who were now safe on the other side—could speak, they saw him rise with a shrill cry and his arms tossed upward from the water, and then disappear in a vortex, which the moonlight plainly showed to be crimsoned with his blood.

Attracted by this, others of these voracious monsters swam towards the spot, where an evident contention took place for the fragments of his body ; and such was the unthought-of end of Jocelyn Stapleton !

Meanwhile, terrible was the work that was taking place in the city. Many of the British residents, who on the first fear of a rising took refuge in the fort, had now returned to their dwellings, trusting to assurances of the 6th Regiment, and all these were barbarously mutilated before death ended their miseries. One entire family, consisting of three generations, they burned alive. In other instances, the nose, ears, lips, fingers, and toes were chopped off, and then the limbs were hacked, till the shrieking victim perished of loss of blood.

Poor little innocent children were bayoneted or brained against the stones before the eyes of their shrieking parents, who perished next. Upwards of fifty Europeans were thus destroyed in the night. Those fiends did not permit even their own countrymen to escape, for the wealthy banker, Peero Mull, had his house sacked, and the shops of many opulent natives were destroyed. "The destruction in the

European bungalows was wanton and insensate," says the editor of the *Delhi Gazette;* "the furniture was broken into fragments, the glass and crockery utterly smashed, and even the canvas of the punkahs cut into shreds."

And now, before recurring to my own miseries and adventures, I shall detail those of some of my friends in the fort of Allahabad, which I was never fated to reach.

————— · ————

CHAPTER XXXVIII.

BLANCHE REFLECTS.

THE streets of Allahabad are about half a mile distant from the fort, or were so then ; and during the four or five days subsequent to our friends finding shelter in it, wild mobs of mutineers and rioters were seen rushing to and fro, plundering, burning, and murdering any stray European or Indo-Briton whose place of hiding they discovered. By day under a hot blazing sun, and by night under the baleful dew, the little garrison manned the ramparts, throwing shot and shell, grape and canister, from the guns and mortars, to scatter and destroy those Indian devils wherever they were to be seen and whenever they came within range.

The fort held by our people was once unequalled in beauty, but has gained in strength what it has lost in external appearance. Occupying a strong position at the confluence of the Ganges and Jumna, it is of great extent, and is defended towards the rivers by bastioned walls of polished red free stone. In the inner side, the fortifications are of very regular construction and of great strength, though the interior is finely planted with trees.

Many of the edifices within it are ancient; among the

latter erections is an arched and subterranean excavation, alleged to be part of an underground passage to Delhi, which is only three hundred and ninety miles distant ! Within the principal gateway, which is Grecian in design, is a pillar composed of a single stone, forty-two feet high, about three feet in diameter, covered with Sanscrit inscriptions, and said to be the pestle with which Bheem Sing, a Hindoo giant, was wont to pound his *bhang* in a mortar.

It was beneath the walls of this fort that, until the days of the Emperor Shah Jehan, the Hindoos were wont to indulge in the pleasant luxury of cutting off their *own* heads, as an offering to the holy Ganges.

The Europeans now dared not venture to make a sortie from the fort, lest in their absence their Sikh compatriots might mutiny, and then their last place of shelter would be lost. The Sikhs seemed to have but little sympathy, however, with the mutineers, though their religious principles were deduced from those of Nanik, a Hindoo philosopher or deist, whose chief doctine was universal toleration : so the Sikh soldiers in the fort of Allahabad behaved nobly, and were literally " true to their salt."

The volunteers, who were now compelled to fight for their lives and the lives of those who were dear to them, were told off in three small companies, and on the morning of the 7th the little garrison was strengthened by the sudden and welcome arrival of fifty of the 1st Madras Fusiliers (now H.M. 102nd Foot), whom Neill—the energetic and the provident— had sent on from Benares. As soon as tidings of the mutiny at Allahabad reached him he came on himself with these men, getting over seventy miles in two nights, relays of natives being compelled to push the cars which contained them.

On the day after his arrival, the whole of the revolted 6th marched from the station under a Mohammedan priest, who unfurled the green flag of the Prophet, entrenched them in a strong position, and proclaimed himself vicegerent of the King of Delhi.

Against this man Colonel Neill marched from the fort of
Allahabad with two hundred bayonets, besides artillery and
cavalry ; he assailed the post with vigour ; it was stormed,
and the rebels were routed in terrible confusion.   On this
occasion Jack Dormer won the Victoria Cross, and the Sikhs,
under Captain Brayser, displayed their usual courage and zeal
alike in cutting up the Mohammedans, who were led by the
subahdar Kureem Sing, and the Hindoos, at the head of whom
was the half mad and wholly knavish Kalidasa Ram, who was
winged by Dan O'Regan most successfully.

The troops were then encamped outside the fort, within
which they had now collected for protection fully two hundred
European women, whose fears and privations were terrible.
The heat was intolerable ; cases of sunstroke were frequent,
and those who had duties to perform wore wetted cloths about
their heads.   The dreadful scourge of cholera now came upon
them, and the fort re-echoed with the shrieks of those who
perished.   Seventy fighting men died of it, and in one night
twenty of these were consigned to one huge and uncouth
grave.   Food became alarmingly scarce.   Any native who
sold our people even a handful of rice was mutilated by the
others, and in one instance a baker who had done so was
found with his nose slit and his hands cut off.

Two ladies who were ill in the common hospital died of
sheer fright ; one of these was Blanche's friend, Miss Appleton ; and meanwhile, amid all this terrible scene of misery
and suffering, where was the once gay and giddy Blanche
Bingham ?

For days and nights, with her soiled and tattered attire unchanged, her beautiful hair dishevelled, matted, and in disorder, her vanity, her foibles, *espièglerie* of manner all gone,
she had watched beside the wretched charpoy whereon, in a
huge and desolate room in the barracks within the fort, her
husband lay—wounded, feverish, and hovering between time
and eternity.

Born and bred amid luxury, accustomed from earliest infancy to have every whim and fancy gratified to the full, and to the enjoyment of everything that wealth could procure, they were now reduced to the level of vagrants or gipsies, so far as mere comfort was concerned, and, moreover, were momentarily menaced by disease and sudden death ; for within the fort of Allahabad, as in many other beleaguered places at that time in India, there were many ways of dying.

All privacy was destroyed, and, irrespective of rank, many were compelled to huddle together in one room ; and this sudden change proved the more severe for ladies and gentlemen, accustomed to all the comforts and luxuries of Indian life, to be reduced to their own resources by the desertion of all servants, to have to wait upon themselves, to be suddenly deprived of all conveniences and attendance, and to be absolutely without a change of clothing.

Blanche daily attended to the dressing of her husband's wounds, to fanning his face, and getting him cooling drinks when such could be procured ; and the big, burly, good-natured Englishman saw with pity and anxiety how her soft face became lined and wan, her eyes inflamed and sunken, and gathering something of a wild expression from the scenes and sights around her.

" Take courage, my dear little girl," said he, caressing her hair with his large white handsome hand ; " in time we'll get over all these infernal troubles, which I suppose are an unlooked-for portion of the legacy we inherit from old father Adam, for his little mistake in Eden."

To Blanche, her past life seemed to have been blotted out or to have been like a dream, and as unreal as the present was unnatural. How long was this nightmare to last ? How did it begin ? How and when was it to end ? All that was occurring under her eye, even in the same apartment, was grievous, distressing, and to her of course consisting of most unusual episodes.

In one corner lay a poor lady in silent misery, grovelling on the bare floor. She had seen her husband hacked to pieces before her eyes, after his throat had been slowly but partially cut with a pane of glass ; for most ingenious in their modes of torture were these Oriental savages.   In another was a poor bereaved mother mourning a missing—too probably a slaughtered—child.   She had a hundred little anecdotes to tell, tearfully and despairingly, of her lost pet—her little angel.   She was *so* different from all other children ; she had so many pretty peculiarities, never seen before in one so young and tender ; and now—now all that remained of her was a lock of flaxen hair, a broken doll, and an empty frock.

It was sad, sad—the child whose chubby hands should never more caress her face, and whose soft dimples she could never again " devour with kisses."

" Dead — dead ! Oh no, doctor—*not* dead !" she heard another cry despairingly, as she cast herself on the prostrate and yet warm form of the handsome young husband, to whom she had been wedded but a month before, and whose breast a ball had pierced that morning.   " Oh, do not tell me that he is dead !" she continued, while a mist gathered before her eyes, and all around her seemed a dream.

" May the heavens be your bed, poor thing !" said Dan O'Regan, as, by the doctor's orders, he laid his kind yet strong hands upon her, and carried her to another apartment, and covered up the distorted dead face, lest its memory might blast her sight and haunt her mind for ever.

These and a thousand other episodes of misery were caused by those wretched mutineers ; and Blanche could remember that, on the morning of the very day they revolted, the chaplain had been preaching " Peace on earth and good-will towards men," when he might have taken his text from the third chapter of Joel, " Beat your plough-shares into swords and your pruning-hooks into spears ; let the weak say, I am strong."

I was supposed to be destroyed, and Henriette too, for Sir

Harry told how I had rescued him, and in doing so had im-
perilled my life ; and Blanche listened to him gravely and
sadly. Had she any remorse for all the mischief she had
wrought us ? I doubt it much, and fear that if safe she
might have played the same game again ; but now—*now*,
menaced with danger and death in so many ways, she began
to reflect ; and she saw in the far distance, as it were, a
flaxen-haired little girl, with beaming eyes and innocent face,
guileless, and unsuspecting evil, and thinking not of it : it
was herself as she had left her mother's arms, and when she
first came, a tiny girl, to white-haired uncle Dormer at
Thorsgill Hall.

How different she was now ! And in fancy she saw the
hall as it seemed in those days—its red walls, towers, and
oriels shining in the sun, its waving woods and green
meadows, the gardens and the terrace, with the old ruin
behind so full of gloom and awe—and felt that never more
might she be in those happy days of childhood and inno-
cence, or see those scenes again.

Amid her present misery, she looked back with remorse to
the folly and duplicity of her past though brief life. Oh, was
the game worth the candle ? If spared, how different she
thought she should be. She might have perished, as poor
Henriette and so many more had done. Her mad wild love
for Stapleton seemed to have passed away, and she could
but shudder when she thought of his awful and unusual end.
The glamour by which her fancy had surrounded him was all
dispelled, and when viewed dispassionately, his many faults
came prominently forward ; she saw in him only the *blasé* and
treacherous man of the world, and began to consider that she
had made a great escape.

And her husband was lying there on that wretched charpoy,
feeble as a child, doubly wounded, faint and feverish. She
shuddered amid her own thoughts as she caressed him, for
the once strong man was now as weak as a child.

" Oh, Harry darling, for sweet Brighton once again !" she

murmured in his ear as she fanned his flushed face : "Brighton
with the breezy pier and the band, the green fields, the sunny
terraced houses, the white cliffs, the cool waves rolling on the
beach, and the fresh odour of the seaweed ! How different
is the heat of this most dreadful Allahabad !"

" Anywhere but here, little woman," he sighed ; " anywhere
out of this hot breathless place of disease and death !"

The poor fellow was grateful for the unwonted tenderness
and attention of his flirting little wife, and added, with earnest
and affectionate manner,

" My poor Blanche, I wish to heaven you were safe beyond
the Calcutta ditch, and you shall go with the first party that
leaves this for down country."

" But not without *you*, Harry. You surely wish me to be
with you ?" she asked with clasped hands.

" Not here—not here, certainly."

" There is no one whose duty and desire it should be to be
by your side but poor Blanche's. Do say that you will keep
me with you."

She tried to get up one of her old playful smiles with a sore,
sore heart, but as she gazed on the pale face and heavy eyelids of her patient, it died away.

" And Henriette, my poor Henriette !" she would mutter to
herself. Like me, she had long since given her over for dead,
and could but pray for her, and hope that her body, once so
fair and sweet and tender, had found some fitting grave at
least in the land of her destroyers.

So passed the days in the fort of Allahabad, and as her
husband's wounds and health progressed favourably, and fresh
mutinies were occurring at Futtehpore and Fyzabad, they,
with some others, thought of obtaining conveyances with a
guard of Europeans under Jack Dormer, and making their
way to Lucknow, where our battalion was in garrison and
Sir Henry Lawrence commanded ; and this they utimately
achieved in safety, though some of their companions perished
of sunstroke by the way.

As a European servant they took with them my man O'Regan, who proved to them invaluable on the journey and when there.

CHAPTER XXXIX.

THE SEVEN DACOITS.

THE dawn was at hand, when stiff, cold, drenched with dew, sick at heart, giddy in the head, and sorely athirst, with an intense dull pain under the left ear where the mutineer had struck me down, I staggered up and became conscious of all that had passed overnight. A cloud of smoke shrouded the entire locality of the cantonments, and amid it I could hear voices, cries, and strange noises, showing that the work of destruction and tumult still went on there, though I doubted not that every European who had not escaped must by this time have perished.

The recollection of Henriette Guise as I had last seen her came instantly upon me ; Henriette, bound like the Andromeda of the classic fable, and helplessly exposed, not as she was to one monster, but a multitude of them. Helpless as a Christian martyr in the Coliseum at Rome.

Infuriated by the cruelty and treachery of the natives, my heart became full of merciless and savage thoughts ; I brooded only on destruction and revenge, for true it is that all the passions of the wildest savage may at times, and under certain impulses, be found in the breast of the most civilized European. In spite of all that preachers urge, one is tempted to think that we have our hell—our purgatory—or whatever it may be, on earth. " Hell is not here or there," some one has written;

"in the nether regions, or in the darkness, or in the valley of Tophet. It is in the hearts of those who turn the angels of compassion and patience out of doors, and give themselves over to the fiends of furious desire and bitter anger."

The longing I had to destroy some of those who had slain so many innocent people was fated to be terribly gratified before long.

In India black darkness always precedes the dawn; there is no gradual twilight stealing in with its tints and shadows, no grey daybreak; and while that blackness lasts we can hear the shrill screams of the odious jackal, as he luxuriates till the last moment on the carrion—perchance a dead corpse —that lies in the nearest nullah.

As the sunlight came flashing in, the glossy leaves of the peepul-tree shone and glittered above me, for the long jungle grass among which I had hidden overnight was on the skirts of a tope, or thicket. I had lost alike my sword and revolver; both had been taken, when or by whom I knew not.

I had but two thoughts: to be armed, and to make my way to the fort of Allahabad; but without weapons of some kind I feared my object would never be accomplished. Looking sharply and keenly about me in all directions, I saw that no one appeared to be moving near me; that I was perfectly alone and free to pursue the way that led to the fort; but in doing so I had unfortunately to pass the place where we had made the temporary stand, and where I had rescued Calvert so fatally for myself.

Several dead bodies were lying there among the grass; six of them that were European were horribly mutilated, and in three instances headless. The corpse of a sepoy of the 6th lay across his Minié rifle, of which I hastened to possess myself. I then tossed the dead wretch over on his back, and taking his pouch with its ammunition—the famous greased cartridges—I threw the belt over my left shoulder, and, in-spired with fresh courage, struck at once into the high-road, carefully loading and capping as I proceeded, and in total ignorance that the fort was at that very time beleaguered by the mutineers, who were also rioting amid rapine and outrage in the city.

What machines we had been in Allahabad, I reflected with a sigh. When not for duty, after parade, we dozed in the verandah, smoked cheroots in our shirt-sleeves, studied the thermometer, the Army List, *Allen's Indian Mail,* or the last English paper, lounged in the mess-bungalow ; dinner over, it was billiards, a little loo—not always " mild play "—devilled bones, with iced brandy-pawnee, and then to bed, to sleep if the mosquitoes would permit it ; but now, by Jove, we had all a change with a vengeance !

I had not proceeded a hundred yards between some fields of wheat and barley, when I heard a musket discharged on my right, and a half-spent bullet rolled along the dusty road past me. A distant shout followed, and I perceived seven natives, armed with knives and matchlocks, running through the grain towards me. One of them carried a European head in a *bhooza*-bag, or receptacle for chopped straw. " Whose head might it have been ?" thought I.

As the odds were against me, discretion was the better part of valour here ; so there was nothing for it but to take to my heels ; and with my heart burning with just indignation and rage, I ran with a speed I had never exerted in the cricket-field, and quitting the high-road dashed into a thicket, followed by this hostile party, all of whom had but one object in pursuit—to take my life, after no doubt subjecting me to prolonged and exquisite torture ; for these wretbhes loved to study and to play with human agony to the last breath. I was soon beyond range of their matchlock balls ; but they were more than *within* the range of my Minie rifle.

Facing about at six hundred yards' distance, and trusting to the skill I had won at Hythe and Tilbury, I levelled the barrel over a branch of a tree and picked off the nearest rascal, he who carried the human head. I saw him go down with his heels up, as he fell with a shriek, and again I resumed my flight, reloading as I went.

The effects of the blow from the musket-butt I had received overnight now became apparent. I grew giddy while running through the long jungle grass and luxuriant undergrowth. I staggered in my pace and more that once stumbled heavily and painfully against the stems of the trees. I then found that the six dacoits or thieves—for such I supposed them to be—lithe, light, active, and perfectly nude—all save the cummerbunds that girt their brown and sinewy forms—were rapidly gaining upon me ; and I knew but too well what my fate would be if maimed by a chance bullet, and more than one of these began to strike the trees around me, lopping off branches and whitening the bark.

Halting again and facing about, at a place which the natives deemed consecrated—a little clear spot, in the centre of which was a slab of stone, whereon were rudely sculptured the figure of a mounted man holding forth his hand to that of a woman on foot—for there in past times a suttee, or widow-burning, had taken place—I fired another shot at three hundred yards ; and as two of my pursuers were in a line, my ball finished off both ; and this summary mode of procedure rather cooled the ardour of the remaining four, who now paused for a time and uttered revengeful yells, and as they all did so in unison, I conceived it to be the signal for succour.

The thicket there was literally alive with wild monkeys, which seemed to become all the wilder when I fired the musket, as they scampered like evil spirits from tree to tree, grinned at me, mocked, jabbered, and in many instances swung downward from the branches by their tails.

Though the dacoits seemed inclined to discontinue the pursuit, they still fired at me ; so, after hastening to get beyond their range, I opened upon them again. I was now sensible of one of the evils attendant on much smoking. I had not enjoyed a cheroot for many hours, and the nervous consequence of the sudden deprivation made me dread the accuracy of my aim, especially when my ammunition was so scarce, for I had but a cartridge or two left. Scarcely daring to breathe, I fired, and a fourth robber bounded upward and fell heavily on his face, for doubtless I had shot him through the brain.

The memory of all I had seen and undergone last night—of the poor victim bound to the gun-carriage—was too fresh not to inspire me with a very lust for vengeance and destruction. I missed a couple of shots, but in a minute or less had knocked over a fifth by a ball through one of his thighs. On this the remaining two fairly turned and fled. It was now my turn to pursue ; and intent on revenge and punishment, I twice dropped firmly down on my right knee, and with my left elbow planted on the left knee, taking sure and steadfast aim, shot both the rascals through the back, with as little compunction as if they had been jackals--with as little certainty as they would have felt in slaughtering me, one who had never wronged them. The black head disappeared in each instance, and a pair of bare feet, beating the air instead, showed that I had not fired in vain.

I had disposed of the whole seven.

I drew a long sigh of relief, and leaned against a tree to consider what was to be done now. I was totally without food, or the means of procuring it. Some of those fellows might perhaps have bread, fruit, or chupatties in a wallet ; but fearing that one of them might only be severely wounded, or shamming dead, and shoot me if I drew near, I did not think it prudent to return and overhaul them. I once more began to penetrate into the wood, not without remembering unpleasantly that in Bengal there were other perils to encounter than armed natives, in the form of wild boars, tigers, wolves, and panthers.

On reflection, I conceived that, as the whole country was now up in revolt, and every black man's hand was lifted against the Europeans, any attempt to reach Allahabad was vain by day, and that I must wait till nightfall, and then endeavour to make my way thither in the friendly darkness.

No man knows what he can do till he tries; and thus encouraged by my recent skirmish, victory, and escape, I was not without hope of ultimately making my way to the fort, and thanked my stars that my dark-green rifle-jacket made me by day less conspicuous in the forest than I should have been if clad in the scarlet of the Line; but my European face there was no disguising, unless by untwisting my last cartridge and mixing the powder with water as a dye; but around me there was no water to be seen.

I was oppressed by intense thirst, consequent on the exciting and harassing events of the past night and morning and the barbarous slaughter of so many friends, and so toiled on amid the jungle in search of a nullah where a runnel might be.

Suddenly I found the wood becoming more open, the trees scattered and farther apart, and I saw a portion of the roadway, which I recognized as being that which led directly to the fort; but the sights I came upon by the way—two Europeans dead, partially stripped, and minus noses and ears; and a little further on, the body of a fair-skinned woman, though an Indo-Briton, bound to a tree by a tent rope—drove me back to the shelter of the friendly wood; and again I toiled on in search of water, oppressed by the fast-growing heat of the morning, for though the trees were lofty, the tope was far from cool, and even there the fiery sun peeled the skin off my ears and cheekbones; I could feel the burning wind hot as the death-blast of Bundelcund—and was in terror of a sunstroke, and hence of losing my reason.

I now remembered that when on a hog-spearing expedition with Joe Lonsdale, poor Captain Birch, and some others, I had seen in this same wood a rock-hewn temple, called in Sanscrit the "keylas," or paradise, an old and totally deserted place, but in which there was a koond, or cistern, that was always full of pure water; and judging from the position of the sun the direction in which it must lie, I proceeded at once in search of it, little foreseeing the perilous trap it was to prove for me.

A sudden and steep ascent in the ground soon informed me that I was near it. I trod on confidently after coming upon the traces of an ancient path, now nearly hidden by the luxuriant undergrowth, and ere long the grotesque peristyle of the temple rose before me, with the dark recesses that yawned behind it—the gloomy interior of the place.

Hewn out of the solid rock, nine gigantic caryatides, or figures half human and wholly monstrous in design, supported on their heads the cornice of the edifice, the black depths of which receded into the bowels of the sloping hill beyond. Excavated as a place of worship, it had, however, long been abandoned by the Brahmins, who told the most absurd legends and stories of its antiquity; and hence an undergrowth of jungle and luxuriant weeds—thick as the leafy labyrinth that surrounded the palace of the Sleeping Beauty, and nearly as impenetrable—grew around it now.

With great difficulty I found my way through a network of wild vines, giant yellow gourds, enormous leaves, and prickly brambles, and went straight to the sacred koond, or marble cistern—a miracle of mysterious carving—which was filled with water, that flowed from the mouth of a sculptured cow, and which stood before a grotesque and towering monstrosity in red stone, supposed to represent the sacred bull Nundee. I had no cup or drinking vessel, but in the cool, clear, delicious, and refreshing water I dipped my whole face and hands, and drank as those alone can do who are so sorely athirst as I was then.

I was now about to withdraw, when the draught of pellucid water proved so alluring—more than ever had been the most sparkling iced Moselle or Clicquot—that I returned and drank again, and thought regretfully that I was without a canteen or other vessel to fill with it.

As this rock-hewn temple—like those of Elephanta, Ellora,

and many others throughout India—was quite forsaken by the Hindoo priests, and, as being now the alleged abode of a ghoul and the scene of many unholy rites and spectral appearances, was shunned by people of all creeds, it occurred to me that I could not find a safer shelter for a time ; and as its interior was delightfully cool, I climbed up into a species of niche or recess in the rock-hewn wall—a wall formed out of a mass coeval with the world—and lay down to reflect on my whole situation and the chances of my ever getting to Calcutta if this wild work went on, as there was every prospect of this terrible contagion spreading over the whole peninsula.

I looked sadly back to the time when I was last in that quaint temple with Joe Lonsdale, who made its echoes ring to his favourite song, " When we're far from the lips of those that we love," etc., and how our companions laughed at his strange comments on the, to him, incomprehensible sculptures which covered the walls ; but which were in fact the poetical history of Rama, famous for his warlike exploits, who conquered the King of Ceylon, a terrible giant who had carried off his queen and kept her prisoner in the castle. This castle Rama stormed, and slew the giant, in commemoration of which the Hindoos hold a great festival every year, and so highly do they venerate his character, that it is their custom in saluting each other to repeat the name of Rama ; but in this temple the carvings had all been defaced and blackened by order of Aurungzebe, to show his contempt for the religion of the Hindoos.

Save the voice of a bulbul, which sang long on the spray of a bush in the peristyle, all was still as death there. The notes were beautifully sweet and plaintive, but the song was short and never varied. After it ceased the silence was intense and oppressive. Within the temple there was not, as in the jungly wood around it, the loud hum of the insect life that pervaded every leaf and flower. Of all the sufferings, deaths, and outrages I had seen yesterday—which now seemed an age ago—one alone haunted me beyond all the others, one was ever present, goading me to madness as I imagined all its details—Henriette bound to the gun-carriage. Ill as I knew she was, I hoped at times that terror might have killed her, terror of a situation so awful, and so ended all her sorrows.

"There are some crimes," says a writer on the revolt in Rajpootana, "that have the stamp of greatness in them, for the authors or perpetrators of which we may have a feeling akin to respect; but there are others which excite only our contempt and disgust for their meanness as well as guilt, and it is in crimes of this kind that the Indian mutiny abounded."

Weary with over-tension of the nervous system, and feeling at times half stunned from the blow of the musket-butt, I wished to sleep and bury all thought; but could not, dared not sleep—though I fell into a kind of waking doze amid which the sense of peril and sorrow was ever present.

From this uneasy kind of slumber, just as evening was closing, I was roused by something stirring near the cistern below me, and lo! there were two hyenas, male and female, quietly taking a draught at it; after which they lay down in a corner, no doubt their accustomed lair, and proceeded to gnaw certain dry bones of a suspiciously human appearance that were among the grass, an occupation which suggested unpleasantly that mine would prove to them a much more acceptable repast.

CHAPTER XL.

THE VILLAGE OF THE DEVIL-WORSHIPPERS.

MY unwelcome visitors were of that striped species peculiar to India and Africa. All unaware that the hyena was such a coward in daylight, and was valiant only in the dark, when, if undiscovered, these two might furiously spring up and reach me, I lay still, scarcely daring to breathe, and intent only on creeping back, if I could do so unnoticed, a little way out of their sight.

This was no doubt their den, for, as Buffon tells us, the hyena is a solitary creature, and makes its lair in the caverns of mountains, in the clefts of rocks, or holes burrowed for itself in the earth. I had but one charge left; fortunately it was in the rifle, and I now regretted that in my haste I had not provided myself with the dead sepoy's bayonet.

I felt in a serious dilemma, for if I shot one, the other might spring upon me; if I missed my aim, which at a distance so short was barely possible, or if the cap snapped, I might be assailed by both.

Some large dry leaves that lay in the recess—drifted there probably by the wind—rustled as I moved, and then both these terrible animals raised their heads from the back of the koond and simultaneously looked at me. I felt my ears tingle at the moment, and something like cold water traverse my spine. I had never flinched before lead or steel; but the teeth and claws of two wild monsters such as these were perils of a very different kind. They looked at me steadily and showed their tusks like a dog snarling, their shaggy brownish-grey manes beginning to bristle the while, as I thought preparatory to making a spring, and I already seemed to feel by anticipation their ravenous jaws fastening on my throat; so now I cocked the rifle.

If ever the hyena laughs, it is said to do so when the intentions of mankind are baffled by its wiles ; and its laugh is an old proverb, as we may find in Webster's *Duchess of Malfi* and *As you like it;* and now each of those two that had me trapped as it were, and at their mercy, uttered strange sounds, like the sobbing of a man combined with the lowing of a calf.

I aimed steadily at the male and softly pulled the trigger. The sharp report of the rifle rang with a hundred reverberations that seemed to rumble and echo in remote and distant recesses, leading me to suppose that the excavations of the keylas went far into the heart of the hill ; and when the smoke cleared away, I saw the larger or male hyena on his back, pawing the air and writhing in the agonies of death, the ball having passed through his head and formed a silver-like star on the side of the cistern beyond, while his partner had vanished into the wood.

I now resolved to quit the place, lest the report of the rifle might bring hither certain human hyenas, whom, in my solitary and now defenceless state, I had no desire to encounter ; so again I issued into the tope, when darkness was beginning to deepen about the undergrowth and stems of the trees, even while the last flush of the set sun yet lingered redly on their topmost branches.

In a few minutes all would be involved in gloom, and night would favour me in my attempt to reach the fort.   Marking well the point at which the sun had gone down, I made my way through the feathery jungle grass and matted creepers till I struck upon the roadway once more, and proceeded in that direction which I conceived to be the right one, between fields of tall Indian corn ; but a sudden turn of the path brought me almost face to face with a man—too evidently a sepoy sentinel.

Shrinking down instantly, I crept slowly and stealthily into the grain for concealment.   A sentinel being posted thus led me naturally to infer that an armed force under a native officer

must be close at hand, and after creeping a little way farther
on, by the blaze of a large fire burning in an open place,
where the wild colocynth grew in great abundance, I discovered a party, evidently an out-picket of the 6th Bengal
Native Infantry, muffled in their dark-blue great coats, with
their white cross-belts outside, sitting or lying around it chatting, laughing, and smoking or chewing betel.

Against the pitchy blackness of the as yet moonless sky the
bright flames of the watchfire stood strongly up, and cast a
ruddy light upon their dark-brown visages and gleaming eyes,
and on the sombre figures of their sentinels, four in number,
pacing up and down upon their short beat, the red sheen
glancing like fireflies on the polished blades of their fixed
bayonets ever and anon.

In the centre of the roadway, and pointing along it, was a
field-piece, doubtless loaded with grape ; and when I saw it
the vision of poor Henriette flashed upon me, and once again
my very soul seemed to shudder within me.

From scraps of their conversation I learned that this party
was under a subahdar ; that the fort of Allahabad was completely invested by rebels and *budmashes* to the number of
several thousand men ; and that they had placed a guard at
the bridge of the Jumna under Kureem Sing.   Hence, for me
to proceed in either direction was worse than useless now.
Which way was I then to turn—whither bend my steps—
without money, food, or arms, in a land where all men's
hands would be uplifted against me ?

Benares and Mirzapore were nearly seventy miles distant ;
but in both these places the troops had revolted, so I might
as well remain where I was as attempt the task of reaching
either.   My whole situation seemed alike desperate and hopeless, yet hundreds—ay, thousands—in India were in the same
predicament, and many, after long wandering and sufferings,
perished miserably in the end.

In the other direction, towards Sultanpore and Fyzabad, so
far as I knew, the country was still quiet ; but the latter place

was nearly a hundred miles distant, and in such a climate how was I to reach it on foot?

Two things were imperative in the first place—to quit the dangerous vicinity of the sepoy picket, and to obtain food, if such could be had, by cunning or force, ere my strength failed through want of it; for, save the draught of water at the temple, nothing had passed my lips since I left the mess-bungalow of the 6th on the preceding evening.

In that populous district I knew that some village could not be far off, and I hoped to find in an unwatched temple or way-side shrine the cakes, wine, and sweetmeats usually placed by the devout before the idol as offerings, that are often carried off by the birds of the air.

When I quitted my hiding-place among the grain, and be-took me once more to the highway, the night was calm and lovely. The newly-risen moon was in the south-west, and the sky, dark before, was now studded with countless brilliant stars. Unseen insects were chirping and buzzing as if the time were noon, and the frogs were croaking them-selves hoarse in the shining pools and marshes by the way-side.

The barking of dogs ere long announced my vicinity to a village, of which I soon came in sight, near the residence of some wealthy zemindar, or landholder of rank; an old fort, the round towers of which crowned a high rock close by it. The place consisted of a single street, having some fifty or so native dwellings on each side, surrounded by a low mud wall, closed by a gate at either end, and above the roofs and trees within it I could see the little white dome of a marble temple shining in the light of the moon.

That all might be quietly abed and, as I hoped, asleep, I waited patiently until the dial of my watch indicated ten o'clock ere I ventured to climb over the wall, in hope to find the temple empty and some offerings on its altar; at least, I could get a draught of pure water from its tank. Even before this dreadful revolt there was often a difficulty in obtaining water from a well, as the natives—Mussulman and Hindoo alike—will not permit the "unbeliever" to use their lotahs or brazen drinking vessels. With the Brahmins, the sacrifice of caste is the destruction of life beyond the grave; but the sacrifice of life in this world, whether yours or theirs, is less than nothing.

All was still in the village save the sharp bark of a dog occasionally; a few lights yet lingered in some of the mud-and-bamboo-built edifices, and I approached the white-domed temple with growing confidence. Before it was a large white marble tank, amid the clear water of which there floated some leaves and flowers of the scarlet lotus, the largest and most beautiful of the nymphæas to be seen in India.

I was just about to drink, when, as my evil genius would have it, I was interrupted by the sudden appearance of a number of men and women, who issued from a side lane into the centre street, and proceeded in a kind of procession towards the adjacent gate, to perform what I afterwards learned was named a "devil-dance."

I shrank down behind the enclosure of the tank, and as they passed by me remained unseen; but now I dreaded to enter the temple, and crouching near it, watched them attentively. It chanced that the village I had thus ventured into was occupied almost exclusively by a sect more peculiar to southern India than to Bengal—the *Shanars*—among whom Satan is worshipped as a deity, under various strange and uncouth names, and who have a deep reverence and regard for all exorcists, whom they deem the direct offspring of the devil, and by general consent are allowed to be, and supposed to be, on the most friendly terms with the world of demons.

Having sold themselves to the service of the great enemy of mankind, these men are supposed to be particularly wicked; yet the lower orders firmly believe in their power as exorcists and casters-out of devils,

These persons, I saw, were about to have a fiend expelled from the person of a young woman. First marched the exorcist, a wild-looking fellow attired in a cummerbund and turban, carrying a broom, a large nail, and a hammer in his hands. Then came the young woman bearing two large stones on her head, accompanied by her relatives and friends. On reaching a few trees that grew within the gate, they halted, and the exorcist said to her :

"Which is your tree ?"

She indicated one in particular, but with a very faint voice.

The exorcist then took hold of her hair, which was very flowing and luxuriant. He twisted it into a knot, through which he drove the nail, during which strange process he repeated certain *mantras*, or charms. The girl then fell down, or rather hung for a minute, half suspended by her hair, till it gradually gave way, when she sank on the ground, when all her friends began to dance frantically, hand in hand, around her, firmly believing that now the devil had been cast out, and that she was liberated from the power of the prince of evil.

I was so absorbed by their strange proceedings, that I forgot for a minute or two the prudence that was so necessary, and had half risen from behind the water-tank before the temple. The moonlight shone full upon my face, and in an instant several recognised in me one of the fated Europeans.

They rushed towards me with shouts of " A Feringhee ! a Feringhee !" But as they were all unarmed, and I instinctively held my empty rifle at the charge—and they were ignorant that it was unloaded—none of them would dare to lay hands upon me ; but their noisy outcries brought a dangerous rabble out of an adjacent caravanserai, where probably they had all been asleep on felt mats and carpets, dozing off their hempseed and bhang. They were about thirty in number. Many of them brandished only long bamboos, but some were very differently and more dangerously armed.

Their yells were horrible, and as like unto those of fiends as were their frantic gestures. They were full of mad joy and all the lust of cruelty to find one white man so completely at their mercy. Two or three pistols were fired at me; but in the very haste with which they were levelled their bullets went wide of the mark.

Among them, with disgust and rage I recognised my late kitmutgar, Rao Sing, the small, slimy, lean, and mahogany-skinned Hindoo with the stealthy gleaming eyes—the des-troyer of Azuma—whom I was yet powerless to punish, and who was now armed with a formidable tulwar. There, too, were Khoda Bux, and one who seemed the most active of my assailants, the Meah Sahib, Abdul Khan, a wretch who had more than once dined at our mess, and who in times past was a frequent lounger at the band-stand. His doubt whether my musket was loaded kept him at a little distance, but he continued to shout, "Get thee to hell, Kafir dog! Strike, strike! slay, slay! Bismillah, the raj of the whites is over!"

Conspicuous among them was a Mahratta horseman, clad in a quilted chintz tunic, with a light shirt of mail over it; a steel morion with a turban twisted round it. He had on steel gauntlets that reached to the elbow, and he launched his heavy Mahratta spear at me, uttering the old war-cry of his people as it stuck quivering in the earth:

"Hur, hur, O Mahadeo! the hills are on fire!"

"Let us throw him down the old dry well, as we did the Mehm Sahib," suggested one, "and leave him there to die; we can come and watch him daily while he lasts."

(The Mehm Sahib! To whom did they refer? Oh, would it be Henriette!)

"Death to all the slayers of the sacred cow!" cried Khoda Bux. "It is the orders of the King of Delhi that not one shall be spared of all the accursed Ghora-logue; so let us blow him from the cannon at the Ranee's gate."

"But we shall then lose his head; and for each of these the King of Delhi gives ten rupees," said Rao Sing reflectively.

"The cannon, the cannon!" cried others, as they ran off to fetch it from the gate of the fort.

My blood ran cold now, and for a second or two all my past life came crowding, flashing back, as it were, into memory. Death seemed very close then and inevitable. Alas! for the many "new leaves turned over," but never made into a volume; the noble plans formed, yet never carried out; the good intentions conceived, never to be fulfilled!

They who had left the rest soon came rushing back to announce that the gun had been spiked.

They were accompanied by the naked fakir Kalidasa Ram, who was armed with a lathee, or iron-knobbed club. Their yells and injurious epithets redoubled now, and in their frantic eagerness to assail me they impeded each other, and I knocked down two or three with the butt-end of my musket.

"Dog and son of dog! thou pig and eater of dirt!" they cried, hissing like snakes through their clenched teeth.

"Cowards," said Kalidasa Ram, taking care, however, not to advance the while, "do you all quail before one man? Remember that you are the subjects of the King of Delhi— that Delhi where a son of the house of Timour once more sits upon the peacock throne! Think, think, O people, if each of you were to contribute but a handful of sand, you might bury all the Europeans in India under one sand heap!"

Thus urged, Rao Sing, who had been gathering Dutch courage from a mouthful of bhang, came slowly towards me; as he did so passing a finger along the edge of his tulwar with grim significance, and grinning horribly and malevolently the while, till I sprang forward and by one blow of the clubbed rifle dashed his jaws to pieces and hurled him to the earth ten yards off

In my blind desperation, I was about to fling myself among the rest, when suddenly an aged Hindoo, who appeared as suddenly as if he had sprung out of the ground, threw himself between us, crying :

"Toba ! toba ! (Shame !) Hold, for the love of Bhowani !"

"It is Sivaji Bulwant, the Shastree. Do *you* dare to interfere with us ?" asked Abdul Khan furiously, for, as a Mohammedan, he despised the Hindoos.

. "Remember that the mother of the murdered sleeps ; but the mother of the murderer never knows sleep."

"Poh !" said Kalidasa ; "my mother was long ago laid in the mud of Mother Gunga."

"Hold, I command you !" continued the Shastree with arms outspread between us.

"What stuff is this ?" said Abdul Khan, appealing, sword in hand, to the Mahratta horseman ; but as a Hindoo, the sudden intervention of the Shastree, though it surprised, nevertheless seemed to impress him with respect.

"By the holy mother of the gods—by Sir Mata Bhowani— I have sworn to protect him !" said the old Hindoo, whose hair was as white as the thistledown, and whose sunken eyes seemed to blaze with fire. On this the crowd, who were all Hindoos, save the lion of Chutneypore and an armed man, who seemed to be his attendant, shrank back, and began to melt away, some retiring to their dwellings and others into the caravanserai.

I was saved, though I could scarcely realize the fact. After high and fierce tension of the nervous system, there was a singular revulsion in the emotions of my heart, and I felt utterly confused, as my protector, whom they had named Sivaji Bulwant led me by the hand into his house beside the temple and carefully closed and secured the door behind me ; but for more than an hour after I seemed still to hear yells and cries of the fanatic rabble, and to see their black gleaming eyeballs flashing with cruelty and ferocity.

CHAPTER XLI.

THE HOUSE OF THE SHASTREE.

I HAD undergone so many perils in such a short space of time—the fight and retreat towards the fort; the encounter in the wood with the dacoits, at all times desperate ruffians, who go in gangs and devote their lives to outrage; the meeting with the hyenas in the deserted temple; and lastly, this "shindy" in the village, suffering all the time from a contusion in the head, without food or rest for so many hours—that the light seemed to leave my eyes, and when the old man who had saved me closed his door behind us I reeled and nearly fainted.

Sivaji Bulwant, whose protection was now accorded to me, was a Shastree—one learned in the Shastras and all the holy writings of the Brahmins, and hence was held in the deepest respect by all Hindoos. Though aged, he was a tall, well-built, and, for a Hindostanee, fine-looking man. His forehead was both high and broad, with bushy white eyebrows over eyes that were not black, but of a dark steel-grey. Save a lock behind, his head was shaved, and a phrenologist would have marked with pleasure the prominence of all the organs of intellect and benevolence. Though a mass of wrinkles now, his brown face had evidently been handsome in youth, and though haughty in contour, his mouth expressed kindness and good-humour.

To rehearse the conversations by which I obtained a knowledge of him and his character would, from the inflated nature of his phraseology, only weary the reader; suffice it that while with him I learned that he was a man of note, and known far beyond that obscure village in Allahabad as a deep Sanscrit scholar, profound in the strange metaphysics of the

Vedas, an astronomer, and a devout Brahmin, who had made many pilgrimages and shone in religious festivals at the conglomeration of villages called Conjeveram, Gya, and Nuddeah, once the capital of Bengal, and at Benares, the grand seat and centre of all Brahminical learning.

His little dwelling, which adjoined the temple I had intended to enter, and in which he officiated, was a model of neatness and cleanness.   Daily its floors of white clay were sprinkled with cool water by his female servants, and covered with designs in coloured chalks, and his usual seat, a divan, was decorated with the lotus and other flowers.   The walls were covered with quaint frescoes, all religious subjects and legends; Krishnu in the tree, with the milkmaids' clothes which he stole when they were bathing in the tank; Ganesha with an elephant's head; Bhowani, the six-armed, fighting the demon Maheswur, and a host of other figures half human, half beast, and all those

> "Gorgons, hydras, and chimeras dire,"

in which the Indian mythology excels.

Over every door was an inscription in Sanscrit committing the apartment to heavenly protection; and a little private temple containing his own household gods—hideous little bronze idols—adjoined the library of the Shastree, whose female servants, when not otherwise occupied, were generally busy with their spinning-wheels in the verandah that overlooked his garden.

It was rather a relief to find that some humanity remained in that land of blood and outrage; and old Sivaji the Shastree was indeed humane; and as he was one who had ever led a life of virtue, feeding the hungry, caring for the aged, the lame, and the blind, and relieving every kind of human suffering, he was viewed by the Hindoos as a saint, and was never known to be without the red eye of Siva on his forehead, in memory of the thousand years of darkness that befell the world when— but for a single moment—Parvati, when lying on the bosom of that god, in playfulness placed her hand upon his two eyes, and to prevent a recurrence of such a calamity, he created a third in the centre of his brow.

More enlightened and liberal than many a Christian clergyman, Sivaji maintained that though there were many religions in the world, even as there were many fruits and flowers, that all religions, if they were sincerely practised, must be acceptable to God.

I have said that I was on the verge of fainting when I entered his dwelling. The kind old Brahmin saw this, and by his orders a servant promptly brought me boiled rice poorees, curry, soft pancakes, and other simple fare, on fresh plantain leaves, with a draught of cool water from the tank of the temple close by.

Sivaji told me that the water was blessed, and hence that it was equally good for baking, cooking, or drinking. However, I must own that, after all that I had undergone, I thought an infusion of cognac would have improved its good qualities.

Of the European woman who had been flung down the old well, and left there to die of bruises and starvation, he could tell me nothing, as he was absent from the village at the time.

" The world is great," he added ; but there is a short path from every part of it to heaven, so let us hope that now she is there."

Deep indeed was the sleep that came upon me when I lay down on the thick felt matting, which was the only bed he could give me, and the setting sun of the next day was fading on the towers of the Ranee's fort and the dome of the village temple when I awoke, to find the Shastree, with a snow-white turban round his shaven head, seated on his divan enjoying the eighth sensual delight of the Hindoos—chewing a huge quid of betel-nut, concerning which I remembered a legend told me by Azuma when we were in the dawk-bungalow at Benares.

A nymph of heaven had fallen in love with a young Hindoo, and invited him to meet her in her celestial dwelling, when, having observed the joy-imparting virtues of the betel, then a plant peculiar to heaven alone, on bidding her adieu, he brought a sprig of it to the lower world, and hence its propagation all over India.

I awoke from my long slumber greatly refreshed, but still too weak to attempt to leave the house which sheltered me; and I remained there an entire week with the Shastree, who, though a zealot in his peculiar religion, did not, as a Mohammedan or Christian might have done, attempt the task of converting an unbeliever, for such would have been worse than useless, as I had no caste, even of the lowest kind, in his estimation; yet, like poor Azuma, he used to talk of Aqui, god of fire ; Yama, king of hell ; Varuna, god of the sea ; and so forth, till my brain became addled.

I was not the only Feringhee whom he had saved ; for in the apartments of his women the Shastree told me that he had a little white child, sick and dying, which had been found in his garden, and whose mother was the woman that the mutineers had thrown down the dry well.

Horrible though this information was, it was some relief to me to learn that the poor victim who had perished thus was a stranger to me, and not one in whom I was so keenly interested ; and yet, strange to say, it was in the house of Sivaji the Shastree, I was fated to hear some certain tidings of Henriette Guise.

There I remained in safety, intent only on recovering my strength, obtaining arms, and reaching any post occupied by our troops.

The house was never molested, though more than once a few of my late assailants assembled before it with the invariable yell of " Deen ! deen !" and a beating of tom-toms—the " Indian drum," of the famous quartette in which I had more than once joined when at Thorsgill Hall ; and now it sounded aught but pleasant in the village of the devil-worshippers.

I was glad that I had punished the villain Rao Sing so severely. The blow with the clubbed Minié rifle had probably killed him, as his face was completely smashed by it ; but the encounter had brought that of his victim vividly before me, the gentle Azuma, whom I seemed to see still in the simple *saree* or robe, of the Hindoo women, of light blue silk with white stripes, wound several times around her lithe form and over her graceful head on the left side, whence the end, with its heavy fringe of silver tissue, used to fall over her shapely back and shoulder.

On the morning of the fifth day I had been with him, Sivaji Bulwant, on returning from service at the temple, informed me that two natives wished to speak with me, and were in the court.

" But I am without weapons," said I.

"These men are unarmed," he replied, " and one is a travelling fakir."

"Then admit them, if you please."

He clapped his hands ; the curtain covering the doorway of the apartment was withdrawn, and Khoda Bux—whilom Dormer's thievish kitmutgar—and Kalidasa Ram, smeared as usual from head to foot in rancid ghee and ashes, stood before me, their dark faces rippling with smiles of insolence and malevolent triumph.

They did not speak, and for nearly a minute I remained silent, as if my tongue was loaded, and I cannot describe the utter loathing and intense hatred with which I viewed those wretches, who came so complacently before me, who had so recently menaced my life, and who were, I knew, steeped in the blood of our helpless women and children and of our unarmed civilians.

" Well, you scoundrels—you infamous assassins—what do you want with me ?" I demanded sternly.

" The sahib will not learn much if he speaks to us thus," retorted Kalidasa Ram.

" You, wretch, were cognisant of the death of the girl Azuma in the cantonments," said I.

" She was about to reveal to you the secrets of our people.

What mattered her death? A few years more and she would
have been too old for marriage, and must have been shaven
and degraded, or married to a khanjur," replied the fakir,
referring to the form of devoting women to the temple, when
their right hand is wedded to a dagger.

"To the point—your business, and then begone."

"We know where the Mehm Sahib Geeze is ; she whom
we took from the house of Calvert Sahib," said the fakir with
a grin, which expanded to a laugh when he saw how agitated
I became by his reference to Henriette.

"She is alive ?" I asked breathlessly.

"Yes, and safe, or was so yesterday morning."

"You have seen her, then ?"

"I saw her at sunrise yesterday," replied the fakir, for
Khoda Bux spoke but little.

"She is near us then ?" said I eagerly.

"Farther off than you think."

"Where is she kept a prisoner?" I demanded, making a
step nearer my inodorous visitor.

"That is our secret."

"Speak out, wretch, or by the heaven above us I will
strangle you !"

"Nothing would be won by that save your own death,
accursed Feringhee !" hissed the fakir through his teeth, while
his eyes glared with hate.

"Could she escape from her place of confinement ?"

"Not alone."

"With your aid, then ?" said I, willing to temporise with
these men.

"Yes."

"And what is the price of your services ?"

"A thousand rupees, sahib," said Khoda Bux, who had not
yet spoken.

"I have not even an ana ; but if you will come to me at
Fyzabad you shall receive the money, which I will pay you
with gratitude," I replied, with a voice that broke in emotion.

For I rejoiced to think that Henriette yet lived, and that she might be saved by my means ; but anon my soul sickened at the imagination of all she *might* have undergone in hands so merciless. Then a natural suspicion occurred to me, and I said:

" How am I to know that you are not deceiving me ?"

" See, sahib," said Khoda Bux, drawing from the pocket of his chintz coat a handkerchief and ring which I thought I had seen Henriette Guise wear, and in a corner of the former was her name written by herself.

" You will leave me these ?"

" Oh, yes, sahib," replied the ex-kitmutgar.

I placed them in my breast-pocket, and then said, with growing sternness and suspicion :

" What proof have I that rascals such as you did not steal them ?"

" This," said Khoda, presenting to me that which he really seemed to have forgotten, a little note written in the native ink with the point of a reed, and from Henriette.

" My dear Captain Rudkin," it ran briefly, " the bearer says that he knows where you are, and that you can ransom me. My sufferings have been dreadful—maddening ! Yet I am safe now, though a prisoner here."

" Here—where ?" I asked.

" Does she not tell you ?"

" No."

" Then, as I have said, that must be our secret. In eight days hence," said the fakir, " I shall come or send Khoda to Fyzabad for the thousand rupees, and if he does not return in safety she shall be cut into kabobs."

" What proof have I that you will keep your part of the bargain and restore her ?"

Then the fakir swore by the most sacred oath that can bind a Hindoo that he would convey her hither himself in a pal-kee, and with this promise I was forced to be content, and we parted ; leaving me all eagerness to reach Fyzabad, where I knew we had a garrison, and I should find no difficulty in

20

raising the money among the officers ; but Fyzabad was a
hundred English miles distant, and how was I to reach it on
foot?

The Shastree had gone to his temple for mid-day prayer,
and I was left for a time to my own reflections. To speculate
on where or with whom Henriette was proved alike vain and
perplexing ; and I sat like one in a dream reading over and
over again the few words her hand had traced but yesterday.
How intensely I longed to see her and hear from her own
lips all she had undergone !

Many horrible stories incident to the mutiny now occurred
to me. We have been told of officers shooting their own
wives to save them from falling into the hands of the revolters
alive ; and though I do not believe there is one authenticated
instance of any such tragedy taking place, the awful indignities and atrocities heaped upon the ladies at Delhi and in
many other places were true beyond all doubt. Investiga-
tions made upon the spot have proved this, though the result
of these painful inquiries will never be known to the world,
and it is as well that it should not be.

When Sivaji the Shastree returned, and I told him of my
anxiety to reach Fyzabad and of the absolute necessity there
was for my making the attempt at all risks, he consented to
assist me with all his heart.

He dyed my face, neck, and hands with the juice of some
herb, which darkened and made my eyes smart as if vinegar
had been spirted into them, and fortunately for me, they, with
my hair and beard—the latter now of several days' growth—
were dark. He supplied me with such a plain dress as might
be worn by a native merchant, with the green turban of a
hadji, some chupatties and ghee ; a drinking vessel for water
I slung over my shoulder. The only weapons he could give
me were a kandjur, which I stuck in my girdle, and a lathee,
or loaded club ; and after sunset next day, I prepared to depart, with gratitude in my heart to this good old man, who in
that land of utter heathendom had already attained that idea

of human brotherhood wherein, as Sextius said of old, "each man should feel himself the care-taker of all men under God."

He indicated to me the route I was to pursue, and as soon as the darkness closed, and before the gates were shut, I stole out upon the highway and turned my back for ever upon the hateful village of the devil-worshippers,

---

CHAPTER XLII.

THE NAIB.

MY anxiety to reach Fyzabad was now intense ; my life seemed to have become doubly precious to me, for on it depended the life, the liberty, and safety of Henriette Guise— the soft-eyed and gentle Henriette Guise of the dear old time that seemed so remote now—the autumn at happy Thorsgill Hall ; and in this desire I had found a new object to make existence valuable.

Again would she owe her preservation to me, and eagerly I looked forward to the time of meeting her once more, and hearing from her own lips all that she had to relate ; but I had one great source for surmise and perplexity—where was she concealed, and with whom ?

She had omitted to mention these two circumstances in her brief note and in her haste, never doubting, perhaps, that her messengers would inform me, which they were too wily, too cunning, or too politic to do.

Her engagement with Colonel Stapleton—born of pique as it seemed, concluded perhaps in a moment of weakness or irresolution—was ended now ; yet she could not know how terribly it was so.

For safety I resolved to travel by night only, and calculated

that, being on foot, the fifth day would find me at Fyzabad.
I intended to husband carefully my little stock of chupatties,
that I might not again have to run the risk of seeking food
as I had done at the village I had just quitted ; and felt convinced that to-morrow would see me beyond Pertabghur.

"If I were always thinking of to-morrow I should go mad,"
says a writer ; and this state of mind rather applied at that
time to me ; I had already learned to let to-morrow take care
of itself, and to think that enough for the day were the evils
thereof.   As I knew that, notwithstanding my disguise, I
must avoid all dwellings, baleful effects of the dews by night
were my chief fear, for if I took fever, or otherwise fell ill by
the way, all would then be over with Henriette Guise and
with myself too.

Ere I had left the village far behind me, the gloom of a
cloudy evening had given place to a brilliant starlit night.
I heard thunder at times in the distance ; the atmosphere
was oppressively sultry ; but I was thankful that, notwithstanding these remote mutterings of a storm, no rain
fell.

A few miles brought me to the vicinity of Mow, a little
town famous for its cotton manufactures, and as I skirted the
suburbs, my chief difficulty was to get across the Sorjew river
on which it is situated.   By good fortune I found a small
punt moored among reeds ; I sprang in, slashed through
the painter with my kandjur, and shoving off, paddled or
rather sculled, it across to the other side, when I soon struck
upon the highway once more, and continued my way
north.

Here and there were fields of stunted dhal ; then the country became black and desolate, and the roadway so undefined,
that after a time I missed it and became certain that I was
proceeding in a wrong direction.   The faint grey light of
dawn as it stole in confirmed me in this supposition, and I
looked about me irresolutely.   All around me was as still as
death, save the howl occasionally of the inevitable jackal, the

purr of the jungle cat, and the hum of insect life, all the louder because some of them were shut within the petals of closed flowers.

Before me rose a mountainous range, towards which I perceived a wayfarer journeying, and as the stranger was a woman, and to all appearance a mendicant, I hastened to overtake and question her. She told me that the path we were pursuing led to Pertabghur, and as she pointed towards the hills, I saw that both her hands had been cut off by the wrists, but evidently several years ago.

This had been the work of dacoits, she told me: they had done so for the sake of her bangles, after stabbing and leaving her for dead, as the Indian fashion of adorning women and children with heavy silver bracelets frequently leads to cases of mutilation and murder; for it is a land full of races of men in every conceivable state or stage of civilisation, from the barbarian of the days of Alexander the Great, or later still, those of Mahmoud of Ghizni, to the polished and subtle rajah, and the commercial "darkie" of Calcutta and our large military cantonments.

When the obscure little town of Pertabghur came in sight, I knew that I had now achieved twenty-five miles of my lonely journey, but was beginning to feel very weary after so long a night march; and thus, before the gates would be opened and the workpeople came forth to their work in the fields, I sought the shelter of a wayside thicket, a clump of trees too near the town wall and too small to be the lurking-place of any wild animals; and there I lay down to rest, and to sleep if I could.

In this thicket were two or three lovely baubool trees, or mimosas, the yellow flowers of which filled the air with delicious perfume; and high over all towered one gigantic talipot, a species of palm, the upper flower of which is very large, and when bursting its sheath makes an explosion like the report of a musket; Thumberg says a cannon, which must be an exaggeration.

"Courage," thought I, while casting my weary limbs among the luxuriant and feathery grass. "I have but seventy-five miles farther to tramp, when I shall again hear the beat of an English drum." And I prayed in my heart for strength and endurance to achieve the distance.

A flock of little parroquets and green pigeons filled the grove with life, the former by their strange chattering, and the latter by flitting to and fro ; and in the towering stem of the great talipot were numerous holes, out of which crept large and glittering black lizards with scarlet throats and bright eyes, animals which the Mohammedan shepherd-boys believe to be evil spirits.

I dipped a chuppatie in a runnel, and soaking it well, made my frugal breakfast ; then I examined the point and edge of the dagger given to me by the old Shastree, and coiled myself under a bush to sleep. Prior to this, however, I drew forth the laced handkerchief and the brief note, which, with the ring, a pearl hoop, were relics of Henriette ; and as such I treasured them, being all I might ever see of one who in the past time had been dear indeed to me, and whom her present helplessness and peril made dear to me again ; and memory went back to the old days of love and doubt and hope, before that fatal "fairy" came ; and as I looked at the handwriting of Henriette, it seemed to me in some way characteristic of her calm and purpose-like style, for she was—as Jack Dormer phrased it in his off-hand way—"a compact sensible girl, and all there."

Then I thought of the regiment, and how, had I but twenty rank-and-file of it with me, I should march boldly through these very towns which I was now compelled to avoid and to skulk near, like a gipsy or vagrant in the thickets by the wayside.

I awoke many hours after to find that I had indulged in a sound slumber, and that the sun was now setting in all his glory beyond the town of Pertabghur, the mosque and houses of which stood in black outline against the deep western flush. The fleecy clouds were rolling away before a gentle breeze ; they were tinted with orange, gold, and crimson hues, which gradually faded away as the sun sank down.

Prior to that, seeing all the country round me quiet, and no one on the far extent of road that stretched beyond the town, and trusting, moreover, to the mode in which the Shastree had attired me, though every joint was stiff and every limb was sore, I grasped my lathee, or loaded club, and set forth once more upon my journey, intent on reaching a European dawk, bungalow, or postal station, which I knew lay ten miles beyond Pertabghur, though I greatly feared to find that the inmates had fled or were lying within it slaughtered.

I passed several persons at intervals on the way near Gospoora, but, thanks to my disguise, no particular or unpleasant notice was taken of me, and as the darkness deepened I trod hopefully on, and in a solitary place where the road wound between two green eminences, just as the moon came forth with uncommon brilliance, I drew near an edifice which, from a previously given description, I knew must be the dawk-bungalow — a little thatched house having two rooms for travellers to rest in, a verandah round it, and outside of that a thick prickly pear hedge.

All was silent in and about the place ; yet a light shone steadily from the curtained window of the inner room, showing that it was not without occupants, I listened intently, but heard not the slightest sound. Grasping the poniard with my left hand, and the lathee with my right, I struck on the door with the latter, and then heard the jangle of spurs and a steel scabbard.

The door was opened by a tall, dark-featured fellow, a native, in the uniform of the most desperate, ferocious, and vindictive of all the mutineers—the Bengal Light Cavalry— holding a candle in one hand and his drawn sword in the other.

"I seek shelter and refreshment," said I, drawing back a pace ; " is the bungalow occupied by troops ?"

"No ; I am here alone," he replied, sheathing his sword shooting it home into the scabbard with a jerk. "You are a hadji I see by your turban ; enter in peace."

"Where is the keeper of the bungalow?" I asked.

"In Jehanum, I hope, the accursed Feringhee !" he replied with a vicious grin. "I found the place empty, and am only making a temporary halt here since sunset. There is nothing to drink but water, and nothing to eat except this candle which I found, and the rats have nearly disposed of that."

I had now entered the bare and almost empty apartment. The place had evidently been looted, and with violence too, as some splashes of blood on the wall seemed to attest ; but three chairs and a table were left. My new companion put down the candle, and we now surveyed each other with equal mistrust and curiosity, for the time was one of peril, outrage and lawlessness.

The sowar was a tall and powerful man, a Mohammedan evidently, as nearly all the native cavalry were, for he had not the orb of Siva painted on his forehead. He had wild-looking eyes and enormous black moustaches, so long that they nearly floated over his shoulder scales, giving him an aspect of grotesque ferocity, like the "heavy villain" of a burlesque. He wore the uniform of the 6th Bengal Light Cavalry, silver-grey, faced with orange—a regiment which had Leswaree, Setabuldie, and Bhurtpore on its colours. His jacket was trimmed with silver lace, thereby showing that he was a Naib Rissalder, or native lieutenant.

"May I ask who you are ?" he demanded, eyeing me sharply and suspiciously as I took a seat.

"Yes," said I, pausing to consider what my name and occupation should be.

"Who and what, then ?" he demanded, authoritatively.

"A hadji."

"So I see ; but where from ?"

"The Hadji Hassin Khalid Ebn al Walid, from Poonah last."

"An accursed name !" was his criticism on the cognomen that I had given myself at a venture.

"How ?" I asked, with pretended indignation.

"Because, as the Koran may tell you, one so called put to flight the cavalry of the Holy Prophet at the battle of Ohod."

"If I am thus unfortunate in my name, it is not my fault. I am a dealer in wines ruined by this revolt, and so forced to journey afoot. And you ?"

"I am Osman Ebn Affan, a naib of the 6th Cavalry."

He then proceeded to tell me boastfully and exultingly of the mutinies at Nowgong, Jhansi, and Futtehpore, at which latter place Mr. Tucker, an English judge, sold his life so dearly, and actually shot down sixteen of his cowardly assailants before he succumbed at last ; after which his head, hands and feet were hewn off, and held up by the kotwal, or native mayor, to the insults of the rabble.

"Your regiment you say is the 6th Cavalry ?"

"Yes, hadji."

"Where is it stationed ?"

"At Jullundur."

"Is all quiet there, naib ?"

"Quiet enough now that we have cut off the unclean and accursed ones root and branch," he replied, grinding his teeth. "I am now riding to certain stations in Rohilcund, where the troops have sworn to be true to their salt, to say that *we* will come and kill their officers for them, and save them from breaking their oaths."

"Riding ! Where is your horse ?" I asked.

"At the back of the bungalow."

This information interested me keenly, and at all hazards I resolved to possess myself of the animal. The outrages which he had witnessed in Futtehpore seemed to afford him peculiar satisfaction ; he recurred to them again and again, and my blood boiled while I listened.

"We took our captain sahib, and sent him to drink boiling

water in hell.   His children we dashed upon the stones, and
his wife—ah, yes—well, ha ! ha ! we made fair spoil of ; for
what says the prophet?   The women of all infidels are the
lawful prey of the faithful, who are, as thou knowest, hadji,
forbidden to make friends of Jews or Christians."

Cramming his mouth and pipe with bhang, he proceeded to
tell me other atrocities, and laughed to remember how a
Feringhee fool of a woman wept for her infidel baby—such a
little one it was too—when he tore it from her arms, and brained
it before her face.

"Why," thought I, "should I have the least compunction
about dashing the Shastree's dagger into the heart of a wretch
who thus coolly speaks to me of this infamous massacre of a
poor English officer and his whole family ?"

My blood was tingling ; my fingers itched to clutch his
throat ; and once actually the idea occurred to me of suddenly
stunning him by a blow of my club, binding him hand and
foot with his sash, sticking the flaming candle into the dry
old thatch of the bungalow, and leaving him to retributive
fate.

And while these ferocious ideas were floating in my mind
he was running on thus :

"In all this we do but obey the second chapter of the
blessed Koran, which tells us to kill the unbelievers ' wherever
ye find them, and turn them out of that whereof they have dis-
possessed you, for temptation to idolatry is more grievous than
slaughter ;' and elsewhere 'war is enjoined you against the
infidels ; if this is hateful to you, perchance ye hate a thing
which is better for you; and ye love a thing which is worse for
you, but Allah knoweth, and ye know not ;" and so he ran on
for a considerable time, quoting the Koran as a plea for atrocities, just as the Jews and Puritans did the Old Testament in
other times.   He then wound up by an original piece of
information :

"The accursed English have not been slain in Northern
Rajapootana.'

" Why ?" I asked.

" Because, as a dervish from there told me, they were all changed by the Prophet in a single night into apes, even as the Sabbath-breakers were ; yet they shall not escape Azrail the angel of death, though they may our swords."

" Shabash !" said I approvingly.

"Yes, it is written in the book of destiny that in the hundredth year after Plassy not one should be left alive between Lahore and Calcutta, Simla and Cape Comorin ; even in Ceylon they shall be destroyed ; but what need is there to talk of these things to one who has seen the tomb of the Prophet ?"

" Yes," said I, adopting his own strain, "I have knelt in Mecca, in Om-el-Kora, have kissed the holy kaaba, and drunk well-nigh unto bursting of the Zem-zem well."

" Happy thou !" exclaimed the naib, cramming more bhang into his pipe. " When we have cut the last of the infidels' throats, I too shall go to the mother of cities by the Red Sea. But whither were you bound to night, friend hadji ?"

" For Fyzabad."

" Fyzabad !"

" Yes ; is all quiet there ?" I asked anxiously.

" As yet—as yet," he replied drowsily, as his head nodded and the bhang began to affect him powerfully.

" Is a disturbance expected there ?"

" Yes ; the 17th Native Infantry have shot all their officers ; they are on the march for Fyzabad, and will be there to-morrow."

" To-morrow !" I exclaimed ; and then I thought, " If so, alas for all my hopes of freeing, rescuing, or even of discovering where Henriette Guise is ; and if I fail to meet the fakir, what then may be her fate ?"

It was now more than ever imperative that I should risk all, even life itself, to possess myself of this rascal's horse, and spur on to Fyzabad, and report to Colonel Lennox, who commanded there, the tidings I had heard so opportunely.

CHAPTER XLIII.

I REACH FYZABAD.

"AND you go to Rohilcund, you say, with orders concerning the destruction of the Feringhees?" said I, after a little pause.

" Yes, hadji."

" By whose orders?" I asked, anxious to gain all the information possible ; those of your subahdar major?"

" Oh, no ; he was in the interest of the infidels."

" *Was*, say you?"

" Yes ; so when we found that out, we soon finished him off."

" How?"

" We blew him from a gun. Allah, you should have seen how high his head went into the air!"

"Then you go to Rohilcund by desire of the regiment?'

" No, hadji ; you are very talkative and I am very sleepy."

" Whose, then?" I asked, as his head began to nod and his eyes to close heavily

" Abdul Khan of Chutneypore."

" The scoundrel!" thought I, as my mind went back to the time when he had so aften shared the hospitality of our mess-bungalow.

" When the 6th, with all the faithful, rose at Allahabad, he sent a select party to carry off a certain golden-haired Mehm Sahib, whom he was determined to place in his zenana ; she escaped with her dog of a husband into the fort ; and they brought Abdul a black-haired one in her place, who, I suppose, in time would please him just as well. But now, not another word shall I say to-night," he added, unbuckling and throwing off his sword and belt, " for by sunrise to-morrow I must be many a coss away."

And while the words yet hovered on his lips, his head and

arms were placed upon the table, and he dozed off into a sound sleep.

I sat very still for a little time ; so still that I could hear my own breathing. The golden-haired lady at Allahabad could only, I knew, be Blanche ; but was that other who had become the prisoner of young Abdul of Chutneypore Henrietta? It almost seemed so ; but my time for reflection was past now, that for action had come, and not a moment was to be lost.

I buckled on his sword, blew out the flickering light, and softly quitting the apartment, slipped round to the back of the bungalow, where I found a troop-horse haltered to one of the posts of the verandah, and shaking its ears somewhat disconsolately from time to time. I led the animal by the bridle a little way out on the road, where I deliberately examined the girths and bit, took up a link or so of the curb-chain, adjusted the stirrup-leathers to suit myself ; then I vaulted into the saddle, casting away the naib's valise as a useless incumbrance, and rode at full gallop on my journey north.

Fortunately the animal seemed tolerably fresh, and continued for many miles at a good round pace. Alone and free, on horseback now, and armed—for both the holster-pistols were double-barrelled and loaded—my spirits and my hopes rose together ; for now I could pursue my solitary way with expedition and in comparative safety.

But for this unexpected contingency I could never have reached Fyzabad soon enough to put the troops there on their guard, and by the timely repulse of the rebellious 17th Native Infantry to keep, as I hoped, my appointment with the fakir, who was to achieve the liberty of Henrietta Guise.

As I drew near the district through which the Goomtee flows, the moon became hidden in clouds ; the night was very dark, but fires were burning brightly on certain eminences and hill-forts, which seemed to indicate that the people of the country were up in arms against us ; hence the utmost circumspection on my part was necessary as I rode on.

I was as anxious to have the meeting with the odious and

detestable Kalidasa Ram as if he was my dearest friend.   If
I failed in that—if protracted fighting ensued at Fyzabad,
and hence there would be a difficulty in procuring the ransom
—the effect might, nay must, be fatal for that poor victim of
many untoward circumstances ; so in my excitement, I rode
madly, recklessly on, with loose rein, giving the horse his
head.   This impatience was nearly proving fatal ; for as I
rushed the animal at an almost " impossible " nullah, it came
crash down with me, and threw me heavily on my head.   I
rolled over, but never relinquished the reins.   I was most
severely shaken ; the accident, however, taught me caution,
and I pursued my way at a more leisurely pace.

About two in the morning I rode through the town of
Sultanpore on the Goomtee, a pretty place and pleasantly
situated, and, all unnoticed and unquestioned, gladly left it
behind me.   It was the place where in 1773 the first brigade
of British troops ever employed by Shuja ud Dowlah in Oude
was cantoned.

It seemed an intolerable and almost incredible thing to
find one's self a lurking fugitive now in British India, where
once we had been lords and masters over all the land and all
that was therein ; and if the revolt spread, I began to fear
that we should never be able to stamp it out.   Though the
white officers might be totally destroyed, the native still remained ; and hence the whole internal organisation of every
regiment was kept intact.   The native troops had all our
enormous arsenals, and immense force of artillery and guns
without number ; and they took us by complete surprise
when, by the usual Whig policy, the European force in India
was at its lowest limit.   More than all, they had Delhi now,
with the prestige of a prince of the house of Timour seated
on the peacock throne.   Even had the pretended cartridge
grievance never turned up at all, the sepoys would have found
another excuse for revolting, and in time to come may do so
again.

"We must not forget," wrote a brother officer on this subject, "that the natives of India are capable of combination. We used to imagine that nothing would ever serve to reconcile the Hindoos and Mohammedans to act in concert against a *third* sect. Experience has proved the fallacy of this. The antagonism of religious animosity is not irreconcilable, and though the great revolt has shown us how badly the co-operation of different bodies of rebels were managed, it has proved that different races and sects can suppress mutual enmity when they have a common object in view."

While reflecting on these things, a ride of fifteen miles beyond Sultanpore brought me in sight of the lights of Fyza-bad while yet the morning was dark.

Fyzabad (or the City of Abundance) is in the kingdom of Oude, on the south bank of the river Dewah, and adjoins the ancient capital of the famous Hindoo demi-god Rama. It contains, as the statists tell us, the palace of Shujah ud Dow-lah, wherein a thousand widows survived him, many hand-some tombs, and an unfinished fortress, which he had commenced on the extensive plan of Fort William at Cal-cutta.

The garrison at this momentous crisis consisted of the 15th Irregular Cavalry, and the 6th Oude Infantry, the 22nd Bengal Native Infantry, and a battery of Horse Artillery.

My extreme satisfaction at having accomplished my lonely and dangerous journey with such safety and unexpected celerity was fated to be clouded by some unpleasant sus-picions in a few minutes.

" Hookam durr ?" challenged a sentinel of the 6th Oude, as I came cantering towards the gate of the fort.

" Friend !" I replied instinctively in English ; on which the fellow instantly discharged his rifle, the ball from which whistled past my ear. I then called to him in Hindostanee, and for a moment began to fear that the place was in posses-sion of mutineers. On this he expressed his astonishment, adding that he thought from my reply I was an Englishman : and then, on seeing my disguise, he asked in a low whisper if I was a messenger from Azimghur, where the 17th were quartered.

"I am not, you scoundrel!" I said sternly; "and the fact of your firing because I replied in English, and then believing me to be a messenger from Azimghur, implies some secret understanding among you, and this must be looked to."

On this he had the effrontery to laugh, while coolly reloading his musket.

The report of the latter having brought the mainguard under arms, I told the officer in command that I was a fugitive from Allahabad, and required instantly to see the commandant, Colonel Lennox, as I had an important message for him. So I passed in without more ado. In that exciting time, the mere circumstance of a sentinel firing haphazard at an individual approaching his post, seemed not worth inquiring into or making a fuss about, as we must have done had it happened at the Tower or Knightsbridge Barracks.

Having gained once more, after so many risks, the friendly shelter of a British barrack, after finding myself among comrades and friends, certain that in a few hours I should have the ransom required for Miss Guise, and have achieved a satisfactory arrangement concerning her with her captors, I could little foresee—in the uncertainty of all human affairs—that twenty-four hours later would behold the garrison of Fyzabad scattered far and wide, and myself a prisoner in the hands of the enemy, and menaced again with suffering and death.

But I am proceeding too fast.

I soon roused Colonel Lennox, who received me half-dressed, for this was no time for ceremony, and I reported the assurance that I had received that the revolted 17th Native Infantry were in full march against his post from Azimghur in the province of Allahabad; with the mutiny in the city, of which he and all his officers were already cognisant; and I added, that from the conduct of the sentinel at the gate, the fraternisation with his garrison was but too probable.

The bugles were now ordered to sound the "assembly," and by gun-fire every officer was at his post, and all means were taken to ensure a warm reception for the 17th ; and here I found in the minds of the married officers the same keen cutting doubts and harrowing anxiety concerning the faith of their men, and the safety of their wives and families. On their own lives, as soldiers, these brave fellows set but little value ; yet true it is, as Byron has it,

> " Leaving a small family at large
> Bothers the heroic in a charge."

Food and rest I required imperatively ; but ere I could take either, I applied to my friend Jones, of the Horse Artillery, whom I had last seen at Dumdum, for the thousand rupees, telling him of the greasy visitor I expected on the morrow probably, and with joy and alacrity he promised to let me have them at once. But I was never fated to require them, as events at Fyzabad, as elsewhere in Bengal, followed each other fast and furiously.

I was now within sixty English miles of Lucknow, where my battalion of the brigade was in garrison, and where—after achieving the freedom of Henriette Guise—I resolved to make every effort to rejoin.

Jones told me of some of those incidents which I have related in their places to preserve the coherence of my narrative ; the retreat from the cantonments to the fort of Allahabad ; who had perished and who got shelter there ; the terrible fate of Stapleton ; and the departure to Lucknow of my faithless " Fairy " and her husband, escorted by a party of Europeans under Jack Dormer.

" By Jove, you have had an adventurous time of it !" he added, as we breakfasted together in the mess bungalow of the 22nd N.I.—coffee, broiled chicken, and a tasty mess called mango-fool, composed of milk, sugar, and green man-

goes, seemed as if food for the gods after all I had undergone. " Poor Miss Guise," he continued, reverting to the
sufferings of Henriette, " she always seemed to me the belle-
ideale of a thoroughbred English girl. With all my heart, I
would to God we had her safe behind our batteries! I hope
that fakir fellow will keep his appointment."

" My perplexity and anxiety will be terrible if he fails me,"
said I, rather appalled by the chance.

" As for the thousand rupees—"

" How can I ever thank you for them, Jones ?"

" By not talking about them. We should have raised ten
times that sum to save any European woman from the hands
of wretches such as these rebels. I used to admire the girl
immensely at Calcutta ; have been at more than one *burra-
khanna* (grand dinner) in her father's swell place at Chowringhee. But there sound our artillery trumpets ! What the
deuce can be up? A row likely. Well, if these niggers,
Moslem and Hindoo alike, are so deuced fond of their
various paradises, we shall send a few of them there pretty
sharply from the mouth of a twelve-pounder—a mode of ex-
tinction they don't fancy much."

" Yet they nearly served me so," I replied with a species of
shudder, remembering the views of the village mob and the
cannon at the Ranee's gate.

" Have a weed, Rudkin, and excuse me, for now I must be
off to my troop like a bird, old fellow."

I thankfully accepted a cigar from his proffered case ; and
then Jones, a tall, fair-haired, and purpose-like officer, whose
naturally fair English complexion had been burned to tawny
red by the Indian sun, took his sword and pith helmet, and
left me.

His cigar proved indeed a luxury, such as I had not enjoyed for some time ; and now, ere it was half-consumed,
worn out with all I had undergone, I dropped into a profound
slumber on a sofa in the mess-room, and it lasted for hours.
unbroken by the sounds around me, by the voices of those

who clattered heedlessly in and out, with their steel scabbards dangling behind them,—shouting for beer, soda iced, brandy-pawnee, and tiffin from the butler,—and by noises which became much more alarming in the cantonments without.

CHAPTER XLIV.

IN VAIN.

WHILE I had slept, two companies of Native Infantry had been told off to support Jones's battery of Horse Artillery, and every precaution had been taken for defensive operations, in expectation of the arrival of the 17th. At ten in the evening an alarm was sounded in the lines of the 6th Oude Irregular Infantry, and all their drums beat. This roused me effectually, and buckling on the only weapon I possessed— the sword taken from the naib, Osman Ebn Affan—I sallied forth into the barrack-yard.

" Load with grape !" I heard Jones cry, as his battery prepared for action, and the fuses were lighted and the limbers cast off.

" Forward !" cried the senior subahdar, or native captain, of the two companies ordered to support the guns. There was a flashing of steel amid the darkness as the fuses were reflected on the blades of bayonets, and the artillery guard advancing deliberately crossed them over the touch-holes of the guns, effectually preventing their use by the gholandazees, or gunners. The white officers, in command but nominally now, felt that all was over with them and their men.

Colonel Lennox now came hurriedly on the ground, and ex⋅

plained that the alarm among the Oude regiment was a false and needless one, and ordered the two companies to rejoin their battalion, leaving but one sentry over each gun. We then found that a general revolt of the whole garrison was taking place by a preconcerted scheme ; for in complete military order, led by their native officers—ignoring altogether the presence of the European—the 15th Irregular Cavalry took possession of the magazine, and planted patrol parties round the entire cantonments, that none might escape without permission.

Jones and I went once more to where his guns were posted, but were not permitted to approach them. Sword in hand, a subahdar named Dhuleep Sing, the prime leader of the mutiny, said :

" Sahibs, if it is necessary to guard these guns, I will take care of them. Retire to the quarter-guard, and no harm shall be offered to any of you. We will prove true to our salt."

" But what if the 17th come in ?" I asked.

The subtle villain smiled, for then he knew the work of murder would begin without delay.

At that moment I heard a native captain, a Mohammedan, who was disposed to prove faithful, cry in broken English to the Oude Irregulars.

" Tam you Hindoo pandies — you 'ave provoked dis row !"

On this a musket exploded ; his brains were blown out, by whom I know not, and he fell on his face with arms outspread.

The mutineers now became dreadfully excited ; but some, who were not so bad as the rest, flocked round us, and frankly urged us to fly, as they would not be answerable for our lives a moment after the 17th marched in, and they might come at any moment.

" To your ranks—fall in, men !" cried the commandant, making a last effort to preserve order.

"Oukha hookam mut mâno !" cried the subahdar Dhuleep Sing, savagely shaking his sword ; "humara hookam chulte !" words which mean in English, "Don't attend to his orders -- *I* am in command !"

Finding the revolt general and hopeless, the handful of Europeans — the exact number is unknown to me -- with their families and one or two native servants, hurried to the bank of the Gogra river, and embarking as best we could in native boats, shoved off into the stream about two in the morning, with the intention of making our way to Garruckpore.

My own peril did not in the least affect me ; I had but one thought now—that of Henriette Guise abandoned to her fate. Too evidently now it seemed that I should never be able to succour her, and should never hear of her more. It was a conviction most sad and terrible to contemplate.

I was on board the same budgeree with Jones and two other officers ; she was leaky and heavy, and we made but little way with our four paddles, for mistrusting the natives, we could not accept the services of any. The other boats were lighter, better manned, and soon left us behind. There was no moon, which was fortunate for us, but the sky was full of brilliant stars. At a point called Adjoodea we were hailed by a patrol of the 15th Cavalry, who rode close to the water-side. They ordered us to bring to, or we should be fired on ; but as this announcement only caused us to redouble our efforts in silence, a couple of carbines flashed redly out from the river's bank ; and throwing up his arms wildly, poor Jones, struck by a ball in the region of the heart, staggered from his seat, fell into the water, and was swept away without a groan.

They did not fire again, and rode off in the opposite direction, uttering cries of derision ; but in rounding a sandbank we had a fresh peril to encounter, for we came suddenly upon the bivouac of the whole 17th regiment.

We could see their red glaring watch-fires, their muskets piled in an orderly way in lines, by companies, glittering in the light ; we could see the dark groups moving to and fro ; heard their voices, and saw others lying asleep upon the ground, for their right flank was almost within pistol-shot of us. We ceased rowing lest the sound might reach them ; and as the boat most fortunately drifted close in shore, where it was completely concealed by a heavy fringe of mangrove-bushes, we urged her along for some hundred yards by grasping these with our hands. Then muffling the oars with our handkerchiefs, and feeling puzzled the while to think how the boats ahead had escaped unseen, we once more resumed our seats, and pulled with all our vigour.

I was seated in the bow ; we had the stream with us, and though our powers of rowing were lessened now by the loss of poor Jones, the boat went through the water with greatly increased speed, till suddenly I felt a terrible shock, and in a moment found myself with my two companions floundering breathlessly in the deep river. Our craft had struck some sudden rock, snag, or other obstruction, and was now floating away from us on the current, hopelessly capsized.

Instinctively I struck out for the shore, which I reached in safety ; but not so my unfortunate companions. Each had but time to utter a pious invocation to heaven, and after rising once or twice, they sank for ever. So accustomed was I then to danger, that this terrible catastrophe affected me less at the time than it does when I think of the whole brief scene now after the lapse of years.

On scrambling up the bank, my first reflections were that I was still near the camp of the 17th regiment, whose fires I could see ; and that fortunately, as I thought, I had by chance landed on the Lucknow side of the stream, which otherwise I must have been unable to cross.

All that day and the subsequent night I lurked in an adjacent jungle, where I dried my saturated clothing as well as

I could, unable to leave the place of concealment—for the dye put upon my face by the Shastree had now passed away (as the polished back of my watch, when improvised as a mirror, informed me)—while the 17th remained in camp and the patrols of the 15th Irregular Cavalry were still hovering about.

At last, to my infinite relief, they all disappeared, having no doubt marched off towards Delhi, the great centre and focus of the revolt.

Wild grapes and gourds were my sole sustenance in the jungle, and I lay there filled by the keenest anxiety to reach Lucknow, and thence, at the head of a party, to make some effort for the rescue of Henriette—the poor girl who trusted me, and who at that very time was no doubt full of anxiety and hope; then I would indulge in reverie amid the breathless heat, dreaming dreams, as I had often done before by the side of a green breezy hill in the "bonnie north countrie," or while gazing into the red changing embers of a sea-coal fire at home, thinking of many things that might never come to pass, hopes that were far away now, and wishes that might never be fulfilled.

One longing ever recurred to me.

Oh, to be again with the Rifles ! was my incessant thought and crave. With Dormer, Lonsdale, Prior, and all those fine young fellows, who were always as happy and merry as if youth was to last for ever. How vile, cruel, pitiful, and degrading seemed this skulking existence ! Oh, to be once again at the head of my company—those hardy and gallant fellows who had gone like a whirlwind, storming up the steep rocks at Alma, who had routed the Russians again at Inkermann, and had ferreted them like rats out of the ovens and quarries; for once again to hear the merry Kentish bugles ring out the orders to " extend " and " advance," to " close " and " form square," from square to form line and " charge "— to charge upon those dark and treacherous wretches, those destroyers of our women and infants, the line with levelled bayonets, our grand old British line, that has never failed in battle since God created it !

The dawn of the second morning stole into the leafy dingles of my jungly retreat. The sunlight spread over the sky, and the waters of the Gogra, which ultimately join those of the Ganges, seemed to roll as white as milk between their dark-fringed banks of foliage. The masses of cloud were edged with gold by the yet unrisen sun, the dew lay deep on every leaf and in glittering pendant drops on the feathery jungle-grass, the golden-coloured gourds, and the sharp thorns of the prickly pears ; and the little parroquets and brilliant birds of paradise were chattering and chirping as they flew from branch to branch, when I crept forth to reconnoitre, and saw that the 17th regiment had really departed, and that no trace remained but the white ashes of the watch-fires.

Stiff with cold and nearly soaked with dew, the dread of fever compelled me now to set forth in search of another sheltering place and of food ; and I resolved to travel in the direction of Lucknow, due west so far as I could, while the morning air had that delightful freshness which, in a tropical climate, is so soon evaporated by the fierce rays of a cloudless sun.

"What may happen next ?" thought I, while treading along the highway, again without money or arms, unable to achieve much single handed, and conscious that I might only be marching to my doom.

In my desperation to procure something to eat, I ventured near a very small village, where a Hindoo woman, commiserating my forlorn aspect, gave me a draught of milk and some bread unquestioned, and directed me as to the road for Lucknow ; but I had not proceeded three miles when two Mohammedan horsemen, ferocious-like fellows, armed to the teeth, overtook me from the rear. One, with a long pistol cocked in his right hand, commanded me imperiously to follow him to the camp of the 6th Oude Irregulars.

"Why?" I demanded.

"Dare you question me, accursed dog?" he cried.

"I do—why?"

"Because your head is worth a hundred rupees," he replied! "but you shall carry it to the camp on your own shoulders."

"Fire, rascal, if you wlll; but follow you I shall not," said I, becoming blind with fury to find myself bullied thus by a vile mutineer.

He instanly levelled the pistol at my head; but his companion, by a circular twirl of his sword, struck up the weapon, which exploded in the air, saying as he did so:

"Kill all, I say; but these infidels are too easily killed. Allah and the Prophet have not given them much life, certainly; but let us take this one to the camp and make sport with him, as we have done with some of the rest."

This "sport" I knew could mean but lingering torture before death, and I began to conceive the idea of anticipating the latter by rushing at the speaker's throat and attempting to drag him off his horse.

"So be it," replied his comrade with a malicious grin; "there is one great devil in this world and many little devils; but the worst devil of all is a white-face Feringhee in a red coat and pith helmet."

Pulling a piece of rope from one of his holsters, he suddenly and very adroitly looped it round my arm, and making me fast to his saddle-bow, proceeded to drag me along the road in the direction of Fyzabad.

"When your head is off you will be saved the trouble of shaving," said he, laughing, with reference to my grisly beard of many days' growth. "I am a barber, but have now relinquished the razor for the tulwar."

"A barber—thou!" exclaimed his comrade rather contemptuously.

"Yes, and have had under my hands and special care the

sacred beard of Hafiz, the Rajah of Chutneypore—his pride and the terror of all unbelievers."

"Bosh!" said the other; "he has a white female slave, who pulls it, they say, whenever he displeases her."

"True, perhaps; but then she is such a privileged gholaum, as the Holy Prophet calls a slave of the right hand. Whom have we here?" he exclaimed, as, at a sudden turn of the road, a party of twenty horse, riding by threes, clad in light-blue uniforms with scarlet turbans, armed with tasselled lances and having round gilt bucklers slung on their backs, came abruptly upon us at a trot, and on seeing me halted and surrounded us.

"Raj troops!" cried the other fellow, meaning that they were soldiers in the service of some native prince.

I concluded that it was all over with me now, believing that some man among them, who was in the mood for it, might pistol or cut me down.

"Surrender this prisoner," said the rissaldar, a handsome young man, with aquiline features and a thick well-curved moustache.

"To whom?" demanded my captors fiercely.

"The Rajah of Chutneypore; we have orders to glean up all Europeans."

I was immediately released, and the two horsemen galloped off in the direction of the village, swearing by the beard of the Prophet they were sorry that they had not shot me at once.

I now found that I had simply changed masters: and in total doubt of what was to follow, was marched under this formidable escort—all of whom were silent, taciturn, and would afford me no information—away by a cross road among the higher ground.

CHAPTER XLV.

IN THE CASTLE OF THE RAJAH.

THE rissaldar had said that the orders of the rajah were to glean up all Europeans ; hence, from the conduct of his son, I could not doubt but that his highness of Chutneypore wished to do a little private homicide on his own account ; and with this pleasant conviction, together with another that escape was hopeless, I marched silently and doggedly onward, surrounded by my escort, who went at a quick pace.

At last there rose before us a town with a few mosques and minarets surrounded by a wall, and over it on a hill a palatial fortress of Moorish aspect, which I knew from engravings I had seen to be the city and palace of Chutneypore, or Chuttneepoor, for the name is spelt in both ways.

The fort on its volcanic rocky hill overlooked a vast extent of luxuriantly-foliaged and finely-cultivated country, rising above the dead level of the plain like a ship above the sea, to the height of five hundred feet. On passing through the narrow and tortuous streets, where, but for my Raj escort, the scowling Mohammedan population would soon have made "kabobs" of me, and by some tanks in which alligators brought when young from the Ganges or the Goomtee, were floating amid the flowers, ooze, and lotus-leaves, we began to ascend by a winding way the hill on which the stately dwelling of the Rajah stood.

En route we also passed the looted and defaced mansion of her Majesty's late Resident, whose skull was then hanging in a bhoosa bag at the Kotwallee, to which he had been dragged through the streets and there slain by Abdul Khan, the eldest son of Hafiz.

I knew that the latter prince was very fond of sport—of fishing and pig-shooting—and that he so loved to combine

the pleasures of the chase with those of the zenana that he
had a balcony built outside the wall of that important part of
his mansion overlooking a jungly thicket, and there he spent
a great portion of every day with his hookah and coffee, his
favourite wives about him, and a few loaded rifles and juzails,
to have a quiet shot at any passing pig or other game ; and
as we proceeded upward we heard a shot or two in the air
from the balcony in question, thus indicating that he was
there.

We were soon within the walls of the guarded fortress. As
we passed the embattled gate, over which two long iron
24-pounders frowned, I gave a last backward glance upon the
green landscape below, and wondered if ever I should be permitted to look on Nature's fair face again.

The castle was fair and lofty, with a round tower at each
corner, and loopholed battlements terminated the lofty wall,
on which the green banner of the Prophet was flying, for the
Rajah and all his people were Moslems. The colour of the
edifice was—I write in the past tense, as Colin Campbell's
Highlanders blew the whole place to atoms after Lucknow—
a muddy grey, somewhat like the tint of our coats after trench-
work in the Crimea, as mud or clay baked hard in the hot
sunshine was a great element in its construction.

Within this fortress were the white walls and terraced roof
of a mansion nicely plastered with chunam, while certain windows of the round towers at the angles, as they opened inward, indicated that they were occupied as a portion of the
general dwelling, with which they were connected by galleries,
and were, as I afterwards found, occupied by soldiers, servants, and gholaums. On the inner side of the banquette
were cannon mounted all round on new carriages, with piles
of new shot between them. Others stood loaded night and
day before the gates, all serving to indicate that his highness
the Rajah was prepared for any mischief or emergency.

The vast number of attendants hovering about in this large
and stately place ; the double relays of palkee or palanquin

wallahs stretched lazily under the verandahs ; the grooms with long chowries fanning pink-tailed white horses ; the men leading hunting cheetahs about ; the soldiers that lounged and loitered in all quarters, smoking bhang or cleaning their arms ; the tailors and other craftsmen at work in odd corners ; the kitmutgars and other Indian domestics, who were intent on doing nothing,—all served to show that we were within a princely dwelling, for the Rajah had an income of some hundred thousands per annum.

I asked the rissaldar, after he had halted his party, if Abdul Khan was in the palace ; and was told, without any of those injurious epithets or adjectives now applied to us unfortunate Kaffirs, that he was supposed to be at Allahabad.

I gathered a little relief from this answer, and reflected that I might long since have perished under merciless hands in the camp of the 6th Oude Regiment ; and now hoped to find, ere the return of his son, some protection at those of the Rajah, as some return for the free exercise of our garrison hospitality to him at "the city of Allah."

I begged the rissaldar to bring me at once before the prince his master, as any certainty, however terrible, to an impatient spirit like mine is preferable to a harrowing suspense.

He told me politely that it was impossible just then, as his highness was among the ladies in the zenana, and could not be disturbed ; but that after evening prayer he would no doubt see me, and meantime all my wants should be fully attended to.

I inquired if there were any other European prisoners in the fortress, and after a hesitation that was very marked he replied in the negative.

Hope gathered more strongly in my heart when I found myself conducted by a kitmutgar to a comfortable apartment, where other attendants came, who, with ill-concealed aversion, gave me a bath, " shaving-tackle," and ere long, on a large silver tray, that which proved most welcome, dinner, Indian though it was.

There were some instances of officers and their families who had been saved from the first fury of the mutineers, being protected by rajahs and zemindars or other landholders, as Rees tells us, either from a desire to propitiate government, in the event of our being successful, or in order to sell them for slaughter to the insurgent leaders, should they continue in power, and utterly crush the East India Company; and in the end I found that his highness of Chutneypore—unlike the merciless frantic Abdul his heir—was exactly one of those politic hypocrites, who, anxious to serve two masters, had resolved to keep friends with both parties—a fortunate circumstance in the end for more than one.

My room was a spacious one, nicely covered by a Persian carpet, with a pillow, or gaddu—a round bolster covered with rich velvet—placed at one end as a seat. The walls were all arabesqued and inscribed with sentences from the Koran; and after my dinner—which consisted of various kinds of curry and sweetmeats—was despatched, together with a couple of bottles of pale ale—the plunder doubtless of some European house, most probably that of the poor Resident—a prepared hookah was brought, and I lolled on the soft gaddu, enjoying the unusual luxury.

Overcome by all I had undergone, I was about to drop asleep, when I saw several Mohammedans in the courtyard without, spreading their carpets and consulting prayer-compasses as to the exact direction of Mecca; then turning their tawny faces that way, they proceeded to their orisons very devoutly. I now knew that the time to see the Rajah and to learn my fate would soon be at hand, and rousing myself, began to frame the speeches I resolved to make him.

Anon I heard the clink of spurs, and the copper-coloured rissaldar came to say that "his highness was at leisure now, and would shed the light of his august countenance upon me;" so starting from my velvet bolster, I rose and followed him with a heart whose pulses were greatly quickened.

We left our boots at the door of an apartment, and were

ushered in.   What was to follow this interview Heaven alone
knew.

My late adventures had been so stirring, "the *entourage* so
strange," to quote an adventurous writer, "the people" among
whom I had been thrown so "wild," the life I led so unique,
that I used to argue the point with myself whether I was the
same individual, or in my normal condition ; whether perchance I had not died in one or other of my near escapes,
and been born anew into a fresh planet."

The Rajah was seated on a divan of yellow silken cushions,
smoking a magnificent hookah, to which a little girl, clad in
spotless white muslin, attended, with its snaky coils of gold
and scarlet silk lying on the carpet round her.   He was
plainly attired for an Oriental of rank, as a single diamond
ornament sparkled in his turban ; but there was an oppressive
sense of magnificence and luxury in his general surroundings.
An open arcade, formed of gilded horseshoe arches, that
sprang from red-marble pillars, formed one side of the apartment, showing the flowers and shrubbery of a lovely garden,
in the centre of which a brazen fountain spouted and
sparkled ; while beyond was the zenana, with all its windows
jealously closed by curtains of scented grass-cloth.

As usual, the hair, beard, and moustaches of Hafiz were
carefully trimmed and oiled, and over his shoulders was a
handsome shawl stamped with the Persian mark ; another
was round his waist, and therein was placed that which I
never saw him wear in the cantonments, a kundjar, its hilt
sparkling with precious stones.

I have already said, when mentioning his appearance at
Blanche's reception, that his figure was small, his face of
course dark, and his eyes cunning in expression.   On this
occasion I regarded him earnestly, and could not determine
whether he regarded me with hostility or friendship ; his
general air was one of Oriental stolidity and indifference.

He signed to the rissaldar to withdraw and wait outside,
and from this I augured well.   I bowed low when he took

the amber mouth-piece from his lips, and with a little nod said :

"Sahib, you are welcome to Chutneypore. The rissaldar did not come on these budmashes who had you a moment too soon. I hope your wants have been attended to ?"

This was most encouraging, so I replied, "Thanks to your highness, yes, in every respect."

"Shabash (that is well) !"

"We have not had the pleasure of meeting since these unhappy events came to pass ; but I trust that in you I shall find a friend," I now ventured to say.

"You shall, sahib, so far as I can be one ; but for how long it is impossible to predict. I have not yet declared for the King of Delhi ; but whether his troops or yours are the first that we shall see before our wall is unknown. We are all in the hands of Fate. Our kismet is written on our brows at the hour of our birth, and is always there, although we see it not."

I bowed in silence, for I knew precisely what all this meant.

If the mutineers were defeated, I should be a free man ; if they proved victorious, the green banner of Timour's descendant would be hoisted and short work made with me.

"I have endured great privations and encountered many perils since the revolt at Allahabad," said I.

"*Kootch purwanni* (never mind)," he replied, smiling ; "they are all over now."

"By the heat my organs of vision are so relaxed, and at times all things before me present but a confusion of black and white."

"A little rest and rose-water of Ghazepore will make that all right," said he, smiling.

He now desired me to be seated while coffee was served. We had a curious disjointed conversation on the then state of matters in India, and I detected that he would gladly have had a thousand Europeans in his hands as hostages to Fortune. From this, I feared that I should be detained a pri-

soner till the termination of the war—a prisoner in secret,
within so short a distance of my comrades, a thought to me
altogether intolerable—and already I began to meditate an
escape.

"Ah, sahib," said he with undisguised regret, "this revolt
has been ill managed, and ruined by the impatience of the
3rd Cavalry at Meerut. Had *all* the preparations gone
secretly on for one year more, by the ninety-nine attributes of
Allah, you had lost every acre of India in one day?"

I felt that there was some truth in this. Warming a little,
he now referred to a well-known but absurd report, then very
current in Central India.

"Your Queen—who is she that she should dare propose to
take our noble zemindars of Oude and the high-caste Brahmins over the *kala-pawnee* (sea), and marry them to the
chunam-faced daughters of accursed unbelievers? Excuse
me, captain sahib, but are they not so?"

In vain I attempted to soothe him by saying, in his own
phraseology, that this was "an invention of the father of lies,"
vowing by every stone in our mosques that it was so.

"Your mosques—*your* mosques!" said he disdainfully, and
thus reminding me by his manner that I was a prisoner rather
than a guest; "you Kaffirs build places, I know, wherein you
worship, as you imagine; but what says the twenty-fourth
chapter of the Koran? 'As for the unbelievers, their works
are like a vapour in a plain, which the thirsty traveller thinketh
to be water, until when he cometh thereto and findeth it to be
nothing.'"

All this was a little tiresome to a man whose life was hanging in the balance; but I was compelled to temporise, and
thought with disdain how often at the mess of our battalion
his highness, who quoted the Koran like a Dervish or Moolah,
had broken the laws of the Prophet by being bundled off in
his palanquin with a good "skinful" of sparkling hock and
moselle. Remembering those times, I said to this politic
Rajah :

22

"I trust that your highness, as a faithful subject of her Majesty, will kindly send me under military escort to Lucknow, the nearest of our posts, if possible."

"There is likely to be plenty of rough work ere long at Lucknow," he replied, knitting his brows at the word "subject," which at that moment was an unfortunate phrase ; but while his eyes flashed, the real desire of his heart was betrayed.

"Feringhee, you are a fool ! That which has been predicted by the Prophet must come to pass—the destruction of all unbelievers. It is at hand, and I believe your *raj* is over."

"Not exactly yet, Rajah."

"How—why !"

"Because that which is foretold is never rightly known until is *has* come to pass, and we are not ruined yet. Remember what Hyder Ali said after his rout to Cuddelore : ' The defeat of many will not destroy these accursed Feringhees. I may ruin their resources by land ; but I cannot dry up the sea.' "

"Wah, wah—true ; but we must not quarrel," said he suddenly, as if somewhat impressed by the truth of Hyder's remark ; "I am going to shoot to-morrow—will the sahib accompany me ?"

"To the fields ?" I asked with mistaken eagerness, as the hope of escape dawned on me.

"No," said he with a malicious smile, as if he divined what was passing in my thoughts ; "no, that is too much trouble in this hot season. I shall send syces to beat the woods, and we shall try our skill from the castle wall."

"I have always heard that your highness was a splendid shot," said I, and the remark was not flattery but truth.

"To-morrow I mean to use an English gun, and you shall see what you shall see," he replied proudly and confident in his skill.

"And you will use the greased cartridge ?" asked I with a little malice in my turn.

" The Prophet forbid, though I have some casks of them."

" How then ?"

" You shall load it for me."

" With pleasure," said I.

He then made a sign that our interview was over, and trusting that something would " turn up," I retired with a low bow, and, weary and worn, threw myself on the charpoy provided for me.

So passed my first night in the castle of Chutneypore.

But our shooting resulted in events which, though they came about very simply, were nevertheless so strange, that the following part of my story almost resembles the coincidences of a novel.

CHAPTER XLVI.

I RIVAL THE RAJAH IN SHOOTING.

THOUGH as a soldier accustomed to sleep with ease anyhow or anywhere, and to wake without an emotion of surprise at finding myself in a strange place after a long, deep, and dreamless slumber, I must own that I *was* puzzled for a minute or two concerning my whereabouts next morning, till all the events of the preceding day flashed with coherence upon me.

" One would require more lives than a cat for Indian service now," thought I ; "but how about getting out of this huge trap, Chutneypore ?"

I have said that Hafiz was fond of sport ; thus I had barely breakfasted, when the rissalder appeared, and said that his highness with his guns and attendants awaited me ; and in the early morning we joined him at a part of the ramparts overlooking the open country, where the silvery mists were rising from the rice and paddy fields, those of corn and maize, the dark-green jungles and the shady tops of beautiful trees, the graceful palm, and the blooming baubool.

I gazed earnestly along the winding road, which led, I knew, to Lucknow, where a caravan was visible proceeding in that direction, and wistfully I watched it for a moment—the quaint and wild-looking escort mounted on camels and horses, all gaily trapped, their lances, bucklers, and matchlocks of steel flashing in the sunshine, and two great elephants with scarlet howdahs towering over all.

The Rajah received me with politeness, almost cordiality, and his attendants, who had not the same reasons for acting with the policy which led him to spare the life of a solitary British officer, regarded him with surprise and me with hate and aversion in their eyes.

One of our ordinary rifle-muskets was now handed to me, and as the Raj troops of Chutneypore were all armed with the ancient matchlock, it was considered altogether a marvel of a weapon in construction and lightness. I carefully loaded it with one of the obnoxious cartridges, and then capped it, a fresh source of wonder to the observers. The flint-musket they could understand; but the percussion cap was quite another thing. I then handed it to Hafiz, who waited with characteristic Oriental patience for some time, till the shrill cries of the syces who were beating the thickets below the castle-wall were heard, and then a wild pig of enormous size, his bristles shining like silver in the morning sunshine, and looking among the bright green leaves as clean as if he had been daily washed and brushed, came trotting past, about a hundred yards distant. Hafiz aimed and fired instantly.

"Shabash! Shabash!" cried his attendants, clapping their hands as usual, for he never missed, and approval of his skill was expected in the form of applause. However, in this instance these exclamations of "Well done!" were rather inopportune; the pig only kicked out with his hind legs, as if the

ball had struck the turf somewhere near him, and then he
trotted leisurely away into the wood ; for Hafiz had not sighted
the rifle—a process of which he knew nothing—and had fired
at a fifty-yard range.

Looking rather perplexed, he knit his brows and desired me
to reload, which I did in silence.

Ere long a couple of similar pigs appeared about a hundred
and fifty yards off. Hafiz selected one, aimed carefully, but
missed again, on which his perplexity and irritation increased.
He fired repeatedly, in every instance missing, till his dark
face flushed with anger, while silent wonder was very plainly
expressed in those of his attendants. At last he violently
threw down the rifle with contempt.

"Pah ! your Feringhee gun is a bad gun," said he, taking
up one of his beautifully mounted Affghan juzails, the stock of
which was elaborately inlaid with ivory, mother-of-pearl and
silver work.

"Will your highness permit me to have a shot with the
English rifle ?" I asked.

"Certainly ; at what will you fire ?"

"Anything that is within range."

"There is one of our syces who is beating the wood," said
the Rajah with an undisguised sneer ; "I think, however, that
he will be pretty safe."

"I beg to differ from you."

"The man is fully five hundred yards off."

"I could hit him easily at a thousand ; still I should prefer another mark, and so I think would he if consulted in the
matter."

Upon a piece of ruined wall there was at that moment
perched one of those fowls I have described as seated on the
cornice of Sir Harry Calvert's house, a gigantic *argill*, or
species of heron, the adjutant bird, so called by our soldiers
in consequence of its erect posture and military strut. Among
Brahmins, who hold it in great veneration, I dared not have
selected such an object to fire at ; but my spectators were all

Mohammedans. The bird sat as still as if cast in bronze, being doubtless gorged with serpents, lizards, and toads, which it devours in abundance ; and it was now, doubtless, dozing sleepily in the sunshine.

"Does your highness see yonder bird ?" I asked.

"Barely ; why it is half a cross distant."

"Not quite so far," said I smiling ; "but it is fully eight hundred yards from us."

"And you pretend that you will hit it ?" he exclaimed.

"I do not pretend but mean to do so."

"It might as well be at Allahabad or Mecca for all the mischief you can do it," said the Rajah, whose followers exchanged smiles of doubt and derision. " But how do you know so well that it is eight hundred yards distant ?"

"By my knowledge of distance. I have been drilled to study it, and to judge of it, for the instruction of others."

"In Allah's name, fire then !" said he with a scornful laugh, in which the rest joined, alike from inclination and duty.

Feeling that, after such confident assertions, much depended on my coolness and accuracy of aim, or I should be disgraced before and derided by those who now crowded near us, I carefully loaded, capped, and adjusted the rifle, having the backsight fully up, and the slide on the scale placed to a nicety ; but yet I knew that I had never used this particular weapon, and that as the figuring is sometimes fallacious, I might miss after all. Having previously ascertained "the pull" of the trigger, I took a steady aim on the Hythe principle, and restraining the breath, fired.

Bang went the rifle, ping rang the conical bullet, and then we saw the great bird rise from the ruined wall for an instant and spread out its wings, with which, in another moment, it beat the turf as it fell, rolled over and finally lay still.

Great was the astonishment of the Rajah at this performance, of which any one of our crack shots would think little now ; but the subadars, jemidars, naicks, and so forth, of the

Raj garrison, who watched me closely—for in that perilous and warlike time every trick of fence and every hint that could be given in the exciting game of homicide was valuable—now began to gaze at each other with surprise and on me with fresh aversion, while not a few muttered audibly of mantras and magic spells.

Since then I have hit many a bull's-eye at a greater distance with a breech-loader on a sweltering day at Wimbledon, or in the long breezy glen of the Braid Hills ; but such weapons and feats of workmanship were unknown in the days of that bantling of the Whigs, Nana of Cawnpore.

" Shabash !" said the Rajah, patting me on the shoulder ; but fearing to mortify him the spectators remained silent. " You shall teach me to do this."

" With pleasure."

" Her highness the Ranee must see you shoot, and she shall do so before sunset this evening.   Meantime we shall have a game of puchese and a pipe.   Do you play puchese ?"

" Yes."

" You do everything," said he approvingly.

" Everything but believe in the Prophet—the accursed Kaffir !" said a not unfamiliar voice ; and on turning I was confronted by the savage Meah Sahib—Abdul Khan—the eldest son of Hafiz, who had just arrived.

" Silence, son," said the Rajah ; "I have promised the sahib my protection, and he shall have it, for he has eaten of our bread and salt."

" So be it," replied Abdul, with a reverence to his father ; " but Inshallah (please God), my time may yet come."

Dissembling my hatred, rage, and contempt—any exhibition of which would have been as useless as unwise—I joined the Rajah in a game of puchese—twenty-five—which is not unlike backgammon, and is played upon a board with cowrie-shells and men, while with a sullen scowl the Meah—for so the eldest son is always named in a Mohammedan family—strode away to the apartments of the Ranee, his mother.

CHAPTER XLVII.

WHAT OCCURRED IN THE ZENANA.

OUR game of puchese was a very protracted one ; but after it and tiffin was over, the Rajah invited me to show the Ranee a specimen of my skill with the rifle, as she and other ladies were fond of overlooking his shooting from the balcony of the zenana.

The syces were once more sent into the woods below the castle rock ; and though usually no male foot save those of Hafiz and Abdul might profane that *sanctum sanctorum*, the zenana, the former conducted me to the place where he usually spent some hours every day, rifle in hand, " potting " the pigs and wild fowl in the thicket below ; and I was presented as a " burra sahib " (*i.e.* great gentleman) to the Ranee and several ladies who were closely veiled, though she showed her face, which might once have been pleasing, but had utterly ceased to be so then.

So I was actually in the zenana, or nearly so ; that wonderful place——

" Where languid beauty kept her pale-faced court."

It was rather brown-faced in this instance. I had certainly passed through the gate of it, and the balcony where the Ranee received me was outside the wall ; but an arcade of open horseshoe-shaped arches showed me an apartment beyond, vaulted with Saracenic groins, a tesselated floor of black and red marble, and arched niches formed of the purest and whitest chunam, containing vases of freshly-gathered flowers ; the walls were painted with beautiful arabesque foliage, interwoven with texts from the inevitable Koran, done in gold leaf.

On low divans of elegant workmanship, covered with the richest Chinese silk or Persian carpets, and attended by female servants, who fanned them when too weary to fan themselves, listlessly idle, inhaling essences or strewing about the petals of flowers, were some of those whom he Rajah kept hidden from the world , but my sudden appearance so near their forbidden dwelling excited them at once to rouse themselves and speak.

The wife of the Rajah was never without her hand-mirror, for though old and withered, wrinkled and mummified in aspect, she was as vain as a European coquette of twenty.

"Fan my face," I heard her say to one ; "my hands, my feet," to others ; "some Ghazepore rose-water—quick !" to a fourth , but on my being presented, she rose from her divan and greeted me very politely.

A large yet slender ring of fine gold hung from the septum of her aquiline nose. It was partly open, with a ruby at each end. Rubies dangled from her ears, and diamonds and pearls were about her dress wherever she could place them.

To please her, I fired several shots at very long ranges, when the syces beat some wild pigs and other game across the open dingles of the wood far down below—a wood where all the barnyard fowls common to Europe were cackling or crowing—in each instance knocking over my quarry, to the unconcealed astonishment of the Ranee and other ladies, as the performances of Hafiz had never exceeded a hundred and fifty yards, and seldom so distant as that, while I was firing at eight and nine hundred ; so such shrill exclamations of "Shabash !" ensued, that many more spectators came crowding to the archways which opened to the balcony, and among these was one whose figure startled me, as from her station and bearing I was certain she was a European, though her face was veiled, and she was muffled in one of those shapeless coils of muslin called a *saree*, consisting of many yards, usually worn by the Mohammedan women. Moreover, if farther proof were wanting, I could see that her hands were as white as snow, and, though covered with native rings, most beautiful in form and delicacy. In one she carried a *vina*, or guitar, with frets and steel and copper strings. She had golden *vullails* round her slender wrists, and a *varan malai*, or necklace, formed of nearly fifty double pagoda coins, encircling her neck ; and from all this I augured that she was a favourite.

A low cry escaped her ; she came swiftly towards me, and threw up her veil.

" *Henriette !*" I exclaimed, in a voice unlike my own.

At another time she might have laughed, even as Blanche would have done, at our mutual masquerade of dress ; but, alas, there was no thought of laughter in us then. Indeed, I had a great lump in my throat, and a strange choking sensation there suggestive of suffocation.

So she was indeed Henriette, looking as beautiful as ever, with an expression of tender uncertainty in her timid eyes— eyes that were dark, yet full of liquid light and tears and joy —as we clasped each other's hands with a mutual warmth at meeting as if we had been rescued from the grave, which was indeed the case. Ours was not a situation for ceremony, and for some moments we were silent, with my right arm round her, and her sweet face on my breast, when she sobbed hysterically, our stolid Oriental spectators looking wonder· ingly on us the while, at such a scene in such an unwonted place.

The surprise of the Ranee at this sudden burst of emotion was mingled with a little indignation at what she deemed our impropriety.

" Sahib, is she your kinswoman ?" she demanded of me.

" No ; but the dearest of my friends."

" So it would seem," was her dry response.

The Rajah—who had seen much more of that which she had not, the usual intercourse of English society at Benares, Calcutta, and elsewhere, and moreover being aware of the terrible situation of the Europeans, which made them as it were all kindred at that time in India—was by no means either surprised or offended with the joy and sympathy expressed by us at a meeting so utterly unexpected ; and as her head drooped on my shoulder there flashed back on my memory the strange dream I had in the verandah of the cantonments at Allahabad—the dream interrupted by poor little Azuma.

"O Captain Rudkin, Captain Rudkin, can it be reality this ?" she kept repeating, with a strange intensity of expression gathering in her eyes ; while I strove to reassure her, and seated her on a divan, feeling that our shooting was over for the day. I was so excited that I could not have hit an elephant at fifty yards. An attendant, by the Rajah's order, now gave her in a crystal cup a kind of liquid sweet-meat, consisting of rose-leaves, conserved with orange-flowers, lemon, and Visna cherry. She then became a little more composed, and Hafiz, who had betaken him to his hookah, said :

"The Koompanie Bahadoor at Calcutta thinks he is powerful ; so did the Sultan Ackbar ; and so have all such since the days of Mahmoud of Ghisni ; but beauty—beauty such as yours is more powerful than all the powers on earth !"

Though Henriette Guise did not understand a word of this, which was said in Hindostanee, the brow of the old Ranee grew black, and she fanned herself violently.

"True," said Abdul Khan, who, unknown to me, had been looking on with a darker scowl than ever: "She is a veritable tulip cheek ; but, like the apples of Isthkather, she is sweet on one side and sour on the other."

"What do you mean, Meah Sahib?" I asked with affected calmness, sensible that there was a more terrible necessity for temporising now.

"Sweet to you apparently but sour to *me*. So one day must end all this !" replied Abdul, grinding his teeth and twisting up his moustache, while I could see that poor blanched Henriette regarded him with a painful degree of terror.

So it was from this fortress that she had contrived to communicate with me, through Khoda Bux and the fakir, to whom she had ventured to throw her note, ring, and handkerchief over the wall of the zenana. They had told her that her message had been duly delivered to me at the house of Bulwant the Shastree ; but as no answer came from Fyzabad, she believed in her heart that I had either perished there or somewhere else, and so concluded herself lost for ever beyond all hope.

"We live in a stirring and most terrible time, dearest Miss Guise," said I, taking her hands once more in mine.

"Terrible, indeed, Captain Rudkin ! Only think, it is quite the persecution of fate with me. After having fever at Allahabad, after discovering—discovering—" she paused, and hastily added, " to be torn from my bed to face the jaws of death, and perhaps worse than death, and now to be a prisoner here ! And you—you——"

" I have risked and saved as many lives as if I had been a grimalkin, and yet every hour have a tenth to look after," said I with a smile to reassure her.

I begged of the Rajah permission to hear her story, which he at once accorded, and in a very few words I told her mine. She inquired eagerly about her cousin Blanche and Sir Harry Calvert. They were safe, I said, down country somewhere— saying that which I hoped to be the case.

" Thank heaven !" she exclaimed, " for I once heard Rao Sing, your servant, say that the Mehm Sahib Calvert was destined for the zenana of Abdul Khan."

Stapleton she never inquired about, which I thought strange ; but when speaking of him she shuddered and covered her eyes with her hands, and was the first to tell me of his dreadful fate, which Khoda Bux had related to her, in his broken English, with remarkable gusto.

While we conversed thus, Zeena the Ranee watched us with a mingled expression of fear, so much so that her husband took the amber mouthpiece of his hookah from his lips and said :

" You look at the Mehm Sahib as if she had the evil-eye !"

" Perhaps she has," replied the Ranee sharply.

" Well, if you fear it, take it out of her," said he, referring to an Oriental superstitition that this can be removed by passing the hand over the possessed person, from head to foot, and pressing the backs of their hands against their temples ; but the Ranee only smiled disdainfully.

CHAPTER XLVIII.

BOUND TO GUN.

SHE told me that on the night of the mutiny at Allahabad she was lying awake in bed, full of very sad and depressing thoughts ; she was thinking of other places and times—of Thorsgill Hall, and much that had happened there—when suddenly various alarming sounds startled her. She heard shouts and wild halloos ; the incessant cry of *Deen !* Then the sound of bugles, of trumpets, and the frequent report of muskets in the cantonments.

Through the green jalousies of her windows the red light of a conflagration—the flaming bungalows—began to gleam ; she heard the rush of many slippered feet in the verandah without ; her door was dashed open, and ere she could attempt to escape, Rao Sing and Khoda Bux, followed by many other native ruffians, rushed in. A wild and despairing shriek escaped her as she was torn from her bed, and with fiendish exultation borne away by them into the night air.

and bound with a cord to a gun.   In this fashion they meant to convey her into the city ; but the stand made by our skirmishers drove her captors, with the gun, back to the cantonments, where, but for the timely intervention of others, a dreadful fate awaited her.

When all hope was dead, and she about to swoon, she felt herself unbound from the cannon, and lifted into a luxurious palkee, or litter, with a kubdeh, or gilded pine-apple—a sign of royalty—on its top ; the rabble fled and she found herself surrounded by a party of Raj troops under Abdul Khan, who had come for the express purpose of carrying off Blanche, whose fair dazzling complexion and golden hair made her seem a veritable divinity in that land of mahogany skins ; so, failing to capture one cousin, he was forced to content himself with the other.

He warned her in broken English that she should never see that land of the Feringhees, England, again, as it was to become a province of the King of De' ' ; that the raj of Jan Bool—is he a god of the Feringhee —and of the Koompanie Bahadoor (Governor-General) was gone now—gone for ever.

" Allah Ackbar," she heard Abdul say to the rissaldar ; "what a houri she is !   I would have preferred the Mehm Sahib Calvert with the sunny hair ; however, I may get her yet, as I have offered sixty gold mohurs for her."

Sorrow and misery are often deadened or relieved by the sensation of sudden motion ; but poor Henriette told me that when in the palanquin, and when the doors were closed and a pleasant breeze came through the open blinds, as the bearers trod swiftly along singing their monotonous songs, she drew the coverings over her and sank back on the pillow, with only a bewildered sense of utter horror of all that might yet be in store for her—one who was so tender, feeble, and helpless, so terrified and stricken.

She felt desolate—most desolate !   The secret of Blanche and Stapleton had passed completely out of her mind.   Her

home, her parents and friends, never should she see them
more, and they would never know her fate. Who had escaped
and who had perished at the station, where doubtless the
horrors of Meerut and Delhi had been acted again ! Had I,
whom she considered her chief friend—how cold the word
seemed now !—fallen with the rest?

Her old life seemed to have passed suddenly, but completely, away ; and a new and terrible one had come in its
place. In whose hands was she now, and whither being taken
—to friends or foes ? Was this state of things—all she had
undergone, all she dreaded—a dream, or a horrible reality?
She could not fashion even a prayer, and yet her agonised
heart was full of deep and prayerful thoughts. She was
somewhat relieved when Abdul opened the door of the litter,
and looking in admiringly, said kindly, in broken English :

"Sleep if you can, you require it, Mehm Sahib."

The bearers were often changed during the night, for they
journeyed many miles, and she could hear the monotonous
tramp of her cavalry escort under Abdul and the rissaldar ;
but she dropped into dull deep slumber that lasted many
hours, till she was awakened by the sudden cessation of
motion, the sitting down of the litter, and a voice crying :

"Gosha, gosha ! Murdana, murdana !"

This means " Private, private !" the usual warning when
Mohammedan ladies leave or enter a mansion ; and then she
found that she was in the zenana of one whom she had so
often seen at Allahabad—Hafiz the Rajah at Chutneypore.

She had been treated with every kindness ; the chief boredom amid her sorrow and fear being the alternate admiration
and attentions of the father and son. At first she felt an
emotion of deep and sincere gratitude to the latter, whose
timely arrival had saved her from greater indignities, and from
a fate at the thought of which her soul sickened and died within her. He had saved her honour and her life ; he had treated
her with every respect and kindness ; yet she read a future
peril in the expression of the young man's eye.

When she first came among them the darkness of her eyes and hair occasioned no comment amongst the ladies of the zenana ; but the pure whiteness of her skin was to them a perpetual source of wonder and speculation. So were the form and delicacy of her hands and feet. They were certain that she possessed some secret, some spell or charm, and were wont to roll up her sleeves to the shoulder and open the bosom of her dress to discover where the white painting ended but these more than " nut brown maids " sought in vain.

Ere I left her I gave her such assurances of hope as my own heart scarcely possessed, and she wept freely when the Rajah pretty plainly hinted I had been there long enough —that there could be no more shooting now ; and then I retired, feeling happier and lighter of heart than I had been for many a month. Yet this new emotion of joy became blended with anxiety for the release of Henriette, whose position was full of peril—the admiration of the two gentlemen mentioned on the one hand, and the fiery jealousy of the Ranee on the other ; which might prompt violence, poison, mutilation of her beauty—I knew not what—for these people were capable of anything.

Gladly would I have spent every day with her who was my old love, but that of course could not be permitted. Without full permission I could enter her guarded abode no more, and even to venture an inquiry concerning her was sufficient to make the little Rajah frown ; thus I had to feign an outward bearing of indifference, while my feelings were keenly interested, during the course of that "instruction in musketry," through which I had now to put not only the Rajah, but also his more waspish son, from whose importunities it was becoming evident that no time was to be lost in getting Henriette away ; but how?

> "It is said that a lion will turn and flee
> From a maid in the pride of her purity.'

Abdul had often quailed before the calm, grave, and some

times haughty expression of Henriette's face, and emotions of
rage gathered in his heart as he felt this conviction. Moreover, he was suspicious and jealous, vulgarly jealous, of me ;
for he had witnessed our mutual emotion at meeting ; so once
he said to me in his hoarse guttural Hindostanee :

" Her voice is as sweet as the flower-bells in the Garden of
the Blessed, her breath is as the roses of Irem, and her bosom
as the buds thereof ; but yours, Feringhee, she shall never be.
I would rather see her cut into kabobs and stuck on skewers
in the Kotwal !"

I could gather from the tone and bearing of the Rajah—
alternately polite, even kind, or haughty and cutting—how the
conflict varied in the world without ; whether fresh mutinies
were recurring with success, or being crushed with severity.
I knew that Abdul was daily in the apartments of his mother
the Ranee, and was thus too probably in the society of Henriette. This filled me with constant anxiety and fear, and
these emotions increased when I learned that on the day of
some great festival which was approaching, the Rajah, with
all his attendants, was to proceed in procession through the
streets to the great mosque, while Abdul was to remain behind, in absolute command of the fort and palace.

One great barrier to his love-making was his ignorance of
English, and hers of Hindostanee. Another was the frequent
presence of his father, perched on a soft divan with his hookah
in his mouth and an absurd leering expression of admiration
in his eyes.

They knew that I alone could interpret some of her wants
and wishes, so by the influence of the Ranee I was permitted
to see her twice again. Bright joy filled her eyes when we
met ; I could see that the poor girl clung to me as a friend,
brother—as something dearer than either. As I was to her
once, so was I fast becoming again; but my new rival's
mode of pressing his suit was, to say the least of it, a singular
one.

" All women taken in time of war are the slaves of those

23

who take them," said Abdul to me one day; "and she shall be mine—she and many more, too."

"But Meah Sahib, she was carried off in time of peace. It is an outrage against all law," I ventured to urge.

"Thou liest!" he hissed through his teeth: "and but for my father I would send your head to the Kotwal in a bhoosa bag."

"I would that you and I were out by the side of yonder wood, alone with our swords," said I through my clenched teeth; for it was impossible to forget how savagely he had tried to take my village near Allahabad. And now for one little anecdote that will illustrate his character.

"She is a lotus-flower—Allah forgive me for using an accursed Hindoo simile!" said he. "She is a bird of paradise then, as gentle as a humming-bird and as soft-eyed as a gazelle. I love her. Will you tell her so in your own language, sahib, and in the fashion of your own people? And I shall give you my right hand in token of amity."

"Thanks very much," I was about to reply, with the contempt the offer merited. "I shall give you my hand, however," I was beginning to temporise, when I suddenly perceived that the hand of the treacherous scoundrel was armed with that which his flowing dress partly concealed—a malicious and deadly weapon (in the shape of steel tiger's-claws) which fits on the fingers, and would have torn mine to pieces.

I drew back, and pointing to this favourite old weapon of the Mahrattas, told him pretty plainly what a coward I deemed him.

"Beware of what you say, Feringhee dog!" he exclaimed sternly, menacing my face with the claws.

"Why should I beware?" I asked furiously, losing all control over my temper.

"Because in three days I shall command her alone; and the tongue sometimes cuts off the head."

With this menace he left me.

I knew well what he referred to. The third day from that was the one of the festival.

CHAPTER XLIX.

ABDUL BAFFLED.

FROM this period our adventures—when I say ours I mean those of Henriette Guise and myself—would fill an average-sized three-volume novel, if detailed in full. We were told of revolts and massacres at Gwalior, at Futteghur, and finally of the dreadful affair at Cawnpore. These were sources of undisguised exultation; but when tidings came of Havelock's march with his army of vengeance, the Rajah somewhat changed in tone and said:

"As for these revolters, I fear me they are like unto him who built a minaret and destroyed a city to do so, or him who sold his vineyard and bought him a wine-press."

When he told me of the awful massacre at Cawnpore, I knew not whether to consider the story false or true, or a mere exaggeration of sufficiently terrible realities.

I have said that I was twice again permitted to spend an hour or so with Henriette, and I found our position was becoming most perilous. We were "on that frontier land where love and friendship approach so closely, that where the one domain ends and the other commences may well occasion mistakes." We had strange little confidences to make; moreover, we had been lovers once. Oh, it was easy to slide into the old life again! for when a man and woman have ever been *more* to each other than mere friends, they can seldom meet as only such again.

The friendship—why so cold a word after the sweet past time?—well, the love I felt for Henriette seemed to give me a right of property in her, very different from the emotion which filled the breast of that Mohammedan toad, Abdul Khan, who generally watched us with a scowl.

The human heart must cling to something. The magic spell that she who was once "my fairy" had thrown over me was broken now, and all my regard for Henriette was fast returning; but circumstanced as we were, whatever my eyes said my lips were silent, lest I might seem to be taking advantage of her helpless situation. She was a clinging creature, loving, tender, and true.

Amid the terrors and uncertainty of the present time it was difficult to indulge in retrospection of the past, or in pleasant anticipations of the future—a future that might never be; and during the two other interviews I had with her, such was almost our sole recreation. Thus we almost revelled in memories of old Thorsgill Hall—where doubtless we were long since numbered with the dead—of our moonlight rambles on the terrace before it; the older ruin, with its vaulted hall and the *panier de morte;* of Rokeby's green woods; of the sylvan grotto and the foaming Tees; and of all we said and did before Blanche came there; and then we spoke of the splendours and pleasures of Calcutta, which neither of us might evermore see, till the Rajah, surprised and offended at the rapidity of our utterances, and the mutual animation of our manner, interrupted us somewhat roughly; and this drew a sudden blush to the now white face of Henriette.

"Did your highness remark how she reddened when the Rajah addressed her?" I heard a veiled woman whisper enviously to the Rance.

"Who do you mean?" asked the latter.

"Who could I mean but the Feringhee Mehm Sahib—the white gholaum?"

"No. Are you jealous, that you watch her so?"

"I jealous of a Kaffir! Allah forbid! Yet the Kaffir is a fair woman, and his highness is only a man."

The Ranee's eyes flashed with a dusky fire. The seeds of

open jealousy began to ripen in her breast, and in this I feared fresh perils for Henriette ; for this evil passion now possessed father, mother, and son alike.

"She is as beautiful as the Rose of Cashmere," continued the veiled speaker ; " and what flower in all India rivals it for brilliancy of tint or delicacy of perfume ?"

"Inshallah," muttered the Ranee, "but I shall find some means to end all this."

Low though she spoke I heard her.

The Rajah did not hear this, as he was busy speaking to Henriette, who turned to me in perplexity.

"Please, dear Captain Rudkin, to tell me what he *is* saying !"

"He tells you that he will make this place to you even as Amherahad is."

"What place is that, and where is it ?"

"A city of Jhinnistawn—he calls it the City of Sweets—in Fairyland—the country of Delight.

"Then please to tell him that my knowledge in geography never went so far ; and the old fool should be ashamed of tormenting me thus."

Though he knew not a word she was saying, something in her tone and manner offended Hafiz. His eyes sparkled with resentment ; he made a sign haughtily for me to retire.

With these dangerous people I was compelled to leave her, and the farewell glance of her soft pleading eyes—an electric glance—went like an arrow to my heart.

She might suffer at the hands of the Ranee, and I at those of Abdul, who was quite capable of having me quietly removed by poison ; in which case Henriette would be lost—though in what way I could succour her, closely watched and guarded as we both were, was far from apparent then—and the dreaded day of the festival was now close at hand. However, a friend was nearer us than we could have anticipated But it was sad for a girl so young and so gently nurtured as Henriette Guise to have her life all at once plunged into mystery and terror, suffering perplexity and the hourly terror of a horrible death at the hands of barbarous Orientals.

To me, on reflection, it seemed altogether an intolerable state of things that, in this age of progression, a young English lady should be menaced by perils suited only to the barbarous ages of the Crusades or of the Moors in Granada ; yet so it was, for we were among a people totally unchanged in manners or ideas since those days, and, indeed, older times.

There was a tender and imploring sadness of expression in the dark eyes of Henriette when I left her—an expression that haunted me. They said as plainly as possible, " When, where, how, shall we meet again ?" And as I dreamed of it I recalled the words of one who wrote thus of such eyes, under circumstances that were not precisely similar : " He remembered the old delight of them, the mystery of them ; and perhaps he thought that in a little time he would be able to awaken the old light in them, and rejoice in the gladness, and be honestly and wholly in love with his future wife."

Wife ! Oh, would that, could that ever, ever be.

And now to anticipate a portion of my story which came to light afterwards, when certain prisoners were in our hands, and the business of flogging, hanging, shooting, and blowing them from the guns, if not lucrative, proceeded most briskly.

The day of the festival came, and, as he had intended to do, Abdul Khan remained in the fort. It was a Friday—which is enjoined by the Koran to be always held as a festival, in remembrance of the Prophet having made his first entry into Medina on that day ; and on that day, too, it is asserted the creation was finished ; so it is styled *yawm al joma*, or the day of assembly.

Accompanied by his attendants, the Rajah left the palatial fort in great state. First when two squadrons of his Raj horse, armed with lance, sword, and buckler, splendidly mounted and equipped ; a regiment of infantry armed with matchlocks followed ; then came servants of all sorts, even to his cooks and barbers, gaily attired. The Rajah was on horsebhck, preceded by a band whose music was more wonderful than melodious ; his led horses ; the Ranee and several ladies of the zenana seated in gilded howdahs, panelled with mirrors, on magnificently-caparisoned elephants, trapped in scarlet and gold. These howdahs had blinds of wire, which enabled the inmates to see without being seen. Then came many ze-mindars, or landholders, dressed in fine silks, satins, and kim-bobs covered with jewels coarsely set in native fashion, each with a golden-hilted or silver-gilt tulwar by his side, and pistols or blunderbuss loaded ; for these men always went with their arms thus, just because their fathers did so before them. Then came four pieces of cannon, well horsed by Aus-tralian nags with the gholandazees in blue jackets, and tur-bans, and trousers of scarlet marching by the wheels ; a white elephant gorgeously harnessed, with the green-silk banner of the Prophet floating from the mimic castle that crowned its back, and with two silver kettle-drums—an affectation of absolute royalty—swaying on each side of it ; a squadron of lancers under the young rissaldar closing the rear.

The wild barbaric music ; the tom-toming, roaring of gongs, the tramping of feet, the trumpeting of the elephants, and the rumbling of the artillery died away on the hot breeze, as this picturesque procession wound down the side of the green and wooded hill, through the arched gate and the tortuous streets of the city, in the direction of the great mosque ; and Abdul watched it with a grim smile on his swarthy visage—a smile of gratified pride—as he thought how much grander would be the display when " the raj of the Koompanie was over ;" and then a brighter expression spread over his face when, from the gun-battery on which he stood, he looked up to that part of the zenana where he knew that his intended victim was to be found.

"I have slain her people without mercy,"he muttered—"true ; but that was only in obedience to the laws of Allah and the Pro-phet ; and too often when thinking of her I have forgotten my

duty to the one and the laws of the other—he who lies at Mecca
For her love I would forego—but that is unnecessary—my
hope of that paradise which the Prophet has described in
words beyond the vocabulary of every human tongue ! But
she is here— here on earth within my reach ; while paradise,
with all its dark-eyed girls reposing on couches, each hollowed
out of a single pearl, with their scarfs of green and floral
wreaths that breathe of the odour of heaven, may be—well,
perhaps doubtful after all !"

The fort deserted by all save the guards, even by the
Moolah, Abdallah Ebn Obba, who acted as his mother's chaplain ; the zenana empty of all but a few of its oldest and
plainest-looking inmates ; its usual attendants away with the
Ranee and other occupants of the gilded howdahs,—he knew
that *she* would be completely at his mercy ; and at the risk
of a mortal quarrel with his father, whose policy he derided
and despised, he resolved to compel her to love him, even
should he carry her off to the nearest post held by the rebels,
and cast his lot with them for weal or woe. And who or what
was she, he thought, that he should trifle with her? Though
lovely beyond all the loveliness he had ever looked upon, he
considered her but the outcast daughter of an alien and un-
believing race, whom he yet hoped to see exterminated from
sea to sea, and from Lahore to Ceylon ; a Feringhee, a prisoner, a slave taken in just war, who, but for the timely
arrival of himself and the rissaldar, must long since have fed
the jackals, like the white women who were now lying in
scores outside the palace walls of Delhi.

To deaden all sense of pity, danger, or risk, Abdul Khan,
after placing a sharp khundjar in his shawl girdle, imbibed a
strong dose of maddening bhang, while conning over for the
hundredth time the tender speeches his extremely slender stock
of broken English would enable him to make ; speeches in
which he thought to describe the depth of his love—a passion
of which he had no more conception than an Ashantee.
While thus engaged, he looked with grim triumph to the

point of his finely tempered khundjar, thinking it would win him, through terror of death, what he never could gain from her love ; and as the fumes of the bhang mounted to his excited brain, the black and dastardly thought occurred to him, that rather than she should become the prize of another, he would ultimately destroy her, gallop to Cawnpore, and join the Nana of Bithoor, that incarnate fiend, at whose behest the terrible well of Cawnpore had been filled to the brim with the slaughtered women and children of the European residents.

With his eyes on fire now, he gave a wild and stealthy glance about him, to assure himself that he was unobserved ; for there was a method in the temporary madness as well as the general villainy of the Meah Sahib, and then he took his way deliberately to the now empty apartments of the Ranee, beyond which he knew she was in one which he had never entered, as it was occupied specially by Henriette, who— when the Rajah did not command her attendance to amuse him with the vina, which she had rapidly learned to play, or to witness his shooting in the balcony—usually secluded herself there ; avoiding the Ranee and all the rest, who, she knew, were openly jealous and envious of her white beauty.

The unusually voiceless silence of the place encouraged the hopes of Abdul ; for he knew that hours must elapse ere the procession returned from the mosque. He paused for a moment as he softly crossed the tesselated floor ; for with the usual Mohammedan courtesy he had cast aside his slippers, and already in imagination he held Henriette in his arms, rending aside her veil, covering her pale face with hot kisses that were odorous of bhang, and pressing her with frenzy to his breast.

" Another minute," thought he, " and all this will come to pass ; but stay—I must not alarm her ; it shall be soft entreaties first, and stern coercion after. If the Feringhee slave repel me——"and at that idea he panted rather than breathed, he clenched his strong white teeth, and an expression came over his dark face and gleaming bloodshot eyes—bloodshot with the maddening drug and the fierce passion that inflamed him—an expression which it was fortunate poor Henriette could not see, as it made Abdul look so like one of his native tigers.

"Shookr Allah," he exclaimed, "it is time to put an end to all this! She will implore mercy in her own tongue, no doubt; but I cannot understand it."

Above the entrance to her room was painted among beautiful arabesques of green and gold, this sentence from the thirty-seventh chapter of the Koran, describing the Mohammedan heaven:

"And near them shall lie the virgins of paradise, refraining their looks from beholding any save their spouses, having large black eyes, and skin like the eggs of an ostrich covered with feathers from the dust."

This Abdul deemed a good omen; for though the comparison seemed strange, the Orientals think that nothing resembles the delicate skin of a woman so closely as the egg of the ostrich. He drew back the blue-silk hanging which in the little Saracenic arch-way served for a door, and as a sense of her presence within stole over him, he strove to appear calm and even smiling, adopting, as he conceived it, a winning exterior to hide alike the fierce passion and wild resolution that were agitating his lawless heart.

The apartment was small, but beautifully and tastefully decorated. Floored with alternate squares of rose-coloured and snow-white marble, it had two painted windows that opened towards the city, with vases of fresh flowers in them under the uplifted screen of scented grass-cloth. Its hangings were all of the most delicate blue silk, and in the centre was a blue-velvet divan, about four feet square and two feet high, fringed and tasselled with silver bullion, and thereon lay the pretty vina with which he had so often heard his intended victim perform.

Restraining his breathing, while dusky fire glared in his dark gleaming eyes, he looked all round the apartment; she

was not visible, but in a corner of it was her charpoy, or bed
the stead or stock of which was carved out of fine dark wood,
elaborately inlaid with silver, ivory, and mother-of-pearl, and
gracefully draped with white mosquito curtains, which,
as they were drawn very close, he had no doubt concealed
her from his view.

Weary with a sleepless night, perhaps, she was no doubt
slumbering now, when a startling waking awaited her; for
Abdul was certain that she was not taken by his father into
the city, the festival at the great mosque being a solemn and
religious one.

He drew nearer and listened. How softly the poor girl
must be breathing, or how soundly asleep, the delicate folds
of the curtains hung so still. He listened for a few seconds
intently, and then could no longer restrain his curiosity and
desire to see her asleep.

With hot and trembling hands he drew back the curtains.

The bed, like the chamber, was *empty;* there was no one
there.

In his speechless astonishment at a circumstance so unexpected, Abdul felt the pillows; but, like the coverlet, they had
evidently been undisturbed since yesterday. It would appear
that during the past night it had not been slept in. Where
was she concealed? Where placed? He looked wildly round
him. How was she spirited away, and by whom? Was she
dead or alive? Had the Ranee's jealousy caused her destruction? He remembered with terror that he had observed a
bright but unfathomable smile on her wrinkled visage as she
had ascended into her gilt howdah that morning. To him it
seemed a strange smile of malice and triumph. Perhaps the
Rajah had conveyed her away to some residence unknown,
fearing the blandishments and personal attractions of his
worthy son and heir.

All these questions, and many more, occurred to him un-
answered; one strange and unexplainable fact alone remained; she was no longer in or about the zenana. His

first impulse was to grasp his khundjar; but there was neither a voice to stifle with loathsome kisses nor a white bosom to stab if she repelled him.

He hurried away to the subahdar of the guard; ordered three alarm guns to be fired towards the city, and their triple boom was pealing in the sultry air when, remembering suddenly that for two days he had not seen *me*, with assassination in his heart, he rushed away in search of me, with what success a little time will show.

CHAPTER L.

I BECOME A HURKARU.

AND now to explain the mystery of the last chapter. To me all chance of our escaping together from that strong and securely-guarded hill-fort seemed an impossibility, though at that terrible time all Bengal teemed with stories of strange hair's-breadth escapes, too often ending in recapture and horrib'e death.

It was a Napoleonic saying, that " an impossibility is only a difficulty to be surmounted;" but without aid from within, it seemed hopeless to think of getting outside our prison, and the law or doctrine of chances was no doubt against any more successful escapes for me in that land, so fruitful then of dangerous and desperate scenes ; yet life is precious, and I would gladly have run the hazard again ; but though I was totally unable to assist her, my whole heart shrank from the thought of leaving Henriette. Speedily, however, I found that there was another inmate of Chutneypore quite as anxious as myself for her absence therefrom.

This was the Ranee, who, with a woman's keen instinct in such matters—an instinct rendered all the more acute by jealousy — had shrewdly suspected that I took a deeper interest in Henriette than mere friendship required or warranted.

I have said that for two days Abdul Khan had not seen me, and my disappearance came about in this way.

On the evening of the last day I had seen her, I was lying on my charpoy, weary and full of anxious and bitter thoughts, when I was suddenly visited by the Ranee's friend, the aged Moollah, Abdallah Ebn Obba, a little attenuated man, having piercing black eyes under shaggy and impending brows that were now white with years. He wore a vast green turban and flowing robes of spotless white, with a great rosary of sandalwood, having ninety-nine beads strung thereon, dangling from his left wrist. Though of a totally different race, there was in his aspect and bearing much that reminded me of my former protector, old Sivaji Bulwant the Shastree.

" In the name of the most Merciful !" said he, folding his hands and bowing his head.

I repeated the usual greeting, and requested him to be seated, while feeling intensely surprised by a visit so unexpected ; but he lost no time in acquainting me with the object of his mission.

" I come, captain sahib, by order of her Highness the Ranee," said he ; " and I have to ask you if you are the brother or the husband of the white lady who is the prisoner of the Rajah ?"

" I am neither, most reverend Moollah," I replied, with growing interest and wonder, and with fear of his ultimate object.

" Her lover, then--for such the Ranee thinks you?"

I shook my head, for any admission might be perilous at such a time.

" What then ?"

" Her friend only—as I said once before."

" Do friends in your country weep and embrace when they meet ?"

" Consider the strange circumstances under which we did meet."

He shrugged his shoulders with an air of contempt, as Mohammedans never manifest emotions of tenderness or surprise.

" Her great beauty," said he, " has roused the ready jealousy of the Ranee ; but she need not fear, for the Rajah sees that the fair slave may be the cause of dissension between him and his son, the Meah Sahib, and has, I know, an intention of presenting her to the King of Delhi."

" To the King of Delhi !" I repeated mechanically, and in a breathless voice, for this was the old wretch at whose behest forty-eight young ladies were so infamously used within the palace, and then abandoned to the rabble in the streets.

" Yes ; what is there so surprising in that ? The revolt is spreading fast and far, and if he is successful, Hafiz will naturally desire to win favour with a son of the House of Timour."

" Does the Ranee know of this—this terrible intention ?"

" No ; hence my visit to you.   She pities you and the poor white lady, and proposes to give you and her the means of escaping."

For some seconds I was too agitated by this unexpected intelligence to speak ; so the Moollah remained silent, stolidly watching the effect of his words.

" This is not a snare, I hope ?" I asked, having now learned to suspect the purpose of every native.

" Snare ?" replied the Moollah, with the slightest tone of indignation. " What object has she, what object have I, in seeking to delude you ? Her plan is this ; that I disguise you as a Hurkaru of the Rajah, for as such you can freely pass the gates of the fort unquestioned, and come to my house beside the great mosque, where you shall learn our further plans."

" And—and the lady ?" said I, with an imploring voice.

" Shall be free to-morrow ; but for that your aid is requisite. Do you agree ?"

" Oh, can you ask me such a question ?" I asked, with my hands clasped. " But you swear to me that she shall be free ?"

" What need is there of swearing? Who but you, an un-believer, in all Oude or Rajpootana, would doubt the word or question the promise of Abdallah Ebn Obba ?"

" Pardon me, reverend sir," I was beginning, when he said curtly, while rising from the divan on which he had been seated cross-legged :

" Do you accept or decline ?"

In what terms and with what broken utterances I poured forth my thanks, I know not now ; but he promised to revisit me in an hour ; and the frame of mind in which I passed it the reader may conceive, but I cannot describe. I remem-bered how at one of our interviews, when hopeless myself, I had sought to encourage hope in Henriette.

" This fort seems of vast strength, and closely guarded too," she had said, with her eyes full of tears.

" The very idea that it is so secure may enable us to get out of it," said I ; " do take courage, Miss Guise."

" Here you might call me Henriette," she replied, with a haggard smile.

" My dear friend Henriette, then ?"

I had greatly dreaded the jealousies of the father, the son, and Ranee, who all three might easily have been prompted to an outrage on a being so helpless as Henriette ; but this proposed transmission of her to the old tyrant at blood-stained Delhi was a new peril which I could not have anticipated, and at the hazard of my life I was more than ever ready to engage in any attempt to rescue her. I now felt that without achiev-ing her liberty my own would be valueless ; and I could not but reflect how strange was the coincidence that we were thus thrown together at Chutneypore, and that save for the

mere incident of the rifle-shooting from the balcony I might
never again have heard of her existence. In that case, what
might have been her future? I shrank from contemplating
it.

Fain would I have thanked the Ranee in person, but that
was impossible. How distinctly her face came before me,
with her large rolling black eyes, her small brown shrivelled
features, a mass of puckers and grotesque wrinkles, her nose-
ring, and her rubies !

Punctually at the stated time, the Moollah Abdallah came
again, and drew from under his flowing white robes a disguise for me, a jacket and dootee, or breeches of yellow-and-
black cotton, with a white turban, together with some kind of
pigment sent by the Ranee to darken my complexion. I
attired myself with a heart that beat lightly, and with the aid
of a pair of scissors completely altered the trim of my beard
and moustache. The Moollah then placed in my hand the
badge, or weapon, of my office, a short stout staff, about the
size of a constable's bâton, painted with alternate rings of
red, yellow, and black, and having at the upper end a large
cotton tuft of the same colours, from amid which there projected a lance-head as long as a bayonet of fine steel, with a
point as sharp as a needle.

" Soobhan Allah (Praise God), your own mother would not
know you," said the Moollah approvingly. " Now, as one of
the Rajah's Hurkarus, or foot-messengers, no man dare stop
you on the highway."

I grasped the formidable weapon with a firm hand, and felt
that I would have extremely little compunction in using it
against any one who interfered with me.

" Let us go now—we shall pass out of the fort together—
ere the evening prayers begin," said Abdallah, and I prepared with alacrity to obey him, at the same time resolving
that if I failed to achieve the release of Henriette, I would
return and surrender myself to Hafiz.

Dusk was closing now, and I must admit that when the

subahdar commanding the guard at the gate of the fort ordered the klinket, or little wicket, therein to be unbarred to let us pass out, my heart beat painfully with excitement, for every instant I might be missed and an alarm given. As we hastened down the winding way towards the gate of the town, I often turned and looked to the towering masses of the hill-fort, then tinted almost with crimson in the last light of the sun that had set, its purple shadows deepening into black where the round towers projected from the crenulated curtain-wall that connected them ; and ever and anon, till we fairly entered the town, my gaze went up to that portion of the building in which I knew the zenana was, for *she* was there ; but how she was to be got out of it was as yet perfectly beyond my conception, and the taciturn old Moollah failed as yet to enlighten me.

As we passed through the darkening streets, I soon became sensible of the value of the disguise he had given me, for in my character of Hurkaru all made way for me, and without risk or molestation we reached his house beside the great mosque. It was a small but well-built edifice, like others there, having extremely small windows, so made for the double purpose of keeping the rooms cool during the hot winds and to prevent opposite neighbours from overlooking them.

Ere I would seat myself or partake of the simple refreshments he offered me, I implored the Moollah to inform me of his farther plans, which were simple indeed, and yet not without perils to be encountered. At midnight I was to return to the Rajah's fort, place myself beneath the balcony, from which we used to shoot, "and there the Mehm Sahib would be lowered down to me." Then horses would be given us, and we should set out on the morrow.

Still I had painful doubts, for these Mohammedans were so utterly cruel and barbarous, so given to sport with the tenderest affections of their European prisoners, that it was quite possible this poor victim might be lowered down to me without her head.

No episode was too terrible for the then state of life in Bengal.

CHAPTER LI.

HOW WE SUCCEEDED.

I LISTENED nervously to every sound in the streets without, fearing that I should be missed, pursued, and traced, but grew calmer after the dead silence and stillness peculiar to all Mohammedan towns—the barking of pariah dogs excepted, after the booths and bazaars are closed and all the people in doors—fell upon Chutneypore ; and a little before midnight we once more repassed the town-gates, which the guard opened to us unquestioned, and in the dark proceeded towards the appointed place, past the ruins of the Resident's house.

To avoid exciting unnecessary suspicion or attention, which might prove dangerous, after we were both missed, it was arranged that, when we had the lady with us, we should not return to Abdallah's house by the way we had come ; but that we were to cross the stream which nearly encircled the base of the hill on which the fort stands, and make our way to a little private door that led to the mosque, and of which he had the key.

" Who are to lower the lady down to us ?" I asked.

" Two men-servants of the Ranee," he replied.

" Men—men in the zenana ?" I asked with surprise.

" No ; in a room beneath it, to which she will be conveyed."

The dreadful suspicion of which I have hinted again flashed upon me, so after a little pause, I said,

" Is not this perilous work ?"

" Very, captain sahib—perilous indeed."

" I mean, what will prevent these men talking of this affair ?"

" One very sufficient reason—neither has got a tongue in his head," was the composed reply.

" Mutes ?" I exclaimed.

" Yes ; and were they in any way to indicate what they had done, the Ranee would send their heads to the Kotwal."

" If no light should be visible ?" I suggested.

" Inshallah ! in that case we can but return to my house," was the composed reply of the Moollah, who shared neither my fears nor anxieties.

Absurd though this my second disguise, melo-dramatic though the whole enforced situation, my thoughts flashed back to the days at Thorsgill Hall, by mere contrast probably, and to the lovely close-mown lawn where I had wandered so often with Henriette ere Blanche Bingham came ; and its sunny terrace, with the sweet odours of the roses, jasmine, and honeysuckle that clambered about the mullioned oriels. Should *we* ever see that place again ?

Anon came memories of the regiment—of the now almost forgotten mess-table covered with gorgeous plate, some of it as old as the days of the old 95th, and with it the faces of Tom Prior, Joe Lonsdale, Jack Dormer, and others in that corps, which had been my happy, though wandering, home. Should I ever see *them* again ?

In two days, perhaps, or—never.

Had that other life, to which I looked vaguely, wonderingly back, a real existence—that life of which Henriette seemed the link—or was the horrible present a reality or a fitful nightmare ?

The night was fortunately an extremely dark and moonless one. The city was still and gloomy, as if it were the abode of the dead. Not a light was visible in any part of it. After a time even the voices of the pariah dogs passed away ; but

24—2

the howls of a pack of jackals resounded in the wood, through which we approached the fort—the same wood into which I had shot on that, to me, most eventful day, from the balcony of the zenana. Fitfully they came to the ear, and were blown away by the passing night wind.

The sky was starry, and across it the crape-like clouds were hurrying in heavy, dark, and weird-like masses, while silent sheet-lightning lit at times the flat horizon, and then the walls and towers, the domes and minarets, or other masses of the sleeping city, were seen to flash out of the darkness that involved them, in strong black outline, for an instant, but an instant only.

As we ascended the hill-side, above us towered the tall façade of the zenana, and other buildings which Havelock's Highlanders blew to atoms after their advance to Lucknow. I looked upward with intense anxiety—with emotions more keen and exciting than I felt when, with the ladder-party, I crept up the slope at the storming of the Redan before Sebastopol.

Oh, was it really to be that Henriette Guise was to owe her safety, her life perhaps, a second time to me? There was no light visible at the place where we expected to see one; but I could discern a white female figure on the balcony outside the horse-shoe arches. Was she there? I asked; but the Moollah averred that the person we saw was the Ranee awaiting us.

Suddenly a clear white light shone out for a moment from one of the windows. It was the appointed signal, and on seeing it, the Moollah clapped his hands thrice. It was then extinguished. All that followed now was like a dream, and passed as quickly as the events of one. I heard a faint half-stifled cry of alarm, and saw at a window below the balcony, but about twenty feet above me, another white female figure, whose garments fluttered in the wind as she was lifted out and lowered softly down by ropes attached to a chair in which she was seated, and to which she was secured by a turban cloth—

an English arm-chair, no doubt part of the "loot" of the Resident's mansion.

In another moment I had Henriette in my arms, and was hurrying her down the slope towards the river, a tributary of the Ganges. We had no time to waste on words—no time for ceremony, questions, or explanations—then. All these were reserved for a future hour ; and silently, but hand in hand, we hurried on after the old Moollah Ebn Obba, who gathered up his flowing skirts and led the way with all the speed he could exert to a ford on the stream, which was fortunately somewhat shallow.

The water, however, rose nearly to my waist, when lifting Henriette in my arms I bore her through it so carefully that not an inch of her dress was wetted.

"O Captain Rudkin," she said in a quick breathless voice, as her head rested for a moment on my shoulder, " how good, how kind you are to me !"

She was sobbing now, and too excited for words.

"Goodness and kindness are but cold emotions," I replied with a swelling heart. "Do you not know that I would die to protect or serve you ? I saved you once from fire, and do so now from water," I added, making a feeble attempt at a jest.

"Oh, deep indeed is the debt of gratitude I owe ! And that good old man too ! This escape has been all his own plan. But for him—for you——"

Her voice was completely broken now, and she clung to my arm in silence as we followed the stolid and taciturn Moollah round the exterior of the town wall—a rampart of sun-baked mud—for half a mile, till we reached the private gate of which we had the key.

While her soft arm and tremulous little hand clung to me, my heart beat high with joy and pleasure even then. Henriette and I were no more engaged than we had been at Thorsgill Hall, and yet somehow I had a feeling that we were so ; though, save what the eyes said, nothing of love had passed between us, in India at least. After proceeding for some time in silence, my thoughts began to take the form of words.

" Miss Guise," I began, in a voice that faltered ; " oh Henriette—do permit me to call you so—how is all this to end with us ?"

" Heaven only knows !" said she, mistaking my meaning.

" We cannot continue to be—to be——"

" What, Captain Rudkin—victims always ?"

" No—friends only."

" Why not ? how ?" she asked ; and even then I felt her arm half withdrawn from mine.

" After our sweet past time at Thorsgill—how far off that past seems now ! and after the agitating present ?"

" Why not friends ?"

" Why not something nearer, dearer—more tender ?"

" Scarcely," said she coldly ; and then she added, in a touching voice, " You are indeed my dearest friend ; but ah, Captain Rudkin, this is not a place or time—circumstanced as I am—for you to talk thus, and to me !"

" Most true. I pray you to pardon me."

She pressed my arm slightly, as if to assure me that it was granted ; but I felt that her tiny rebuke was a correct one ; and at that moment our guide opened the little gate and ushered us into a silent, empty, and narrow thoroughfare that led direct to his house. We did not reach it a moment too soon, for already the ruddy dawn was gilding the domes of the mosque, the galleries, and open cupolas of the minarets ; the rich masses of the trees, yet heavy with the refreshing dews of the past night, and exhaling the fragrance of the tuberoses, orange flowers, and limes in the garden of Abdallah Ebn Obba, when all the ground gave forth that pleasant odour which is peculiar to the early Indian morning, and which, as a writer has it, " mingles so peculiarly with every other perfume."

A few persons were now in the streets, hastening to the mosques rosary in hand ; for already the shrill cries of the muezzins, shouting the beginning of the *azan*, or call to prayers, " Allah ho ackbar !" (God is victorious), were echoing from every minaret in the city.

We passed the whole of that day concealed in the house of the good Moollah, as he deemed it rash to travel at a time when, if our flight were discovered, armed Raj Horse would be sent to scour the roads in every direction. All that day was spent in the sweet society of Henriette, and it passed, though anxiously, most swiftly, for we had a thousand things to talk of and notes to compare. I ventured, however, on no more love speeches. Keen anxiety gathered in my heart when I gazed on the pale and worn face of Henriette. From long suffering and continued over-excitement she seemed so nervous and agitated, that I feared she might become feverish, or fall ill on my hands, when all her strength was most required to achieve our ultimate safety.

Everything continued quiet to all appearance in the fort and city, and the morning of the solemn festival dawned ; and listening intently for every sound that might indicate alarm—the discharge of a cannon, the beating of gongs, or the tramp of searching cavalry—I sat in Abdallah's garden, watching the ruddy light tinting everything with streaks of fire—the heavier the dew, the deeper the tints ; the tall rugged trunks of the talipot palms were glowing in scarlet against the pale grey of the western sky, and the stream through which I had borne Henriette had splashes of gold, amber, and even crimson, on its current, as it rolled away between groves and jungles, peepul topes, and fields of waving rice and paddy, on its way to the holy Ganges.

I then turned to meet the soft sad smile of Henriette, who held out both her hands to me.

To her I was kind, tender, and most scrupulously respectful in manner ; we were so singularly, so terribly placed ; so awkwardly, and yet so happily, thrown together. But how could I be otherwise? Neither of us felt quite at ease; and yet the perilous circumstances under which we were should have made us completely so.

The Ranee had provided horses for us at the house of Abdallah, with arms for me—a tulwar and brace of pistols. Henriette was disguised as a Parsee woman, to be called a daughter of Peeroo Mull, the banker at Allahabad (if we were stopped or questioned), sent by the Rajah to Lucknow in care of a Hurkaru. The horses furnished for us were Arabs; not those kicking brutes from Australia now becoming so common in British India.

Selecting a time when all in the city were rushing to see the Rajah proceeding in state to the great mosque, we quitted Chutneypore by the Moollah's private gate, and rode at full speed along the highway towards Lucknow, which we expected to reach about nightfall, making allowance for seeking shelter in some grove during the oppressive heat of the day.

We were not fated to see Lucknow quite so soon.

We had barely ridden a mile when three pieces of cannon —24-pounders at least—boomed from the western wall of the fort, above which their thin white smoke was seen floating upward in the morning air; and by this signal of alarm, as well as the hoisting of a scarlet flag on the zenana, we concluded justly that our double disappearance had been discovered by Abdul Khan, who for his own ends and purposes had remained in the fort and palace.

CHAPTER LII.

THE TOMB IN THE WOOD.

As I rightly conjectured that an immediate pursuit would be made along the road that led to Lucknow, I deemed it wise to make a détour, and struck into that which led, as I supposed, towards Shahabad in Oude. This of course took us somewhat out of our route ; but in my character of Hurkaru, and, moreover, as I spoke Hindostanee better now than ever, I had little or no fear of our making our way safely if we could avoid the Rajah's mounted horsemen, who would be certain to examine my companion closely.

Till nearly noon we rode on without seeing a trace of pursuers, and, after getting some most necessary refreshment at a dawk-bungalow, I conducted Henriette into a dense wayside grove to avoid the sultry midday heat, under the effects of which she was well-nigh fainting. There was an additional reason, which I did not confide to her. If pursuers came this way, and the keeper of the bungalow were questioned, the fact of her having been seen with me would cause the country to be strictly searched. I had incidentally learned that in this grove were some spacious ruins, and among these I resolved to seek shelter and concealment, perhaps till the morrow.

The wonderful luxuriance of the thicket, through which our horses made their way with extreme difficulty, greatly impressed Henriette ; for there, high over the jungle grass, towered canes that were sixty feet in height ; oleanders, ever the pride of the Indian jungle ; the flowering baubool, a pyramid of crimson and gold ; while in some places the thorny and prickly shrubs, with blades like sabres and serrated like saws, the dense, dark, and impenetrable masses of wild foliage and rank luxuriant vegetation, would have opposed the march of an army, unless its van were most active pioneers.

Beneath, the brushwood was full of insect life, filling the whole air with a drowsy, incessant, and monotonous hum ; above, the trees were alive with richly-plumaged birds, glowing in scarlet, yellow, and purple : blue jays, green pigeons, crested woodpeckers, ring-necked parroquets, the slender fly-catchers, and the lovely little tailor-bird, which sow leaves together with their sharp bills, and swing therein aloft in their sweetly-scented nests.

Exclamations of delight that were almost childish in their joy escaped Henriette as we piloted our way into the heart of the jungly tope, and some that were certainly expressive of extreme satisfaction escaped me, when suddenly we came upon one of those large, massive, and ruined buildings, half temple, if not wholly--a tomb—such as may be found scattered all over India, the relics of past ages, and of the races which have conquered and succeeded each other.

Therein I resolved to find Henriette shelter for a time.   On farther examination I was certain the edifice was a tomb of the Patan times, but I did not tell her so.   I assisted her to alight, relaxed the girths of our horses, and knee-haltered them, and after carefully looking to the priming of my pistols —the Ranee had provided me with a flint-lock pair—I stuck them in my girdle and led her inside.   There I hoped she would find repose—sleep if she could—while I kept guard against visitors, perhaps such as those that surprised me in the rock-hewn temple near Allahabad.

Though our perils were not yet over, nor could they be until we were within the sound of her Majesty's drums, I felt a deep and pure emotion of joy in being alone with Henriette and in being the sole protector she could cling to.   All this situation far exceeded my wildest hopes when I had been the prisoner of Hafiz, and when she and I were both in that mood of mind when any change of place or circumstances nearly—

anything involving action—would have proved a relief to mind and body, and when I first hailed the plans of the Ranee with transport and gratitude, though in serving us she was to a great extent also serving herself.

The edifice was square, and externally measured about eighty feet each way, with a domed roof, having an orifice at its apex to admit light, and was entered by an arch of Moorish form supported by twisted pillars, two on each side. Before it were two giant figures of red stone, which had doubtless kept guard there for centuries ; and now the matted weeds and jungle grew high above their knees. In many places the solid masonry was rent into great fissures by the tamarind and peepul trees that grew between the stones, and forced them asunder. In some parts the carving was elaborately beautiful, for true it is, as Bishop Heber says, "those Patans built like giants and finished their work like jewellers."

An altar-like block of red marble in the centre, with three steps round it, seemed to indicate that some one was interred beneath it—a contemporary, perhaps, of Mohammed Ghori ; but whether a renowned warrior, a favourite beauty of the harem, an omrah of the empire, or a holy Suyd, nothing remained to show. I do not think there is a "John Murray" for British India, otherwise I might fill a long chapter by a minute description of this edifice, for then I was more interested in Henriette Guise than an examination of its details, and I was distressed to see her looking so weary and so pallid.

Cutting down a quantity of the soft feathery jungle grass with my sharp tulwar, or native sword, I made therewith a couch for her in a corner, and seated myself near her on a stone. Our situation was very peculiar, in our absurdly strange costumes, together and alone in that wild and lonely place ; and so Henriette seemed to think, as she looked up at me from time to time from her pillow of grass, and always with a smile in her pale face and dark thoughtful eyes—a smile that, though sweet, was sad, yet full of brightness and a winning

beauty, so different from the half-mischievous and wholly triumphant smile of Blanche.

The forest without was, I have stated, full of animal life,
and teeming with noisy sounds ; but under the shadowy dome
of our strange abode all was as silent as a tomb should be ;
and through the circular aperture overhead one of those long
rays of golden light that fell in flashing flakes athwart the
trees without shone brightly and steadily down, till it faded
away on the inward curve of the otherwise dark dome, which
it served but partially to illumine.

"We are lost here like the babies in the wood," said I.

"But I hope we won't be found like them, covered up with
dead leaves," replied Henriette, looking up at me with that
smile which was so peculiarly her own, and which made the
pulses of my heart to quicken.

I was beginning to feel certain that this sweet girl loved me
still, though doubtless to anyone—even her dearest friend—
she would have denied it, and perhaps, after the delusion—
the snare—into which I had fallen with her cousin, she may
have felt a little anger at her own weakness ; but how true it
is that we cannot always control our own hearts !

Once inadvertently my hand rested on hers, and I was conscious that she did not draw it away, as on that evening in the
library at Thorsgill—that particular evening on which so
much depended, and which, from the many changes we had
seen, and the stirring events that had surrounded us, seemed
to have passed ages ago.

Unlike the rattling and flirting Blanche, Henriette had con-
tracted in her soft face an expression of calmness—almost of
seriousness from her habit of speaking little and thinking a
great deal ; yet her mind was full of enthusiasm for all that
appertained to poetry and art, and her imagination was rich
and active.

She knew, I hoped, my feelings towards her now ; a glance
of the eye, a touch of the hand, must have told her all ; yet I
resolved not to venture to speak of love, situated as we were

then, and doubtless she appreciated this delicacy of sentiment; and though neither of us approached the subject, we were both in fancy back among the ferns of Thorsgill Chase, and in the ivied ruins by the Greta and the Tees, or in the arbours of the old garden, with its ribbon borders of verbena, calceolarias, petunias, and lobelias, with backgrounds of dahlias and rhododendron.

The hours stole on, the shadows fell westward, for evening had come apace.

We had ceased to speak; her eyelids drooped, and at last she slept. I was so happy that she did so, knowing that sleep would restore her wasted strength; and while she slumbered softly as a child, I could gaze unwatched and unseen on the delicate beauty of her face, her closed long lashes, and, to quote a pleasant writer, "the placid sweetness of her unkissed lips."

CHAPTER LIII.

A LOST LINK FOUND.

OVERCOME by all she had undergone, Henriette slept the entire night; and during all the hours of it I watched near her with my sword and pistols beside me. The feathered tribes were all in their nests; the fire-flies alone were flashing to and fro. No sound stirred in the wood without, save when a branch, or a large leaf too heavily laden with dew, drooped, and a shower that sparkled in the moonlight flashed like sudden rain upon the jungle-grass and yellow gourds below. The still night passed on; and so, while listening to her soft breathing, and sometimes a little muttering, when she dreamed of danger, as dawn drew near it, I too, though awake, was in dreamland. There was a kind of intoxication in the sense of her silent presence, in being so near her, and all alone with her for such a time, and in such a lonely place.

The poor girl, who should have been dreaming of a new bonnet or a new dress, was doubtless haunted by visions of sepoy mutineers and other yelling demons in the shape of Indian rebels.

The dawn came in. Between the tall trees there fell patches of golden light that gradually stole down their stems; a wild cock or hen would flash from tree to tree, and I could see the shining tail of a long green snake as it crept slowly into a bush. Rank and strong in odour was the leafy jungle then, moistened by the heavy dews of night and fostered in the sun's fierce heat by day.

At last Henriette awoke with a start, and looked about her for a moment with astonishment, till she remembered where she was.

"I have been sleeping, and now it is evening, to judge by the light," said she, half rising from her couch of grass.

"Nay," I replied, "it is dawn."

"Dawn! have I been asleep all night?"

"Thank Heaven, you have."

"And you—you?" she exclaimed.

"Have watched you, as a mother would her child."

"Asleep a whole night, my dear good friend! How selfish of me!"

She held out her hand, and I took it between mine caress-ingly.

"My poor friend," said she, "how haggard you look!"

"I have been sentry all night," I replied with a smile.

"Ah, Heaven, if you should become ill!" she exclaimed.

"Don't think of such a thing, for what would then become of you?"

As we looked in each other's eyes there suddenly came into them that expression which we see but once in life, and which there is no mistaking. Each made the other's heart to thrill, ånd as I drew her towards me, I could but say, in a hushed voice,

"I love you, dearest Henriette, as you know I first loved you—before—before—"

"Blanche came?" she whispered.

"Yes."

We sat long and silent, with her head on my breast, till she said, in a low and broken voice,

"I do not ask you how much you loved Blanche, or if you have loved another since; but I know well that you loved me then—before she came. I can only hope that—that—"

"What, darling Henriette?"

"That you love me truly now."

"I love you more passionately and fervently, more adoringly, because you are so trustful, gentle, and true. The past has gone beyond us; we can but strive to take care of the future."

"I knew that when Blanche came to Thorsgill Hall she would lure you from me, as she pitilessly did."

"But," said I, smiling, "I once overheard you say to her, when you were together gathering roses under my window, and she asked if you would accept me, that you would certainly *not*."

"My reply was, 'Certainly not, without my papa's full consent.' Had you heard all the sentence—"

"How much misery might have been averted!"

A pretty blush crossed her pale face, as she said with a coy smile,

"To me it seems that in making this admission I have proposed to you, not you to *me*."

"In love we are equal, and it would matter little if you had done so, for I know that you—"

"Always loved you; and so I did and do, dearest Lancelot" (she had never called me by my Christian name before); "and oh, how much do I owe you!"

And this girl—a rose without a thorn, a dove without gall —I had deserted for a showy flirt like Blanche Bingham !

"Stapleton—" she began, and paused ; while at the utterance of his name, which grated unpleasantly on my ear, a kind of spasm passed over her face.

"You could never have been happy with that man—if the rumour of your engagement was a true one."

"I was tricked into a sort of engagement by Blanche. I did not look for happiness. God alone knows what I thought. Perhaps I hoped that there was in store for me that which a writer describes as 'a chance of dropping into some sort of stagnant happiness,' which might reconcile me to my life."

"My poor Henriette ! And you thought that marrying Stapleton would—"

"Put you out of my head."

"Yes."

"But never out of my heart," she replied, with innocent candour. "O Lancelot, I did love you dearly, long before that night of the fire, when I half hoped we might die together."

"How sweet it is to hear you say that you loved me !"

"Yes, and would have married you had you asked me ; but you lingered, had doubts apparently."

"Of my success, yes."

"Doubts which *I* could neither remove nor explain ; and then Blanche came, and too speedily she eclipsed me by her mere flippancy, for such it was."

And so, while loving me, she had engaged herself to the worthless Stapleton, and been on the verge of committing what General Bounce calls "that species of moral suicide which is described by the vulgar adage of cutting off one's nose to spite one's face, and which produces the most incomprehensible of all vagaries—marrying out of *pique*."

I had loved Blanche certainly, and would have done so still, had she not proved so false and fickle a fairy ; but I was glad to find that Henriette did not look upon me as a species of widower who never meant to marry again.

Heedless of the outer world, its dangers all forgotten, we sat long and happily in that old ruin. All was still around us, save the rustling leaves of the sunlit peepul-trees, as the breath of the hot Indian air stirred them, and the twittering of the gorgeously-plumed birds, which were songless ; but even with lovers there comes a time when the world will force itself upon them, and I began to remember the necessity for making an attempt to reach Lucknow, which could not be very distant from where we were.

I got our horses in readiness, looked closely to girth and stirrups, gave a last glance at my pistols, swung my dear companion into her saddle, and in a few minutes saw us clear of that lovely grove, and once more out upon the dusty highway.

From a wayfarer whom we passed—a pilgrim Fakir, whose left arm, as a self-imposed penance, was bound above his head, and had been so for years apparently, as it was odiously shrunken and withered up—I obtained the alarming information that a great body of insurgents were marching to Lucknow, and had actually halted within twelve miles of that place, which Sir Henry Lawrence was making every effort to defend to the last extremity.

He was, or more likely pretended to be, ignorant of the exact position of the rebel forces ; thus our approach to Lucknow, from which we were then fifteen miles distant, would require all my care and circumspection, lest we should fall in with some of their scouts or patrolling parties.

Our pilgrim informant had scarcely left us, to trudge barefooted on his long and weary way to Hurdwar, when at a place where the road went over the crest of a gentle eminence, between two fields of tall yellow Indian corn, we suddenly saw, about a quarter of a mile distant, and in our front, a party of horse : and so keen had my eyesight become by the necessity for exerting it, that I knew them in a moment to be some of the Raj troops of Chutneypore ! Their lances and bucklers were sufficient to convince me of this, and, if further proof were

25

wanting, the circumstance of their uttering a simultaneous shout and brandishing their weapons on seeing us was enough to convince me that we were recognised or suspected, and that their intentions were hostile.

Putting spurs to their horses they rode with increased speed towards us, and came on rapidly before I could quite decide what direction to take, as they were most unluckily between us and Lucknow, having no doubt pushed on in that direction during the night, while Henriette and I were in the ruin.

To avoid them at all hazards was imperative in the first instance, and yet the idea flashed upon me that we might only be riding into the jaws of a greater peril—the assembled forces of the mutineers that were menacing the station.

A road that branched off at right angles from that by which the horsemen were advancing was the only way we could take, and ere we reached it they were so close that we could hear their cries, the clatter of the hoofs, and I could distinctly make out their leader to be Abdul Khan.

"*Feringhee bong chute !*" ("You rascally English !") was their shout from time to time.

"Are they mutineers ?" asked Henriette, whose face was blanched with terror.

"No, my poor darling," said I, with a tone of intense commiseration ; "they are some of the Rajah's troops led by the Meah Sahib his son."

"By Abdul ! we are lost, lost after all ! Oh, what a fate yours will be !" she exclaimed in a mournful voice.

"Think not of me, dearest Henriette ; but keep a firm hand on your bridle, and we may distance them yet. Fortunately our horses are fresh after a whole night of rest."

"On, on then ! But unluckily I have neither whip nor spur."

"See, see, yonder already are the gilded domes of Lucknow !"

I pricked her Arab in the flank with the short pike given

to me as a badge of my pretended office, and the animal
bounded on before me, while I rode in the rear, as the sowars
had now begun firing.

"Do not be alarmed, dearest," said I; "even the best
dragoons fail to hit when firing from the saddle. We are not
yet within pistol range, and fortunately these rascals have
neither carbines nor matchlocks."

For nearly six miles our flight and their pursuit continued
thus, and as yet the way before us seemed clear and the adjacent country quiet ; but I became sensible on looking back
that two horsemen, being better mounted than the others, had
distanced them all, and were fast overtaking us. One of
these I knew to be Abdul Khan, and with this knowledge the
blackest fury gathered in my heart. Was she perhaps to be
torn from me after all, and after escaping so much, to suffer
at his hands a fate worse than death? My own doom, I
knew, would soon be sealed.

The expression of her poor little white face, as she looked
round from time to time, maddened me ; its strange beauty
seemed almost to have disappeared, for terror, sorrow, and
horror were blended in her features now. Accustomed though
we had been to so much and such incessant danger, I felt the
present peril the more keenly than any that had preceded it.
The events of the last few hours had made life more valuable
and Henriette dearer than ever to me ; and then we were so
close to Lucknow that protection, hope, and perfect liberty
were all at hand. Was the light of a new and great joy about
to be extinguished for ever?

Abdul and his companions were so close, that it was imperative to face about and try to rid us of one or the other ;
so calling to Henriette to ride on—which she did not do—I
reined up my horse, wheeled him round, and in less than a
minute they were close to me.

As the sowar came first, aiming at him by the eye, and
judging the distance correctly with all the force I could exert,
I launched the heavy club and spear at him, and I think it

must have buried itself in his chest, as he threw up his arms with a wild cry, tumbled back over the crupper, and rolled on the road in agony ; while, with his eyes flashing out the hatred, jealousy, and triumphant malice that rankled in his cruel heart, his dark visage purple with fury, his reins loose over his left arm, a pistol in each hand, and a tulwar between his teeth, Abdul Khan came like a demon on me.

He fired both pistols at once, and then hurled them at my head. Both balls missed ; but one took effect in the head of my horse, which sank under me. In a moment I was out of my stirrups and stood tulwar in hand, on my defence, resolving to kill Abdul and possess myself of his horse ; but suddenly I heard a strange cry from Henriette—a cry of *delight* —and an English bugle sounding cheerily "the advance," on which a score of Riflemen, soldiers of my own regiment, in their dark-green uniforms, black belts, and white puggerees, started out of a thick leafy grove close by, led by Joe Lonsdale.

"Fix bayonets !" he cried. "Come on, my lads ! Go at them like bricks. If we can't beat the d——d niggers, we'll die game, anyhow."

But at the sight of them Abdul turned his horse, and fled at full gallop with all his followers, while some of the Rifles, surrounding me with their sword-bayonets fixed, proceeded to question me rather roughly, and one who actually laid his hand upon my throat proved to be Dan O'Regan !

CHAPTER LIV.

IN LUCKNOW.

I HAD barely spoken when the Riflemen recognised me.

"Hurroo! hurroo!" cried Dan O'Regan. "By the mortial but it's the master himself, alive and hearty after all; and Miss Guise too! Oh to the Lord where have you been, and how have you been treated?"

Poor Dan fairly blubbered with joy, and we all shook hands heartily, he squeezing those of Henriette with such excessive good will that she evidently winced.

To describe the satisfaction of Lonsdale and my more humble comrades would be superfluous here; and after a few explanations on both sides, Joe informed me that the story of the pilgrim was quite true; that the insurgents were really within ten miles of Lucknow—of which place they had resolved to take possession, and enjoy the luxury of another massacre such as those at Cawnpore, Meerut, and elsewhere; and that he had, most luckily for us, been sent out with a scouting party, by order of Sir Henry Lawrence, to reconnoitre and discover their exact whereabouts.

"So bravo, Lance," he concluded; "you have just arrived in time to share in what Marryatt calls "the all-absorbing occupation of killing our fellow-creatures.'"

"If those horrible sepoys can be deemed so, Mr. Lonsdale," said Henriette, with the first genuine smile I had seen on her face for a long time, as the Rifles now began to retire towards the town, in which I was glad to hear that all friends in the regiment were well.

"You are welcome to the hospitalities of Lucknow, Miss Guise," replied Lonsdale, looking with pleasure into her soft sweet face; "but I fear that ere long our dinners will become a mere make-believe, like the feasts of the Barmecides. By

Jove, Rudkin, what a rum turn-out this is of yours!" added Joe, with reference to my disguise. "What is the part you have been playing in this new cast?"

"The character of a Hurkaru to the Rajah of Chutney-pore," said I, laughing for the first time these many, many weeks.

"It is said that old scoundrel has gone over to the enemy at last."

"The appearance of his son here in arms this morning confirms the rumour," said I. "Even in this disguise I could not have escaped him but for you and your party."

"And you, Miss Guise?"

"Oh, I was to be passed off, if possible while veiled, as a daughter of Peeroo Mull, the Parsee banker. The costume is simple, is it not?"

"Very," replied Lonsdale, laughing; "but I fear I should not like to figure in the Row, even with you, or walk down Regent Street with Rudkin; but we can rig him out anew at Lucknow. I am sorry to say that there are no end of dead fellows' traps there."

"Your own appearance is not very distingué," said Henriette; and I was glad once more to hear her laughing outright; for by this time she had learned that her cousin was well, and Sir Harry recovering from his wound. And, sooth to say, the attire of Joe and his party showed that they had undergone pretty severe work since the battalion had quitted Allahabad. All use of the razor had long since been relinquished; their dark uniforms were patched with pieces of red cloth and other colours; by incessant use, I could see that the browning was nearly worn off the barrels of their rifles; while by constant exposure to the sun those parts of their faces that were not hidden by hair were burned to a somewhat Indian tint indeed. But Joe was as happy and in as high spirits as ever; and it was from him that I got the first really authentic information of Stapleton's terrible end.

"If the poor fellow hadn't been gobbled up," he added,

"he'd have come in for a good pot of money on the Calcutta races, as I know he made a heavy book against horses that were his own. Deuced clever dodge, that."

When he spoke of Stapleton I glanced uneasily at Henriette; but she had gone a few paces before us, and was stooping from her horse answering some questions which the soldiers were asking her with honest interest and commiseration.

" You have a rough time of it, I fear, in Lucknow," I said, surmisingly.

" Yes, we are in harness day and night—Lawrence is indefatigable. By this time I was in hopes to have cut India—the service too, perhaps."

" How so, Lonsdale ?"

" At Allahabad I spun a rupee in the air as to which of those rich girls I would propose to, and proposed, as you know. If accepted, I had resolved to go home on a medical certificate, or without it ; those blessed lacs of hers would have made me independent even of the Governor-General. But now that is at an end, and it is no use crying over spilt milk," added Joe philosophically. " In Lucknow I was on the point of being hooked by a nice girl, daughter of the Chairman of the Poppy and Pepper Board ; but she went down country, while I was left lamenting. I believe every man in this world has a wife sent into it specially meant for *him*, if he could only find her ; but as he generally picks up some other fellow's intended, hence half the mistakes in life. Where mine may be it would be hard to say—as far off, perhaps, as from the first of January to the top of St. Paul's ; our great Sandhurst problem. But here we are in Lucknow ; that is the Residency ; yonder is the Emambara ; and to the left of it lies the Bhoosa Guard."

The expression of Henriette's face was now one of genuine brightness as we entered that which we deemed a haven of repose after perils too terible almost to think of, and saw the red-coated sentinels at their posts, and the Union Jack flying on the summit of the Residency. All seemed to speak to our hearts of home and protection; and for the time we both forgot that the rebellion was still spreading; that help was far away, and the insurgents within ten miles of us.

Blanche was then in Lucknow, as she had been in Allahabad, before me; but it stirred now no chord in my heart to know that in less than an hour, perhaps, I should see the fair face of her who had fooled me—the woman I had so weakly allowed myself to love.

She had called that love a *flirtation*. Such merely I now deemed it must have been; for when I looked at Henriette, and tenderly lifted her from her horse when we had reached the heart of the garrison, I half imagined I had never loved before—or never loved other than her, who was now so dear to me.

This beautiful city, which was ere long to become the scene of so much terror, suffering and disaster, is on the south bank of the Goomtee; a river which rises among the hills of Kumaon and joins the Ganges below Benares. Lucknow is a place of vast antiquity, and was long the residence of the Nabobs of Oude. Though its streets are narrow, tortuous, and irregular, it possesses many stately khans, handsome mosques with gilded domes, and Hindoo pagodas that loftily cut the sky line, especially those of the noble Emambara, which contains a mosque and the mausoleum of Asoph-ud-Dowlah. But now the whole of that building had been utilised as a hospital for sick and wounded officers. The former were generally victims of that deadly pest the cholera, which had broken out in the garrison, together with small-pox; both of which made me tremble for Henriette. The native population at this crisis numbered fully two hundred thousand souls. From the north Lucknow is approached by a bridge of iron and another of stone, having eleven arches, thrown across the Goomtee.

Aware that the insurgents from several quarters were coming against him in great force, Sir Henry Lawrence had not been idle in Lucknow. The extensive range of buildings known as the Residency was placed in a state of defence. At every commanding point cannon had been mounted ; a store of provisions was laid in ; and the native troops in garrison appeared, as yet, quite as interested as ourselves in making a vigorous defence. Henriette and I had not got in an hour too soon, as a little time longer saw the city invested on every side.

The Residency was crowded with ladies and other European women, making in all three hundred and fifty helpless beings ; but for whose presence our battalion and the slender 32nd, or the gallant Inglis's Cornish lads, might soon have cut a path with the cold steel to Agra, as we were far from sanguine of succour coming from Calcutta. Thousands of coolies were employed at the batteries, stockades, and trenches, on which they worked while looking forward to the time when they should have the luxury of cutting all our throats. The treasure was buried, and all the ammunition of which we had fortunately an ample store, was brought into the Residency ; and there, as in the Muchee Bhawn—an edifice originally the castle of the ancient Sheiks, when Lucknow was but a village—I beheld the most animating scene on entering ; for there were mingled European and Indian soldiers, gloomy prisoners in irons, hundreds of native servants and coolies carrying weights on their heads or dragging battery guns, rattling field-pieces to and fro among carts and camels, elephants, bullocks, and horses ; and there, too, was the roar of many noises and many voices, amid which the sound of a warning drum was heard occasionally, or the lively notes of a Rifle bugle, as orders were issued or detach- ments mustered.

The ramparts of the Muchee Bhawn commanded the stone and iron bridges on the north ; the south and western parts of Lucknow had been levelled, that the fire of its guns might be unimpeded ; towards the east it was commanded by the Residency, and overlooked the most populous and frequented

thoroughfares.   Everywhere its walls were well armed with
cannon, and when these were of light calibre, jingals—immense blunderbusses moving on pivots—were placed ; but
these walls were old and crumbling, so that a time came
when the reverberation of our guns would have shaken them
to dust.   However, luckily, the natives believed it to be im-
pregnable.   There Major Francis of the Bengal Native Infantry commanded, with two companies of Europeans, Captain Alexander's battery of horse artillery, a mortar battery,
and the gate-gun.

The Kotwal, or mayor, had shown himself zealous in our
cause ; but there was every chance of the vast population
rising and joining the insurgents when they came near.
Moreover, the city was full of Mohammedan fanatics, whose
hatred of the Christians was never concealed.

Good old Sir Henry Lawrence was so active that he frequently lay on a pallet near the guns of the Bailey-guard
Gate, that he might in person see his orders carried out ; and
he had organized a body of volunteer cavalry, consisting of
officers whose regiments had revolted, clerks, and others,
under Captains Ratliffe of the 7th Light Cavalry, and Boileau
of the Oude Irregulars, in addition to a body of English
Civilian Infantry ; for every European had now to fight for
his life, and the lives of all who were dear to him. Moreover,
they had nothing else to do ; business was at an end, and
each man found his " occupation gone."

To inflame the people against us, all Oude was full of
ridiculous stories, very similar to those circulated in England
against the Scots Highlanders in 1745.   We were alleged to
be slayers of men and women alike, and that we always refreshed ourselves after a day's work by a dainty slice off a
young child, and that we had amongst us wonderful specifics,
made from the bones of children killed for that purpose. But
all this belongs to history rather than to my narrative.

It is needless to say how warmly we were welcomed by my
Colonel, by Tom Prior, Jack Dormer, by every officer and

man of the battalion, as we were supposed to have perished long ago at Allahabad ; and we had quite an ovation up to the gates of the Residency.

"And Lady Calvert, Jack," said I, "how is she ?"

"Well, but not jolly," replied her cousin ; "she has become a regular saint. She was one of those we used to call 'officers' girls'—a gay and flirty rattler ; now, by Jove, she has become a model of marital propriety."

I could hear all this with indifference now.

" She is in the Residency, of course ?"

" No," replied Jack, " in a place where she is more useful."

" Where ?"

"At the Emambara, among the sick ; we'll find her there."

" Come, cousin Henriette, take my arm, and we shall join her."

From the terrace of the Residency, whence we could look down on the shining domes, the splendid mosques, and palaces, the gilded minars of the city, with its gardens, parks, and trees, we proceeded towards that which was soon to become a crowded place of suffering—the stately Emambara, where already Dr. Gargill and the medical staff were busy among the sick.

CHAPTER LV.

AT THE EMAMBARA.

FRESH congratulations, explanations, welcome, and wonder awaited us there. Blanche wept with excitement and joy; and I really believe that in her impulsive effusiveness she was about to embrace me ; but I think that something in the expression of my eyes repelled her.

What a change was there in all our relations ! She was still "fairer than a fairy," as the old general had said, but was as altered in aspect as in her surroundings. It was not with her now as it had been at her "receptions" at Allahabad, or at the bandstand, where every man—horse, foot, and artillery, with the C.S.—hovered about her, and was led to imagine that *he* was the courted guest or favourite escort, by her winning manner and sweet yet now conventional smile. How many men had she lured and led on in the past time, and then crushed by the announcement that she was engaged, or, to some of less consequence, married. Like those of many other ladies within the fortifications, her dress was sorely soiled and in tatters ; her golden hair was no longer dressed to perfection, but its shiny and still marvellous masses were simply, as she apologetically said, "knotted up anyhow." Her lovely white arms were bare above the elbows now ; I could remember the time when she would have "handled" them so as to show the dimples there ; but that period was past with her, and past for me too.

She whose fondest visions of earthly glory had been gaiety, balls and glitter, pleasure and splendour, carriages, horses, déjeuners and kettledrums, flirtation and adulation, was to be seen now surrounded by the sick and ailing, the wounded and the suffering, with a mob of orphaned little ones clinging to her tattered skirts. I regarded her with wonder ; and

Henriette and I, as we looked at each other, seemed to ask, was this Sister of Charity—for such she had become, to all intents and purposes—this changed woman, the same Blanche Bingham we had known, and who had carried on a senseless and dangerous flirtation with Colonel Stapleton, for which we both forgave her now?

She was in total ignorance of how much we knew of that affair; otherwise, even in that place, and at that time, her manner would, in receiving us, have been less assured.

Her chief daily occupation had been nursing her husband, whose injuries, received in the skirmish on the night of the revolt, gave him serious alarm in a climate so warm, especially as the doctor feared they might gangrene. I found him looking rather wasted; his fair beard grown greatly in volume, his head more bald, and his large blue eyes somewhat sunken and keen in their expression. He was lying on a charpoy, with a poor coverlet spread over him. It was near an open window, from which we could see the enormous branches of that banana tree which all who were then in Lucknow will remember growing close by the Emambara; and Blanche was bathing and fanning his face with Rimmel when we first entered the large, bare, and desolate-like apartment.

He held out his hands to us with genuine cordiality, and laughed at our disguises.

"I have not words to express my delight to see you both again, and in perfect safety!" he exclaimed; and added again and again, "it's miraculous, by Jove—positively miraculous!"

"I do hope, Sir Harry, we are safe here," said Henriette, for lack of something else to say.

"Scarcely, cousin—we are cousins, you know, Henriette," said the *blasé* ex-guardsman, looking at her admiringly, and caressing her little hand in his huge fingers; "but I am glad to see you look so well after all you have undergone. Well! by Jove, Henriette, you are the handsomest girl I have ever seen, bar one—my little Blanche!"

I felt now inclined to say, "Bar none."

With the first honest and genuine emotion I had seen in
her eyes since we had met in India, Blanche now said to
me, while taking my hand in a burst of warmth between
both her own, which trembled as she drew me a little way
apart,

"You saved my Harry on that dreadful night, at the risk
of your life, and with the loss of your liberty. And I—I—"
she spoke in a low and broken voice—"I thank you with
a fervour known to God alone! Never, never can I sufficiently
tell you, Captain Rudkin——"

"I was Lance once," said I smiling.

"Well, then, my dearest friend Lancelot Rudkin, how am I
to express my gratitude?"

"By not speaking of it," I replied, in a low tone, "I did but
my duty—or as he would have done for me."

"You had no jealousy?"

"None—that emotion, if I ever had it, was dead, I beg you
to be assured."

"It was noble of you!"

"Why the devil should I have come out here to soldier?" said
Sir Harry querulously. "I have a fine old place in the mid-
land counties—a stately house, a lovely park, twenty thousand a year when what I owe the twelve tribes is paid, money
in the funds, and timber worth thirty thousand more. I was
a lunatic ever to come to India."

"But for which," said his golden-haired wife coyly, "you
would never have met *me*."

"True, dear little Blanche," he replied, and with that conviction the fair-whiskered giant was consoled.

"You will soon be well—quite well—you dear, dear, delightful old thing!" said Blanche, with something of her old
manner ; and the burly Saxon smiled and caressed her.
Well, I thought, as I have said, that he was looking older and
more grizzled ; service and wounds had not improved the
"Brighton plunger" of her letter to Thorsgill, her "first love,"
as she had assured Jack Dormer he was. Drawing me aside
again,

"Did you see Stapleton perish?" she asked, in a voice so low as to be heard by me alone.

"No," said I coldly and curtly.

"It was a horrible death?" said she sighing.

"Most horrible ; but," I added, looking straight into eyes that once were so much to me, "it did not occur a moment too soon."

"How?"

"For your happiness," said I pointedly.

"My happiness !" she repeated in a breathless voice, while growing so painfully pale that—remembering the change that had come over her nature—I pitied her, and hastened to speak of something else.

There was a time when I could little have imagined that I should ever come to have merely a platonic friendship pure and simple with my dazzling little fairy, and that there was *another* who would be dearer still ; but to this state of the heart may we be brought, by attraction on one hand and re-pulsion on the other.

Ignorant of all this, and of the change that had come over me and "the spirit of my dream," Jack Dormer, thinking the regard she showed for Calvert might annoy me, resolved to cut short the interview, and carried me off to the mess bun-galow. So ended this most unexpected meeting—this dis-jointed conversation and extraordinary visit.

"I've good news for you fellows to-day," said Joe Lonsdale, as we entered ; "our messman has actually contrived to get a sheep, though it seems to have had deuced hard times of it before this ; so we'll have some dinner to-day, and that, I may tell you, Rudkin, is not a frequent meal now with the Prince Consort's Own in Lucknow, and we are glad to eat our meat without even that *one* sauce which Voltaire said the English only possessed, though they had three hundred and sixty-five religions. I have contrived to collar a bottle of Clicquot, so we'll have a drink, Rudkin—you can't have had much tipple since that row at Allahabad. You'll like this.

I have tried all kinds of fruit squeezed into champagne, and think that a sliced apple—a good Devonshire pippin if you can get it—is the best after all."

"We have only one glass among three of us," said Dormer; "a ten-inch shell exploded in the butler's pantry, so we have scarcely a utensil left."

"Well," added Joe, "we can use it by turns, like a spooney pair at a pic-nic ; and what's the odds so long as you're happy ?"

"Seen the garrison orders to-day, Joe ?"

"No—anything up, Jack ?"

"Yes, we are detailed for this affair at Chinhutt to-morrow."

"The devil we are !"

"Fact, my dear boy ; and every one says it may prove a general engagement perhaps."

"Are these pandy devils in possession of Chinhutt ?"

"Yes ; and we must drive them out—go at them like old boots !"

"It seems that some of the Volunteer Cavalry under Lieutenant Campbell were scouting, and on seeing a body of eighteen mutinous sowars break from a wood, made a dash at them, so great was their ardour ; and on pursuing them for some distance, till they had to retire, they found the whole enemy's force in possession of Chinhutt, and had to come back without having achieved the real object of their expedition—which was to ascertain the probable strength of the enemy."

"So, Rudkin, you are like to enjoy a little shooting tomorrow," said Joe with a sigh as we finished the bottle.

CHAPTER LVI.

THE BATTLE OF CHINHUTT.

At half-past three next morning, ere the rising sun had gilded the domes and minarets of Lucknow, while the dew lay deep on every herb and tree, and the guns and shot piles on the batteries glistened as if they had been rained on ; when all, as yet, was still in the populous city below, and calmly the dark blue Goomtee, which is there about a hundred yards in breadth, was flowing under its bridges, our warning bugles sounded, and then the drums of H.M. 32nd Regiment ; and "rigged out," as Lonsdale phrased it, in the uniform and accoutrements of one of ours who had died some time ago, I hastened to join my company.

Prior to doing so, I went to the Emambara, to take farewell of Henriette, who, having heard that some fighting was likely to ensue, was up and attired to receive me. She had now relinquished the fantastic, though for a time most necessary, costume of yesterday. A cool and simple dress of light brown-holland, trimmed with rose-coloured ribbons, displayed her handsome figure, as the loose, wide sleeves did her shapely arms, for cuffs and collars were luxuries unknown in Lucknow then.

Her fine dark hair was now dressed as of old, and I thought she never looked more beautiful than on this morning, when, after all we had undergone, we might be parting to meet no more !

Her lips were quivering, she began to weep the moment she saw me, and when I drew her to my breast, she looked up at me with eyes that, though dark, were soft as the starlight of the Indian summer ; love unspeakable was in their expression. What delight it was to think that those eyes and their proprietor were all mine !

26

"I am going to the front with the regiment, darling," said I, with a smile to reassure her; "to the front for a little time."

"To the front—will—do you think there will be any fighting?" she asked in a husky whisper.

"Most likely, we must knock some of those fellows on the head, to keep them out of Lucknow."

"May God protect you, dearest!" she said imploringly.

"I trust He will for your sake; we have escaped so many perils before, that I'm confident I shan't be hit now, darling."

"But you may be taken prisoner."

"Never!"

"How so?"

"I shall die first! Abdul Khan is among those fellows; only think of my falling into his hands!"

She buried her face in my breast, till the very marks of the thick black braid on my jacket were impressed on her soft cheek and delicate brow.

"You are to be my wife, Henriette—take courage."

"Oh, this is no time or place for marrying or giving in marriage," she urged piteously.

"That I know—but you promise."

"Yes," said the poor little hushed voice.

"Trust to me, and be mine—I mean in the time to come."

"Trust you!" she said in a low earnest voice, while her eyes were full of eloquence; "well do you know how I love and trust you."

"By the first dawk-boat down country, I shall write to your father concerning our engagement——"

"Our engagement—how new—how strange it sounds!"

"And seek his permission, my darling."

Money considerations, fear of "Papa's views," and of his proverbial "pumping in the study," were all forgotten now or cast to the winds. We had been so much and so strangely thrown together! Had I not twice saved her life, and was she thus not doubly my own, even had she loved me less than she did. A spasm crossed her face, for again the bugles sounded, and I knew that the men were " falling in," and that we must part at last.

" How red and sunken your eyes are, Henriette !"

" Oh, Lancelot dearest, dearest Lance—I have spent, for months past, many a sleepless night—nights of tossing from side to side—of wide-eyed, weary longing for the morning, though it might only bring me fresh sorrow and danger ; but never have I spent such a night as the last."

" Why, my love ?"

" I knew that the orders were out—that you were going to fight ; was not that more than cause enough for me ?"

" It is my 'occupation,' as it was Othello's," said I, smiling.

" But, oh ! I love you so much—so much—and if—if——"

Her little lips quivered and her voice died away again.

" Tush !" said I, laughing ; "there are some fellows who are very hard to kill, and I begin to think that I am one of them. Take her, Blanche, and be kind to her till I return," said I to Lady Calvert, for *she* was standing unnoticed but observantly by, with a half smile on her face ; and as I hastened away the eyes of her cousin followed me, with an expression in which love, sorrow, and worship were singularly combined, and which haunted me during the operations of this eventful day.

Our colonel was already on horseback in front of the battalion. He was a brave and fearless fellow, and had the conviction, after many most hair-breadth escapes in the Crimea, the Gwalior and Sikh campaigns, that he would never meet his death either by shot or steel—a comfortable state of mind to attain at that time in India.

" Fall in the Rifles !" (how welcome a sound was his voice of old authority.) " Gentlemen, have your companies quickly proved, and the ammunition cast loose in the pouches—we have not a moment to waste."

These orders were rapidly obeyed, and the battalion wheeled into line.

"Fours—right!" followed, and from the right, away we went at a swinging double for a time, with rifles at the trail, and in less than half an hour our dark-green uniforms were changed in hue by the white sand, which in hot weather is there driven about by the wind, and pervades everything.

It was exactly four in the morning when we moved off. We were accompanied by the 32nd (Queen's), only two hundred and fifty strong; one hundred Sikh cavalry; thirty-five Gentlemen Volunteers on horseback; a few of the 13th N.I., who as yet remained loyal; a body of armed native police; an 8-inch howitzer drawn by an elephant, and ten horsed field-pieces worked by native gholandazees. The morning was close and suffocating. Even the elephant seemed oppressed, and lumbered slowly along, but after a march of five hours we reached the village of Ishmaelgunge, and formed in order of battle on the Chinhutt road, under the immediate orders of Sir Henry Lawrence, a resolute-looking man, having prominent cheek-bones, a long straight nose, a moustache, and long goatee beard, but no whiskers.

The few men of the 13th were thrown to the front as skirmishers; we, with the 32nd, lay in the hollow of the road to the left under the village; in the centre were the mortars and cannon, and the Sikhs were on the extreme right of all. We were fainting with heat. Rum, water, and biscuits were with the baggage; but no refreshments were offered to our men, who, after a long march, buckled and accoutred, were already beaten by the morning sun which glared, like a furnace, right into their faces.

We knew that the enemy were in Chinhutt, a large village situated on the edge of a spacious lake, near the hunting-seat of a former king of the district; but we were fatally ignorant that they were not about four thousand strong, as some treacherous spies had represented, but mustering *sixteen thousand* men, with seven batteries of thirty-six pieces of cannon ; so we had fallen into a perilous trap !

One of their chief commanders was the Meah Sahib Abdul Khan, who had so fully committed himself by the murder of our Resident at Chutneypore, and aiding in the siege of Alla-habad, that to think of forgiveness from our government was hopeless, so most of his father's Raj forces were posted in Chinhutt against us.

We opened fire with a nine-pound gun, and as the report rang in my ears, my thoughts flashed back to the pale face of her who loved me, and I did pray earnestly in my heart to be spared for her sake.

Then a shell from our 8-inch howitzer, thrown at a range of 1300 yards, burst right over the heads of the enemy's prin-cipal column. On this, their guns opened fire all at once, and the booming roar of them on the ambient air of the echoing valley soon became awful. They were splendidly worked, and hence the slaughter among us became terrible.

Steadily we kept closing up, ignorant as yet of their num-bers, knowing only that their guns were very numerous, that we must quickly grapple and have it out with them ; so steadily and shoulder to shoulder, the slender, though grand old British line went on. Much is said about the necessity now for loose formation and so forth ; but I am weak enough to believe in the magnetic influence of the "touch of the elbow," the "shoulder-to-shoulder" of the old Highland toast.

As we scrambled forward over very broken ground, to my surprise I saw an European—an English woman, who had rashly followed the troops thus far, looking after us with eager and haggard eyes.

" Can I serve you, my poor woman ?" I asked.

" No you can't, sir, thank you, kindly, I am only looking for my poor Tom," she replied in a broken voice.

" Where is he ?"

" In number two company of the 32nd ; I see the company,

but, oh, I can't see my own Tom. I only know he's there, and——"

Ere she could utter another word she was torn in pieces by a cannon shot, and I turned away sick at heart.

Again I was under fire! Again I heard the fierce hum of the round shot; the crash as it struck some solid object, or the awful *squash* of a human body; again I heard, as in the Crimea, the vicious *ping* of the conical rifle-bullet, so different from the whistle made in air by old Brown Bess's ball; but I had been in the Crimea, so the feeling of a quicker beating of the heart, the dread of a sudden death, or, worse still, of a dreadful mutilation, did not haunt me now. I had also got over that propensity for the frequent and involuntary change of position, so usual in some men when they are for the *first* time under fire.

The little village of Ishmaelgunge being filled with the enemy's sharpshooters, a fierce, but sputtering fire of musketry was maintained by them from among the green compounds, the houses and trees, till white smoke hid the whole position in that quarter.

Colonel William Case, at the head of the 32nd, gallantly led them up to it, but fell, struck by a bullet. It is supposed that had he lived he would have succeeded in clearing the village at the bayonet's point, but his death seemed suddenly to dishearten his men, who paused and lay down under shelter of a green ridge, from whence they fired on the enemy as fast as they could cast about and load. On seeing the colonel fall, Captain Bassano rushed to his assistance. He was choking in his blood and breathing heavily.

"Captain Bassano," said the colonel faintly but firmly, "leave me to die. I have no need of assistance now, and your place is at the head of your company."

A few minutes afterwards he expired. Meanwhile Major Bruère, with a few of the 13th Native Infantry, and Lieutenant Birch, with the Sikhs, on the right of our force, replied to the fire of the enemy with great spirit; but that fire was simply overwhelming. Splendidly drilled and skilfully handled by their own native officers, the manœuvres of the sepoy rebels were admirable ; and it has been confidently asserted that had their leader obeyed his instructions to the letter, not a man of our force would ever have reached Lucknow to tell the story of the fight.

As our battalion went forward in extended order by alternate files, the light puffs of smoke from the enemy's muskets floated up from every rugged ravine, green bush, and the tall waving jungle grass, as we gave them shot for shot ; but ere long our bugles sounded to close to the centre, as they were coming on against us regiment after regiment, in quarter distance columns, and all with their colours flying in the proper places. The police force we had brought with us deserted *en masse*, and then, wheeling about, opened fire upon us. The rascally native gunners next cut the traces of their horses and began to abandon the cannon, and accompanied by a few terrified Sikh cavalry, the elephant with the howitzer was trotting leisurely home along the Lucknow road.

To make matters still more serious, a vast force of the enemy's cavalry, all clad in the Company's silver grey with red facings, and led—as my field-glass enabled me to see— by Abdul Khan and his friend the young rissaldar, came pouring on in one unceasing tide towards our right, in the direction of Lucknow, with the view of cutting us entirely off.

The whole ground between Ishmaelgunge and Chinhutt was now covered by one moving mass of men, whose steel ramrods, bayonets and musket-barrels were flashing in the blazing sunshine, amid the white rolling clouds of smoke. In a few minutes one body of cavalry, led by the rissaldar, and fully five hundred strong, was so close to our flank, that the colonel had to throw back two companies on the wheel to prevent them from encircling us.

"As somebody has it," said Joe, "I am a good average

Christian if you don't push my Christianity too far, but hang me if I don't put that pandy's pipe out !"

As he spoke he took up a short rifle, whose owner was lying on his back mortally wounded in the chest, and blowing balls of bloody foam from his lips, while his eyes were glazing fast in the hot sunshine.

Quietly adjusting the sight, Lonsdale took a steady aim at the rissaldar, who, turning in his saddle, was calling on his men to follow him, while he brandished his sabre aloft. The ball pierced his lungs ; he fell on his horse's neck, and then rolled heavily over on the turf below ; on this his men reined up irresolutely.

"Devil burn me," exclaimed O'Regan, "but that rapparee is knocked over and past praying for. Shouting on the Prophet too—well, may every nigger go to the devil his own way."

To us it was a moment of awful suspense, for our battalion was thinning fast. With the front rank kneeling, the two companies referred to poured in a concentrated volley, which made the horses plunge, swerve, and recoil, while the column trembled as if a single object ; and now a dashing deed was done.

Amid the dense smoke that enveloped us, for in the hot, still, breathless air, it ceased to rise or melt away, I heard a voice cry——

"Threes right—trot !" And out from among some trees came our little band of *thirty-five* volunteer cavalry led by Captain Ratcliffe of the 7th, "Front form—forward—charge !" followed rapidly, and these brave fellows, who but a few weeks before had been seated quietly at their desks in the city, dashed on at full speed with flashing swords uplifted.

The mutineers never bided the shock ; threes about they went, and fled at the gallop. "Five hundred cavalry and two guns to be hunted by thirty-five sabres," said one of the latter ; "it was a miserable fact !"

For a minute the ground in our front was thus clear, and

remembering that the rissaldar had not been unkind to me when in Chutneypore, though I had never learned his name, but only knew him by his rank as leader of a *Rissala*, or troop of Independent Horse, I went over to where he lay on his back dying, with his teeth clenched and tufts of grass clutched fatuously in his fingers. He prayed me to get him water for the love of Allah when he recognised me ; but not a drop was there to cool the parched tongue of any man in the field.

" I am dying I know, sahib--and your turn will come in its time," said he faintly ; "the people of each religion go to heaven their own road, even as they tread on through time, for generations and generations, their own way."

His right sleeve had been rolled up above the elbow, to enable him to use his sword more freely, and I perceived that there was bound about his arm a band of fine silk, which had been rent in his fall, and I saw within it a metal amulet, and a scrap of parchment, with some Arabic words written thereon ; but this talisman had failed to save him from Joe Lonsdale's bullet. He asked of me if the Meah Sahib had escaped ? and when I replied in the·affirmative, he told me that Abdul had sworn seven times by every vow a Moham- medan deems most holy, to enter Lucknow at the point of the sword, and to possess himself of my head and of the Ferin- ghee lady of whom I had robbed him.

Our bugles were now sounding to retire, and we had not a moment to lose, as the strength of the enemy was beyond our power to pierce or drive back. We retreated with all speed, yet having incessantly to face about and fire on the yelling columns that followed us. I passed close to where poor Colonel Case of the 32nd was still lying by the side of the road, with his sword grasped and his sightless eyes wide open, with the corpses of his men around him. There too lay Lieutenant Brackenbury of the same regiment dead, and Thompson the adjutant mortally wounded. Bassano had a leg broken, but got away by the assistance of a soldier.

Many of our poor fellows were so severely wounded as to be unable to rise : yet while retiring, we could see them fighting, some on their knees—fighting like true British bull-dogs to the last, till they were finally slaughtered. Many more, parched with thirst and worn with fatigue, fell down exhausted and were sabred by Abdul's cavalry. Others were struck by apoplexy.

Captain Stevens of ours had a leg wounded, and after limping with us for five miles fell a little to the rear, and was instantly destroyed.

Throughout all that most disastrous day the brave old Sir Henry Lawrence was seen riding about in the most exposed places, amid a terrific fire of round shot, grape, and musketry ; and when at last—sorely pressed by the enemy, both horse and foot—we reached to Kokrail bridge over the Goomtee, he wrung his hands in the agony of his mind, and exclaimed,

"My God ! oh, my God ! my poor soldiers ; and I have brought you to this !"

At the bridge, men, women, and children of all ranks crowded around us with vessels containing water, of which we all drank with a thirst that seemed savage. Among them I saw poor Mrs. Case, looking wildly into the ranks of the 32nd for her husband, who was lying dead at Chinhutt. We effectually prevented the pursuers from crossing the iron bridge ; but the daring Abdul with his cavalry forded the river below it, and in the hope perhaps of fulfilling his double vow, actually entered Lucknow near the Motymahal, and rode to the gates of the Khas Bazaar, scouring the whole south and east part of the city.

The guns on the Muchee Bhawn, worked by a few officers alone, drove the foe from the stone bridge, and from that day the siege of Lucknow, which might never have been but for our luckless expedition to Chinhutt, virtually commenced ; and how it was to end—unless in the destruction of us all— not one in the city could then foresee !

CHAPTER LVII.

ABDUL FULFILS HIS VOW.

FOR five long months Lucknow was fated to be, as some one has phrased it, "our wretched harassed home," ere the final crisis came ; and the last home it proved for many.

To recapitulate the succession of scenes and sights of sorrow and agony—of death by the bullet, by the bayonet, by small-pox and cholera, would but weary and appal the reader, while I am compelled to admit that no human pen is adequate to depict them : and many a gay fellow, who, when lounging in the windows of "the Rag," was particular to a degree about his kid gloves, satin ties, and bandolined moustache, and who would lispingly condemn this, that, or the other thing as "dooced bad form," was now fain to darn his own pantaloons, or patch his boots, if, fortunately, he had a pair to patch. While fair, gentle, and highly-bred women, once accustomed to all the luxuries and refined elegances of Anglo-Indian life—to have every thought, wish, and want attended to by a horde of native servants—were now reduced to serve themselves and others who were unable to do so.

Amid all this my heart bled most for them ; and for one in particular, my tender and dove-like Henriette, like others, now compelled to attendance on the wounded, and to almost menial drudgery.

The letter which I had proposed to write to her father was never written ; for, blockaded as we were on every hand, there were no means of despatching it ; and, I may here state, that ever since her disappearance after the revolt of Allahabad, her whole family, believing that she had perished, wore mourning.

By the thousands of the foe without, the slender "handful" of British in Lucknow were most thoroughly hemmed in,

and soon made to feel sensible of the horror and peril of
their completely isolated situation. The whole city became
suddenly alive with shot and shell. All the prisoners who
had been released from gaol, and all the native servants,
deserted to the enemy ; after which all Europeans crowded
into the fortifications, where many who had been accustomed
to dwell in magnificent mansions were glad to content them
with the most miserable little huts. After the first attack, Sir
Henry Lawrence decided that the Muchee Bhawn must be
abandoned, but the greatest difficulty was how to convey his
wish to the officer commanding there. I volunteered to leave
the security of the Residency and make the attempt, but he
declined, saying, " there is no chance of success."

Our rough telegraph worked ill. Some time elapsed ere
we could attract the attention of the little garrison in the
Muchee Bhawn, and when that was achieved, a dreadful fire
was opened on the flat roof of the Residency where the telegraph was being worked ; and the order to blow up the fort
and retreat to us had barely been accomplished, ere the
whole machinery was torn to pieces by grape.

Twelve at night was the appointed time, and most anxiously
we awaited it, for every advantage was on the side of the
mutineers, and every European life was most valuable. To
distract the attention of the besiegers we opened a heavy fire
upon them as the hour drew nigh, and this had the desired
effect ; so the whole force, with their guns and treasure, came
safely in. The explosion followed after the last man fired the
train. I felt the earth shake beneath my feet ; a volume of
fire seemed to fill the entire Muchee Bhawn ; there was a
dreadful sound as if the world was uplifting, and an immense
cloud of black smoke that obscured the stars, announced to
the city that 240 barrels of gunpowder, and 594,000 rounds
of ball and gun ammunition had destroyed the ancient fortress.

Our last shelter now was the Residency and its adjacent
buildings, all of which had been connected by earthworks

and improvised as a fortress. The former was a beautiful and well-built mansion, with lofty apartments, shady verandahs, and stately porticoes. It contained three floors in addition to the *tyekhana*, or handsome underground rooms, built as a refuge from the extreme heat in summer. In this edifice was crowded about a thousand persons; officers with their wives and families. Fresh air might be taken on the flat roof, but it was far from being a safe promenade, although high above all the other buildings.

As the firing was incessant, deaths by the bullet, and the not less deadly pestilence, were also incessant; but no man's loss was so universally regretted as that of Sir Henry Lawrence, who was mortally wounded one morning by a shell which fell into the Residency and burst near his bed, in which he lay weary and worn, and in the act of dictating some orders to Captain Wilson. An enormous fragment smashed his left thigh, and two days subsequently he expired in the greatest agony; after which the command fell to Brigadier (afterwards Sir John) Inglis, of the 32nd Regiment. Deep was the despondency that sunk upon us all when Sir Henry died, and many said aloud that our last hope was gone.

Some days we underwent a perfect hurricane of shot from jingals, cannon and muskets; often there were more than ten thousand of the latter blazing on the Residency at once. No place was safe, and many unfortunate ladies were killed or wounded in their apartments. Ere long the rebels took to firing billets of wood, pieces of iron and telegraph wire, copper coins and bullocks' horns—anything that was calculated to slay or mutilate. At an average our loss was ten men per day.

Hourly we watched the direction in which we hoped to see the gleam of bayonets announce that succour was coming, for rumours had reached us of old Colin Campbell and his hardy Highlanders; but the hours became days, and weeks, and months, during which we lived and toiled in the midst of death and suffering.

Among all the women in Lucknow, Blanche was now a bright example—as veritable a Sister of Charity as little Sister Louise Marie, who nursed me so tenderly at Bulganack. Doubtless she thought of the fate of Stapleton with horror, and with sorrow too, and how greatly a longer intimacy with him might have perilled herself ; and how much of selfish folly and coquetry there had been in her past life ; and so, perhaps, amid the suffering she witnessed daily, some tears of contrition and self-abasement may have escaped her. She who, as a child, had been full of childish fear in the darkness of night at Thorsgill Hall, now saw shells bursting and cannon shot crashing through the solid masonry, and could ere long look at them quietly.

" No fear of me," said she, more than once ; " I shall be brave for my Harry's sake."

But his illness seemed a very lingering one, and truly the atmosphere of the place was not calculated to restore health rapidly. The heat was intense ; dead bodies were decomposing in every direction ; the churchyard graves were shallow and full ; the air was pestilential, and we were pestered by clouds of great, cold, and clammy flies, that had been feeding on the unburied corpses which abounded within the range of our guns outside the works.

By natives whom we thought we could trust, letters enclosed in quills were despatched to General Havelock, then on his march to Cawnpore, imploring aid ; no less than twenty of these were sent by twenty different men, who must have proved faithless, as the succour did not come. I began to wonder how much longer this kind of thing could continue, our numbers were diminishing so fast. How long should I escape for *her* sake ? Would a time come when, like so many others, I might be knocked on the head, wrapped in a rug, thrust into a dhooley, and borne to a shallow hole in which some other corpses lay ? Then I would thrust the thought aside ; and taking my place in an embrasure among my own privates, would blaze away with a rifle, till the barrel grew too hot for the hand.

So fatal were the bullets of the enemy, that the wounded were fewer than the killed ; and now came a fatal night, when I was to lose one of my best friends. My company, with one of the 32nd, was detailed for a night sortie ; and just as evening was closing, I paid a visit to my friends at Calvert's rooms, in the Emambara, without hinting, however, of the additional peril I had to encounter.

I found Henriette with a little orphan girl, whose parents had perished, seated on her knee, and nestling in her soft neck. She was endeavouring to brighten the child by her smiles ; but the latter was struck by the anxious expression in her sweet face, and said :

"Mamma smiled at me just so."

"When, darling ?"

"Just before those terrible sepoys tore her from papa's arms at 'Allahabad, and I have never seen either of them since."

Little sobs followed, for she scarcely knew what she referred to.

The face of Blanche seemed, like that of Henriette, sorely worn ; her rosy lips, " once made for saucy speeches and sunny smiles," were quite blanched.

" You have done too much nursing to-day," said I, taking her hands kindly in mine.

" Yes ; I fear so."

" You have become very good and kind."

" Would that I were better !   I have been so silly and frivolous ; a foolish little thing, Lancelot."

" Oh—I am Lancelot again, am I ?" said I, laughing, in spite of myself.

" Yes ; you are to marry Henriette. She was the wife nature intended for you, not a giddy thing like me."

"And now I must go," said I, "being wanted at the batteries as usual."

Henriette looked at me with anxiety; but she had become so used to see me come and go, that on this occasion she had no special fear when I bade her adieu, and went forth with a strong confidence in my heart, knowing that it was in her tender keeping, and feeling for the nonce a bold trust in the future, with a certainty that succour would come. I felt so happy in the earnest love of Henriette, a love without cloud or doubt, that the air around me seemed actually full of musical sounds: yet what were they? The whistle of the red shell soaring high in air; the thundering crash of its explosion; the whizzing of grape; the heavy thud of the round shot, as it buried itself in the earth, or tore down a mass of brickwork; yells, cheers, groans, and the last sighs of the dying!

Oh, such a medley of anything but sweet sounds we had in Lucknow then; and one sound there was more exciting than all—the occasional shout of "A mine!"

And she thought I was going forth to the batteries "as usual," perhaps to Ommaney's, from whence I so often saw the lights in those rooms of Calvert's in the Emambara which I knew were occupied by her and Blanche. How different from the time when I had so often watched her bedroom light from the terrace of ivied Thorsgill Hall!

The object of this little sortie was to destroy, with its occupants, a house belonging to a merchant. It had been taken by the enemy, and from the windows of it they picked off our men by dozens. There was in particular one deadly marksman among them whom our soldiers named "Bob the Nailer," an African eunuch of the late King of Oude, whose double-barrelled rifle was becoming a source of terror, so Brigadier Inglis came to the resolution of destroying the place, if possible, and all that were in it.

"I have been almost without food to-day," said Joe Lons-

dale, as he and I proceeded to the muster-place together;
"matters can't go on this way for another month!"

"Shall we be on the face of the earth then?" asked Tom
Prior, our second-lieutenant.

"In it more likely," said I gloomily, as I thought of all that
Henriette was compelled to risk and endure.

"Duck down—down—here comes a shell!" cried Joe, and
describing a fiery arc in the air, a large bomb, with its fuse
burning clearly, came whistling over our heads, and exploded
with a mighty crash at a little distance. For an instant we
could see each other's faces in the darkness, and while lying
nearly flat on the ground I felt a fragment pass over me;
"this is one of the trifles incident to life in our Indian
mundane sphere," commented Joe; "a close shave this was
for all of us; well, this kind of work pays off my darkie
creditors at Allahabad, and saves me the bother of taking
arms against a sea of troubles, and all that sort of thing."

Joe gave a little sigh, as if he gathered satisfaction from
the reflection, and carefully lit a cigar while the men fell in.
Uniforms few or none of us had now, or if we had could we
have worn them, the heat was so intense by night as well as
by day. We, the three officers, were in dark jersey shirts
and flannel trousers, over which we wore our sword and
pouch belts and revolver cases; and often when counter-
mining the latter weapon was wanted on a moment's notice
to scatter some wretch's brains against the earthen wall, when
a sudden fall of the soil brought us instantly face to face with
the foe. We had with us a party of the 32nd Regiment, under
Lieutenant M'Cabe, a brave fellow, who had served in all the
battles of the Affghan campaign, in China, and elsewhere,
and who had won his commission at Mooltan, where he was
the first man to plant the British standard on the ramparts.

Quietly and silently we loaded, fixed bayonets, and stole
out of Lucknow towards the house, which we reached unseen
in the gloom of the night, though it was full of the enemy.
The time was one of keen excitement as we got close under

27

the walls of it ; every moment I expected to hear a shout of
alarm, and a blaze of musketry opened on us from the
windows, for at that very time " Bob-the-Nailer " was perched
on the flat roof of it busy with his rifle, returning the fire
which Jack Dormer and other of our officers, were maintain-
ing against him from the top of the Residency in the dark,
solely to divert his attention.

By a rifle-shot we blew the door open, and rushing in burst
all over the place. In every room we found sepoys asleep,
overwhelmed by fatigue, bhang, and other excesses, and all
undisturbed by the incessant report of the African's rifle
ringing overhead, or the occasional shelling that was going
on elsewhere. Every man we came upon was instantly
bayoneted, and Dan O'Regan made his way to the roof,
where he shot and threw over the terrace the terrible African
who had put to death so many brave Europeans.

This was all achieved without our losing a man ; but as we
were returning—the distance to the trenches being only seven
hundred yards—a random shot from a three-gun battery,
which the enemy had in an adjacent garden, struck poor Joe
Lonsdale on the right hip-joint, and literally smashed his
whole body ! The strange sound made by the ball as it
fairly doubled him up was dreadful to hear.

" Rudkin—Lance, old fellow," said he in a voice like a
sigh, " you'll write to mother—and—and tell her all about it
—that I died game—and the regiment too."

I could only clasp his hand, which was beginning to feel
cold already, as the blood was gushing from every artery and
vein in torrents.

" God bless you. Lance—good-bye, lads," said he in a voice
that was barely heard. His head turned to the right side,
and all was over. My poor jovial friend was gone ; gone to
that unknown shore which is washed by the waves of eternity.

His body was so mutilated that it was with difficulty we
could get it conveyed, athwart three rifles, across the space
between the Brigade Mess and Deprat's house, and by day-

light next morning he was laid in his last home. A foot or two of difference in our positions would have made his fate mine. I sorrowed for him long and deeply, at least as deeply as men may do who are situated as we were then, and ever face to face with death and calamity.

The great Mohammedan festival of the Mohurrum was now at hand, and as the observers thereof are more than usually fanatical and bloodthirsty, our prospects were fast becoming desperate ; for, as a writer says, we " knew only too well that every individual drop of blood in our veins, every eye, nerve, and bone, would be considered a graceful offering in the cause of Islam." This festival lasts forty days, and when the ninth has expired comes the Night of Butchery, when a massacre of goats paves the Moslem's path to heaven ; and we never doubted but that a most furious and combined attack upon the riddled and shot-riven Residency would be deemed a more acceptable substitute.

Thus with growing and gnawing anxiety did we look for those succours from without, by which the wretched survivors in Lucknow could alone be saved. The absolute terror of the ladies for the lives of their husbands and children was more than ever painful to see. We had many widows among us now, and many fatherless little ones, and every day's strife added to the number ; but why protract this portion of my story !

After our partial relief by the gallant Havelock, we still remained blocked up in that fatal place, though we could better defend ourselves ; but November came and found us still besieged, and still starving and fighting in Lucknow. Prior to that we had tasted a little of the sweets of revenge.

One dark night a sudden and furious attack was made by a strong force of the enemy upon a portion of our trenches, and while our attention was attracted by a mine sprung in another quarter, they actually carried a part of the works by the bayonet, led by a man of undoubted bravery, whom I heard shouting from time to time —

"*Leea! leea! jalloo bahadour!*" (meaning "the entrench-
ment is taken—advance, my braves!")

To enable us to direct our fire and distinguish friend from
foe, an officer of Engineers lit two or three gigantic blue
lights on an angle of the works. Steadily these burned in
the airless Indian night, and most strange, weird and wild
was the ghastly effect on the dreadful scene in the stormed
trench, where our men in broken masses grappled fiercely
and furiously with the enemy—all of whom were duly maddened by bhang—stabbing with the flashing and gory bayonet,
or braining them by the butt-end whirled upon their skulls at
full swing.

The red gleams of the musketry at times, the flashing of
swords and tulwars were all visible as if at noon, and the
brown faces of the sepoys, their black sparkling eyes and
white glistening teeth, tinted blue by the glare, resembled
those of incarnate fiends, or the demons of a Christmas
pantomime.

Illuminated by the same weird lustre rose the masses of
the buildings in the Sikh square and the Brigade Mess, and
I could even see the walls of the Kaiserbagh, half a mile
distant, shining in the wondrous gleam.

Brief but desperate was the struggle, and long ere the
lights died out, we had completely repelled the attack by the
bayonet chiefly, and had scoured the trenches, moreover
taking several prisoners, among others their leader, whom
Tom Prior disarmed and actually dragged in by the throat.
It was on this occasion that I saw a very remarkable effect
from a wound inflicted on a subahdar of the 17th Bengal Infantry. A grapeshot tore away his bowels, and actually
wreathed them round a rose-bush that grew in an angle of
the trench. He rose instantly, grinned in my face, and then
fell dead, for the vertebræ had been uninjured—at least so
Doctor Gargill afterwards told me.

Tom's prisoner proved to be no other than the Meah Sahib,
Abdul Khan of Chutneypore, whose atrocities the Brigadier

resolved to punish without an hour's delay after dawn. With Nusseer-ood-de n, a sowar of the 3rd Cavalry, Khoda Bux (Dormer's ex-kitmutgar), and two others whose names I have forgotten, he was tried by a drumhead court-martial. They were all sentenced to be blown from the guns; and it is but justice to say that they met this revolting death with a heroism worthy of a better cause.

The bearing of Abdul was grave without effrontery, and as he was bound to the field-piece with the muzzle planted between his shoulders, and his arms bent by ropes behind him to the wheels, he repeated aloud that part of the Koran which is always read to the dying, and which ends thus : "When the blast of the trumpet shall sound, all that is in heaven and on the earth shall be smitten with terror, except the chosen of the Lord, all men shall appear before him, humbly and prostrate."

The portfires fell on the vents of the five guns; the salvo rung; the group vanished in smoke, and a shower of gory human fragments ascended into the air to fall in a horrid shower upon the earth !

Thus was Abdul's vow, that he would get into Lucknow or die in the attempt, fulfilled—fulfilled to the letter !

CHAPTER LVIII.

HOW THE SIEGE ENDED.

My narrative is drawing to a close.   After this striking episode, in which from personal reasons I felt an interest so deep,
we had to return to the daily work of fighting the enemy, and
being battered by them in return—starving, often hungry and
sorely athirst—and hoping almost against hope that relief
would come to us ere long.

From the daily task of facing death and enduring toil—my
sword-belt never off—it was nevertheless delightful to be able
to turn from time to time to the sweet gentle face of Henriette ; so that at last I began to feel as if I endured it all for
her alone.   Though it was the chance of war and duty that
made me one of the defenders of Lucknow, I identified the
fact with the necessity for her protection, and in this view of
the matter I seemed to be fighting for her alone.

At last there came a day which I shall never forget—the
16th of November.

I had left Henriette with strange and vague forebodings of
evil in my mind, and had gone to my post at the Bailey
Guard Gate, with Dormer, Prior, and a strong party of ours,
to work a large gun which was placed there, in opposition to
two which the enemy had at the Clock Tower, four hundred
yards distant.   The long months of over-excitement the girl
had undergone was telling upon her health and appearance
now ; and though there was no change in her firm white arms
and dimpled hands, no hollow to spoil the oval of her cheeks,
her pallor alarmed, and the general expression of her face
haunted me, and while telling off my men to their places by
the Lancaster gun, I had on my lips an unuttered prayer
that succour might soon come, were it but for her sake
alone !

We were all becoming dreadfully emaciated and worn out by want of food and by excess of toil; while the deadly work in which we had been engaged so long, and the savage emotions with which we regarded the merciless foe, had gradually imparted a wild kind of hawk-like glare to our eyes, and a grim knitted expression to the muscles of the forehead.

"Even the little children in Lucknow began now to think like soldiers," says one who has written on the Siege, "and they became, as it were, fond of the 'game of war.' I heard one urchin of five years say to another, 'You fire round shot, and I'll return shell from *my* battery!' Another, on getting into a rage with his playmates, said, 'I hope you may be *shot* by the enemy.' Others (playing with grape-shot in lieu of marbles) would be heard to say, 'that is clean through his lungs;' or, 'this wants more *elevation*,' for these young scamps picked up all the expressions of the artillery, and made use of them in their games."

We knew that succour was coming now; but knew not precisely from what point or *when* it would come; our great dread being that it might only arrive too late.

On this day a desultory fire of cannon, and occasionally of musketry, was going on all round the Residency as usual; but the enemy were redoubling their efforts at some points, and hence at the Bailey Guard we had hard work of it to keep our ground against the two guns opposed to our one; while the clock-tower above them was manned by a few picked marksmen so much ducking and dodging were necessary as we fired the piece and dragged it back when recoiling, to reload.

"I wish we had some bitter beer here," said Prior with a genuine sigh, as he took off his pith-helmet for a moment to wipe the heavy perspiration from his temples; "working this Lancaster gun under a blazing sky makes one's clay want moistening inwardly. I never thought to turn artilleryman; but what's the odds, and so forth, as poor Joe used to say."

We had barely been in the battery ten minutes when casu-alties began to occur.

One poor fellow of ours, a corporal, working like the rest in his shirt and trousers, with sleeves rolled above the elbow, while in the act of charging home the gun, was struck by a bullet through the embrasure, and after reeling away for some yards like a drunken man, fell heavily on his back, with the blood deluging his shirt and spirting from a wound in his breast on which he placed his finger, his eyes looking wildly upwards the while.   Then one of his comrades bent kindly over him and raised his head.

" That bullet has finished me," said the wounded man in a low voice ; " they have hit me twice before—but—but have done for me at last !   I'm dying, Jack—I feel it."

" Pray to God then, comrade," said the other with more fervour than we usually found in Lucknow.

" I have too long forgotten Him, Jack," replied the corporal despondingly.

" But He ain't a-forgotten you—be assured of that."

What further passed I know not, as it was my turn to level the gun, and when again I looked round all was over.   The corporal was lying dead with Jack's coat spread over his face : and a few yards farther off lay poor Jack himself expiring with a canister-shot in his throat.

" How strange it is," said Dormer, " as some one says, that life should go out of our organism when lead goes in !"

" Not at all strange," said I ; " but one or two more of our poor fellows are over their troubles at last."

" Yea, sir, verily," said a quaint-looking old Scripture Reader' who had been attached to the 6th B. N. Infantry, but had not made many proselytes in that distinguished regiment, and who had now perched himself under the shelter of a deep sand-bag rampart very near us ; " they are indeed over their sorrows ; but has not the House of Ahab always suffered for his sin from the time of Elijah, whom the ravens fed, until now ?"

"Very likely," replied Tom Prior; "but stand clear of the gun, old fellow, or you'll have the recoil on your reverend toes."

Suddenly we heard an increased sound of cannon and of musketry too, but in a quarter where all had been hitherto still, and each man looked inquiringly in his comrade's face, while every eye grew brighter.

"That firing is in *rear* of the enemy," said I; "the sound comes from the direction of Secunderbagh!"

"Can these pandy devils be fighting among themselves?" suggested Dormer; "the Mohammedans against the Hindoos?"

"Scarcely, though that may come when they have finally settled us," said I.

"God!" exclaimed a veteran sergeant; "if it should be the relieving force!"

The firing grew manifestly nearer and nearer, and inquiries and suggestions rained thick on all sides as to what it could portend; and so interested were we, that we ceased to handle the gun, and crouching close to the parapet listened, with our hearts beating thick and fast.

Anon the firing lulled a little, and then there was wafted towards us on the soft Indian breeze another sound—that strange wild cadence, of which so much has been made in many melodramatic versions of our story.

It was the *pipes* of the steadily advancing Highlanders!

Then we knew that relief had come, and that we were saved at last—that old Colin Campbell—Campbell the brave, the resolute and the prompt—he who when asked by the Premier when he could start for India, replied, "to-morrow,"—was bursting at the bayonet's point through the enemy's rear, and breaking for ever that zone of fire which had begirt us so long!

Next we heard the bugles of the 64th—the Staffordshire—cheerily sounding the "advance." For a moment a great hush fell upon all in the batteries, as if each man mistrusted his organs of hearing ; then there rose a universal shout, mingled with a hearty hurrah, and cries of

" They are coming ! they are coming round from the Alambagh !"

Then as the glad tidings spread like wild-fire, many a mother wept when she embraced her rescued little ones, and many a husband clasped his wife to his breast—as I did Henriette—with a new joy never known till now.

" To the Lancaster gun again, my lads !" cried I ; " and now to silence those beggars in the Clock-tower."

Inspired by new fervour and fury, we worked the heavy gun like madmen—handling it as if it were a mere toy—and long ere we could see the red coats, the green tartans of the Highlanders, and the fluttering pennons of the Lancers, or the rest of that force which was breaking through the enemy, the guns in the Clock-tower were silenced, abandoned by all but the dead, and we were left in quiet possession of the Bailey Guard.

To relate how Campbell advanced from Cawnpore to Lucknow with a slender force, whose hearts were maddened by the sight of the Nana's slaughter-house ; how he stormed the Dilkhousa or Hunting Palace; carried the strongly garrisoned Secunderbagh after a most dreadful struggle, as every sepoy fought with a halter round his neck ; how Peel's Naval Brigade disposed his 68-pounders, " very much as if he were laying the Shannon alongside an enemy's frigate ;" how Wolseley, of Ashanti fame, stormed the Mess-house at the head of a company of the Perthshire, would be to include here facts that belong to history.

Suffice it to say that resistance was everywhere vain. Mercy was never given, and never asked. Like a flash of lightning, the bayonet's deadly thrust was followed by the shout of " Cawnpore—remember Cawnpore ;" hence in the Secunderbagh alone more than two thousand wretches met their well-earned doom.

Need I say that the joy of those the victors saved was too deep for words—too deep for aught but tears?

* * * * * *

CONCLUSION.

I HAVE said that Lucknow was relieved on the 16th of November.

On that day three months Henriette and I were married, and had left Chowringhee on board a stately P. and O. Liner, doubly happy amid our joy that we were quitting India for ever, after all we had undergone—our cross-purposes, mistakes, and deadly perils.

She it was who in reality had stirred all the depth of my heart; who had made my existence a part of her own, and had taught me that affection is love and passion is not!

The great steamer was crowded; many were going home with us now; also sick of the land we were leaving; broken in health, in spirit, and in heart; for many were the widows and orphans of the fallen; but I felt myself the happiest man on board, when with Henriette and the Calverts I watched the low and dark-green jungles of marshy Saugor sinking in the blue evening sea.

Thus Henriette was mine after all, so strangely do the wheels of Life and Fortune turn!

In the *Libro d'Oro*, where such names are to be found, that of my "once Fairy" still figures with those of a brood of little Calverts. At —— Hall, Sir Harry has long since become a hearty country-gentleman, learned in mysterious powders for fattening pheasants or physicking harriers; a great enemy of poachers, and curious in the crossing and breeding of all manner of cattle and pigs; while, mindful of

the terrible lessons taught her in the Emambara, Blanche
and the Vicar's wife go hand-in-hand in the matter of parish
schools and Dorcas charities, blankets, coals, and soup; a
promoter of the associations for clothing the young Ashan-
tees and Fiji Islanders, and for the evangelisation of every
place but England.

Since the dark and stormy days of the Indian Mutiny all
has been happiness with *us;* but ever and anon my mind goes
back to its stirring events, and to the faces of those who
perished.

Far away from "God's Acre," they lie in the hideous
battle trenches ; yet the brave hearts that moulder there
might serve to consecrate the city of the Sultan or the desert
of Sahara.

THE END.

BILLING AND SONS, PRINTERS, GUILDFORD, SURREY,

GEORGE ROUTLEDGE & SONS'
RAILWAY CATALOGUE.

⁎ *The columns of prices show the forms in which the Books are kept —e g., Ainsworth's Novels are kept only in paper covers at 1/, or limp cloth gilt, 1/6; Armstrong's only in picture boards at 2/, or half roan, 2/6.*

Paper Covers.	Limp Cl. Gilt.					Picture Boards.	Half Roan.
		AINSWORTH, W. Harrison—					
1/	1/6	Auriol ...	...	...	...	—	—
—	—	Boscobel ...	...	...	...	2/	—
1/	1/6	Crichton ...	...	...	...	—	—
1/	1/6	Flitch of Bacon ...	...	...		—	—
1/	1/6	Guy Fawkes ...	...	...		—	—
1/	1/6	Jack Sheppard ...	...	...		—	—
1/	1/6	James the Second	...	...		—	—
1/	1/6	Lancashire Witches	...	...		—	—
1/	1/6	Mervyn Clitheroe	...	...		—	—
1/	1/6	Miser's Daughter	...	...		—	—
1/	1/6	Old St. Paul's ...	...	...		—	—
1/	1/6	Ovingdean Grange	...	...		—	—
1/	1/6	Rookwood ..	...	...		—	—
1/	1/6	Spendthrift ...	...	...		—	—
1/	1/6	Star Chamber ...	...	...		—	—
1/	1/6	St. James' ...	...	...		—	—
1/	1/6	Tower of London	...	...		—	—
1/	1/6	Windsor Castle ...	...	...		—	—

Ainsworth's Novels, in **17** vols., paper covers, price 17*s.* ; cloth gilt, £1 5*s.* : 8 vols., cloth, £1 5*s.*

ALCOTT, Louisa M.—
See "RUBY SERIES," *page 23.*

ARMSTRONG, F. C.—

Paper Covers.	Limp Cl. Gilt.					Picture Boards.	Half Roan.
—	—	Medora ...	...	...	...	2/	2/6
—	—	The Two Midshipmen	...	...		2/	2/6
—	—	War Hawk ...	...	...		2/	2/6
—	—	Young Commodore	...	...		2/	2/6

The Set, in 4 vols., cloth 10*s.* ; or boards, 8*s.*

Paper Covers.	Limp Cl. Gilt.		Picture Boards.	Hf. Roan.

ARTHUR, T. S.—

| 1/ | 1/6 | Nothing but Money ... ... | — | — |

AUSTEN, Jane—*(See page 23.)*

BANIM, John—

| — | — | Peep o' Day ... . | 2/ | 2 6 |
| — | — | Smuggler ... ... | 2/ | 2/6 |

BARHAM, R. H.—

| 1/ | — | My Cousin Nicholas ... ... | — | — |

BAYLY, T. Haynes—

| 1/ | — | Kindness in Women ... ... | — | — |

BELL, M. M.—

| — | — | Deeds, not Words ... ... | 2/ | 2 6 |
| — | — | The Secret of a Life ... ... | 2/ | 2 6 |

BELLEW, J. C. M.—

| — | — | Blount Tempest ... ... | 2/ | — |

BIRD, Robert M.—

Nick of the Woods ; or, The Fighting Quaker   2/   —

CARLETON, William—

1/	—	Emigrants...	—	—
1/	—	Fardarougha the Miser	—	—
1/	—	Jane Sinclair, &c.	—	—
1/	—	Tithe Proctor	—	—

Carleton's Novels, 5 vols., paper covers, 5s. ; cloth, 7s. 6d.

CHAMIER, Captain—

—	—	Ben Brace	2/	2 6
—	—	Jack Adams	2/	2 6
—	—	Life of a Sailor	2/	2 6
—	—	Tom Bowling	2	2/6

Chamier's Novels, 4 vols., bds., 8s. ; cloth, 10s.

COCKTON, Henry— *Cloth.*

—	—	George Julian, the Prince ...	2/	2/6
—	—	Stanley Thorn	2/	2/6
—	—	Valentine Vox, the Ventriloquist	2/	2 6

Cockton's Novels, 3 vols., bds., 6s. ; half roan, 7s. 6d.

Paper Covers.	Limp Cl. Gilt.		Picture Boards.	Cl. Gilt, with Frontispiece.
		COOPER, J. Fenimore—		
		(SIXPENNY EDITION *on page* 20.)		
1/	1/6	Afloat and Ashore; a Sequel to Miles Wallingford	2/	2/6
1/	1/6	Borderers ; or, The Heathcotes ...	2/	2/6
1/	1/6	Bravo : A Tale of Venice ...	2/	2/6
1/	1/6	Deerslayer; or, The First War-Path	2/	2/6
1/	1/6	Eve Effingham : A Sequel to "Homeward Bound" ...	—	—
1/	1/6	Headsman	2/	2/6
1/	1/6	Heidenmauer : A Legend of the Rhine	2/	2/6
1/	1/6	Homeward Bound ; or, The Chase	2/	2/6
1/	1/6	Last of the Mohicans	2/	2/6
1/	1/6	Lionel Lincoln ; or, The Leaguer of Boston	2/	2/6
1/	1/6	Mark's Reef ; or, The Crater ...	—	—
1/	1/6	Miles Wallingford ; or, Lucy Hardinge	2/	2/6
1/	1/6	Ned Myers ; or, Life before the Mast	—	—
1/	1/6	Oak Openings ; or, The Beehunter	—	—
1/	1/6	Pathfinder ; or, The Inland Sea...	2/	2/6
1/	1/6	Pilot : A Tale of the Sea ...	2/	2/6
1/	1/6	Pioneers ; or, The Sources of the Susquehanna	2/	2/6
1/	1/6	Prairie	2/	2/6
1/	1/6	Precaution	—	—
1/	1/6	Red Rover	2/	2/6
1/	1/6	Satanstoe ; or, The Littlepage Manuscripts	—	—
1/	1/6	Sea Lions ; or, The Lost Sealers	—	—
1/	1/6	Spy : A Tale of the Neutral Ground	2/	2/6
1/	1/6	Two Admirals	—	—
1/	1/6	Waterwitch ; or, The Skimmer of the Seas	2/	2/6
1/	1/6	Wyandotte ; or, The Hutted Knoll	2/	2/6

Cooper's Novels.—The Set of 18 vols., green cloth, £2 5s. ; boards, £1 16s.

The SHILLING EDITION, 26 vols. in 13, cloth, £1 19s. Also 26 vols., cloth gilt, £1 19s. ; paper covers, £1 6s.

See also page 20.

Paper Covers.	Limp Cl. Gilt.		Picture Boards.	Half Koan.
		COOPER, Thomas—		
1/		The Family Feud	—	—
		COSTELLO, Dudley—		
—	—	Faint Heart ne'er Won Fair Lady	2/	—
		CROLY, Rev. Dr.—		
—	—	Salathiel	2/	2,6
		CROWE, Catherine—		
—	—	Lilly Dawson	2/	2,5
—	—	Linny Lockwood	2/	2,6
—	—	Night Side of Nature	2/	2,6
—	—	Susan Hopley	2/	2,6

The Set, 4 vols., cloth, 10*s.*

CRUIKSHANK, George—

The following Volumes are illustrated by this renowned
Artist :—

Dickens's Grimaldi, *on page* 6.
Mayhew's Two Books, *on page* 14.
Mornings at Bow Street, *on page* 17.
Several of the Octavo Novels, *on page* 22.

Paper Covers.	Limp Cl. Gilt.		Picture Boards.	Half Koan.
		CUPPLES, Captain—		
—	—	The Green Hand	2/	2,6
—	—	The Two Frigates	2/	2,6
		DANA, R. H., Jun.—		
1/	—	Two Years before the Mast ...	—	—
		DICKENS, Charles—		
—	—	Grimaldi the Clown ...	2/	—
		DUMAS, Alexandre—		
1/	1/6	Ascanio	—	—
1/	1/6	Beau Tancrede	—	—
1/	1/6	Black Tulip	—	—
1/	1/6	Captain Paul	—	—
1/	1/6	Catherine Blum	—	—
1/	1/6	Chevalier de Maison Rouge ...	—	—

Paper Covers.	Limp Cl. Gilt.				Picture Boards.	Hf. Roan.
		DUMAS, ALEXANDRE—*continued.*				
1/	1/6	Chicot the Jester			—	—
1/	1/6	Conspirators			—	—
1/	1/6	Countess de Charny			—	—
1/	1/6	Dr. Basilius			—	—
1/	1/6	Forty-five Guardsmen ...			—	—
—	—	Half Brothers			2/	2/6
1/	1/6	Ingenue			—	—
1/	1/6	Isabel of Bavaria			—	—
—	—	Marguerite de Valois			2/	2/6
1/	1/6	Memoirs of a Physician vol. 1			2/6	3/6
1/	1/6	Do. do. vol. 2				
1/	1/6	Monte Cristo ... vol. 1			2/6	3/6
1/	1/6	Do. ... vol. 2				
1/	1/6	Nanon			—	—
1/	1/6	Page of the Duke of Savoy ...			—	—
1/	1/6	Pauline			—	—
1/	1/6	Queen's Necklace			—	—
1/	1/6	Regent's Daughter			—	—
1/	1/6	Russian Gipsy			—	—
1/	1/6	Taking the Bastile, vol. 1			2/6	3/6
1/	1/6	Do. vol. 2				
1/	1/6	Three Musketeers ...			2/6	3/6
1/	1/6	Twenty Years After ...				
1/	1/6	Twin Captains...			—	—
1/	1/6	Two Dianas			—	—
—	—	Vicomte de Bragelonne, vol. 1			2/6	3/
—	—	Do. do. vol. 2			2/6	3/
1/	1/6	Watchmaker			—	—

Dumas' Novels, 19 vols., half roan, £2 17s.

EDGEWORTH, Maria—

TALES OF FASHIONABLE LIFE :

1/	—	The Absentee			—	—
1/	—	Ennui			—	—
1/	—	Manœuvring			—	—
1/	—	Vivian			—	—

The Set, in cloth gilt, 4 vols., in a box, 8s.

EDWARDS, Amelia B.-

—	—	Half a Million of Money ...			2/	2/6
—	—	Ladder of Life			2/	2/6
—	—	My Brother's Wife			2/	2/6

Paper Covers.	Limp Cl. Gilt.		Picture Boards.	Half Roan.

FERRIER, Miss—

—	—	Destiny	2/	2/6
—	—	Inheritance	2/	2/6
—	—	Marriage	2/	2/6

The Set, 3 vols., half roan, 7s. 6d. ; in boards, 6s.

FIELDING, Thomas—

—	—	Amelia	2/	2/6
—	—	Joseph Andrews	2/	2/6
1/	—	Tom Jones	2/	2/6

Fielding's Novels, 3 vols., half roan, 7s. 6d. ; boards, 6s.

FITTIS, Robert S.—

—	—	Gilderoy	2/	2/6

GERSTAECKER, Fred.—

—	—	Each for Himself ...	2/	2/6
—	—	The Feathered Arrow	2/	2/6
—	—	Sailor's Adventures	2/	2/6
—	—	The Haunted House		
—	—	Pirates of the Mississippi ...	2/	2/6
—	—	Two Convicts	2/	2/6
—	—	Wife to Order	2/	2/6

The Set, 6 vols., half roan, 15s.

GRANT, James—

	Picture Boards.	Half Roan.
Aide de Camp	2/	2/6
Arthur Blane ; or, The Hundred Cuirassiers...	2/	2/6
Bothwell : The Days of Mary Queen of Scots	2/	2/6
Captain of the Guard : The Times of James II.	2/	2/6
Cavaliers of Fortune ; or, British Heroes in Foreign Wars	2/	2/6
Constable of France	2/	2/6
Dick Rodney : Adventures of an Eton Boy ...	2/	2/6
Fairer than a Fairy	2/	2/6
First Love and Last Love : A Tale of the Indian Mutiny	2/	2/6
Frank Hilton ; or, The Queen's Own... ...	2/	2/6
The Girl he Married : Scenes in the Life of a Scotch Laird	2/	2/6
Harry Ogilvie ; or, The Black Dragoons ...	2/	2/6
Jack Manly	2/	2/6
Jane Seton ; or, The King's Advocate ...	2/	2/6
King's Own Borderers ; or, The 25th Regiment	2/	2/6

	Paper Covers.	Limp Cl. Gilt.				Picture Boards.	Half Roan.

GRANT, JAMES—*continued.*

	Picture Boards.	Half Roan.
Lady Wedderburn's Wish : A Story of the Crimean War	2/	2/6
Laura Everingham ; or, The Highlanders of Glen Ora	2/	2/6
Legends of the Black Watch; or, The 42nd Regt.	2/	2/6
Letty Hyde's Lovers : A Tale of the Household Brigade	2/	2/6
Lucy Arden ; or, Hollywood Hall	2/	2/6
Mary of Lorraine	2/	2/6
Oliver Ellis : The 21st Fusiliers	2/	2/6
Only an Ensign	2/	2/6
Phantom Regiment ; Stories of "Ours" ...	2/	2/6
Philip Rollo ; or, The Scottish Musketeers ...	2/	2/6
Queen's Cadet	2/	2/6
Rob Roy, Adventures of	2/	2/6
Romance of War ; or, The Highlanders in Spain	2/	2/6
Scottish Cavalier : A Tale of the Revolution of 1688	2/	2/6
Second to None ; or, The Scots Greys ...	2/	2/6
Secret Despatch	2/	2/6
Shall I Win Her?	2/	2/6
Under the Red Dragon	2/	2/6
White Cockade ; or, Faith and Fortitude ...	2/	2/6
Yellow Frigate	2/	2/6

Grant's Novels, 34 vols., cloth, £4 5*s.*; boards, £3 8*s.*

GRIFFIN, Gerald—

Paper Covers.						Picture Boards.	Half Roan.
1/	—	Colleen Bawn	...	...	...	—	—
1/	—	The Rivals	...	...	...	—	—

Griffin's Novels, 3 vols., cloth, 4*s.* 6*d.* ; paper, 3*s.*

"GUY LIVINGSTONE," Author of—

						Picture Boards.	
—	—	Anteros ...	...	...	...	2/	—
—	—	Barren Honour	...	...	...	2/	—
—	—	Brakespeare ...	...	...	...	2/	—
—	—	Breaking a Butterfly	...	...	2/	—
—	—	Guy Livingstone	...	...	...	2/	—
—	—	Maurice Dering	...	...	...	2/	—
—	—	Sans Merci ...	...	...	...	2/	—
—	—	Sword and Gown	...	...	...	2/	—

The Set, in 8 vols., cloth, £1 4*s.*

Paper Covers.	Limp Cl. Gilt.						Picture Boards.	Half Roan.

GREY, Mrs.—

1/	—	The Duke ...	...	...	...		—	—
1/	—	The Little Wife	...	...	...		—	—
1/	—	Old Country House ...		...	...		—	—
1/	—	Young Prima Donna		...	...		—	—

The Set, in 4 vols., 6s., cloth gilt.

HALIBURTON, Judge—

—	—	The Attaché...	...	...	...		2/	2/6
—	—	Letter-Bag of the Great Western ...					2/	2/6
—	—	Sam Slick, the Clockmaker			...		2/6	3/6

Haliburton's Novels, 3 vols., cloth, 8s. 6d. ; paper covers, or boards, 6s. 6d.

HANNAY, James—

—	—	Singleton Fontenoy...		...	...		2/	—

HARLAND, Marion—See RUBY SERIES, *page* 23.

HARTE, Bret—See *page* 24.

HAWTHORNE, Nathaniel—

1/	1/6	The House of the Seven Gables			...		—	—
1/	1/6	Mosses from an Old Manse			...		—	—
1/	1/6	The Scarlet Letter ...		...	...		—	—

HOOD, Thomas—

—	—	Tylney Hall...			...		2/	2/6

HOOK, Theodore—

—	—	All in the Wrong	...	...	...		2/	2/6
—	—	Cousin Geoffry	...	...	...		2/	2/6
—	—	Cousin William	...	...	...		2/	2/6
—	—	Fathers and Sons	...	...	...		2/	2/6
—	—	Gervase Skinner	...	...	...		2/	2/6
—	—	Gilbert Gurney	...	...	...		2/	2/6
—	—	Gurney Married	...	...	...		2/	2/6
—	—	Jack Brag ...	...	...	...		2/	2/6
—	—	The Man of Many Friends...		...			2/	2/6
—	—	Maxwell ...	...	...	...		2/	2/6
—	—	Merton ...	...	...	...		2/	2/6
—	—	Parson's Daughter ...		...	...		2/	2/6
—	—	Passion and Principle		...	...		2/	2/6
—	—	Peregrine Bunce ...		...	...		2/	2/6
—	—	The Widow and the Marquess			...		2/	2/6

Hook's Novels, 15 vols., half roan, £2 ; Sayings and Doings, 5 vols., half roan, 12s. 6d.

Paper Covers.	Limp Cl. Gilt.		Picture Boards.	Half Roan.
		JAMES, G. P. R.—		
—	—	Agincourt	2/	—
—	—	Arabella Stuart	2/	—
—	—	Black Eagle	2/	—
—	—	Brigand	2/	—
—	—	Castle of Ehrenstein	2/	—
—	—	The Convict	2/	—
—	—	Darnley	2/	—
—	—	Forest Days	2/	—
—	—	Forgery	2/	—
—	—	Gentleman of the Old School ...	2/	—
—	—	Gipsy	2/	—
—	—	Gowrie	2/	—
—	—	Heidelberg	2/	—
—	—	Huguenot	2/	—
—	—	King's Highway	2/	—
—	—	Man at Arms	2/	—
—	—	Morley Ernstein	2/	—
—	—	Philip Augustus	2/	—
—	—	Richelieu	2/	—
—	—	Robber	2/	—
—	—	Russell	2/	—
—	—	Smuggler	2/	—
—	—	Stepmother	2/	—
—	—	Whim	2/	—
—	—	Woodman	2/	—

The remainder of the Works of Mr. James will be published in Monthly Volumes at 2s. each.

		JEPHSON, R. Mounteney—		
—	—	Tom Bulkley of Lissington ...	2/	—
		KINGSLEY, Henry—		
—	—	The Harveys...	2/	2/6
—	—	Hornby Mills	2/	2/6
—	—	Old Margaret	2/	2/6
—	—	Stretton	2/	2/6
		KINGSTON, W. H. G.—		
—	—	Albatross	2/	—
—	—	The Pirate of the Mediterranean ...	2/	—
		LANG, John—		
—	—	Ex-Wife	2/	—
—	—	Will He Marry Her?	2/	—

Paper Covers.	Limp Cl. Gilt.		Picture Boards.	Cloth.
		LEVER, Charles—		
—	—	Arthur O'Leary	2/	2/6
—	—	Con Cregan	2/	2/6
		LE FANU, Sheridan—		
—	—	Torlogh O'Brien	2/	—
		LONG, Lady Catherine—		
—	—	Sir Roland Ashton	2/	2/6
		LOVER, Samuel—		
—	—	Handy Andy	2/	2/6
—	—	Rory O'More	2/	2/6
		LYTTON, Right Hon. Lord—		
—	—	Alice : Sequel to Ernest Maltravers	2/	2/6
—	—	Caxtons	2/	2/6
—	—	Coming Race	2/	2/6
—	—	Devereux	2/	2/6
—	—	Disowned	2/	2/6
—	—	Ernest Maltravers	2/	2/6
—	—	Eugene Aram	2/	2/6
—	—	Godolphin	2/	2/6
—	—	Harold	2/	2/6
—	—	The Last of the Barons	2/	2/6
—	—	Leila	} 2/	2/6
—	—	The Pilgrims of the Rhine ...		
—	—	Lucretia	2/	2/6
—	—	My Novel, vol. 1	2/	2/6
—	—	Do. vol. 2	2/	2/6
—	—	Night and Morning	2/	2/6
—	—	Paul Clifford	2/	2/6
—	—	Pelham	2/	2/6
—	—	Pompeii, The Last Days of ...	2/	2/6
—	—	Rienzi	2/	2/6
—	—	Strange Story	2/	2/6
—	—	What will He Do with It? vol. 1 ...	2/	2/6
—	—	Do. do. vol. 2 ...	2/	2/6
—	—	Zanoni	2/	2/6

Sets of Lord Lytton's Novels, 22 vols., fcap. 8vo, cloth, £2 15*s.*; boards, £2 4*s.* (*See also page* 18.)

		MAILLARD, Mrs.—		
1/	—	Adrien	—	—
1/	—	Compulsory Marriage	—	—
1/	—	Zingra the Gipsy	—	—

Paper Covers.	Limp Cl. Gilt.		Picture Boards.	Half Roan.

MAXWELL, W. H.—

Paper Covers.	Limp Cl. Gilt.		Picture Boards.	Half Roan.
—	—	The Bivouac	2/	2/6
—	—	Brian O'Linn ; or, Luck is Every-thing	2/	2/6
—	—	Captain Blake ; or, My Life ...	2/	2/6
—	—	Captain O'Sullivan	2/	2/6
—	—	Flood and Field	2/	2/6
—	—	Hector O'Halloran	2/	2/6
—	—	Stories of the Peninsular War ...	2/	2/6
1/	—	Stories of Waterloo	2/	2/6
—	—	Wild Sports in the Highlands ...	2/	2/6
—	—	Wild Sports in the West	2/	2/6

The Set, in 10 vols., half roan, £1 5s.

MARK TWAIN—

(*See* " AMERICAN LIBRARY," *page* 24.)

MARRYAT, Captain—

(*See also pages* 19, 20.)   Cl. Gilt.

Paper Covers.	Limp Cl. Gilt.		Picture Boards.	Cl. Gilt.
1/	1/6	Dog Fiend	2/	2/6
1/	1/6	Frank Mildmay	2/	2/6
1/	1/6	Jacob Faithful	2/	2/6
1/	1/6	Japhet in Search of a Father ...	2/	2/6
1/	1/6	King's Own	2/	2/6
1/	1/6	Midshipman Easy	2/	2/6
1/	1/6	Monsieur Violet	—	—
1/	1/6	Newton Forster	2/	2/6
1/	1/6	Olla Podrida	—	—
1/	1/6	Percival Keene	2/	2/6
1/	1/6	Phantom Ship	2/	2/6
1/	1/6	Poacher	2/	2/6
1/	1/6	Pacha of Many Tales	2/	2/6
1/	1/6	Peter Simple	2/	2/6
1/	1/6	Rattlin the Reefer	2/	2/6
1/	1/6	Valerie	—	—

The Set of Captain Marryat's Novels, 16 vols. bound in 8, cloth, £1 5s. ; 16 vols, cloth, £1 4s. ; paper, 16s. ; 13 vols. (Steel Plates), cloth, £1 12s. 6d.

MARTINEAU, Harriet—

Hf. Roan.

Paper Covers.	Limp Cl. Gilt.		Picture Boards.	Hf. Roan.
—	—	The Hour and the Man	2/	2/6

Paper Covers.	Limp Cl. Gilt.		Picture Boards.	Half Roan
		MAYHEW, Brothers—		
—	—	The Greatest Plague of Life ...	2/	2/6
—	–	Whom to Marry and How to Get Married	2/	2/6

These two works have Steel Plates by George Cruikshank.

Paper Covers.	Limp Cl. Gilt.		Picture Boards.	Half Roan
		MAYO, W. S.—		
—	—	Kaloolah	2/	—
1/	—	Mountaineer of the Atlas	—	—
		MILLER, Thomas—		
—	—	Gideon Giles, the Roper	2/	—
		MORIER, Captain—		
—	—	Hajji Baba in Ispahan	2/	—
—	—	Zohrab the Hostage	2/	—
		MURRAY, The Hon.—		
—	—	Prairie Bird	2/	—
		NEALE, Capt. W. J.—		
—	—	Captain's Wife	2/	—
—	—	Cavendish	2/	—
—	—	Flying Dutchman	2/	—
—	—	Gentleman Jack	2/	—
—	—	The Lost Ship	2/	—
—	—	Port Admiral	2/	—
1/	—	Pride of the Mess	—	—
—	—	Will Watch	2/	—
		NORTON, The Hon. Mrs.—		
—	—	Stuart of Dunleath	2/	—
		OLD CALABAR—		
—	—	Won in a Canter	2/	—
		OLD SAILOR—		
—	—	Land and Sea Tales	2/	—
—	—	Top-sail Sheet-Blocks	2/	—
—	—	Tough Yarns	2/	—
—	—	The War-Lock	2/	—
		PALISSER, Captain—		
—	—	The Solitary Hunter	2/	—

Paper Covers.	Limp Cl. Gilt.		Picture Boards.	Half Roan.
		PORTER, Jane—		
—	—	The Pastor's Fireside	2/	2/6
—	—	The Scottish Chiefs	2/	2/6
—	—	Thaddeus of Warsaw	2/	2/6
		3 vols., half roan, 7s. 6d.		
		RICHARDSON, Samuel—		Cloth.
—	—	Clarissa Harlowe	2/6	3/6
—	—	Pamela	2/6	3/6
—	—	Sir Charles Grandison	2/6	3/6
		The Set, 3 vols., 10s. 6d., cloth.		
		SAUNDERS, Captain Patten—		
—	—	Black and Gold: A Tale of Circassia	2/	—
		SCOTT, Lady—		
1/	—	Henpecked Husband	—	—
—	—	Marriage in High Life	2/	—
—	—	The Pride of Life	2/	—
—	—	Trevelyan	2/	—
		SCOTT, Sir Walter—		
—	—	Antiquary	2/	—
—	—	Guy Mannering	2/	—
—	—	Heart of Midlothian	2/	—
—	—	Ivanhoe	2/	—
—	—	Old Mortality	2/	—
—	—	Rob Roy	2/	—
—	—	Waverley	2/	—
		SIMMONDS, P. L.—		
—	—	The Arctic Regions	2/	2/6
		New Edition, 1875.		
		SKETCHLEY, Arthur—		
—	—	Mrs. Brown at the Crystal Palace	1/	—
—	—	Mrs. Brown at Brighton	1/	—
—	—	Mrs. Brown at Margate	1/	—
—	—	Mrs. Brown on Dizzy	1/	—
—	—	Mrs. Brown on the Liquor Law ...	1/	—
—	—	Mrs. Brown on the Alabama Case	1/	—
—	—	Mrs. Brown at the Play	1/	—
—	—	Mrs. Brown on the Grand Tour ...	1/	—
—	—	Mrs. Brown in the Highlands ...	1/	—
—	—	Mrs. Brown in London	1/	—
—	—	Mrs. Brown in Paris	1/	—

Paper Covers.	Limp CL Gilt.		Picture Boards.	Cloth.

SKETCHLEY, ARTHUR—*continued.*

—	—	Mrs. Brown at the Sea-side ...	1/	—
—	—	Mrs. Brown in America	1/	—
—	—	The Brown Papers, 1st Series ...	1/	—
—	—	The Brown Papers, 2nd Series ...	1/	—
—	—	Mrs. Brown on Women's Rights ...	1/	—
—	—	Mrs. Brown at the Skating-rink ...	1/	*shortly.*

SMEDLEY, Frank E.—

—	—	The Colville Family	2/6	3/6
—	—	Frank Fairlegh	2/6	3/6
—	—	Harry Coverdale	2/6	3/6
—	—	Lewis Arundel	2/6	3/6

The Set, in 4 vols., cloth, 14*s.*

SMITH, Albert—

Hf. Roan.

—	—	Christopher Tadpole	2/	2/6
—	—	Marchioness of Brinvilliers ...	2/	2/6
—	—	Mr. Ledbury's Adventures ...	2/	2/6
—	—	The Pottleton Legacy	2/	2/6
—	—	The Scattergood Family	2/	2/6

The Set of Albert Smith's Novels, in 5 vols., half roan, 12*s.* 6*d.* ;
5 vols., boards, 10*s.*

SMOLLETT, Tobias—

—	—	Humphrey Clinker	2/	2/6
—	—	Peregrine Pickle	2/	2/6
—	—	Roderick Random	2/	2/6

The Set of 3 vols., half roan, 7*s.* 6*d.*

STERNE, Laurence—

Cloth.

1/	—	{ Tristram Shandy, and { Sentimental Journey } ...	2/6	3/6

STRETTON, Hesba—

—	—	The Clives of Burcot	2/	2/6

SUE, Eugene—

—	—	The Mysteries of Paris	2/	2/6
—	—	The Wandering Jew	2/	2/6

THOMAS, Annie—

—	—	False Colours	2/	—
—	—	Sir Victor's Choice ...	2/	—

VIDOCQ—

—	—	The French Police Spy	2/	—

Paper Covers.	Limp Cl. Gilt.		Picture Boards.	Cloth.

WETHERELL, Elizabeth—

Paper Covers.	Limp Cl. Gilt.		Picture Boards.	Cloth.
—	—	Ellen Montgomery's Book-case ...	2/	2/6
—	—	Melbourne House	2/	2/6
1/	—	My Brother's Keeper	--	—
—	—	The Old Helmet	2/	2/6
—	—	Queechy	2/	2/6
—	—	Two Schoolgirls, and other Tales...	2/	2/6
—	—	The Wide, Wide World	2/	2/6

"Whitefriars," Author of—

Hf. Roan.

Paper Covers.	Limp Cl. Gilt.		Picture Boards.	Cloth.
—	—	Cæsar Borgia	2/	2/6
—	—	Gold-Worshippers	2/	2/6
—	—	Madeleine Graham	2/	2/6
—	—	Maid of Orleans	2/	2/6
—	—	Owen Tudor	2/	2/6
—	—	Westminster Abbey	2/	2/6
—	—	Whitefriars	2/	2/6
—	—	Whitehall	2/	2/6

The Set of 8 vols., cloth, gilt top, 24*s.*

TROLLOPE, Mrs.—

Paper Covers.	Limp Cl. Gilt.		Picture Boards.	Cloth.
—	—	The Barnabys in America	2/	2/6
—	—	Love and Jealousy	2/	2/6
—	—	One Fault	2/	2/6
—	—	Petticoat Government	2/	2/6
—	—	The Ward	2/	2/6
—	—	Widow Barnaby	2/	2/6
—	—	The Widow Married	2/	2/6

YATES, Edmund—

Paper Covers.	Limp Cl. Gilt.		Picture Boards.	Cloth.
—	—	A Waiting Race	2/	2/6
—	—	Black Sheep	2/	2/6
—	—	Broken to Harness	2/	2/6
—	—	The Impending Sword	2/	2/6
—	—	Kissing the Rod	2/	2/6
—	—	The Righted Wrong	2/	2/6
—	—	The Rock Ahead	2/	2/6
—	—	Running the Gauntlet	2/	2/6
—	—	Two by Tricks	2/	2/6
—	—	The Yellow Flag	2/	2/6

Anonymous—

Paper Covers.	Limp Cl. Gilt.		Picture Boards.	Cloth.
—	—	Bashful Irishman	2/	—
—	—	Mornings at Bow Street	2/	2/6
—	—	Adventures of a Strolling Player ...	2/	—
—	—	Rodenhurst	2/	—

LORD LYTTON'S NOVELS AND ROMANCES.

KNEBWORTH EDITION.

Crown 8vo, green cloth, 3s. 6d. each.

Eugene Aram.	Devereux.	What will he Do with
Night and Morning.	My Novel. Vol. 1.	It? Vol. 1.
Pelham.	My Novel. Vol. 2.	What will he Do with
Ernest Maltravers.	The Disowned.	It? Vol. 2.
Alice.	The Coming Race.	Leila and the Pil-
Last Days of Pompeii.	Godolphin.	grims of the Rhine.
Harold.	Paul Clifford.	Falkland and Zicci.
Last of the Barons.	Zanoni.	Kenelm Chillingly.
Lucretia.	Rienzi.	The Parisians. Vol. 1.
The Caxtons.	A Strange Story.	The Parisians. Vol. 2.

Complete Sets, 27 vols., brown cloth, price £4 14s. 6d. ; or in half-calf or half-morocco, £9 9s.

LORD LYTTON'S MISCELLANEOUS WORKS.

Uniform with the Knebworth Edition of the Novels.

England and the English.	Caxtoniana.
Athens ; Its Rise and Fall.	Quarterly Essays.
The Student.	

To be followed by other Volumes, including the Dramatic and Poetical Works of Lord Lytton.

WORKS OF CAPTAIN MARRYAT.

An entirely New Edition of the Works of Captain Marryat, crown 8vo, bound in blue cloth, price 3s. 6d. each ; printed from entirely new type, with Six original Illustrations by the best Artists.

Peter Simple.	Percival Keene.	Pacha of Many
The King's Own.	Japhet in Search of	Tales.
Frank Mildmay.	a Father.	Valerie.
Midshipman Easy.	Rattlin the Reefer.	The Phantom Ship.
Jacob Faithful.	Newton Forster.	Monsieur Violet.
The Dog Fiend.	The Poacher.	Olla Podrida.

The Set, 16 vols., half-roan, £3 3s. ; cloth, £2 16s.

SIR WALTER SCOTT'S NOVELS.

Containing the Original Steel Plates designed by CRUIKSHANK, TURNER, MACLISE, and others. Crown 8vo, red cloth, 3s. 6d. each.

Waverley.	Antiquary. [moor.	Abbot
Guy Mannering.	Bride of Lammer-	Kenilworth.
Old Mortality.	Black Dwarf.	Pirate. (Aug.)
Heart of Midlothian.	Ivanhoe.	Fortunes of Nigel.
Rob Roy.	Monastery.	(Sept.)

(*The other Volumes Monthly.*)

ROUTLEDGE'S ANECDOTE LIBRARY.

Each Volume containing 192 pages, bound in fancy boards.
Price 1s. (Postage 2d.)

Scotch.	*J. A. Mair.*	American.	*Howard Paul.*
Irish.	*P. Kennedy.*	Theatrical	*Percy Fitzgerald.*
English.	*Tom Hood.*	Naval.	
Legal.	*John Timbs.*	Military.	

ROUTLEDGE'S STANDARD SERIES.

Paper covers, 1s. each; limp cloth, 1s. 6d.; postage, 3d.

1. **Essays by Lord Macaulay.** Reprinted from the *Edinburgh Review;* contains the famous Essays on MILTON, JOHNSON, BUNYAN, and others.

2. **Miscellaneous Writings of Lord Macaulay.**

3. **The Rev. Sydney Smith's Essays,** from the *Edinburgh Review*, 1808-18.

4. **Ditto, 1818-27.**

5. **Specimens of the Table Talk of S. Taylor Coleridge.**

ROUTLEDGE'S SIXPENNY NOVELS.

Two Columns on a page. Without Abridgment. (Postage 1d.)
CAPTAIN MARRYAT.

Peter Simple.	Japhet, in Search of	Olla Podrida.
King's Own.	a Father.	The Poacher.
Newton Forster.	Mr. Midshipman	Percival Keene.
Jacob Faithful.	Easy.	Monsieur Violet.
Frank Mildmay.	The Dog Fiend.	Rattlin the Reefer.
Pacha of Many Tales.	The Phantom Ship.	Valerie.

Also, in Volumes, in boards, 2s., or cloth, 2s. 6d.

Vol. 1. King's Own—Frank Mildmay—Newton Forster—Peter Simple.

,, 2. Pacha of Many Tales—Jacob Faithful—Midshipman Easy—Japhet.

,, 3. Phantom Ship—Dog Fiend—Olla Podrida—Poacher.

,, 4. Percival Keene—Monsieur Violet—Rattlin—Valerie.

The Set in 4 vols., boards, 8s.; cloth, 10s.

COMICAL AMERICAN BOOKS.
6d. each.

Artemus Ward, his Book.	Major Jack Downing.
Artemus Ward's Travels.	Nasby Papers.
Biglow Papers.	Orpheus C. Kerr.

SIXPENNY NOVELS—*continued.*

J. FENIMORE COOPER.

Afloat and Ashore.	Mark's Reef.	Prairie.
Borderers.	Mercedes.	Precaution.
Bravo.	Miles Wallingford.	Red Rover.
Deerslayer.	Mohicans (Last of	Satanstoe.
Eve Effingham.	the).	Sea Lions.
Headsman.	Ned Myers.	Spy.
Heidenmauer.	Oak Openings.	Two Admirals.
Homeward Bound.	Pathfinder.	Waterwitch.
Jack Tier.	Pilot.	Wyandotte.
Lionel Lincoln.	Pioneers.	

For Second Titles see page 5.   £ *s. d.*

The 28 Volumes bound in 7, cloth, gilt edges   1   1   0
    Do.   do.   cloth 0 17   6

The Volumes are sold separately, 2*s.* 6*d.* cloth ; 2*s.* boards.

Contents of the Volumes :—

Vol. 1.   Spy—Pilot—Homeward Bound—Eve Effingham.
 ,,   2.   Pioneers—Mohicans—Prairie—Pathfinder.
 ,,   3.   Red Rover—Two Admirals—Miles Wallingford—Afloat
        and Ashore.
 ,,   4.   Borderers—Wyandotte—Mark's Reef—Satanstoe.
 ,,   5.   Lionel Lincoln—Oak Openings—Ned Myers—Precaution.
 ,,   6.   Deerslayer—Headsman—Waterwitch—Heidenmauer.
 ,,   7.   Bravo—Sea Lions—Jack Tier—Mercedes.

SIR WALTER SCOTT.

Abbot.	Guy Mannering.	Pirate.
Anne of Geierstein.	Heart of Midlothian	Quentin Durward.
Antiquary.	Ivanhoe.	Redgauntlet.
Betrothed.	Kenilworth.	Rob Roy.
Bride of Lammer-	Monastery.	St Ronan's Well.
moor.	Legend of Montrose,	Surgeon's Daughter.
Count Robert of Paris	and Black Dwarf.	Talisman.
Fair Maid of Perth.	Old Mortality.	Waverley.
Fortunes of Nigel.	Peveril of the Peak.	Woodstock.

The Set of 25 Vols., bound in 4 Vols., green cloth, 15*s.* ;
half roan, 17*s.* 6*d.*

This Edition is also to be had in Volumes, each Volume containing 4 Novels.   Boards, 2*s.* ; cloth, 2*s.* 6*d.*

Vol. 1.   Waverley—Monastery—Kenilworth—Rob Roy.
 ,,   2.   Pirate—Ivanhoe—Fortunes of Nigel—Old Mortality.
 ,,   3.   Guy Mannering—Bride of Lammermoor—Heart of Mid-
        lothian—Antiquary.
 ,,   4.   Peveril of the Peak—Quentin Durward—St. Ronan's
        Well—Abbot.   [*More Volumes shortly.*

SIXPENNY NOVELS—*continued.*

EUGENE SUE.

THE WANDERING JEW.	THE MYSTERIES OF PARIS.
Pt. 1. The Transgression, 6*d.*	Pt. 1. Morning, 6*d.*
,, 2. The Chastisement, 6*d.*	,, 2. Noon, 6*d.*
,, 3. The Redemption, 6*d.*	,, 3. Night, 6*d.*
Complete in 1 vol., 2*s.*, boards,	Complete in 1 vol., 2*s.*, boards,
or 2*s.* 6*d.*, half roan.	or 2*s.* 6*d.*, half-roan.

VARIOUS AUTHORS.

	Paper Covers. s. d.	Cloth Gilt. s. d.
CUMMINS (Miss). The Lamplighter	0 6	1 0
DE FOE. Robinson Crusoe...	0 6	1 0
DE QUINCEY. The Opium Eater ...	0 6	—
FIELDING. Tom Jones. Part 1. ...	0 6	—
Do. do. Part 2. ...	0 6	—
The Two in One Vol....	1 0	—
GOLDSMITH. Vicar of Wakefield ...	0 6	1 0
GERALD GRIFFIN. Colleen Bawn...	0 6	—
HOLMES. Autocrat of the Breakfast Table	0 6	1 0
Do. The Professor at the Breakfast Table..	0 6	1 0
Also, the Two in One Vol. ...	1 0	1 6
IRVING (WASHINGTON). The Sketch Book	0 6	1 0
LAMB (CHARLES). Essays of Elia...	0 6	1 0
Do. The Last Essays of Elia	0 6	1 0
Also, the Two in One Vol. ...	1 0	—
SMOLLETT (TOBIAS). Roderick Random...	0 6	1 0
STERNE (LAURENCE). Sentimental Journey	0 6	—
Do. Tristram Shandy ...	0 6	—
Also, the Two in One Vol. ...	1 0	—
STOWE (Mrs.). Uncle Tom's Cabin	0 6	1 0
SWIFT. Gulliver's Travels ...	0 6	1 0
VICTOR HUGO. Notre Dame	0 6	—
WETHERELL (Miss). Queechy ...	0 6	1 0

ROUTLEDGE'S

SIXPENNY MINIATURE LIBRARY.

Cloth, gilt edges. (Postage 1*d.*)

The Language of Flowers.	The Ball Room Manual.
Etiquette for Gentlemen.	Carving.
Etiquette for Ladies.	Toasts and Sentiments.
Etiquette for Courtship and Matrimony.	How to Dress Well.

www.ingramcontent.com/pod-product-compliance
Lightning Source LLC
Chambersburg PA
CBHW030941110726
47900CB00004B/1085